THE FALLEN LEAVES

If you bury the past bury it deep

JOHN REGAN

ISBN-13:9781082152245

DEDICATION

To Vicky with love. My biggest fan and harshest critic. Without which I would never have finished this book.

ACKNOWLEDGMENTS

It goes without saying that to produce anything worthwhile, requires help from others. The process of writing a book such as this is aided and abetted by numerous people. Some of who only subtly assist, and others, who profoundly do so. My thanks go to anyone who however small, contributed to this novel. My principal appreciation, however, is to the people who purchased and read my first four books: The Hanging Tree, Persistence of Vision, The Romanov Relic and The Space Between Our Tears. Your support is greatly appreciated. Many thanks go to my writing friends for their invaluable support and help in making this book possible. Finally, to anyone who is reading this book. I hope you find it enjoyable, and any feedback is always appreciated.

September 2019.

DISCLAIMER

Many of the places mentioned in this book exist. However, the author has used poetic license throughout, to maintain an engaging narrative. Therefore, no guarantee of accuracy in some respects should be expected. The characters depicted, however, are wholly fictional. Any similarity to persons living or dead is accidental.

CHAPTER ONE

The man and woman watched from the front of their van as a thick-set individual staggered from the pub. He stopped and tugged the collar of his coat up high. Reaching into his pocket, he pulled out a flat cap and pressed it firmly onto his bald head. He paused, lit a cigarette and drew deeply on it, before carrying on along the dimly-lit street away from the pub.

The female shifted inside the cab of the van and placed her hand on the arm of her male friend. 'You know what to do?'

'Yeah.' He pulled a ski mask over his head and eased his giant frame out of the vehicle.

She watched, her eyes scanning the length of the road, as her partner trailed the bald man along the footpath before catching up with him fifty metres from where she parked. The bald man spun but could do nothing as a fist struck him square on the chin. He fell backwards and cracked his head on the pavement. Groaning he attempted to sit, instinctively reaching inside his coat pocket for his gun. The large man bore down on his helpless victim, and as the prone man's fingers found the handle of his weapon, the thud of his assailant's boot kicked him into unconsciousness. He grabbed the collar of the limp figure and pulled him into an alleyway as the van slid to a halt next to them. The woman jumped out, raced around to the rear and threw open the doors.

'The coast's clear,' she whispered.

The big man, his unconscious victim draped across his shoulders, lumbered forward and dropped the cap-less individual into the back. He jumped inside, pulled the motionless figure to the rear of the vehicle and jumped out. Slamming the doors shut, he hurried around to the driver's side as the woman scanned up and down the road before climbing in next to him. She patted his arm and smiled, he smiled back, found the gear he sought, and roared off as the curtain to an upstairs bedroom fell silently back across the window.

The huge, hooded figure entered the barn. He stared across at the bald, naked man. A rope attached around his throat, his feet bound and tethered to the floor, making movement difficult. Strolling across to his victim, he stopped, picked up a bucket of water and threw it over the man. He let out a gasp, the cold liquid rousing him rudely from unconsciousness. Drenched and shivering, he stared wide-eyed at his captor as the figure made his way over to a table close by. From it, he lifted a large hunting knife and allowed the tethered man to see the blade. He writhed against his shackles, the gag stretched tight across his mouth preventing much sound, only a muffled cry escaping from him. Eyes bulging, as the hooded figure edged closer.

The captive's eyes darted to his right as a young woman stepped forward from the darkness and joined her companion. She edged closer and pulled the gag from the tethered man's face. 'Billy Turner?' she said.

'What if I am.' He sneered.

'Amanda Hewitson?' she asked.

'Never heard of her.'

The woman glanced at her companion. 'This could be harder than we thought.'

The huge man stepped forward and pressed the tip of the knife onto Turner's chin. A small trickle of blood ran the length of its blade.

'What happened to her?' she said.

'I don't know what you're on about.'

She lowered her eyes and sighed. 'You could make this easier and a lot less painful for yourself. My friend here—'

'Fuck you! I don't know what you're on about. I've never heard of Amanda Hewitson.'

'I *know* you have.' She patted her companion on the arm. 'Let me know when you've found out everything.'

He nodded, put down the knife and eased off his bomber jacket. She viewed the tethered man again, shook her head and headed towards the door.

The woman re-entered. The unconscious man hung limply from his bonds, as blood dripped from the end of his nose and onto the floor in front of him.

'Did he talk?' she said.

The big man lowered his head. 'Those bastards raped and murdered her.'

'Did he give you names?'

'Yeah. Three. Do you want me to finish him?'

She looked towards the man. 'He's a particularly nasty piece of work, this one. I know all about Billy Turner.'

He held out the knife to her. 'Do you want to do it, then?'

'No. I'll leave that to you.' She turned away, paused, and spun back around. Snatching the knife from her companion, the woman ambled towards their victim. 'On second thoughts ...'

She handed the knife back to the big man. Their captive groaned as blood dripped from between his legs.

Patting her friend on the arm, she stared directly at him. 'I'm sending a message to his employer. Make sure he gets it.'

The big man grunted and moved towards the groaning victim. He placed the tip of the knife in the middle of his chest, and the tethered man's eyes opened wide. He pulled and rocked against his fetters, their tautness allowing only the smallest of movement. The woman walked off, the door closing with a loud bang behind her. A high-pitched whine escaped the prisoner's mouth, as his captor, slowly, meticulously, went to work.

One week earlier – The huge figure crept across the garden towards the house. His graceful movement belied his size. He paused at the wall of the property, quickly glanced both ways, and steadily made his way around to the rear. He reached into his jacket and pulled out a piece of paper, studying the crude drawing for a couple of seconds. Satisfied, he pushed it back into his pocket and carried on across to a set of French doors. He gave his field of vision one last look, then reached for the handle. The door opened, and the man slid silently inside. He waited a few moments for his eyes to adjust to the darkness, and then hurried across to the far side of the room. A large floor to ceiling wooden wall stood before him. The man glanced to his left, and touching one panel at a time, counted across, stopping at the fifth panel in. Tracing his finger along the bottom of the decorative beading, he found a small, almost invisible hole. The panel clicked open as his finger found the button. The door to a safe lay behind. Pulling the rucksack from his back, he dropped to his knees and rummaged through it.

Conrad Hudson sat at a table with a brandy. He took a sip and flicked over the page of the document in front of him. The phone rang.

Hudson tossed the paper aside, placed the brandy glass on the table, and answered.

'Yes, Taffy?'

'The manor's been broken into.'

Hudson stood. 'What?'

'Someone's blown the safe.'

'When?'

'One of your staff phoned me. He said there wasn't an answer when he called you.'

Hudson grabbed his jacket. 'I must have left it in the car. They haven't phoned the police, have they?'

'No.'

'Good. We don't want them poking their noses into our business.'

'They left the money, Boss.'

Hudson slumped back onto the seat. 'What?'

'They didn't take the money. Whatever else you had inside—'

'Jesus, Taffy.'

'What was in there?'

Hudson blew out hard. 'Documents. Information on everyone.' He looked upwards. 'They knew what they were after.'

'The people you use? The names—?'

'Yeah. But not everything. I split the information up. There's some incriminating stuff, but probably not enough to cause us trouble.'

'Right. Anything else?'

Hudson paused. 'The lads ...'

'What about them?'

'... I kept a dossier on each of them.'

'Why would you do that?' Taffy said.

'In case they turned on me ... on us.'

'And me?'

'I didn't keep anything on you. I swear. I trust you, implicitly.'

'Ok. We're checking the CCTV, to see if it comes up with anything.'

'I want them to pay for this.'

'We need to catch them first,' Taffy said.

'They'll be in touch,' Hudson said. 'They want something.'

'If not money ... What?'

'I don't know. I really don't know.'

Six months earlier – Jean Cooper entered the pub and made her way into the back room. She glanced about. A man sitting at a table in the corner attracted her attention, and she headed over.

The man stood and offered his hand, smiling pleasantly. 'Harry Prentise,' he said.

She shook his hand and sat opposite. 'Mr Prentise. You said you had some information?'

'I thought we'd eat and drink first.'

She frowned at him. 'Mr Prentise ... I haven't come here to socialise.'

'Call me Harry.' He smiled. 'Perhaps just a drink, then?'

She briefly stared at him. 'A red wine.'

'Any particular type?'

She rummaged through her handbag and took out a mobile. 'Merlot,' she said, studying the phone.

Harry placed the drink in front of her and sat back in his seat. He clasped his hands together and fixed his stare on her. 'I'll get straight down to brass tacks, should I?'

'Please do.'

'I've reason to believe Conrad Hudson had something to do with your husband's disappearance.'

She rolled her eyes. 'So you said on the phone. As I told you, I don't believe you. Conrad would—'

'And yet you're here,' he said.

'Have you proof?'

He shrugged. 'Proof is hard to come by.'

She stood. 'Clearly, this is a waste of both our time. If you have proof, go to the police.'

'Please, Mrs Cooper.' He indicated for her to sit.

She slumped back onto the chair. 'I'll give you five minutes.'

Harry looked across into the far corner of the room and waved a young woman across. She ambled over and joined them.

'This is Jen,' Harry said.

Mrs Cooper nodded at the woman. 'Jen.'

Harry leant back in his chair. 'Tell her.'

Jen faced Mrs Cooper. 'Conrad Hudson had something to do with my sister's disappearance.'

Mrs Cooper sneered. 'And have *you* any proof?'

Jen glanced back at Harry. 'Nothing concrete.'

Mrs Cooper cocked her head. 'This is all hearsay. My husband stole money from the council and left. Probably with one of his many floozies.'

'Your husband and my sister were seeing each other,' Jen said. 'I spoke with her ex-flatmate.'

Mrs Cooper fixed Jen with an ice-cold glare. 'I don't doubt it. As I was saying …'

'She disappeared, too,' Jen said.

'She may have left with Alex,' Mrs Cooper said.

Jen shook her head. 'She'd have been in touch. I was incredibly close to my sister.'

Mrs Cooper closed her eyes and pondered. 'Look … If any of this is true … If Conrad had anything to do with Alex and your sister disappearing, I need proof. Then we inform the police.'

'Colin Pybus,' Harry said.

'What about him?' Mrs Cooper asked.

Harry tapped at his upper lip with his index finger. 'Colin knows something. More than he's told us.'

Mrs Cooper folded her arms. 'Go on.'

'He won't talk,' Jen said. 'He won't tell us all he knows. He's scared of Hudson. But he hinted Alex and Amanda were an item.'

Mrs Cooper rolled her eyes again. 'What did he say exactly?'

'He knew my sister. He had a soft spot for Amanda, I could tell. When I mentioned I was looking for her, he apologised but said he couldn't help. He implied he knew what happened.'

'And this involves Conrad, how?'

Harry leant forward. 'I know you and Conrad Hudson are close.'

'My relationship with Conrad is no concern of yours.'

'But what happens if it's true?' Jen said. 'What if Conrad had something to do with them both disappearing?'

'Then I would need proof. I loved Alex greatly, despite his ... failings. But I would need proof, and then we could inform the police and have him arrested.'

'Perhaps if you talk with Colin Pybus?' Harry said.

'I don't know him that well. If he hasn't told you two anything, what makes you think—?'

'She was only seventeen,' Jen said. 'Seventeen.'

Mrs Cooper leant back in her chair. 'Perhaps there is a way.'

Harry looked up. 'Yeah?'

'You could work for Conrad and ... Well ... Find out what you can, I suppose.'

'Why would he employ me? He doesn't know me from Adam.'

'He's always on the lookout for men. I could vouch for you. Or rather, have someone he trusts vouch for you.'

Harry glanced at Jen. 'Great.'

Mrs Cooper narrowed her eyes and studied him. 'I understand this young lady's interest. But what's yours, Harry?'

'Robin Slaney,' he said.

'I don't think I know him.'

'Robin Slaney was a gardener for Conrad Hudson,' Harry said. 'He disappeared around the same time as Alex and Jen's sister, Amanda. He's my brother. That's my interest.'

'Disappeared?'

'Yeah,' Harry said. 'He's never been heard from since. Don't you find that a little strange, too? Three people who went missing at the same time and no one has heard from then since.'

Mrs Cooper stood. 'I'll be in touch,' she said, as she walked away.

Jen leant closer to Harry. 'What do you think?' she said.

'So far, so good.'

Jean Cooper watched as Harry and Jen exited the pub and got inside separate vehicles. She took out her mobile and called.

'Hi, Jean,' a male voice said.

'Tony. I need a favour.'

'Anything.'

'A friend of a friend is looking for a job. He's a sound bloke. Just the type Conrad would want.'

'And you want me to put in a word?' Tony said.

'If you could. I'd do it myself, but you know how suspicious Conrad is. He values your opinion. I'm sure if …'

'No problem, Jean. Send him around and I'll sort him out.'

'Thanks, Tony. I appreciate this.'

She hung up and searched through her contacts again.

Harry answered. 'That was quick.'

'I'm going to text you a name and address. Tell him I sent you.'

'Will Conrad go for this?' Harry said.

'He will if Tony, the guy I'm sending you to see, vouches for you.'

'Great.'

'Your past … Your brother? Will Conrad be—'

'Conrad won't be able to link us. He was only my half-brother. We have different names.'

'Have you been in trouble with the police?'

'Bits and pieces,' Harry said. 'Is it a problem?'

'Quite the opposite. Conrad likes people who've been in trouble with the law. Keep in touch. Let me know how it goes.'

'I will.'

Harry hung up and phoned Jen. 'We're in.'

'Great,' she said. 'The friend I was telling you about?'

'Yeah.'

'He said he'll help me. When should we begin?'

Harry pondered. 'Leave it a few months. Give me a chance to work on it and gain Hudson's trust. Then you and your friend can do what you like.'

He hung up again and dialled.

'Yeah,' a male voice said.

'She's gone for it. She's going to get me into Hudson's firm.'

'Brilliant. What about me?'

'We'll let Jen and her friend do the dirty work,' Harry said. 'Once we've created a few vacancies, we'll get you in. Sit tight. I'll be in touch.'

Three months later – Jen put down her book and snatched up her mobile. 'Harry? Long time, no hear.'

'I've been busy with Hudson. Winning his trust.'

'Has it worked?' Jen said.

'Yeah. But he has a guy working for him, his right-hand man, who doesn't trust me.'

'Won't it be a problem?'

'I don't think so. I just think he doesn't like how close I've got with Hudson. That's all.'

'Have you managed to find anything out?'

'Not yet. However, Colin Pybus has been in touch. He wants to speak to us again.'

'Really?'

'Yeah. That's what he said. Can we meet and I'll take you around to his place?'

'Do you think—?'

'I can't see him getting in touch with me unless he was going to tell us something.'

'Where, when?'

'Can you get across to Middlesbrough?'

'Yeah.'

'I'll pick you up this afternoon,' Harry said. 'He lives in a place called Acklam. Meet me in the carpark of the Cornerstone Hotel. Three o'clock.'

Harry, standing with Jen, knocked on the door. They waited a couple of moments before the door opened. Colin Pybus stood there. Jen gasped.

'Are you ok, Colin?' she said.

Colin lowered his eyes and padded along the hallway into a room. He carefully lowered himself into an armchair and motioned for the other two to sit.

'Sorry about the mess,' he said.

'Are you sure you're—' Harry said.

'Cancer,' Colin said.

Jen stretched across and clasped hold of his hand. 'Oh, Colin. I'm so sorry. Are they—?'

'There's nothing they can do. Too far gone. I …' He coughed and reached for a glass. He gulped greedily at the liquid and grimaced. 'Even drinking is painful. The bloody medicine they gave me …' He glanced upwards. 'If I had a gun …'

'How long?' Harry said.

'Weeks, a couple of months, maybe. Anyway …' He smiled at Jen as tears collected in his eyes. 'You're the image of her.' He placed a hand on Jen's cheek. 'Beautiful, just like Amanda.'

Jen clasped hold of his hand again. 'What happened, Colin?'

He started to sob. 'I couldn't save her … I warned Alex … I told him it was dangerous.' He wiped at the tears as they cascaded down his cheeks.

Harry edged nearer. 'Tell us everything.'

CHAPTER TWO

Graveney showered, dressed and made his way downstairs. Heather was busy in the kitchen, making breakfast. He put his arms around her waist and kissed her on the cheek.

'Put a bib on Max, will you?' she said.

Graveney picked one up and placed it around the neck of his son, who played with a toy in his highchair.

'Morning, Max,' Graveney said, gently rubbing the top of the infant's head. Max briefly glanced up and giggled at his father, before resuming his play.

'Where are the other two?' Graveney said.

Heather placed a plate on the table. 'Louisa's gone for some milk. Give Luke a shout.'

He strode to the threshold of the kitchen. 'Luke!' He listened and heard movement from the bedroom above, a confirmation his son was up.

Graveney finished his breakfast and wiped his chin. He looked towards Louisa. 'What are you up to today?'

'Shopping with Heather,' she said. 'My exams are finished. I think a bit of shopping is in order.'

'Can I come?' Luke said.

'Unfortunately not,' Heather said. She picked up her son's empty bowl and deposited it in the dishwasher. 'You've got school.'

Luke groaned and got up from his seat. 'I'm sure they wouldn't miss me for one day.'

'Sorry, mate,' Graveney said. 'It's the law.'

Luke tramped out of the room and collected his bag from the hall just as the doorbell rang. He opened the door to his friend, Tommy, who stood staring at his mobile. Tommy glanced up, grunted at Luke, turned and ambled off.

'I'm off,' Luke said, following his friend.

'See you, son,' Graveney and Heather said in unison.

Heather sat and looked at Graveney. 'What have you got on today?'

'Bit quiet actually, but not a bad thing.'

'Certainly not,' Heather said.

Graveney stood. 'Well, I'll leave you to it.' He planted a kiss on Louisa's head, and then on Heather's cheek. 'Enjoy your day shopping.'

'We will,' the pair said, grinning at him.

Graveney headed into Middlesbrough, stopping en route at Ratano's coffee shop. Becky was still on maternity leave, and he chatted pleasantly with Andrea before completing his journey. Armed with his coffee, he headed upstairs, into his office and opened a file in front of him. Someone knocked.

Hussain popped his head inside. 'The Chief Inspector wants to see you, Guv.'

Graveney picked up his coffee, drained it and dropped the cup into the bin. 'Yeah, ok.'

He tapped on the door and entered. Mac sat behind his desk, talking on the phone. He motioned for Graveney to sit and finished his call.

He looked across at Graveney, held up his phone and tapped it. 'Becky.'

'How's she coping?'

'Very well. Considering they're her first.'

Graveney smiled. 'And you? Those rings around your eyes are getting darker by the day.'

Mac placed on his head. 'Twins at my age. I must be mad.'

'Are the four of us still on for the meal on Friday?'

'If Louisa babysits,' Mac said.

'She will. I'll book a table, shall I?'

'Yeah. About eight.'

'Eight it is.'

Mac leant back in his chair and stroked his chin.

'You look the part behind that desk,' Graveney said.

'You could have had this job. You were stupid not to take it.'

'Not my idea of fun.' Graveney screwed up his face. 'Spending most of my day stuck in an office. I like to get out and about.'

'Yeah. I know what you mean.' Mac coughed and stroked his chin again.

'What is it?' Graveney said.

'What?'

'What is it you have to tell me?'

'You know, Peter,' Mac said. 'That thin-slicing thing of yours is bloody annoying.'

'I know. You've told me before.'

'There's been a body fished out of a pond up near New Marske.'

'Clumsy fisherman?'

Mac tutted. 'No. Not unless he was fishing in a Ford Mondeo.'

'Accident?' Graveney said.

'Not sure. Can you go and have a look? The pathologist and crime investigation team are already on site.'

'What else? What is it you're holding back?'

Mac swallowed and took a deep breath. 'Bev's back.'

Graveney's eyes widened. 'Bev?'

'Yeah,' Mac said. 'Bev Wilson.'

'I know which Bev you mean,' Graveney said. 'I thought she was working in Wales?'

'Apparently not anymore. She's moved back up here, permanently. That's what I've heard.'

Graveney stood and turned towards the door.

'I can send someone else?' Mac said. 'If you'd like.'

Graveney shrugged. 'I'll run into her eventually. Now's as good a time as any.'

Graveney and Hussain drove out towards New Marske. Turning off the main road, they travelled for a short distance along a narrow track. Hussain pulled the car up next to the already full, small parking area, and Graveney got out. He stalled, spotting Bev Wilson, bedecked in her usual light blue overalls, some distance away.

Hussain followed his gaze. 'Everything ok, Sir?'

Graveney faced Hussain. 'Yeah, fine. See what you can find out.' Hussain marched off.

Graveney looked over to Bev Wilson again and watched as she disappeared behind the mass of vehicles, pulled the collar of his coat up high, and headed after her.

'Hi, stranger,' he said.

Bev turned to face him. A broad smile spread across her face. 'Peter. Long time, no see.' She moved closer.

Graveney surveyed the scene. 'Well …' Quickly switching into police officer mode, he pushed his hands into his pocket. 'I believe you've got a body for me.'

She cleared her throat. 'Erm … Yes.'

'Accident?' Graveney said.

'Not unless he stabbed himself and drove his car into the lake.'

'Do we know who it is?'

'Not yet. There doesn't appear to be any identification on the man, or in the car. The boot won't open either. I'll check for a DNA match when I get back. You never know, there may be some clue in the boot.'

Graveney smiled. 'Life's never that easy. This afternoon?' He stepped closer to her.

Bev's cheeks flushed a little. 'Probably. I'll ring later.'

Hussain approached the two of them and stopped. Graveney stepped away from Bev. 'It was workmen who found it, Guv. They were draining the pond. New houses are going up around here.'

'Any idea how long it's been in there?' Graveney said.

'There aren't any plates, Guv. Someone went to the trouble of removing them.'

Graveney scrutinised the rusty car. It's windows black with sludge. 'Must have been in there a long time. Over ten years, I'd say.'

'The lads are going to check for the vehicle identification number. But everything's rusted up.'

'Let me know when you have that.'

Hussain acknowledged the pair and headed off.

'Richard got a transfer to Teesside University,' Bev said. Graveney turned to face her again. 'An opportunity he couldn't turn down.'

'It's a free world,' Graveney said. 'You don't need to explain.'

Bev stepped closer. 'I did miss you.'

Graveney glanced about. 'It's difficult. I wanted to get in touch but ...'

'I know.' She stretched out a hand and touched his arm.

Graveney fought the urge to step away. He glanced around again. 'How's the family?'

'Mam's fine but Dad's ailing a bit. That's another reason I came back. She doesn't want him going into a care home and hopefully, I can help prevent that.'

Graveney's shoulders drooped, and he dropped his eyes down. 'How's Aimee?'

'She's great. I've pictures.' Bev fished in a pocket for her phone. She turned the mobile around, and Graveney took it from her. He stared at the face of a little girl.

'She's beautiful,' he said. 'Looks just like her mother.'

'Do you think so?' She tilted her head. 'I think she looks like her dad. It's the dark, wavy hair.'

Graveney looked up from the phone and locked eyes with Bev. They stared briefly at each other before he broke the connection.

'It's a noble thing he's doing ... Richard ... Bringing up another man's child.'

'He's a great dad. Treats her like his own. I couldn't ask for more.'

Graveney forced a smile. 'Does he know?' He took one final look at the phone before handing it back.

'No one knows. I didn't tell anyone. I always manage to skirt around the subject when someone asks. Sleeping dogs and all that.'

'I ...' Graveney shook his head.

'It's better as it is,' Bev said. 'Less complicated this way.'

Graveney's shoulders slumped. He glanced back towards the car. 'I'll look forward to your call.'

'Yeah,' she said. They smiled apologetically at each other and parted. Graveney watched her leave and then trudged back to the car.

Bev rang him late afternoon. She suggested he come across to her and discuss her findings. Graveney agreed. He couldn't avoid her, especially in their line of work. Being in her company made the guilt he felt, which he was usually able to subdue, bubble to the surface. He decided to go on his own, keeping Rav and the others busy with little jobs.

Bev was sitting at her desk when one of her staff showed Graveney into her office. Bev thanked her, and the two of them remained silent until she left.

'New office?' Graveney asked. He glanced around the room, trying to delay the inevitable eye contact.

'Yeah,' she said. 'Much bigger than my old one.'

Graveney smiled. 'You needed a bigger one to house your ego.'

'Haha,' she said. 'I missed your humour. The coppers in Wales were a little too serious for my liking.' She picked up her pad and flicked through the pages.

'Straight down to work, is it?' he said.

'Why? What else did you have in mind?' She grinned, slightly elevating her eyebrows.

'Nothing,' Graveney said. 'Just trying to get back to how we were.'

Bev stared at him. 'Guess what we found in the boot?'

'Another body?'

'Who told you?'

'Nobody.' Graveney's eyes widened. 'I was joking. Don't tell me there was?'

'Yes. Another body,' she said.

'And do we have names?'

'The one in the front was called Sean Grant. He has some previous. Minor stuff, I think.'

'And the other?'

'Alexander Cooper.'

'The councillor who disappeared?'

'Yep,' she said.

'He was supposed to have run off with all that money. A bit before my time, but I remember reading about the case.'

'Well he never got far,' she said.

'Don't suppose you found a big bag of cash?'

She cocked her head and winked at him. 'Nope. But I can afford an extension on my house now.'

Graveney smiled. 'The cause of death. The one in the boot, obviously.'

'Head trauma,' she said. 'Cranium meets a large object. Large object wins. Judging by the state of the skull, he'd have been totally incapacitated. But he may not have died instantaneously from the blow. There are signs on the skull of other injuries.'

'What like?'

'Whoever killed him, continued his attack after incapacitating him. His cheekbones and the bridge of his nose show signs of a sustained, and possibly frenzied attack.'

'A failed planning applicant, perhaps?'

'Obviously,' Bev said. Graveney looked across at her. He'd missed Bev. The banter and good nature they'd once enjoyed. She looked radiant too. Her hair cut a little shorter than he remembered. He continued to observe her as she pushed the hair behind her right ear giving him an unrestricted view of her face.

'The other had been hit on the head as well,' she continued. 'It wouldn't have killed him, but it may have knocked him out.'

Graveney jotted the names in his notebook. 'Anything else? A body tucked in the footwell, perhaps?'

Bev put her hand up to her mouth. 'I forgot to check there.'

'Sloppy, Wilson. Sloppy. Seriously though. Anything else of interest?'

'We're still going over it, but given the time it's been in the water, I'm not sure what else we'll find.'

'Rav ran a check on the car.' Graveney said. 'It was reported stolen by its owner. A Mr Henry Longford.' Graveney consulted his notebook. 'He died five years ago. Nothing suspicious. A respectable gentleman.'

'So,' she said. 'It looks as if someone stole the car intending to dump the body in the boot?'

'Looks that way. The one in the front is puzzling, though.'

Bev narrowed her eyes. 'A falling out among thieves?'.

'Maybe.' Graveney rubbed his chin. 'Well, you've certainly given me plenty to think about.'

'One tries,' she said.

Graveney got up from his seat. 'Thanks again, Bev.' He gripped hold of the door handle.

'Does she know?' Bev said.

He turned to face her. She stood and moved a little closer to him.

Graveney dropped his eyes to the floor. 'When you told me ... I booked a table at a restaurant. I'd intended to tell Heather over dinner.

Get the main course out of the way, of course.' He forced an unconvincing smile as he tried to lighten the mood again. 'But before I could, she told me she was expecting. And I—'

'Couldn't tell her then,' Bev said.

'I could have, and I should have,' he said. 'But I took a coward's way out.'

'I've got something for you.' Bev moved back towards her desk and pulled out an envelope from a drawer. She handed it to Graveney, who took it from her. 'Photos.' She half-smiled. 'Thought you might like them.'

Graveney stared at the envelope for a moment, then pushed it inside his pocket. 'Thanks ... I'll see you later.'

'I'm sure you will.'

Graveney opened the door, paused briefly, feeling he still had something to add, but then left without saying another word.

Graveney was back in his office when Hussain entered.

'I've got some information on the bodies, Guv,' he said, easing himself into a seat opposite to Graveney.

'Fire away,' Graveney said, giving Hussain his full attention.

'Sean Grant, the body in the front seat. He had a bit of previous. Nothing major, though. Theft, GBH, and stealing a car.'

'Any links with the councillor?' he said.

'None we can find so far.'

Graveney drummed his fingers on the desk. 'I think we'd better start off with Sean Grant. Find out who his friends were. Maybe they can give us some information on his background. They might know if he was an acquaintance of Cooper.'

'His mother's still alive,' Hussain said. 'Lives in Grove Hill.'

'Well ...' Graveney lounged back in his chair and placed his hands behind his head. 'We'll start there.'

CHAPTER THREE

Graveney and Hussain pulled up outside an old house. The broken front fence missing several boards, and the gate lay flat in the garden. The two officers walked along the path and tapped on the already slightly open door. No one answered, so Hussain knocked louder.

'All right!' shouted a voice from inside. 'I'm coming.' The door was pulled open abruptly by an unshaven, scruffy man. Graveney eyed him. In his sixties, his hair unkempt, a half-smoked cigarette hung from his mouth.

'What?' he said, glaring at the two officers.

'Mr Grant?' Graveney said.

'Who the hell are you?'

'Detective Inspector Graveney and this is my colleague, Detective Sergeant Hussain.'

'There is no Mr Grant. Mr Grant's been dead years.'

'Is Mrs Grant in?' Hussain said.

The man looked him up and down. 'Brenda!' he shouted. 'A couple of coppers to see you.' The man trudged back inside, slamming the door to the front room shut as he disappeared behind it. A woman descended the stairs and fully opened the front door.

'Yes?' she said.

'Mrs Grant?' Graveney asked.

'Yes.'

'Can we come in?' Graveney said.

She beckoned them inside, and the two officers followed her through into the kitchen. It was surprisingly tidy, given the state of the outside of the house. She ushered them towards two chairs, and the officers took a seat.

'What can I help you with?' she said.

'You might want to sit, Mrs Grant,' Graveney said. The woman did as she was told.

'We're here about your son, Sean,' Hussain said.

Her eyes widened. 'Sean?'

'We've found a body in a car,' Graveney said. 'I'm sorry, we believe it to be your son.'

The woman put her hand up to her mouth. 'A body?' she repeated.

'When did you last see Sean, Mrs Grant?' Graveney said.

She rubbed her face with a shaky hand. 'About seventeen or eighteen years ago.'

'We believe he's been dead for about that length of time,' Hussain said.

'That's impossible.' She crossed her arms. 'Sean lives in Spain. He sent me postcards.'

'Postcards?' Graveney glanced at Hussain. 'When did you last receive one?'

'Four or five years ago.'

The two officers looked at each other, again. 'Are you sure?' Graveney said.

'Yes. I kept all of them.'

'Can we see them?' Graveney said. 'Have you anything else with your son's handwriting on it?'

Mrs Grant disappeared, returning moments later with the postcards. She handed them to the officers and sat back down.

'We've carried out a DNA test, and we're sure it's Sean,' Hussain said.

Graveney held up the postcards. 'It's possible someone else sent these to conceal your son's disappearance.'

'Who would do that?' she said quietly.

'We don't know,' Graveney said. 'Can you tell me who Sean hung around with?'

Mrs Grant paused for a moment. 'Karl and Craig.'

Hussain pulled out his notepad. 'Karl?'

'Smith,' she said. 'And Craig Embleton. Craig's dead, though.'

'Dead?' Graveney said.

'His girlfriend murdered him.'

'Have you an address for Karl Smith?' Hussain asked.

She slowly shook her head. 'No. It was such a long time ago. I think he lived near the Steelworks Club, but I'm not sure.'

'Thanks,' Graveney said. 'We'll let ourselves out. I can get someone to come and chat with you. They can help with your son's funeral and other things.'

The woman didn't respond. She gazed towards the floor with her hands clasped tightly together.

'Mrs Grant?' Graveney said. She glanced up at him. 'Did your son ever mention anyone called Councillor Alexander Cooper?'

She considered for a moment. 'No, I don't think so.'

'Thanks again,' Graveney said. He looked at Hussain, nodded towards the door, and then the officers left.

Once back in the car, Graveney looked across at Hussain. 'See what you can dig up on this Karl Smith and Craig Embleton. I'll have a word with the Guv and see if we can't get a few hands to help us out.'

'Where to now?' Hussain said.

'Back to the station.'

CHAPTER FOUR

Lindsey Armstrong and Jimmy Jefferson had almost finished clearing the house. Lindsey stood in her bedroom, now devoid of furniture, silently staring at the blank walls. The chatter in her head which had once dogged her, now gone leaving her alone with her own inner voice. She was deep in thought as Jimmy entered the room. He put his hand on her shoulder, causing her to jump a little.

'Sorry,' he said. 'I didn't mean to scare you.'

Lindsey put her arms around his waist, hugging him tightly. 'You didn't,' she said, stretching up to kiss him on the cheek.

'There's one more box. Might need a big healthy girl to help me lift it, though.'

'Come on, then.' She took hold of his hand and squeezed tightly. 'Let's go.'

The two of them strolled out, stopping briefly at the threshold of the door. He squeezed her hand again, knowingly.

'You don't leave the memories behind,' he said. 'They come too.'

'I know … I know it's just bricks and mortar, but …'

'We can stay a little longer if you want?'

'No,' she replied forcefully. 'A new start.'

The couple set off down the stairs. Lindsey limped behind Jimmy, her leg still giving her trouble since the accident. They reached the bottom just as Graveney and Hussain walked up the path. Lindsey peered across at Jimmy, as the two officers stopped at the threshold of the open door.

'Lindsey Armstrong?' Graveney said.

Lindsey crossed her arms. 'Who's asking?'

Graveney and Hussain showed their credentials and introduced themselves.

'You'd better come in,' she said. Turning, they headed into the living room.

'You'll have to stand, I'm afraid,' Jimmy said. Following her into the room, he stopped by her side. 'As you can see, we're in the middle of moving.'

Graveney stared across at Jimmy. 'Can we have a private word with Lindsey?'

She glowered at the officers. 'Anything you've got to say you can say in front of Jimmy.'

'I know we're probably not your favourite people.' Graveney said, switching his attention to Lindsey. 'But ...'

'Listen,' Lindsey said. 'Just spit it out. We haven't got all day.' Jimmy took hold of her hand and gently squeezed it.

Graveney smiled to himself. She was feisty, this one, he thought. But there was something just below the surface. For all her bravado, she was worried. Yes, he recognised as much now. She was hiding something, he was sure.

'Sean Grant,' he said, allowing the name to echo around the empty room.

Lindsey clenched her jaw. 'What about him?'

Jimmy's heart beat faster. He edged slightly away from the two officers, resisting the overwhelming urge to leave the room altogether, as he tried desperately to remain outwardly calm.

Graveney fixed her with a deep stare. 'We're speaking with people who knew him.'

'I knew him,' she said. 'But then you already know that. It's why you're here.'

Hussain glanced towards Jimmy and then stared at Lindsey. 'We understand he was mates with a past boyfriend of yours?'

'He knows,' Lindsey said. She cast a sideways look at Jimmy. 'He knows all about Craig.'

Graveney continued to study Lindsey, drinking in her emotions. 'Did you know him well?'

'Of course, I did.' Lindsey smirked. 'He was my boyfriend.'

'I was talking about Sean Grant,' Graveney said.

'I didn't like Sean. He was a waste of space. He got Craig into all sorts of trouble.'

'Is that why you argued with Craig?' Hussain said.

'Read the police file.' Her body tightened. 'I've done my time. I don't have to answer to you.'

'We're just doing our job,' Graveney said. 'We're trying to establish Sean's movements.'

Lindsey hesitated. 'Sean Grant was a bad lot. If he's dead, he probably deserves to be.'

'I didn't say Sean Grant was dead,' Graveney said.

'Oh, come off it!' Lindsey scoffed. 'You bloody coppers think you're so smart. You said you are talking to people who knew him. I naturally assumed ...' She threw out an arm dismissively.

'Have you ever been to Grewgrass Lane, in New Marske?' Hussain said.

Lindsey tapped her foot as Graveney tried to gauge her reaction. 'No. Why?'

'Sean's body was found inside a Ford Mondeo, at the bottom of a lake on Grewgrass Lane.'

Jimmy tried to take in what Graveney said. He almost spoke but stopped himself.

Lindsey shrugged. 'Don't know what this has to do with me?' Jimmy glanced across at her, amazed by her calmness.

'Karl Smith?' Hussain said.

'Another friend of Craig's,' Lindsey said. 'Are we just going to go through all the people Craig knew?'

'Did you know Karl Smith?' Graveney asked.

'Of course I knew him. I knew all of Craig's mates.'

'I don't suppose you know where he lives?' Graveney said.

'Sorry.' She said. 'Lost touch with Karl. Spending fifteen years inside does that. People move on.'

'Have you ever heard of anyone called Alexander Cooper?' Hussain said.

'Wasn't he the councillor who disappeared?' Jimmy said. Moving nearer to Lindsey, he took hold of her hand and squeezed it again.

'That's right, Mr ...'

'Jefferson. Jimmy Jefferson.'

Lindsey looked away. 'I think I saw his name in the papers.'

Graveney strolled around the empty room. 'Are you moving far?'

'Coulby Newham,' Lindsey said. 'Sorry. We're only inviting friends to the housewarming.'

'Your new address?' Hussain said. 'In case we need to ask you about anything else.'

'204, The Meadows,' Jimmy said.

Graveney paused and turned. 'Thanks for your help.' He looked over at Hussain, and the pair moved towards the door. 'We'll see ourselves out.'

Jimmy and Lindsey watched through the window as the two police officers got in their car.

'What do you think, Guv?' Hussain said.

Graveney pondered for a moment. 'Not sure. I thought maybe she knew something about the murder. But, when I mentioned Grewgrass Lane, it surprised her.'

'As if she'd never heard of it?'

Graveney gazed into space. 'Yeah. Not 100% sure about that.'

'What about Cooper?' Hussain said.

'I couldn't tell if she was telling the truth there. Although again, I'm not sure she wasn't hiding something. She ...' He struggled to find the right words. 'She masks her emotions well.'

'We need to find this Karl Smith,' Hussain said. 'It appears as if he's disappeared off the face of the earth, though.'

Graveney glanced back towards the house. 'Maybe he's lying at the bottom of a lake, somewhere.'

'Maybe he is.'

Lindsey and Jimmy let out the lungful of air they'd been holding since the officers left.

'What do you think of that?' Jimmy said.

'I don't know.' She watched as the car drove away.

He followed her gaze outside. 'How did Sean's body get from Roseberry Topping to this lake?' he said. 'Do you think they have anything linking you?'

She turned and looked him in the eyes. 'If they did, I think I'd be at the police station by now.'

'What about this other guy, Cooper?' he said.

Lindsey looked away from Jimmy. He placed a hand on her shoulder and turned her around. 'What is it?' he said.

She lowered her eyes. 'I knew Alex Cooper.'

'Why did you tell the police you didn't?'

'I didn't actually say I didn't know him,' she said. 'I told them I'd read about him in the papers.'

'Come on, Lindsey.' Jimmy huffed. 'Lying will make them more suspicious. Especially if they find out you knew him.'

'I know,' she said. 'It just came out.'

'How did you know him?'

Lindsey swallowed. 'I had a thing with him.'

'*A thing*?'

'An affair,' she said.

Jimmy rubbed the back of his head. 'When did this happen?'

'I was in my second year of college, and I was writing an assignment about what councillors do. How councils work, etc. I met with Cooper at the town hall.'

'And?' Jimmy said.

'He was twenty years older than me and I ...' She thought hard. '... I was a stupid kid. He was a wealthy, handsome councillor, and I fell for his charm.'

'Was he married?' Jimmy asked.

Lindsey rolled her eyes. 'Aren't they always?'

'How long did this last?'

'Six months. We'd meet up somewhere, and Alex would take me to a hotel out of town.'

'What about Craig?' Jimmy said.

'I met Craig through Alex. Alex invited me to an official council function near Christmas and told me to meet him in the carpark after it. I waited, and he was talking to two men. Craig and Sean. Craig must have clocked me, because, a week or so later, I was out with a few friends in Middlesbrough when I ran into him.'

'And you started seeing Craig as well?'

'No. I finished with Alex and started going out with Craig. I think Alex was glad it was over. He probably just found a new shag.'

Jimmy turned away and walked towards the door. Lindsey followed him. 'I'm sorry I didn't tell you,' she said. 'But …'

Lindsey grabbed hold of Jimmy. 'I'm sorry I—'

'Lindsey.' Jimmy faced her. 'I know you had a life before we got together. It's just a bit of a shock.'

'Should I tell the police?' She placed a hand on his arm and moved to touch his face but stopped herself.

'Is this everything?' Jimmy said. 'There aren't any more skeletons in your closet?'

'No.' She stepped forward and touched his face. 'I swear. I was only eighteen at the time. Stupid kid, as I said. Swept away by his money and charm, that's all.'

'But it doesn't answer the questions. What was Sean doing in the car, and why are they asking about Cooper after all these years? He was supposed to have run off with council money.'

'Karl must have something to do with it.'

'Karl disappeared after he tried to kill you,' he said. 'It's a good job you never told the police who was driving the car that tried to run you down.'

'How did Karl manage to get Sean's body from Roseberry Topping,' she said.

'Are you sure he was dead?' Jimmy said.

'I hit him with a branch and Karl examined him. He told me Sean was dead and that I should get away while he dumped the body. There was a hole close by where Sean hid stuff he'd nicked. Karl said he dumped him there.'

'Maybe Sean wasn't dead,' Jimmy said. 'Maybe he was only knocked out.'

'Then he could have got down the hill himself.'

Jimmy rubbed his chin. 'Possibly. We need to know how he died.'

'How do we find out?'

'We'll go to the police,' he said. 'Fabricate a story. Tell them Craig told you he and Sean had a bust-up, and Craig hit Sean over the head with something.'

'What?'

'Be vague. Neither Craig nor Sean are in a position to contradict you.'

'What if Karl turns up?' Lindsey said.

Jimmy pulled her close. 'Karl won't turn up. He'll be miles away. I know it's dangerous, but our life is just getting good. Why should you suffer for something you didn't do?'

Lindsey forced a smile. 'I don't ...'

'What about Cooper?' he asked.

'We were discreet,' she said. 'I don't think many people would remember me knowing him. It was such a long time ago. If the police find anything, I'll just brazen it out.'

'Tell them you met him once for your article. Just say you've only just remembered it was him.'

'It may get the police interested in me?' she said. 'You know how their minds work.'

'But if you don't, and someone remembers you? I mean, it wasn't much time after you were arrested for Craig's murder.'

'I'm sorry for all of this,' she said. 'I wish ...'

'Don't worry.' He looked away and thought for a moment. 'We'll get out of this mess somehow.'

Graveney pushed aside the file on his desk when his phone rang. 'Graveney,' he said.

'I've got Bev Wilson on the line, Sir,' a female voice said.

'Put her through ... Bev,' Graveney said.

'We've found something in the car.'

'A gear-stick and a steering wheel?' Graveney said.

Bev laughed. 'As well as all the usual things you would expect to find in a car ... We found a wedding ring.'

Graveney flicked through his paperwork. 'Sorry, Bev. I'm already married. Nice gesture, though.'

Bev ignored him. 'It's inscribed on the inside. *AJ & MT 20/05/81*.'

'Could be the car owners?' he said.

'Maybe.'

'Anything else?'

'That's it for the moment, Peter.'

'Thanks, Bev. I'll get one of the boys to come over and collect it later today.'

'Ok. We'll talk later.'

Graveney coughed. 'I've seen the photos of ... She really is beautiful.'

'It just goes to show,' Bev said. 'Even ill-judged decisions can turn out for the best.'

'Was it ill-judged?'

'I don't know. Was it?'

'We'll talk later.' Graveney hung up.

Graveney pressed a number on his phone.

'Yes, Guv,' DC Sarah Cooke said.

'Can you check the records and see if we have listed a missing or stolen wedding ring? Inscribed with AJ & MT 20/05/81 on the inside. It's a bit of a long shot, I know.'

'Straight away?'

'Please,' Graveney said.

Graveney was on his third coffee of the day when Cooke tapped on the door and entered. He stretched in his chair, his back aching from sitting all morning.

'The ring, Guv,' she said. 'It belonged to Mary Jefferson. Wife of PC Alan Jefferson.'

'Copper?'

'Yeah. Before your time. She was murdered in 1999 by a person or persons unknown. Her body was discovered near Ingleby Greenhow a few days later.'

'And we're certain it's her wedding ring?'

'Her husband gave a list of jewellery taken from their house,' she said. 'A suspected burglary which went wrong, possibly. The ring was missing when they found the body.'

'Jefferson,' Graveney said. 'That name rings a bell.' He opened his notepad and leafed through the pages. 'Were there any other family members?'

Sarah flicked through the pages of the case file. 'A son. James,' she said. 'Why?'

'Lindsey Armstrong. When we visited her the other day, she was with a man. Jimmy Jefferson.'

'The same one?' she said.

'What do you think?'

'I'm not sure. What are your thoughts?'

'Lindsey Armstrong knew one of the people in the car. Well, at least her boyfriend, Craig Embleton, did.'

'The boyfriend she murdered?' Cooke said.

'Yeah. And the ring, belonging to the murdered mother of her current boyfriend, is found in the same car.'

'Coincidence?'

'*Yeah.*' Graveney scoffed. 'That's likely, isn't it? Maybe we should have a word with Lindsey Armstrong and Jimmy Jefferson.'

'Shall we bring them in?'

Graveney's phone sounded. He motioned for Cooke to wait and then answered. 'Graveney.'

'It's the front desk, Sir. I've got a Lindsey Armstrong and Jimmy Jefferson in reception. She says she needs to talk with you.'

'Put her in one of the side rooms, Geoff,' he said. 'I'll be downstairs in a minute.'

Graveney put down the receiver. 'Well, well.' He smiled. 'It appears you don't need to go and fetch them. They're downstairs.'

'*Really?*' Cooke said.

'Yes, indeed. Fetch me the case file from Armstrong's murder investigation, will you? It may come in useful.'

'What about Mary Jefferson's death?' she said.

'Bring that too.'

Graveney entered an interview room with Cooke and a uniformed officer, carrying a couple of folders under his arm. He took a seat opposite the pair. Lindsey and Jimmy had waited nearly half an hour and not the five minutes the sergeant on the desk promised.

'Can you go with the officer, Jimmy?' Graveney said.

'Why can't he stay?' Lindsey said.

Graveney ignored her. 'We won't be too long.' Jimmy stood, glanced helplessly at Lindsey, and then left with the uniformed officer.

Lindsey's eyes darted about nervously, thoughts from her past making themselves known.

'Are you ok?' Graveney asked. 'Would you like a drink?'

Lindsey glared at him. 'No, I'm fine. Just bad memories, that's all.'

'So,' Graveney said. 'How can we help you, Lindsey?'

'I've remembered a few things.'

'About?' Graveney said.

'Craig and Sean.' She took a deep breath. 'Craig fought with Sean on the night Craig …' Her voice trailed off. She coughed and continued. 'Anyway ... I remember him telling me he hit Sean over the head with something.'

'Something?' Graveney said.

'I can't remember,' she said. 'Craig thought he'd killed Sean, but Sean was only knocked out.'

'Right.' Graveney folded his arms, allowing her to talk more.

'I think … Craig lied to me. Maybe … he'd killed Sean when he hit him.'

'Sean had been hit on the head, Lindsey. The pathology report showed that, but it's not what killed him.'

Lindsey let out an audible sigh. 'How did he die?'

'I'm sorry we're not at liberty to disclose that.'

'Of course,' Lindsey said. 'I understand.'

Graveney narrowed his eyes, sensing she still add more to add. 'Anything else?'

'Alexander Cooper.' She sighed again. 'I met him once.'

'Go on,' Graveney said.

'I was doing a course at college, and one of my assignments was about how councils work. And what being a councillor involved. I phoned someone at Middlesbrough Council to ask if I could meet and interview one of them.'

'Alexander Cooper?' Graveney said.

'Yeah. I only realised after you left the other day who it was.'

Graveney leant back in his chair. 'Where did you meet him?'

'The town hall,' she said.

'Did Jimmy ever meet him?'

Lindsey frowned. 'Jimmy?' Jimmy was just a kid, then. Fifteen, maybe sixteen.'

'What about Craig?' Graveney said.

'I don't know.'

Graveney stared directly at her. 'Are you sure about that, Lindsey?'

Lindsey threw her head back. 'What is this? I came here to assist you. You're so suspicious.'

'From our point of view ... It looks suspicious. Two bodies in a car. And you knew them both.'

'I told you, I only met Alex once.'

'Alex?' Graveney said.

'Yes. That was his name. Sean was Craig's friend. I'd little to do with Sean.'

Graveney picked up the folder in front of him. 'I've been looking through your file.' He studied her as he opened it.

Lindsey peered at the picture, the body of Craig lying in a large pool of blood on the floor of his flat. The way she found him. Her footprints and handprints picked out in the dried blood. Lindsey pulled her eyes away, the shocking scene just as traumatic now, as it had been all those years ago.

'You've no right,' Lindsey said. Tears filled her eyes. 'I've done my time. I don't have to talk about Craig.'

'You see how it looks, though. Craig, Sean, and *Alex*.' He emphasised the name. 'All dead. And what about Karl Smith?'

Lindsey snapped her head around and glared. 'What about him?'

'Maybe he's dead too. Maybe you came out of prison, and you and your boyfriend had some unfinished business.'

'Fuck you, Graveney.' She got to her feet. 'I didn't kill anyone.' She pointed an accusing finger. 'You understand. No one.'

'Sit down, Lindsey,' Graveney said, calmly.

Lindsey slumped back into her seat and sternly folded her arms. 'Jimmy's done nothing. You're trying to pin these murders on us, and it's not on. Jimmy's mam was murdered. Your lot couldn't find who killed *her*, could you?'

'We found something else in the car,' he said. 'A ring.'

'So what?' Lindsey said.

'It was Jimmy's mam's wedding ring.'

Lindsey said nothing. She stared at the photo of Craig again. The page still open in the file.

'You can see where this is going,' Graveney said. 'Jimmy's mam's ring. The person who possibly stole it ... dead. Craig, who may or may not have helped him, dead. Karl, another person who you knew, missing. And a body in the boot which you just happened to know.'

'Are you arresting me?' she spat back at him.

'Not yet, Lindsey,' he said, and got to his feet. 'But don't leave town. We may need to speak with you again.'

Jimmy sat in silence, staring down at his hands.

'Sorry to keep you,' Graveney said, as he and Cooke entered.

Jimmy looked at the officers. 'Where's Lindsey?'

Graveney and Cooke sat opposite him. 'Lindsey's fine,' Graveney said. He studied Jimmy. He appeared nervous. His eyes lowered towards the desk. 'How well did you know Lindsey's boyfriend, Craig?'

Jimmy looked up. 'Hardly at all.'

'What about Alexander Cooper?' Graveney said.

'Not at all. What's this about?'

'Sean Grant?' Graveney continued.

'I knew his face from the estate he lived on, but I never even spoke to him. A friend of mine lived near his parents' house. I would sometimes see him when I went there.'

'We found something inside the car,' Graveney said. 'The car fished out near Marske.' Jimmy nodded. 'Your mother's wedding ring.'

'My mother's ...'

Graveney watched Jimmy closely. He appeared confused, as Graveney thin-sliced his reaction. 'Yes.'

'Are you saying Sean Grant had something to do with my mam's murder?'

'We don't know,' Graveney said. 'But it looks as if Sean was involved somehow. You and Lindsey ... How long have you known each other?'

'I don't know ... Since about 98/99, I suppose.'

'How did you meet?'

Jimmy rubbed his face. 'I had a crush on her. When I was about fifteen.'

Graveney leant inward. 'Your dad ...?'

'I'll tell him about the ring,' Jimmy said. 'He's been sober for about three months. I wouldn't want him having a setback.'

'Of course,' Graveney said. 'Thanks for your help. One of the officers will show you out.'

Graveney and Cooke returned to Graveney's office and closed the door.

'What do you think, Guv?' Cooke said.

Graveney brought his hands together and rested them on his chin. 'Lindsey Armstrong knew Cooper better than she's letting on.'

'So, do you think her boyfriend and Sean Grant killed Jimmy Jefferson's mam?'

'Not sure,' he said. 'The way she reacted over the photo of the boyfriend was strange.'

'In what way?'

'You would expect remorse for what she'd done, but there was none. Just a deep sadness. I'm almost tempted to believe ...' Graveney flopped onto his chair and rubbed his chin. '... She didn't kill Craig.'

Cooke frowned. 'Why would she admit to a murder she didn't commit?'

'Why indeed.'

'And Jimmy Jefferson?'

'I think he was telling us the truth. I don't believe he was involved in the murders at all. However, there's something he's not telling us.'

'What?'

'Something involving Lindsey's boyfriend. When I mentioned his name, there was deep remorse. Guilt even.'

'Maybe he murdered him.' Cooke said. 'If Lindsey didn't, I mean.'

'No. It's not that sort of guilt. It's hard to describe. If Lindsey didn't kill him, I think Jimmy possibly knows who did.'

'Karl Smith is the missing piece,' Cooke said.

'Yeah. We need to find Karl Smith. If he's still alive, that is.'

Graveney watched from his window as Jimmy Jefferson exited the station and made his way over to the waiting Lindsey. They kissed and embraced. 'What is it you two are hiding?' Graveney said to himself, as he watched them disappear out of sight.

CHAPTER FIVE

Graveney, seated behind the desk in his office, looked up as Hussain and Cooke settled onto the chairs in front of him.

'Rav?' Graveney said, looking at the DS.

'We've continued our search for Karl Smith,' Hussain said. 'According to his sister, he was last in touch with his mother in 2005. She died six months later. His relationship with his sister isn't great, so it's not surprising she hasn't seen him.'

'Did he come home for the funeral?'

'No,' Cooke said. 'Karl Smith's sister said he was living in Spain. She sent him a letter, but he didn't reply.'

'Which explains the postcards Sean Grant's mother received from her son,' Graveney said. 'Can we do a handwriting check? Just to be sure.'

'His sister is looking for something with his writing on it,' Hussain said. 'She may have some old birthday cards in the loft. We should have something later today.'

'So ...' Graveney swigged his coffee. 'If Karl Smith was sending the postcards, what would be his motivation?'

'Maybe he was involved in Sean Grant's murder?' Cooke said.

'Maybe,' Graveney said. 'If the handwriting on the postcards matches. However, I think we can be sure Karl Smith was involved. Does that let Lindsey Armstrong and Jimmy Jefferson off the hook though?' He leant back in his chair and rubbed his chin.

'All three may have been involved,' Hussain said.

'We need a motive,' Graveney said. 'Do we have a last known address in Spain for him?'

'I've checked that, Guv,' Cooke said. 'He worked over there in a bar for a few years and then moved on. The trail goes cold in about 2009.'

Hussain grinned. 'We did find something else, Guv. Karl Smith did a bit of driving for a private taxi firm in Middlesbrough. This company was owned, in part, by Alexander Cooper.'

'Interesting,' Graveney said. 'Dig a bit deeper.'

'Cooper's wife comes back from holiday today,' Cooke said.

'We'll pay her a visit,' Graveney said. 'Rav. You keep digging into the link between Cooper and Smith. Sarah can come with me to see Mrs Cooper.'

'Yes, Guv,' Hussain said. He got to his feet and paused. 'What about Alan Jefferson? He needs to know about his wife's ring.'

'Yeah,' Graveney said, deep in thought. 'His son may have already told him. I might just give Jimmy and Lindsey another visit. They're definitely involved in this, somehow. I'm convinced.'

Lindsey and Jimmy endured a restless night in their new house. They discussed the events from the previous day, unsure if the police believed what they had told them. Lindsey faced her boyfriend and kissed him. Jimmy opened his eyes and gazed at her.

'You ok?' she asked.

'Yeah. Why wouldn't I be?'

'You need to speak with your dad today,' she said. 'About the ring.'

'I know. I don't want the police telling him. He's come so far. I wouldn't want him falling off the wagon.'

Lindsey turned away from him. 'Maybe we should tell the police everything we know. Tell them about Karl and how he tried to kill me.'

'I've been thinking about that. If we do, it'll make the police even more suspicious.' He shifted onto his back and stared up at the ceiling. 'The coppers already suspect you had something to do with Sean's murder. If they find out you had an affair with Cooper, they may assume you and Craig were involved in his death too. We need to think this through carefully.'

Lindsey rubbed her eyes. 'And Karl? If he doesn't show up, they may think we had something to do with his disappearance as well.'

Jimmy rolled away and planted his feet on the floor. 'He'll probably turn up. Bad pennies always do.'

'Yeah. You're right.'

Jimmy stood. 'We need to stick to our story and not worry about what might happen.'

'This isn't fair,' she said. 'Why should we suffer for something we haven't done?'

'The past is the past. As I said, let's stick to our story and hope the police lose interest.'

Lindsey climbed out of bed and placed a hand on his back. 'Maggie gets out soon.'

'We'll need to get the room ready,' he said. 'Make it special for her.'

'Are you sure it's ok Maggie moving in with us?'

'Of course it is.' He laughed. 'I'm already living with one convicted murderer. Another won't matter.'

Lindsey smiled. 'I love you, Jimmy.'

'I love you too,' he said.

Graveney and Cooke entered the drive of the large house, pulling up opposite the door. They got out of the car and climbed the short flight of steps. Graveney pressed the bell, and he and Cooke waited. There was a brief pause, and then the door swung open. A woman in her late-fifties stood there.

'Can I help you?' she said.

'Mrs Cooper?' Graveney asked.

'No, I'm her housekeeper. Can I ask who you are?'

The officers took out their credentials and showed them to the woman. Satisfied, she allowed them inside.

'I'll just go and get Mrs Cooper,' she said. 'If you'd like to wait in here.' Pointing to a room to their right, she trudged off.

They waited a few moments before a well-dressed, elegant looking woman came in. Graveney eyed her. She was late-forties, he guessed. Attractive, and with the look of someone who not only never had to work a day in her life, but someone who spent a large part of it pampered.

'Good morning,' she said politely. Indicating for the officers to take a seat. 'How can I help you?'

'I'm Inspector Graveney, and this is my colleague, DC Cooke,' he said. 'There's no easy way of telling you this, Mrs Cooper. We've found the body of your husband.'

Mrs Cooper brought a hand up to her mouth. 'Are you sure it's him? Could there …?'

'Yes, we're sure. There were documents on the body belonging to your husband. We completed a DNA test from a sample of his on file. There is no doubt.'

'I see.' She lowered her eyes and ran her fingers around her wedding ring. 'How …?' her voice trailed off.

'We can't be sure,' Graveney said. He observed her, trying to read the emotions. She appeared to be thinking long and hard before asking a question. He found this odd. Graveney's antenna twitched.

She met Graveney's stare. 'Where was he … found?'

'In a car at the bottom of a lake,' he said. 'Near New Marske.'

'Lake?'

'It's called Tolmby Lake, but it's more of a large pond.'

'I see. Was it an accident?'

'We're confident it wasn't,' he said.

Mrs Cooper looked down and gently stroked the gold band on her finger. 'I'm sorry … Can I offer you a drink? This has come as a bit of a shock.' She got to her feet and moved to the other side of the room.

'Not for me,' Graveney said. He glanced at Cooke. Cooke shook her head.

'Can I ask when you last saw your husband?' he said.

Mrs Cooper poured herself a large gin and tonic and shakily lifted the glass to her lips. She sipped from it. 'In 1999.'

Graveney pulled out his notepad. 'I read the report into your husband's disappearance. It appears Alex left with a large sum of money.'

'Yes. Alex embezzled money from the council coffers for some time, apparently.'

'£130,000,' Graveney said. 'Not a huge sum of money. Even then.'

'They apparently pay you well, Inspector, if you think £130,000 isn't lots of money.'

'It's all relative. This house ...' Graveney pointed around the lavish interior. 'This must be worth quite a bit.'

'Alex had business interests in a couple of local companies. They've done quite well since his disappearance.'

'And before?' Graveney said.

'They were struggling a little.'

He eased forward in his seat. 'Do you think he stole this money to prop up his business?'

'I don't know.' She chewed her lip. 'Back then, I'd little input on that side of his life.'

'Can I ask you about your husband's personal life?' Graveney said. He paused, struggling to find the appropriate words. 'Did your hus—?'

'You're wondering if there were other women? … Alex was handsome and a terrible womaniser. He loved me, but he tended to stray when the urge took him. I turned a blind eye to all his *philandering*. I came from a humble background, and I wasn't about to lose that.'

'You could have divorced him,' Cooke said.

She drained her glass. 'I could have. But I didn't.' She reached into her handbag and removed a cigarette packet, shakily took one and lit it. Drawing deeply. 'What's sauce for the goose.' She smiled at the two officers and then stared at Graveney. 'Besides, I loved him.'

'I see,' Graveney said. 'Can you think of anyone who would want to harm your husband?'

She sneered and looked out of the window. 'Probably a string of irate husbands and boyfriends.'

'One more thing, Mrs Cooper,' he said, pausing until she looked him in the eye again. 'Did your husband ever mention anyone called Sean Grant?'

'Sean Grant?' she said. 'I don't think so.'

Graveney maintained his penetrating stare. 'Thanks for all your help.' He and Cooke stood. He reached into the top pocket of his brown tweed jacket, pausing briefly as a memory pushed for his attention. He felt something, he was sure. A key. He fumbled again with his fingers. There was only a card. 'If you remember anything else, can you ring me?' He handed Mrs Cooper the card.

'Yes, of course,' she said.

Graveney and Cooke got in the car. He glanced over to the window of the property. 'She'd heard the name before,' he said.

'Whose name?' Cooke said.

'Sean Grant.' Graveney raised his eyebrows at Cooke, and she started the engine.

Mrs Cooper waited for the car to exit the drive. Closing the living room door, she picked up her mobile. A man answered.

'Hi,' he said. 'You'll have to make it quick. I've got a meeting with a client in five minutes.'

'The police have been here,' she whispered. 'They've found Alex's body.'

'Where?' he asked.

'In a car. At the bottom of a pond.'

'The one over New Marske?' he said.

'Yeah. How did you know?'

'It's all over the news. It was fished out the other day.'

'I've just got back from the villa,' she said. 'I didn't know.'

'Who was the second body?'

'Second body?'

'The news said there were two bodies in the car.'

'It must have been Sean Grant,' she said. 'The policeman who came asked if Alex, or I, knew Sean Grant.'

'I'll come over later.'

'Tell me you had nothing to do with this, Conrad?'

'Of course not. I thought Alex had done a runner with the missing money like everyone else.'

'What about Sean Grant?'

'No idea. I'll see what I can find out.'

'Have I anything to worry about, Conrad? You would tell me?'

'Jean,' he said. 'I'm as much in the dark as you. Just hold your nerve and don't panic. We've done nothing wrong.'

She searched for another number and dialled. 'Can we meet?' she said.

'Yeah. Why?' Harry said.

'They've found Alex's body. Conrad denies any involvement.'
'You don't believe him?'
'Let's just say, I'm keeping an open mind.'

Conrad Hudson dialled a number. 'It's Conrad. Cooper's body's shown up.'

'Where?'

'In the car they fished out of the lake. It looks as if Sean Grant's body was in there too. See what you can find out from your contact.'

'Ok, Boss.'

CHAPTER SIX

Graveney sipped at his coffee and looked up as Hussain entered. He stood in front of Graveney's desk, shuffling his feet.

Graveney sighed and glanced up at him. 'What is it?'

'We've found something else in the car.'

Graveney held his hands out, palms open. 'And?'

'A bracelet.'

'Why wasn't it found earlier?'

'Apparently one of the guys from forensics discovered it behind the glovebox. It must have fallen out and become lodged there somehow. We were lucky he removed the glovebox.'

'Was it on the list of things stolen from Mrs Jefferson's house?'

Hussain slowly shook his head.

'Come on,' Graveney said. 'Spit it out.'

'It's engraved with a name and a date.'

Graveney threw open his arms. 'And the name is ...?'

'Lindsey.'

Graveney reclined back in his chair and smiled. 'The date?'

'The same date of birth as Lindsey Armstrong's,' Hussain said.

'Have you got it?'

Hussain held out a plastic bag and handed it to Graveney. 'I think we'd better go and chat with Miss Armstrong,' Graveney said, as he gazed at the object in his hand.

Lindsey dressed, and she and Jimmy spent the morning unpacking and arranging the furniture. She placed a vase, replete with flowers, on a table as Graveney's car pulled up outside. Lindsey groaned and watched as Graveney and Hussain got out and headed towards the front door.

'It's the coppers,' she said. Jimmy turned to face her as Graveney knocked on the door.

Lindsey and Jimmy sat together on the settee, across from them Graveney and Hussain. In between the four, a coffee table acting as no man's land.

'Can I get either of you a drink?' Jimmy said, trying to appear calm. The pounding in his chest nearly betraying him.

'I'm all right,' Graveney said. He glanced at Hussain. His junior held up a hand to indicate he didn't want one either.

Graveney focussed on Jimmy. 'Did you tell your dad? About the ring?'

Jimmy glanced at Lindsey. 'I did,' Jimmy said. Lindsey gently squeezed his hand. 'He's ok, I think.' Jimmy continued. 'We're having him stay a couple of days. Just to keep an eye on him.'

'I understand. It must be difficult.' He turned to Lindsey. 'You ok, Lindsey?'

She lifted her head, stared at him, and folded her arms tightly, her brow lowering into a scowl. 'Why don't you just get to the point? You haven't come here to ask how we are.'

Graveney reached inside his jacket pocket and took out the small plastic bag. He placed it on the coffee table in front of the two of them. Lindsey stared at the object, as a little babble of voices in her head started. She rubbed her eyes and tried to push the chatter aside. Slowly it receded.

'It's mine,' she said.

'Guess where we found it?' Graveney said.

'No idea.'

'It was in the glovebox of the car we fished out of the lake. I don't suppose you know how it got there?'

Lindsey closed her eyes tightly and sighed, before blinking them open again. 'I gave it to Sean.'

'This is the Sean who you hardly knew?'

Lindsey tilted her head back. 'Yeah.'

'Why give Sean your bracelet?'

'Sean was a bad influence on Craig. Craig wasn't like him. He was a decent lad who'd got in bad company.'

Graveney glanced at Hussain. 'Funny how many of those I meet,' he said. 'People who've fallen into bad company. Never seem to meet up with any of this bad company, though.'

Lindsey ignored his goading. 'Sean wanted Craig to go on some job with him. I gave it to Sean, along with some money and other bits and pieces, to leave Craig alone.'

'This job …?'

'I don't know,' Lindsey said. 'He never went into details.'

'And did Craig go on this job?'

'He was going to. We argued ...'

'And you killed him?'

'And I killed him.' She wiped away the tears which escaped their bonds and tumbled down her cheeks.

'Is that what happened, Lindsey?' he said. 'Did you actually kill Craig?' The two locked eyes.

Jimmy got to his feet. 'Are you arresting us? Because if you are, we're not saying anything else.'

'Not just yet,' Graveney said. He rose. 'We may need to speak again. Don't go anywhere, will you?'

Graveney and Hussain got back in their car. Graveney, although he couldn't see her, sensed Lindsey was watching them from within.

'Why didn't you arrest them, Guv?'

'There's something not right. They're keeping something from us, but I'm not sure what.'

'Her boyfriend, Craig?' Hussain said. 'She killed him.'

'She didn't kill him. I'm sure of it.'

'Nobody does fifteen years for something they didn't commit. She pleaded guilty. Why admit to it?'

'I don't know.'

'And Sean Grant?' Hussain said.

'I don't think she murdered him either.'

'Jefferson?'

Graveney bit his bottom lip. 'No. I don't think so. There's something not right here.' Graveney stared towards the house and rubbed his chin. 'Dig a little deeper into Councillor Cooper. He may be the key to all this.'

'And Karl Smith?' Hussain said.

'Unless we find him ... we may never know his involvement.'

CHAPTER SEVEN

Graveney stopped on the patio and viewed his handiwork. The garden set out with tables and chairs neatly arranged on the lawn. He headed inside where Heather was preparing food. Max, perched in his highchair, chewed a piece of carrot.

Graveney sauntered across and put his arms around his wife and kissed her on the cheek. 'Need a hand?'

'No. I think I'll cope.'

'I've put all the chairs and tables out. The barbecue only needs a match.'

She half-turned and kissed him on the cheek. 'There is something you could do.'

'Oh, yeah?'

'I think your son needs changing.'

'I'd rather peel those potatoes,' Graveney said.

'I think I've got these covered.'

Graveney moved across to his son, picked him up, and wrinkled his nose. 'I don't think there's any doubt.'

Heather turned to face the pair. 'The nappies are in the front room.'

'Come on shitty pants,' Graveney said.

Graveney stood with Mac, casually pushing the sausages around the barbecue. Heather and Becky relaxed at a table close by. People milled in and out of the house, the garden a hubbub of noise.

Graveney held a sausage up between his tongs. 'These sausages are ready.' People vacated their chairs and headed towards him.

Mac drained his bottle. 'Another beer, Peter?'

'Yeah,' he said, as Mac headed inside. Graveney whipped around as a familiar voice drifted into earshot. Bev stood with her husband,

Richard. Graveney looked down towards Bev's right hand and her daughter holding tightly on to it. He smiled. The little girl's angelic face framed by dark brown, almost black, curls. Bev met Graveney's stare as he brought his head back up, the pair performing a perfunctory smile at each other before looking away.

Graveney stood looking at Max and Aimee, playing inside the sandpit in the corner of the garden. Louisa joined him.

He kissed his daughter as she put an arm around him. 'When did you arrive?'

'Just now,' Louisa said.

'Where's Jonathan?'

'He's got an errand to run and then he's coming over.'

'There's plenty of food left.'

Louisa bent and picked up Max. 'How's my baby brother?' Max, resenting being removed from the sandpit, kicked out his legs as Louisa lowered him back down.

'The little girl's—'

'Bev's,' she said.

'Yeah. Aimee.'

Louisa smiled as the girl peered up at the two adults. 'She's beautiful.'

'She is,' Graveney said.

Louisa looked directly at her father. 'I don't think anyone else suspects.'

He glanced past Louisa, but no one else was in earshot. 'How did you guess?'

'I didn't know for sure, until now. Your face just told me.'

Graveney laughed. 'Ok detective. Have you ever considered joining the police?'

Louisa linked Graveney's arm, looking deeply into her father's eyes. 'I won't say anything.'

'It happened before Heather and I got together. I know that's no excuse, but—'

'Dad,' Louisa said. 'You don't have to explain. I'm not going to judge you. Will you tell Heather?'

He looked towards the house as his wife came outside. 'I don't know.'

'You've got a good life with Heather. Maybe you should let sleeping dogs lie.'

Graveney brought his hand up to her cheek. 'What did I do to deserve you?'

Heather watched the pair from across the garden. She smiled as they hugged and wandered across to join them. 'What are you two plotting?' she said.

'Father and daughter stuff,' Louisa said. She grasped hold of Graveney's arm and beamed.

Heather gazed at Louisa. 'Luke's looking for you. He wants you to take some shots at him. He's decided he wants to be a goalkeeper.'

'Better not disappoint then,' Louisa said. She kissed her father on the cheek and disappeared.

Heather put her arm around her husband. 'Richard and Bev are going. They want their daughter back. Max will have to do without his playmate.'

Heather bent down, picked up the girl and carried her towards the house. Graveney looked on, as Aimee, with her head on Heather's shoulder, looked back at him. He smiled, the child responding with one of her own, and then she was gone.

Graveney turned off the main road and headed for Robin Hoods Bay. He pulled up outside a cemetery, collected the flowers from the back seat and headed inside the graveyard. Removing a scrap of paper from his pocket, with the location of the plot written on it, he walked across to the grave situated in one corner of the churchyard, overlooking a grassy bank. He knelt and removed the now dead flowers from the urn in front of the headstone. He unwrapped his, and placed them in the pot, arranging them neatly. Satisfied, he stood up and viewed the name, *Stephanie Marne*. Phillips was right, it was a lovely spot, he thought. The trees, surrounding the graves, threw a dappled shade across them. He closed his eyes and pictured her flawless face and smiled to himself. But as fast as it appeared, it was replaced by the blood-covered features moments after her death. Her face coated in the sickly-red liquid. Her eyes fixed in a deathly stare. The right-hand side of her head, a mess of brain and gore where the bullet exited. He shuddered and opened his eyes, the image slowly dissolved into nothingness. Turning, he headed back to his car, as invisible songbirds filled the air with their sweet music.

He pulled up outside a small picturesque cottage with roses growing around the door. Its well-tended gardens resplendent with colour. Graveney got out, headed up the path and knocked.

Phillips opened the door. Smiling, he offered his hand to Graveney. 'Peter.'

Graveney shook it firmly. 'Beautiful cottage, Trevor.'

'Come in, I've just put the kettle on.'

He followed Phillips inside, heading through into the kitchen. 'I'm sure I've got some coffee in here.' Searching through a cupboard, he pushed items aside.

'Tea's fine,' Graveney said.

'Are you sure?'

'Yeah. Milk, no sugar.'

Phillips poured the tea and passed Graveney a mug. 'Biscuit?'

Graveney shook his head. 'I visited the cemetery.'

Phillips paused, a plateful of biscuits in his hand. 'I thought you might.'

'It is a lovely spot.'

The older man put the plate on the table, motioning for Graveney to sit. 'We think so.'

'Where's Pam?'

'At her cross-stitch group. You said on the phone you wanted to pick my brains. Not much left up here.' He tapped his head. 'Only a few marbles.'

'Alexander Cooper,' Graveney said.

'The councillor who disappeared with all the money?'

'He turned up the other day. In the boot of a car at the bottom of a deep pond.'

Phillips slid into the seat opposite Graveney and leant forward. 'The one in Marske?'

'Yeah.'

'Saw it on the news. Obviously not natural causes.'

'Nope. I'm looking for anything you can tell me.'

Phillips tapped his chin. 'Not a lot, really. We assumed he'd done a runner with the money. No reason to think otherwise.'

'The money wasn't with the body,' Graveney said.

'The other body? Who was that?'

'A petty criminal, Sean Grant. He knew Cooper, apparently. What did you think of Cooper's wife?'

'Wasn't sure about her. Cooper had a bit of a reputation as a ladies' man. She knew about it. Maybe she got sick of him and had him killed?'

Graveney sipped his tea. 'Maybe.'

Phillips stood. 'I've some of my old diaries locked away upstairs. I was going to burn them or use them in my memoirs. I'll go and get them. See if there's anything inside those.'

Graveney stared out of the window as Phillips returned. 'Not a lot I'm afraid, Peter. Although I've made a note here.' He handed it to Graveney.

Graveney glanced at the page and read. 'Possible connection between Alexander Cooper and Conrad Hudson?'

'Yeah. Just whispers. I was interested because Hudson was already getting a bit of a reputation.'

'Right.' Graveney glanced again at the book. 'You've put a question mark next to Jean Cooper.'

Phillips sat. 'Yeah. I'd a suspicion Jean Cooper and Hudson were having an affair.'

'Really?'

'Nothing concrete,' Phillips said.

'Why the suspicion?'

'I think one of my officers saw Mrs Cooper leaving Hudson's office. He couldn't be certain, though.'

'You didn't check into it, then?'

Phillips leant back. 'Yeah. They knew each other, but we found nothing to lead us to believe they were an item.'

'It gives them the motive to kill Cooper if they were,' Graveney said.

'They both had cast-iron alibis. A couple of influential people vouched for them. Although …'

'Although?' Graveney said.

'People who knew the Coopers well said she was devoted to her husband. Despite his indiscretions.'

Graveney rubbed his chin. 'Maybe she just grew sick of him. Even if they had an alibi, Mrs Cooper and Hudson could have had someone do it for them.'

'They could. But who?'

'I don't know. Sean Grant, maybe.'

Phillips lowered his eyes. 'The other body?'

Graveney nodded. 'Yeah. And one of Hudson's men could've killed Sean Grant.'

Phillips blew out hard. 'I don't envy you this one, Peter.'

'No. It's what we get paid for, though.' Graveney stood. 'I better get going, Trevor.'

Phillips handed him a second notebook. 'Have this one as well. You never know, you may find something in it. My memory is not what it was.'

'Oh,' Graveney said. 'Do you remember a Lindsey Armstrong?'

Phillips rubbed his chin. 'The name sounds familiar.'

'She was sentenced to life for murdering her boyfriend.'

'Ah, yes,' Phillips said. 'I do. Not my case, though. Sid Harris handled that one. Why?'

'Lindsey Armstrong knew Alexander Cooper. She also knew Sean Grant via her boyfriend.'

'The one she killed?'

'Craig Embleton.' Graveney said.

'Right. You think Lindsey Armstrong had something to do with it?'

'Don't know. It's a bit of a coincidence, though. Don't you think?'

'Maybe,' Phillips said.

'There's something she's holding back. I've a feeling she knew Cooper far better than she is letting on.'

'Far better? You mean they were an item?'

'She was only young,' Graveney said. 'But it's possible. Apparently, it was common knowledge in the council chambers, Cooper liked his women young. Nothing to suspect he broke the law, you understand.'

'The right side of legal?' Phillips said.

'Looks that way.'

Phillips stood and picked up the cups. 'Have you read the case file on Lindsey Armstrong?'

'Yeah. Cut and dried.'

'Give Sid Harris a ring,' Phillips said. 'He may remember something. I've still got his number.' Phillips moved over to a dresser and fished through a drawer. 'We play golf occasionally. I've got it in here somewhere.'

Graveney sat in his car and pulled out the little piece of paper Phillips gave him. He dialled the number and waited.

'Hi,' a voice said. 'Sid Harris.'

'Hello, Sid. My name's DI Peter Graveney. You don't know me, but we have a mutual friend. Trevor Phillips.'

'Trevor. Yeah.'

'I'm working on a murder enquiry. And a name keeps cropping up. Lindsey Armstrong.'

'I remember her,' Harris said. 'She killed her boyfriend.'

'Any doubt about that?'

'Cut and dried. She confessed to it.'

'What about forensics? Any doubt there?'

'No,' Harris said. 'She denied doing it at first, if I remember. She said she found him dead and panicked. Plausible, I suppose. But when we discovered the knife—'

'Nothing suspicious there?' Graveney said.

'No. It was hidden in the garden of her parents' house. It had her boyfriend's blood on it, and it matched the weapon which killed him.'

'It says one of your DS's found it?'

'That's right. He, and DC Jones were looking at the rear of her mother and father's property.'

'Jones?' Graveney said.

'I know Jones was implicated in the Oake scandal, Peter. But the internal investigation did a thorough check of all the cases Oake and Jones worked on. I don't think you have anything to worry about.'

Graveney grunted. 'Whenever those two are mentioned, alarm bells start ringing.'

'But as I say, the Lindsey Armstrong case doesn't look suspicious.'

'Yeah,' Graveney said. 'I've studied the case notes, and it does look cut and dried.'

'She clammed up after we found the knife, and wouldn't talk anymore. It came as a huge surprise when she pleaded guilty.'

Graveney pondered for a moment. 'That's great, Sid. Thanks for your help.'

'What case are you working on?' Harris said.

'The Alexander Cooper murder.'

'How is Lindsey Armstrong—?'

'She knew him,' Graveney said.

'Didn't her boyfriend work for Cooper?'

'He did,' Graveney said. 'There are too many coincidences for my liking.'

'The other body found with Cooper?'

'Sean Grant. A mate of Lindsey Armstrong's boyfriend.'

Harris chuckled. 'Christ, Peter. You've opened up a can of worms here.'

'Don't I know it.'

'Maybe …' Harris said. 'Lindsey Armstrong and her boyfriend killed Cooper?'

'I've considered that. But what about Sean Grant?'

'It's a poser.'

'It is. Thanks for your help, Sid.'

Graveney stooped at his desk, flicked through the notebook Phillips gave him. He stopped at a name with a line through it. 'Robin Slaney,' he said to himself. Graveney picked up his mobile and called Phillips.

'Hi, Peter. Did my notebook yield anything?'

'Probably nothing,' Graveney said. 'You've written down a name and then crossed it out. Robin Slaney?'

'Robin Slaney?' Phillips said. 'I can't remember anything about him.'

'At the top of the page, you've written "Staff".'

'Ah, yes. I remember now.' He rubbed his chin. 'Slaney worked for Hudson as a gardener. He was married to Hudson's cook. She was Portuguese, I think.'

Graveney glanced at the book again. 'Anabela Slaney?'

'That was it. By all accounts, she was a bit fiery. Her husband and her were always rowing. She didn't like living in England. Anyway, she left and returned to Portugal a couple of weeks before Cooper's disappearance.'

'And her husband?' Graveney said.

'I think if my memory serves me right …' Phillips said, 'he left to join his wife a little later.'

'Before or after Cooper's disappearance?'

'I think before. That's why I crossed his name off.'

'Did you check up on him?' Graveney said.

'I had one of my DCs do it, I think. It was a long time ago.'

'Can you remember which one?'

Phillip's huffed. 'Christ, Peter. You're feeding on scraps here.'

'I know,' Graveney said. 'I understand not pursuing him vigorously back then. Everyone else believed Cooper did a runner, but we now know he was murdered. Maybe Slaney saw or heard something.'

'Yeah. I suppose it's worth looking into. But it's still a bit of a long shot, though.'

Graveney laughed. 'You know me and long shots, Trevor.'

'I do. You could try someone called Danny Hallbrook. He was a young DC in my department. I probably gave him the task of checking up on Slaney.'

'Is he still working in the force?'

'No. He left ages ago. Became a fireman, I think. Ask Ruth. She keeps in touch with most people from back then. She might know.'

'I will. Thanks, Trevor. I'll let you know if I find anything else out.'

Graveney picked up his phone and dialled. He waited as someone picked up the phone. 'Incident room,' a woman's voice said.

'It's DI Graveney. Is Ruth there?'

'I'll just get her, Sir.'

He waited a few moments as the phone was passed to someone. 'Yes, Guv,' Ruth said.

'Ruth ... Do you remember a young DC who used to work here? Danny Hallbrook?'

'Danny, yeah,' she said. 'He left to become a fireman. Nice lad, but wasn't cut out to be a plainclothes officer. He should've stayed in uniform. Why?'

'I was visiting Trevor today. He said he was one of his DCs.'

'How is Trevor?'

'Loving retirement.'

'Good to hear. Do you need an address for Danny?'

'Yes, please. It's a long shot. But you know me, Ruth. I like to check the smallest of details.'

She laughed. 'I do. I saw Danny a couple of months ago in town. I think he works at Middlesbrough fire station. I'll find out his home address if you want?'

'No, it's fine, Ruth,' Graveney said. 'I'll give the station a ring and pop over and see him.' He hung up, downed the remainder of his coffee and stood.

Someone knocked, and Hussain pushed his head through the gap. 'There's been a body found near Stainton, Sir. Definite murder.'

Graveney dropped Phillips' notebooks into his drawer. 'Murder. Let's get going then.'

CHAPTER EIGHT

The car trundled along the farm track towards the huge barn stood at the end of it. Hussain pulled the vehicle up outside a broad set of wooden doors. Graveney viewed the scene. Forensic officers in blue, entering and exiting the building.

He glanced at Hussain. 'Speak to whoever found him, Rav.' Hussain took out his notepad, and the pair clambered out.

Graveney slipped on a pair of plastic overshoes and overalls and marched towards the barn. A constable lifted the tape strung across the entrance, allowing him through. He stopped at the threshold, drinking in the scene. Someone – a man he supposed – naked and tethered, hung from a rope fastened around his neck. A huge gaping wound stretched from the middle of his chest to just above his groin. Blood covered the bottom half of his body. Below this, lying neatly in a pile in front of him, the man's viscera. Graveney shook his head and wandered closer to Wilson.

Bev Wilson, squatting on the floor near to the man, stood to face Graveney.

He reached her and stopped, raising his eyebrows. 'You invite me to all the best murder scenes, Bev.'

'A particularly gruesome one ... This chap ...' She nodded at the corpse. '... must have upset someone.'

'A name?'

'William Turner. Well, that's what the driving licence says. It was in the pocket of a jacket we found nearby. He's been here quite a few days. Maybe a week.'

Graveney smirked and bent lower to view the corpse. 'Billy Turner.' He tutted loudly. 'I've seen him look much better. And smell better too.'

'It appears,' she said, 'Mr Turner was eviscerated while still alive. I won't be sure until I get him back to the lab. Whoever killed him, cut off his genitals and shoved them into his mouth.'

Graveney sucked in air. 'Now, that's got to smart. Was that done before death too?

'Maybe. Do you know him?'

'Oh, yes,' Graveney said. 'Billy Turner and I have crossed paths on numerous occasions. A nasty piece of work.'

'Karma?'

'Karma with a sharp knife.' Graveney turned to face Bev. 'Any clues?'

Wilson handed him a clear plastic envelope with a piece of paper inside. He viewed it. Although covered in blood, he could see a playing card. 'Jack of Clubs?' he said.

'It was pinned to his thigh with a knife. The knife, I suspect, used to carry out this handiwork.' She looked down at the man's innards.

Graveney sniffed. 'It'll make your post mortem easier. Whoever did this, has done most of the hard work for you.'

'True enough.'

Graveney motioned to leave and paused. 'Let me know when you've finished with him.'

Wilson clasped hold of his arm. 'How are you?' she said.

He paused. 'I'm good. You?'

Wilson glanced at her wedding ring. 'I'm well. I enjoyed the barbeque.'

'Yeah. It was a good day. How's ...?'

'Aimee's fine.'

Graveney lowered his head a little. 'I should get going.' His eyes darted towards the door. 'Duty ..."

'I think about you a lot, Peter. I've tried not to ...'

Graveney rubbed his eyes. 'It's so complicated. We need to talk. Away from work.'

The pair turned as Hussain made his way into the barn.

'I'll ring,' Graveney said. He forced a smile and headed towards his Junior.

Graveney and Hussain drove into the car park of *Hudson Fabrications* and pulled up. They jumped out, marched inside and stopped at reception.

'Conrad Hudson, please,' Graveney said.

The receptionist scrutinised them. 'Mr Hudson is in a meeting.'

Graveney showed his credentials. 'He'll see me.'

She pouted and picked up the phone. '... Mr Hudson. Sorry to bother you, but the police are here ... Yes ... Ok.' She hung up. 'Come with me, please.' Graveney and Hussain followed her as she made her way along corridors and stopped outside a door. 'If you could wait in here, Mr Hudson will be along shortly.' Graveney thanked her and entered the room.

Hudson strode in. Graveney and Hussain, who were looking out of the window, spun around. 'Inspector,' he said. 'To what do I owe this pleasure?' He continued over to a cupboard on the far side of the room and took out a bottle and glass. He held the glass up and smiled at Graveney. 'Will you join me?'

'Billy Turner?' Graveney said.

Hudson poured himself a large measure and slid into a chair. He took a mouthful. 'He works for me. But then you already know that.'

'When was the last time you saw him alive?'

Hudson's eyes narrowed. 'Alive? That would signify he isn't anymore.'

Graveney moved closer to Hudson and perched on a chair opposite him. 'We found him this morning. In a derelict barn near Stainton.' Hudson shrugged, and Graveney continued. 'Near to where they're building those new houses.'

Hudson shrugged again. 'I haven't seen Billy since last week.'

'You and he haven't fallen out, have you?'

'Billy's one … Was one of my best men, Graveney.'

'Billy was a thug. He should've done time for the Johnson girl.'

Hudson scoffed. 'History, Graveney. The girl retracted her statement. If that's all, I am rather busy.'

'Not much compassion, Conrad. Considering he was one of your best men. I'll leave you to it, but we may need another chat.'

'Can't wait, Inspector.'

Graveney and Hussain stood. 'One more thing, Mr Hudson.'

'Yes, Graveney.'

'Do you remember someone called Robin Slaney?'

'Robin Slaney?' Hudson gulped from his glass.

'Yeah. I believed he worked for you?'

Hudson spluttered. 'Worked! He was possibly the worst gardener I've ever had. I only kept him on because his wife was such a good cook.'

'Anabela?' Graveney said.

'Yeah, Anabela.'

'Do you remember what happened to them?'

Hudson drained his glass. 'I can't be expected to remember every person I employed, Inspector. I do have more important things in my life than what my ex-employees get up to.'

Graveney sensed Hudson's annoyance. Understandable, given his dislike for the police, but below this, another emotion briefly came into view before Hudson masked it.

'Indulge me,' Graveney said.

Hudson fixed Graveney with a Baltic stare. 'Anabela couldn't settle. She left and went back to Portugal, I think.'

'And her husband?'

'Robin left a week or so later.'

'You kept him on after his wife left? Even though he was a poor gardener?'

Hudson sneered. 'Maybe I needed my roses deadheading.'

'Did he go back—?'

'Jesus Christ, Graveney. I don't know. I didn't have him followed.'

'Thanks again, Mr Hudson. We'll be in touch.'

Hudson stood, poured himself another large drink and watched as the officers left.

Graveney and Hussain strode towards the door. Graveney paused as he opened it. 'If you need the number of a good florist ...' Hudson glared at him. '... For Billy Turner's widow.' Graveney grinned.

Once outside, Hussain turned to Graveney as they reached the car. 'Who's Robin Slaney, Guv?'

'A name from Hudson's past.'

'What's the connection to the case?'

'The bodies in the car,' Graveney said. Hussain nodded. 'Hudson was interviewed when Cooper went missing. Slaney and his wife weren't interviewed at the time.'

Hussain frowned. 'Why would they be?'

'I spoke to Phillips the other day. He suspected Hudson and Cooper's wife were having an affair.'

'A good reason to have Cooper killed?'

Graveney stopped as they reached the car and the pair jumped in 'No one gave it any thought at the time,' Graveney said. 'They assumed Cooper did a runner with the money.'

'But now he's turned up dead?'

'Exactly,' Graveney said. 'Puts a whole new complexion on it.'

'You think this Robin Slaney may know something?'

'Yeah. Staff often overhear things. Maybe he heard or saw something.'

'Where is he now?' Hussain said.

'By all accounts, he followed his wife to Portugal.'

Hussain rubbed his hands together. 'Are we going on holiday, then?'

'I don't think the Guv would wear that.'

Hussain started the engine and tilted his head back at the factory. 'What about Hudson?'

Graveney stared at the building and pondered. 'It's not unusual for people to show surprise when you blindside them with a question. It was a long time ago. But there was definitely something else below the surface.'

'What?' Hussain said.

'Concern.' Graveney smiled. 'Hudson is concerned.'

'Where to, Guv?'

'Pathology. Bev Wilson will have finished the post mortem on Billy Turner. Then we need to go to Middlesbrough fire station.' Hussain frowned. 'I'll explain on the way,' Graveney said.

Hudson put down his phone and stretched back in his chair. He picked up the bottle, replenished his glass and took a large gulp.

His phone rang. 'Yeah?'

'It's Taffy, Boss. You wanted a word?'

'Get your arse over here.'

'What's up?'

'Billy's dead. The contact of yours in the pathology department?'

'What about her?' Taffy said.

'See if you can find out how he died. I've had Graveney in here quizzing me.'

'Ok. I'll be a couple of hours. What did Graveney want?'

'Robin Slaney,' Hudson said.

'Robin Slaney? What about him?'

'Graveney was asking questions.'

'Why?'

'I don't know. Graveney obviously has something up his sleeve, though. We'll discuss it when you get here.'

'Ok, Boss. See you soon.'

CHAPTER NINE

Graveney made his way into the pathology department with Hussain and headed for Bev Wilson's lab.

Graveney smiled. 'All finished?'

'Just now,' she said. 'Have a seat.'

The pair waited as Bev collected her notes and joined them.

'Right … Mr Turner was eviscerated while still alive. I'm not sure if he was conscious, though.'

Graveney leant forward. 'Mmm.'

'Prior to him having his innards laid bare, someone cut off his genitals and forced them into his mouth as I told you.'

'Someone really hated him,' Hussain said.

'He would probably have been unable to breathe. He may even have passed out. A godsend when you know what happened to him next.'

Graveney screwed up his face. 'Sex crime?'

'Sex crime?' Wilson said.

'Yeah. To mutilate him, especially cutting off his wedding tackle, it has to be something sexual.'

'Possibly,' she said. 'Does that help?'

'Not really, unless we know what Billy Turner did and who he did it too.'

'True,' Bev said. 'But it's a start.'

Graveney stood. 'Anything else?'

'The playing card …' Wilson said. '… has to mean something.'

Graveney nodded slowly. 'It's obviously got some significance.' He looked towards Hussain. 'Get onto the station, and make some enquiries regarding the Mia Johnson case.'

Hussain looked up from his notes. 'Isn't she the girl Billy Turner allegedly raped?'

'He did rape her. The fact she retracted her statement doesn't mean he didn't do it.'

'You think someone in her family had something to do with it, Guv?'

'Maybe.'

Hussain stood, took out his phone and wandered off.

Graveney eyeballed Wilson. 'I'll be in touch.'

She stood and moved closer, placing a hand on his arm. 'What about us two?'

Graveney glanced towards the door Hussain left by, and then gazed into her eyes. 'I think we know where this is heading. If we allow it.'

She bit her lip. 'I think we do.'

Hussain came back in. 'The guys are on to it now, Sir.'

'Ok, Rav.' Graveney turned to Wilson and winked. 'See you later.'

The officers made their way along a series of corridors and back outside. They jumped into the car, and Hussain started the engine. 'Fire station?' Hussain asked.

'Yeah, fire station.'

Graveney and Hussain parked next to Albert Park and made their way over to the fire station. The officers entered the reception and were escorted into an office. The pair waited for a few moments before a man came in. He looked at Graveney. 'DI Graveney?' he said. The two officers stood.

Graveney held out a hand. 'Danny Hallbrook?' He nodded. 'This is my DS,' Graveney said. He gestured towards Hussain, and the three men sat.

'So,' Hallbrook said. 'How can I help you?'

'This is a bit of a longshot,' Graveney said. 'Can you remember Alex Cooper?'

Hallbrook leant in closer. 'The one you've just fished from the lake in Marske?'

'Yeah. What do you remember about the case?'

'Not much,' Hallbrook said. 'The thought was he'd made off with the Council's money. Obviously, we now know that wasn't the case.'

'I was talking with Trevor Phillips the other day, and he mentioned he may have asked you to trace someone called Robin Slaney.'

Hallbrook rubbed his chin. 'He was a gardener for—'

'Conrad Hudson,' Hussain said.

'Yeah. Phillips suspected Hudson was having an affair with Cooper's wife. It was a line of inquiry he wanted investigating.'

'Did you talk with Slaney?' Hussain said.

'No. I telephoned his wife. She'd gone back home to Portugal, and I got the impression there was no love lost between her and Slaney. She was ranting at me down the phone, calling him all sorts. Her English wasn't great, and I couldn't understand a lot of what she said. You know what some of those Latin types are like.'

'What did you tell Phillips?' Graveney said.

Hallbrook paused. 'If I were still in the force, I'd probably lie to you and say I told him I hadn't spoken to Slaney.'

'So, what did you tell him?' Graveney said.

'Nothing. My marriage was going through a rough patch.' He stared upwards and shook his head. 'History now, thank God. I went off sick for a couple of weeks. I said I was ill. In reality, I was trying to patch things up with my ex. She was threatening to stop me from seeing the kids, and, well, you get the picture. When I came back, the investigation was shelved. The belief was Cooper nicked the money and did a runner. Phillips never asked me about Slaney, and I forgot about it.'

'But you got the impression Slaney wasn't in Portugal?' Graveney said.

Hallbrook leant forward. 'I can't be certain, but that's how I read it. The impression was Mrs Slaney was expecting her husband to join her, but he hadn't shown up.'

Graveney looked at Hussain. 'We need to get in touch with Mrs Slaney, and see if he did show up,' Graveney said. 'Anything else you remember from the conversation, Danny?'

'As I said, her English wasn't great. But I suspected she thought her husband had someone else.'

Graveney lowered his eyes and leant in closer. 'What gave you that impression?'

'She mentioned another woman.'

'You don't have a name, do you?' Graveney said.

'No. I don't think she mentioned a name. Just ... Bloody woman. His fancy woman. I remember it was quite comical, with her accent. But she definitely didn't mention a name.'

Graveney fished inside his pocket as he and Hussain stood. He took out a card and handed it to Hallbrook. 'Thanks for your help, Danny. If you remember anything else ...'

'Yeah, no problem.'

The men shook hands, and the officers left. They climbed into the car, and Hussain started the engine. He looked across at Graveney, who was deep in thought. 'What are you thinking about, Guv?'

'This is probably a blind alley, Rav. But ...'

'But,' Hussain said. 'You have a feeling?'

'Yeah. Something doesn't add up.'

'I'll see if I can track down Mrs Slaney.'

'Yeah,' Graveney said. 'And see if you can find anyone who knew her husband. Neighbours of Hudson. Someone might remember him working at the house.'

'If we find him, Guv, he may not talk. He might know nothing, anyway.'

'If he's still alive,' Graveney said.

'You think … he's dead?'

Graveney stared at Hussain. 'Yes. I do.'

'Right,' Hussain said. 'Where to now?'

'The Mason's Pub. Billy Turner used to drink in there. It's as good a place as any to start.'

Graveney and Hussain entered The Mason's public house. The noise in the room lowered to a hush as the two officers ambled towards the bar.

The barman turned away from them. 'Micky,' he shouted over his shoulder. A man came from out of the back and looked at the barman. The man followed the barman's eyes towards Graveney and Hussain.

'Inspector,' he said. 'What can I do for you?'

Two men in the corner got up and hurried from the pub. Graveney's eyes followed them as the pair left. 'Sorry about that, Micky. Looks as if I'm upsetting your regulars. It's putting a dent in your profit margin.'

Micky smiled thinly. 'Don't worry about it. Drink?'

'Billy Turner?' Graveney said.

'He hasn't been in today.'

'When did you last see him?' Hussain said.

Micky glanced across at the barman for confirmation. 'Last week?'

'What day?' Graveney said.

'Tuesday or Wednesday.'

Graveney watched as another customer got up and left. 'What time did he leave?'

'Just before closing,' the barman said. 'About eleven.'

Graveney peered around the bar. 'You've had this place decorated, Micky.'

'Yeah.'

Graveney walked the length of the bar and back again. 'Where did you get the money from?'

'You know me, Inspector. I keep my nose clean. I don't allow any funny business on my premises.'

Graveney waved a dismissive hand at him. 'Save me the testimony, Micky. I've bigger fish to fry than you. Was Billy with anyone?'

Micky slowly shook his head. 'He popped in for a couple of pints.'

Graveney scoffed. 'Why come into this dump. He didn't drop off any packages, did he?'

'As I said, Inspector—'

'Yeah, yeah, yeah. You run a clean boozer. Was Billy picked up? A taxi or car, perhaps?'

Micky looked at the barman again. 'No. I think he walked. He doesn't live far from here.'

Graveney turned and moved towards the door, closely followed by Hussain. 'If you remember anything …' he said, over his shoulder as he left.

Once outside, Graveney stopped and glanced up and down the street. 'We'll knock on a few doors. See if any of the residents saw or heard anything.'

'Turner's wife said she hadn't seen him since Tuesday night, Guv. That tallies with what Micky says.'

'Yeah. Obviously, something happened after he left the pub.'

'Looks like it. I'll take this way, Guv.' He pointed up the street.

'Yeah, ok,' Graveney said. He headed away in the opposite direction to his Hussain.

Graveney spun on his heels as Hussain shouted. His sergeant waved furiously towards him. Graveney hurried along the road and joined his junior.

'This is Mr Cuthbert, Guv. He saw something the other night.'

Graveney studied the elderly gentleman. 'Yeah?'

'I was telling your colleague here,' he said. 'I heard a commotion the other night over the road. When I looked out of the window, I saw a van parked outside.'

'Did you see who was driving it?' Graveney said.

'Not really. It was dark. Then it roared off.'

'I don't suppose you got the colour?'

'A light colour. White, I think.'

Graveney nodded. 'Anything else you remember?'

'There's this.' He picked up a flat cap from inside the house. 'I found this the following morning.'

Graveney took the cap from him and studied it. A dark patch on the brim marred the otherwise clean hat.

'I didn't think anything of it,' Cuthbert said.

'Thanks, Mr Cuthbert,' Graveney said. 'You've been a big help.'

The two officers headed back towards their car. Graveney stopped outside the passenger door and handed Hussain the cap. 'Get this bagged and over to forensics. See if it's Billy Turner's blood on there.'

'Yes, Guv.'

'And get some of the uniform guys to interview the residents, and see if anyone else saw anything.'

CHAPTER TEN

Graveney waved Hussain into his office. 'Anything back from the search of the murder scene?' He pointed to a seat, and Hussain sat.

'Yeah, Guv. We got some good footprint casts. One is small, size four. A woman's Adidas trainer. The other is a size 13 military boot. A brand used by the British army.'

Graveney leant back in his chair with his hands behind his head. 'A man and a woman? Possibly ex-forces?'

'Yeah, looks that way. And this.' He slid a piece of paper across the desk. Graveney examined it. A flier for a pizza shop. Written across the top in ink, Pearl Street. Graveney lifted his head. 'Pearl Street, Middlesbrough?'

'Yeah,' Hussain said. 'They've knocked down a lot of the houses around there. There are some squats, though.'

Cooke popped her head through the door. 'Sorry to interrupt, Guv.'

Graveney beckoned her inside. 'Go ahead.'

'We interviewed the people who own the farm next door to the one where the body was found.' Graveney nodded, and Cooke continued. 'The owner's son was in a field close by, and remembers seeing a white van parked up near to the barn.'

'There was a white van when Billy Turner got abducted,' Graveney said. 'Then again, white vans are common.'

'Don't suppose he got a reg?' Hussain said.

'No, sorry, Rav. Life's never that easy. It was too far away. He thought nothing of it because the developers had surveyors and such like in the area for a couple of weeks.'

'Anyone else spot it?' Graveney said.

'Sorry, Guv. That's about all we have, except ... The farmer said the side of the van, at one time, had something printed on it. It'd been removed, but you could still see the outline. He said it was *S&D or S&B printing, or* possibly *plumbing.* Some of the lads are checking for possible companies. Or any that resemble those names.'

Graveney leant forward. 'Gather a couple more people. We'll drive to Pearl Street.'

Cooke frowned. 'Pearl Street, Guv?'

'Rav will fill you in. I'm off upstairs to see the Guv. Ten minutes, people.'

Graveney knocked and entered Mac's office, easing himself into the seat opposite his friend.

'Peter.' Mac smiled. 'I was about to ring you.'

'We're on our way over to Pearl Street. A couple of leads to check on.'

'How did the interview with Conrad Hudson go?'

'His usual arrogant self,' Graveney said.

'Do you think he's involved in the Billy Turner murder?'

'I don't think so. It came as a surprise to him. He tried to remain cool but beneath his calm exterior, he was genuinely shocked.'

'What's your lead in Pearl Street?'

'We found one of those fast-food fliers near Billy Turner's murder scene. It had an address in Pearl Street written on it. It's a bit of a long shot.'

'Well, keep me informed.'

Graveney stood. 'Will do. Oh …' He stopped at the door. '… Heather wants to know if you and Becky fancy coming over on Saturday. She's planning a little dinner party. All very middle class.'

Mac smiled. 'Will Louisa babysit?'

'I'll ask.'

'If she will … We'll be there.'

Graveney made his way downstairs and into the incident room. He poured himself a coffee and inspected the whiteboard.

DC Jack Roberts approached him. 'Have you a minute, Guv?' he said.

'Yeah. Fire away, Jack,' he said, continuing to look at the wall.

'I've managed to locate Anabela Slaney, or Anabela Cortez, as she is now.'

Graveney turned. 'Yeah.'

'She lives in Portugal. I used an interpreter because her English wasn't great. She verified what you were told. She moved back there in 1999.'

'What about her husband?' Graveney said.

'She moved back because he was having an affair with another woman. She gave him an ultimatum. Either he come back with her, or the marriage was over. The plan was …' Roberts flicked over the page of his notebook. 'She would go ahead, and he would join a little later. He was waiting for his passport, apparently.'

'Don't tell me …' Graveney said. 'He never turned up?'

'He didn't. His wife assumed he'd decided to stay with this other woman. She's never attempted to contact him again.'

'Robin Slaney?' Graveney said.

'We're still trying to trace him. However, I've a name for the woman he was seeing. Helen Trainor.'

'Great work, Jack. Do we have an address for her?'

Roberts smiled. 'We do.' He tore a piece of paper from his book and handed it to Graveney. 'She works as a barmaid in a pub in Guisborough. The Kings Arms. It's on the High Street.'

Graveney rubbed his chin. 'Right. We'll pop across and have a word with her.'

'Now, Guv?'

'No. We've a possible lead in Middlesbrough. Grab your things. You and DS Cooke are coming along with me and Rav.'

Graveney and Hussain drove into Pearl Street, closely followed by another unmarked police car. They drew to a halt. Graveney looked along the road. On one side, a row of terraced houses. On the other, one solitary building stood alone. Open spaces either side of it where it's companions once stood.

Graveney nudged Hussain. 'Do you see what I see?'

Hussain followed Graveney's stare. 'A white van.'

The two officers got out and walked towards the vehicle, stopping close by. DS Cooke and DC Jack Roberts joined them. Graveney peered at the side of the van. A faint outline where a sign had once been.

'*Sid Ponting*,' Graveney said. He turned to face Hussain. 'S&D Printing?'

'Could be, Guv. I'll run a check on the plates.'

A man came out of a house, and spotting the officers hurried along the Street. Graveney headed across the road and intercepted him. 'Excuse me, Sir,' he said. 'You don't know who owns that van, do you?'

The man halted. 'Sorry,' he said, in a thick, east-European accent. 'My English is not good.'

Graveney pointed to the van. 'Who owns the van?'

He pushed his hands into his pockets. 'I don't know.'

Graveney thanked him and allowed him to go.

He quickly disappeared around a corner and pulled out his phone, searching his contacts he stopped at Jen. He glanced back to where he had come from, then pressed dial.

'Yes, Pavel?' Jen said.

'The police are outside the house. They're asking about your van.'

'You didn't tell them anything, did you?'

'Of course not. But someone else will.'

'I owe you one,' Jen said. She thrust the mobile into her back pocket, raced upstairs and burst into a bedroom. 'Joey,' she said. 'We need to go.'

The big man heaved himself up in bed. He put a hand to the large scar which covered the right-hand side of his face. 'What is it?' his speech slow and laboured.

She squatted in front of him, handed him his boots and placed her hands on his shoulders. 'We have to go, Joey. Now.' She kissed him. The man hauled his giant figure from the bed and dressed.

Hussain finished his call. 'It's been reported stolen, Guv. The owner lives in York.'

Graveney beckoned Cooke and Roberts closer. 'Start knocking on doors. See if anyone knows whose van it is.' The two officers marched off. 'Rav. You're with me.'

They headed for the door closest to the van, knocked and waited. Nothing stirred. 'Keep trying,' Graveney said. 'I'll look around the back. He walked to the end of the terrace block and made his way along the alley. At the end, a gate. He tried the handle. It was locked. The fence was high with spikes on the top, and he doubted he could scale it.

He groaned and made his way back towards Hussain. 'Any luck?' he said

'No answer, Guv. But there's definitely someone inside. I saw them through the letterbox.'

'The gate to the alley's locked,' Graveney said.

Roberts and Cooke joined them. Roberts addressed Graveney. 'A woman a couple of doors down said she'd seen a big guy and a young woman getting out of the van. She doesn't know their names.'

'Go back and ask her if she has a key to the alley gate,' Graveney said. 'We'll have two around the back and two at the front. Rav. Go and get the battering ram.'

Graveney turned back as the door to the property opened. A young woman holding a toddler stood there. Graveney stepped forward. 'Is that your van?' he said, pointing at the vehicle.

The woman wrinkled her nose. 'No. It belongs to a big guy who lives in the house over there.'

Graveney followed where she was pointing, and stared at the single house further up the road. He looked at Cooke. 'Grab Jack and Rav.' Hurrying towards the house, he stopped at the car and stretched for his baton. Graveney reeled backwards as the deafening explosion took him off his feet and slammed him into the side of the vehicle. He fell heavily to the floor and raised a hand to his head. The other three officers raced forward, the two police cars wrecked and covered in debris from the now burning house.

'Guv,' Cooke said, the first to reach him. 'Are you ok?'

Graveney struggled to his feet, blood trickled from a wound on his right temple. 'Yeah. But I cracked my head when I fell.'

The four of them turned as the van roared into life. They looked on helplessly as it screeched off, careered around a corner and out of sight.

'I'll call for backup,' Hussain said.

'Jesus,' Roberts said. 'The cars are wrecked.'

'You were lucky, Guv,' Cooke said. 'I think the cars saved you from the blast.'

Graveney stared back at the house. The acrid smell of black smoke emanating from it filled the air. 'I think you're right.'

Graveney came out of a cubicle and made his way into A&E reception.

Cooke stood and met him as he made his way to the door. 'They've found the van,' she said. 'It's been torched.'

Graveney smirked. 'I thought it might be.'

'What did they say about you?'

'Concussion,' Graveney said. 'The usual. Watch out for dizziness etc. Have you filled the Chief in?'

'Yeah. Rav and Jack are briefing him now. We managed to get some descriptions, but they're not great.'

'Go on. Tell me.'

'The guy is tall and muscular. One of the witnesses reckons he's over six-foot-six.'

'Get in touch with The Ministry of Defence. Ask for names of anyone who served, or is still serving, who matches that height. Massive task, I know, but the height should narrow the field a bit.'

They reached the car. Cooke stopped to make a note in her pad. 'You think he was in the forces?'

'The footprints at the murder scene were military issue boots. It's as good a place as any to start. He seems to know his way around explosives too. Look for any from the York area.'

'Why York?'

'It's where the van was stolen from.' Cooke climbed in the car next to Graveney. He glanced across at her and continued. 'The woman?'

'Bit better description. She's mid-twenties. Five-two or three with long, light-brown hair. She may be called Jen.'

'Good. Can we get a photofit done? They're obviously dangerous.'

'Someone is on to it now.'

CHAPTER ELEVEN

The young woman, carrying her handbag, raced from the pathology building, paused and gazed around. A man across the road looked at her and motioned over his shoulder. Quickly, she followed after him as he disappeared around a corner. Stopping for one final look about, she slipped down the side of the building.

A man stepped out from behind a skip, causing her to jump. 'Jesus, Taffy. You scared the hell out of me.'

'Have you got it?' he said.

She pulled a file from her handbag. 'I'll need it back within the hour. The pathologist is on her lunch.'

'Don't worry,' he said.

She grabbed his arm as he took it. 'I mean it, Taffy. I'll be up shit creek if I get caught.'

He shrugged her off and grabbed her by the throat with his free hand, pushing her up against the wall. 'Don't ever touch me again. You got that, Holly?'

'Yeah. Sorry ... It's just ... I'm taking a huge risk.'

He relinquished his grip on her throat and gently patted her cheek. 'Good girl.' He reached into his pocket and pulled out an envelope. '£500. Like we agreed.'

She grabbed it from him. 'Cheers.'

He reached into his pocket and pulled out a small plastic bag with white powder inside. 'I've got something else for you. Something you'll love.'

Her eye's widened, and she rubbed her nose. 'What do I have to do?'

'The usual.'

Nervously, she looked left and right. 'Christ, Taffy. It's broad daylight. Anyone could see us.'

He smirked. 'You'd better make it quick then.' He waved the bag in front of her. 'This is top-notch gear. Not the crap you usually put up your nose. 100% pure.'

She plucked it from his hand, thrust it into her jeans pocket and glanced about. 'Ok. Let's do it.'

'Good girl,' he said, and unbuckled his belt.

Holly filled the hand basin and washed her face with soap and hot water. She viewed herself in the mirror and patted her face dry with some hand towels. The door to the toilet opened, and Bev Wilson came in.

'Hi, Holly,' she said.

Holly startled, viewed Wilson through the mirror. 'Hi, Bev.'

'You ok? You look a little peaky.'

She forced a smile. 'I think I'm coming down with something.'

'Really. Do you want to go home? We haven't much on. I can finish up here.'

Holly glanced at her watch. 'No. I'm fine. Probably a virus.'

'If you're sure,' Bev said.

She looked away. 'Yeah, fine.'

Bev walked towards the door, stopped and turned around. 'You haven't seen the William Turner file, have you?'

'Yeah. I think I saw it earlier. I'll bring it up to your office.'

'Put it on my desk, I'm going out for a coffee.'

'No problem.' She watched Bev leave and glanced at her watch. 'Come on, Taffy,' she whispered to herself.

Conrad Hudson sat back on the leather chair, closed his eyes and relaxed. His phone rang. 'Yeah, Taffy.'

'I've got the information on Billy's murder.'

'And?'

Taffy blew out hard. 'The bastards gutted him while he was still alive.'

'Jesus.'

'They mutilated him as well.'

'Spare me the details. Bring it to the office tomorrow.' Hudson said. 'I've got some information of my own. The explosion in Middlesbrough yesterday. It was the people the coppers are looking for. A bloke and a girl. Graveney nearly died, apparently.'

'Shame,' Taffy said.

Hudson laughed. 'It is. People on Pearl Street must know who this pair are. I'll send Harry down there and see if he can get some information. I want those twats finding and killing. And I don't want it done quick, either.'

'Are you sure you don't want me to go?'

'No. There's something else I want you to do. Tell Harry to take Robbo but keep it low key. The scum who live there will be glad of a few extra quid for their cider and cigs.'

'Will do. What's this other job you want doing?'

'Wayne's been cutting the gear we gave him. I've had a complaint. I want him teaching a lesson.'

'How much of a lesson?'

Hudson stood and closed the living room door. 'Break his legs. Tell him if he does anything like it again, I'll cut them off myself.'

'Ok, Boss.'

Hudson sat back in his chair. Jean Cooper entered and handed him a glass. 'Who was that?' she said.

'Taffy. He has some information on Billy's murder.'

She closed her eyes. 'Don't tell me how he died.'

Hudson rubbed his chin. 'I won't. It was a bit grisly. Are you staying tonight?'

She sidled closer. 'If you want me to?'

'Of course.' He pulled her close. 'What about going upstairs?'

'Ok.'

The doorbell sounded. Hudson scowled. 'Who the hell is this?'

'You finish your drink,' she said. 'I'll go.'

She opened the door, Graveney and Cooke stood outside. Graveney grinned. 'Fancy meeting you here, Mrs Cooper?'

'I suppose you're here to see Conrad?' she said.

'We are. Can we come in?'

'Conrad,' she shouted. 'It's the police.'

Hudson strode into the hall. 'Graveney.' He smiled tightly. 'What do you want?'

'A few words, Mr Hudson.'

He traipsed back into the lounge. 'Make our guests a drink, Jean.'

The two officers followed him. Hudson pointed at a settee. 'Have a seat.' Graveney and Cooke sat. 'Fire away, Graveney.'

'We believe the person or persons who killed Billy Turner have a military background.'

'Really?'

'Do you know of anyone. A soldier. Ex-soldier, perhaps, who has a grudge?'

'Nope.'

'Sure?'

Hudson sipped from his glass. 'Absolutely. But if I remember anyone, you'll be the first I'll ring.' He forced a smile at Graveney.

Graveney smiled back. 'I'm sure I will be.'

Mrs Cooper walked in, carrying a tray of tea and biscuits. She placed them on a table in front of the officers and sat next to Hudson.

Graveney and Cooke left the house fifteen minutes later. They climbed into the car, and Cooke glanced across at Graveney. 'What do you think, Guv?'

Graveney stared back towards the house. 'I don't think he has a clue who the murderer is. He's as much in the dark as we are.'

Graveney's phone sounded. He put it on speakerphone and placed it on the dashboard. 'Yeah, Rav?'

'We've got a possible name. Joseph Purdey, 36-year-old. He fits the description. He was invalided out of the army.'

'What regiment?'

'Royal Logistic Corps. Ammunition Technician, so he'd know his way around explosives.'

'You said he was invalided out?'

'Post-traumatic stress disorder. He was involved in an explosive accident in Iraq. By all accounts, he has mental issues.'

'What about his family?' Graveney said.

'None. He was adopted at birth by a couple who lived in York. His adoptive mother's in a home there, and his father's dead.'

Graveney looked at Cooke, who raised her eyebrows.

'York.' Graveney said. 'So, my hunch was correct … Where the van was stolen from. Good work, Rav. Address?'

'No. He disappeared off the map a couple of years ago. He may have been living rough.'

'What about the woman?'

'Nothing. We're still digging, but Purdey had no known acquaintances called Jen.'

'Ok. We're on our way back. Gather the team for a briefing.'

CHAPTER TWELVE

Joey let out a scream and bolted upright in bed. He thrashed and clawed at the bedclothes.

Jen, woken by the noise, grabbed hold of his arm. 'Joey.' She placed a hand on his cheek. 'You're fine. You're safe.'

He faced her. 'I had the dream again.'

'I know.' She gently stroked his face. 'I'm here. I won't let anything happen to you.' He calmed and lay back down.

'Do you want some blow? It'll help settle you.'

He nodded. Stretching across him, she picked up a tobacco tin, pulled a spliff from it and held it out. His shaking hand finally placed it between his lips.

Jen poured some whisky into a glass as he lit the cigarette.

'Better?' she said. Joey grunted. 'Drink this. I went out while you slept to do a recce. This is your next target.' She opened the file in front of her and passed him a photograph.

Joey eased himself up and studied it. 'Is he a bad man as well?'

'He is. Like the other one.'

He took a long drag from the cigarette. 'We'll teach the bastard a lesson, won't we?'

She kissed him. 'We will.' Standing, she walked across to a dresser in the corner and picked something up.

'What is it?' he said. Joey jumped out of bed and joined her.

'I'm pregnant. You're going to be a dad.'

He smiled and placed his head on her stomach. 'A dad?'

'Yeah. Did you just think I was getting fat?'

The car glided to a halt outside the terraced properties. Harry and Robbo got out and glanced along the road and at the burnt-out house.

Harry gripped his friend's arm. 'Conrad wants it keeping low-key, so no rough stuff. We're to offer them money for information.'

Robbo sneered. The two of them stopped at a house and knocked. The door opened, and a young woman carrying a baby answered.

'Sorry to bother you, love,' Harry said. 'I was wondering if you could give us any information about the people who blew up the house.'

'I've told the police all I know. I didn't really know them.'

Harry pulled a note from his pocket and held it out. 'Anything at all.'

She viewed the note and glanced up and down the street. 'I didn't speak to them. I know someone who did.'

Harry pulled a second fifty-pound note from his pocket. 'Their name?'

'He's a Polish guy. Pavel, I think. Lives at number eighteen. I've seen him talking to them.'

Harry allowed the woman to pluck the money from his hand. 'Thanks.'

'You didn't get it from me, though.'

'Did you tell the police this?' Harry said.

She grinned. 'No. The police don't hand out fifty-pound notes.'

Harry tapped the side of his nose. 'Mum's the word.'

'He won't be in now,' she said. 'He works at a kebab shop on Linthorpe Road.'

Robbo stepped forward. 'Which one?'

She grinned. 'Must be worth another note?'

Robbo sneered. 'I could always knock it out of you.'

Harry grabbed his arm and pulled him away. 'Cool it, Robbo. Go and start the engine.' Robbo glared at the woman and trudged back to the car.

'What's his problem?' she said.

'Ignore him. He's in a bad mood.' Harry pulled another note out. 'The shop's name?'

'I'll do better than that.' The woman picked up a piece of paper. 'I've got a flyer.'

Harry handed her the note and took the paper from her in one swift movement. 'Cheers.' He turned to walk away but stopped and spun around. 'Don't mention this to anyone, will you? Especially the police.'

She snorted. 'I told you … They don't hand out money.'

'Good,' he said. 'I'd hate to send my friend back around here.' He smiled and walked off. The young woman slammed the door.

Harry jumped in next to Robbo. 'Let's go and see where this guy works.'

Jen and Joey followed Harry and Robbo to the kebab shop, keeping enough distance not to be seen. She looked over at Joey. 'It looks like they're after Pavel.'

'How many?' Joey said.

'Two. Can we handle them?'

Joey leant forward. 'Yeah. Do you want me to kill them both?'

'Just the one in the photo.'

He pulled a ski mask over his head and slid on a pair of gloves. 'Do I wait?'

Jen glanced along the road. 'Yeah. There are too many people around. They'll probably follow Pavel home and grab him on the way. We'll let them take him and follow them.' She looked over her shoulder at the vehicle. 'You ok?'

'Yeah.'

Pavel pulled on his coat, trudged out of the shop and headed for home, unaware he was being watched. He stopped as he heard footsteps behind him. The figure held out a gun and pushed him up against the wall.

'I haven't any money,' Pavel said.

A car drew up next to them. 'Get in,' Robbo said.

He did as he was told. The gun pushed into his back, encouraging him inside. Robbo got in next to him.

'Please ...? What is this ...? I—'

'Shut up.' Robbo said.

Harry twisted in his seat. 'We're going for a little ride. We need a chat with you. Do what we ask, and you won't get hurt. You understand?' Pavel dipped his head.

The car moved off and turned back onto Linthorpe Road.

Jen and Joey followed as the car finally pulled into a small industrial estate. They parked a short distance away, and Jen pulled on her ski mask. Joey handed her a pistol. The pair crept from the van towards the car.

Harry turned fully to face Pavel. 'The big guy and the girl who lived near you?'

Pavel looked about. His heart hammering in his chest. He swallowed a lump the size of a golf ball. 'What about them?'

'Where are they?'

'I don't know. They left when the police came.'

Robbo pushed the gun into his side. 'Who are they?'

Pavel rubbed his face. 'He'll kill me if I tell you.'

Harry grabbed Pavel's jacket. 'They're not here. We are. We'll kill you if you don't.'

The driver's door and rear door opened simultaneously. Harry felt the cold steel as the barrel of the pistol rested on his temple. Robbo gaped and was hauled from the car, his gun knocked from his hand. He swung a fist at his assailant, Joey easily swatting it aside. Robbo buckled as he was struck in the stomach, the wind knocked from him. Joey flipped him over and fastened his hands with a cable-tie. Harry slowly swivelled his head and viewed Jen.

'Get out,' she said. 'You too, Pavel.'

The two men hauled themselves from the vehicle. They watched as Joey taped Robbo's mouth, placed a bag over his head and led him to the van.

'You won't get away with this,' Harry said.

'We already have,' she said. The crack of the gun hitting against his head resounded in the quietness of the night. Harry dropped to the floor as darkness swallowed him.

'I told them nothing,' Pavel said. 'Please don't kill me.'

Jen put a hand to his face. 'We're not going to kill you. But you can't stay here. Other men will come looking for you.'

'Where can I go?'

'A friend of mine in York.' She pulled an envelope from her pocket and handed it to him. 'Take the car and go. Dump it on the way. Not in York. You understand?'

He nodded. 'There's £1000 in the envelope and the name and number of my friend. Tell them Jen sent you.'

Conrad Hudson sipped his brandy while watching the TV. His mobile sounded. He muted the television and answered. 'This had better be good, Harry.'

'We were jumped. The big guy and the girl snatched Robbo.'

'Robbo?'

'Yeah. She knocked me out. I'm on Stockton Road, near a church.'

'What about the Pole?'

'He's gone,' Harry said. 'So's the car.'

'I'll send one of the boys. Are you ok? Or do you need to go to the hospital?'

'I'm fine. A few aspirins.'

Hudson emptied his glass. 'Come to my house. I'll get in touch with Charlie and Taffy.'

'Why?'

'I'll explain when you get here.'

Hudson stood and paced. He stopped and rubbed his chin, picked up his mobile and made a call.

Robbo, naked, sat fastened to a chair. He lifted his head as the door opened, and two masked figures entered. The larger of the two strode across to him and ripped the tape from his mouth. Sweat from Robbo's forehead slowly ran the length of his nose and dripped to the floor.

Joey pulled off his mask. Robbo gasped. He stared, unable to take his eyes off the large scar covering one side of Joey's face.

Jen stepped forward and removed her mask. She stopped close to Robbo and spat in his face.

'Amanda Hewitson,' she said.

Robbo's eyes widened. 'I didn't kill her. I wanted no part. Conrad Hudson wanted her dead.'

'Who killed her?'

'I don't know. We drew cards.'

She sneered. 'I know all about your sick card games. Your friend told us.'

He glanced towards Joey as the big man edged closer. 'Please. I don't know who murdered her. It was one of the others.'

Jen pulled a large hunting knife from her back pocket. 'You know what you did.' She held the blade in front of his face. 'This is what retribution looks like.'

Robbo sobbed. 'Please. I have daughters of my own. I didn't kill her. It was one of the others.'

'But you all raped her,' she said.

Robbo gulped. 'I ...'

'Your friend Billy told us. He didn't want to, but my friend here ...' She patted Joey on the arm. '... can be quite persuasive.'

'Please ... I don't want to die. My kids ...'

'Amanda was little more than a kid when you ...'

Robbo sobbed louder. 'Please.'

'Look at you,' she said. 'Your mate held out for some time. At least Billy had balls. Well, for a while he did.' She smiled at Robbo. 'Sympathy's in short supply, my friend. You should've thought about that before raping and killing my sister.'

Robbo lowered his head. 'But I didn't kill her. I didn't kill her.'

Joey tore a piece of tape from the roll and pressed it over Robbo's mouth. The tethered man's eyes widened as Jen lowered the knife to his groin. 'Sorry.' She grimaced. 'This might sting a little.'

As Joey slept, Jen slipped out of the room and pulled on her parka. She wandered outside into the chill night air, took out her mobile and called.

'Hi,' Harry said.

'Thank God you're ok. I thought I'd killed you.'

'I've got a banging headache, though. You had to make it look good. Hudson's got to believe I was jumped.'

'Did you ring him?' Jen said.

'Yeah. He's sending one of the boys over. I'm hoping he'll trust me a little more. Maybe I can find out some more about Amanda.'

'Hopefully.'

'What about Robbo?' Harry said.

'He's dead. Two down, two to go. And then we can go after Hudson.'

'Watch yourself, Jen. He's got men looking for you two.'

'I will,' she said. 'How's Colin?'

'Not too good. Weeks rather than months, I think. He's expecting a visit from Hudson.'

'Will he be ok?' Jen said.

'Yeah, Colin's not bothered. There's nothing Hudson can do to him now.'

'Thank Colin for me, will you?'

'I will.'

'He can tell Hudson who we are.'

'Are you sure?' Harry said.

'Yeah. I want the bastard to know who's coming after him.'

CHAPTER THIRTEEN

Hudson opened the door. Harry, holding an icepack to his head, entered, closely followed by Taffy and Charlie. Hudson led them into the living room. 'Get yourself a drink, boys,' he said, pointing towards the drinks cabinet in the corner.

Harry slumped into a chair. 'What's this all about?'

Hudson glanced at the other two before fixing his attention back on Harry. 'Someone from our past. Amanda Hewitson.'

'Is she the girl—?'

Hudson perched on the edge of his seat. 'Amanda Hewitson is dead. Long story short. She got in the way, and we needed to get rid of her. She was working for Alex Cooper.'

'The councillor?' Harry said. 'Jean's old fella?'

'Yeah,' Hudson said. 'He'd been stealing money off me for years. He was a loose cannon too. We were partners, but Alex wasn't happy with that. He tried to muscle me out. He got Amanda to help him.'

Harry rubbed his chin. 'Right.'

'Needless to say,' Hudson said. 'This goes no further.'

Harry held his hands out. 'Of course not, Conrad. What happened to Alex Cooper?'

Hudson glanced at Taffy and Charlie, before fixing his stare back on Harry. 'Alex overstepped the mark. He stole some money from the council, and I covered it up for him. When the time was right, I uncovered it again. Everyone assumed he'd done a runner with the cash and one of his many, many women.' Hudson drained his glass. 'He was the architect of his own downfall. He had to go.'

'Is that how he ended up in Marske?'

Hudson raised his palms. 'Well, we didn't put him there.'

'So, who dumped Cooper's body?' Harry said.

Hudson stood and replenished his glass. 'I had a young lad called Sean Grant who worked for me. He was a bit dim. He got himself into a bit of bother. I did him a favour, and he was supposed to get rid of Alex Cooper's body.'

'What sort of bother?' Harry said.

'He killed a mate of his. They got into an argument, and he stabbed him. None of this is relevant to us, though.'

Harry downed his drink. 'Sean Grant? Where have I heard—?'

'He was fished out of a car the other week,' Hudson said. 'The one with Alex's body in the boot.'

'So, who killed Sean Grant?' Harry said.

Hudson shrugged. 'No idea. I assumed he'd dumped Alex's body and made off. I thought maybe Sean lost his bottle or something.' Hudson sat back down. 'The lads checked into Sean's background. He had a mate called Karl Smith, who did a bit of driving for Alex's taxis.'

'And this Karl Smith? Where is he now?'

'He disappeared,' Charlie said. 'We think he killed Sean.'

Harry frowned. 'Why would he do that?'

'We don't know,' Hudson said. 'A falling out between thieves?'

Charlie took a swig of his drink. 'The four of us. Billy, Robbo, Taffy and me. We got rid of Cooper and the girl.' Charlie dropped into an armchair. 'Whenever anyone needed removing, we played a little game. We had four playing cards. Three Jacks and the ace of spades. We each picked a card in turn. Whoever got the ace …'

'That way,' Taffy said. 'None of us knew who'd carried out the deed. We'd draw straws, and a couple of us would get rid of the body.'

'Where did you dump her?' Harry said.

Taffy glared at him. 'It's not important. What's important is finding who killed Billy.'

'Of course.' Harry said. 'I didn't mean to ... This girl and bloke who killed Billy and took Robbo? How are they connected to Cooper?'

'They're someone who knew the girl, possibly?' Hudson said.

Harry stood and fixed himself another drink. 'It could be a relation of this girl?'

Hudson stood again, ambled across to the mantelpiece and pondered. 'Maybe?'

Harry took a sip from his glass. 'What do we do?'

Hudson rubbed his chin. 'We've an advantage over the police. They don't know this pair's motive yet. We know about Amanda Hewitson.'

'And the big guy—?' Harry said.

'He could be related too. Dig into Amanda Hewitson's family,' Hudson said. 'See if it throws anything up. A brother, sister … friend.'

'How did they find out about Amanda Hewitson?' Harry said.

Hudson briefly closed his eyes. 'Someone grassed.'

Charlie and Taffy stared at each other. 'Colin Pybus,' Charlie said. 'He was the only other one who knew.'

'Who's Colin—?' Harry said.

Taffy stepped closer to Harry. 'You ask too many questions,' Taffy said. 'Asking questions gets you into bother.'

'Easy, Taffy,' Hudson said. 'The man's just trying to fill in the blanks.'

Taffy sneered and flopped down. 'What about Pybus?' he said.

'I'll pay him a visit,' Hudson said.

Charlie stepped forward. 'Aren't we forgetting about Robbo?'

Hudson closed his eyes. 'Robbo's had it.'

Charlie snarled. 'When we catch these two, they're mine.'

Hudson stood and fixed Charlie with a stare. 'When we catch them.' He looked at each of the men in turn. 'We'll all have a piece of them.'

Taffy narrowed his eyes and continued to look across at Harry. Harry took a sip of his drink and stared back. 'Yeah. We'll all have a piece of them,' Taffy said.

Taffy followed Hudson into the kitchen. 'Can I have a word, Boss?'

'Yeah.'

'Are you sure we can trust Harry?'

'Of course. What's up, Taffy?'

'He asks too many questions for my liking.'

Hudson huffed. 'You worry too much. Tony vouched for him. He wouldn't do that if he wasn't trustworthy.'

'Yeah, I suppose.'

'Get yourself another drink. Stop worrying.'

Taffy made his way outside and made a call.

'Hi, Taffy,' Tony said.

'How are you, old man?'

'Very well. Filling my days with golf and sunshine.'

Taffy chuckled. 'I might move over there myself when I retire.'

'I'll find you a nice little villa.'

'Can I be blunt, Tony?'

'Of course.'

'Harry Prentise? How do you know him?'

'He's a friend of a friend. Comes highly recommended. Why?'

'No reason,' Taffy said. 'I like to know who I'm working with.'

'He straight. Take it from me. I wouldn't put him your way if I had any doubts.'

'Cheers, Tony. Thanks for that. Send my love to Babs.'

'I will.'

Tony rang off and searched for Jean Cooper's number.

'Hi, Tony?'

'I've had Taffy asking about Harry Prentise.'

'Oh, yeah?'

'There's nothing you're not telling me? I've gone out on a limb, here.'

'You know Taffy, he's paranoid. Harry's a good lad.'

'Ok. I'll take your word for it, Jean.'

The inert body of Robbo hung limply, still fastened to the seat, as blood dripped slowly onto the floor.

'It's over,' Joey said. He wiped the blood from the knife and handed it to Jen. She walked forward and placing the playing card onto Robbo's leg, pushed the knife through it and into his thigh.

Harry swung the car through the gates of the hospice. He found a parking spot and pulled up.

Hudson glanced across at him. 'You stay here.' Harry nodded.

He watched as Hudson entered the building, and then took out his mobile. He waited for the phone to be answered. 'Conrad had Alex killed,' Harry said. 'He claims Alex was trying to push him out. He also had Amanda Hewitson killed. I'll ring when I know more.'

Hudson knocked on the door and entered. The room was dark, the curtains still drawn.

'Hello, Colin,' he said.

The man in the bed moved his head a little. 'I knew you'd come.'

'You've been talking,' Hudson said.

He coughed. 'I heard about Billy. I hope he suffered.' He reached for the glass next to him.

Hudson snatched it from the table. 'Who are they? I know there's a connection with the Hewitson girl.'

'Amanda's sister. The guy's an ex-soldier she befriended.'

'You've caused a bit of bother. I came here intending to kill you, but it appears you're almost dead. I'm looking at a bag of bones. A ghost of a man.'

'Do it. You'll be doing me a favour.' He coughed again.

Hudson poured the water on the floor. 'No. I want you to suffer.'

Colin chuckled. 'I've got morphine. I bet you Billy didn't.'

Hudson grabbed him around the throat. 'You scumbag. Betraying your mates.'

'Mates? They deserve to die for what they did to Amanda. I'm only sorry I won't be around to witness it.'

Hudson threw the glass on the floor. It bounced before coming to a rest against the wall. He turned and moved towards the door.

'She'll be coming for you too,' Colin said. 'I bet her friend has a fitting end for you. I'll see you in hell, Conrad.'

Hudson stopped at the door. 'When I've finished with those two, you'll need DNA to identify them.' He opened the door and raced out.

Colin chuckled again. 'I'll reserve a furnace for you.'

CHAPTER FOURTEEN

Graveney sat up in bed. He put a hand to his head as a lightning bolt of pain shot across his temple. Wincing, he closed his eyes, allowing the pain to recede. When he opened them, across the room in the chair opposite reclined Stephanie Marne. She smiled at him. Graveney closed his eyes again and slowly reopened them. She was gone, the chair now empty. He brought his hand to his mouth and gasped as memories tugged at him.

The toilet in the bathroom flushed, and a naked Bev walked out. She slipped inside the covers and draped an arm across him. 'You ok?'

Graveney leant in close to her and kissed her head. 'Yeah. Bit of a headache though.'

'I've got some tablets in my bag.' Bev climbed from the bed and wandered into the bathroom, returning with a glass of water and two pills. She perched on the edge next to Graveney and handed them to him. 'Here, take these.'

Graveney threw the tablets into his mouth and washed them down with water. 'Bev,' he said. 'Is it usual … when you have a bang on the head …?' He paused and rubbed his chin. 'Forget it.'

She took hold of his hand. 'What is it?'

'I saw something.'

'Something?'

'When you were in the bathroom. Out of the corner of my eye.'

She edged closer. 'What sort of something?'

He rubbed his face. 'Nothing really. Well, nothing important. I just saw something. I closed my eyes and when I opened them again, it was gone.'

'Hallucination?' she said.

He shrugged and glanced back at where Marne had been sitting.

Bev placed a hand on his arm. 'It's not unusual for people to hallucinate full stop. It can happen when we're falling asleep or waking up. They're called hypnogogic and hypnopompic hallucinations. Nothing to worry about.'

Graveney forced a smile. 'I suppose.'

'Why? You haven't had any blackouts or dizziness, have you?'

'No. Forget about it. It's not important. What time is it?'

Bev stretched for her watch as Graveney glanced back towards the chair. 'Four,' she said.

'We'd better get going.'

Graveney waited for Bev to leave. After showering and changing, he headed into the reception and paid for the room in cash. Hurrying outside, he checked around the carpark and satisfied no one was about, jumped in his car and started it. He looked down at his phone as it beeped with messages from Rav.

Graveney quickly rang. 'Rav. What's up?'

'I've been trying to get hold of you. We've got another body, Guv.'

'Sorry, bad signal. Where? Who?'

'Tommy Robinson, we think. He's in a bit of a mess.'

Graveney picked up a piece of paper and a pen. 'You're kidding?'

'Nope. Anonymous tip-off.'

'Are forensics there?'

'I think so. They were having a spot of bother getting hold of Bev Wilson.'

'I'm on my way over. Are you at the crime scene?'

'Yeah. It's not far from where the other body was found.'

'Has anyone spoken to the Guv?'

'Not yet.'

'I'll do it. Text me the details.'

Graveney donned his blue overalls and raced towards the building. Rav intercepted him. 'Bev Wilson's in there now, Sir.'

'Where are the others?' Graveney said.

'They're interviewing possible witnesses.'

Graveney marched on. 'Anything?'

Rav exhaled loudly. 'Nothing yet. We think it happened last night.'

Graveney paused at the door. 'Ok. Carry on. Let me know what the others have.' He wandered inside and towards Bev. She blew out. 'How many messages did you have?'

'Two,' he said.

'Six.' She sniggered. 'Next time, we'll do it out of work hours.'

Graveney glanced back towards the door. 'We need to be careful, Bev. We both have a lot to lose.'

She laughed. 'I thought you liked the danger?'

Graveney smiled. 'I do. But—'

Rav returned. 'We may have a piece of luck.' He moved closer and stopped. 'A guy who owns a big house at the end of the lane has CCTV around his property. He said it quite often picks up passing vehicles.'

'Good. But I think we probably know who did this.' He turned towards Bev.

She scrutinised the body. 'At first glance, it's the same MO. Ace of spades pinned to his thigh.'

Graveney sucked in air. 'They really hate these guys. Whatever they did, it must be bad for them to do this to them.'

Bev glanced at the pair in turn. 'Still no lead on the girl?'

'No. We've delved into the guy's background, but we haven't come up with anything yet.'

Cooke appeared at the door. 'Sorry to interrupt, Guv. Can I have a word with Rav?'

Graveney looked at Hussain. 'Are we finished here?'

'Yeah.'

Graveney turned back to Bev. 'When will you have the post mortem done?'

'In the morning.'

'Right. See you then,' he said.

Bev took hold of his arm. 'I enjoyed this afternoon,' she said.

'Me too. I wasn't ...' He paused and looked down at the floor. 'Too rough with you?'

She nudged him. 'No. Not at all.' She lifted his head up with her hand and stared into his eyes. 'I loved it, Peter.'

Graveney glanced over his shoulder. 'I better go.' Bev lowered her head. Graveney hurried off.

CHAPTER FIFTEEN

MIDDLESBROUGH 1999 – Lindsey headed along the hotel corridor, stopped outside the room, and peered back along the length of the hallway. On hearing voices getting closer, she slipped around a corner out of sight and waited. The voices receded. She returned to the door, paused and wiped the palms of her hands on her jeans. Allowing herself one last glimpse in either direction, she knocked.

The door was unlocked and opened. Alexander Cooper stood there. He ushered her inside and glanced outside and along the corridor. Satisfied there was no one there he closed the door behind them. 'Hello, gorgeous.'

Lindsey stepped closer and threw her arms around him. 'I missed you, Alex. So much.'

He kissed her. 'I've got you a gift.' He ambled across the room and picked up a slim, black jewellery case.

She kissed him and plucked the box from his hand as he held it out. Inside was a bracelet. 'It's beautiful.'

'It's inscribed. Look.' Turning the bracelet over, he held it up. Lindsey looked at her name and date of birth. 'Shall I put it on for you?' he said.

'Yes, please.'

Lindsey slid onto her side, her head resting against a pillow, and studied Alex. He pushed his fastened tie up tight to his collar. She frowned. 'Do you have to go already?'

He sat on the edge of the bed and pulled her close. 'Business, gorgeous.' He kissed her on the head and stood, put on his watch, slid on his jacket and moved towards the door. 'Take as long as you want. The room's paid for. I've left some money for you.' He pointed at the dresser.

'I don't want money.'

'Get yourself something nice. A new dress or a jacket.'

She glanced at the bracelet on her wrist and held up her arm. 'But you've already bought me this.'

'I love you,' he said. 'I like you to have nice things. Buy yourself something classy.'

'Who's Amanda, Alex?'

Alex spun around at the door. Lindsey lowered her eyes. 'Her name came up on your mobile while you were showering.'

'Come on, Lindsey. You're not getting all clingy, are you? You know there's no one else, babe.'

'Except your wife.'

Alex grinned. 'You're having a good time, aren't you? I never made promises. It's complicated.'

Lindsey jumped from the bed and hurried across to him. She put her arms around his waist and kissed him. 'I'm sorry I …'

Alex pulled them off. 'Not now, babe. I've got business. I can do without this. I'll see you later.' He left, raced along the corridor and down a flight of stairs. As he reached the bottom, he took out his mobile and called.

'Hi, gorgeous,' A woman said.

'I'm back, babe. I'm on my way over now.'

He made his way outside and into the rear of a waiting car. Craig Embleton peered over his shoulder. 'Where to, Alex?'

He handed a piece of paper to him. 'I've got a postcode. You'll have to programme the satnav.' Slumping back in his seat, he blew out.

'Everything all right?'

'Lindsey's giving me earache. She's becoming too clingy, that one.' He glanced back at the hotel. 'Could be time to move on.'

Craig glanced back through the mirror. 'It's not far. Five minutes.' He put the car in gear and pulled away.

Alex grunted and stared out of the window. 'Good.'

Lindsey pulled on her jacket and looked around the room. Spotting the money on the dresser, five crisp £50 notes, she scooped them up and pushed them into her jeans. She rushed down the stairs and through the lobby, avoiding eye contact with anyone. Once outside, Lindsey pulled a baseball cap from her pocket and pushed it onto her head. She bounded into the street and headed along the road. A car drew up beside her, and the window lowered.

Craig smiled at her. 'Need a lift?'

Lindsey stopped. 'What are you doing here?'

'Just passing.'

'Just passing?'

'Yeah.' He smiled again.

'Just passing in Darlington?'

Craig beamed. 'I picked Alex up and dropped him off. I thought you might be here.'

She jumped in beside him. 'Alex? Where did you take him?'

'A house near the station. Why?'

Lindsey stared outside. 'He's got someone else, hasn't he?'

'I wouldn't know about that. He tells me very little. He did say it was business.'

'Yeah, business.' She scoffed. 'I'm just one of many.'

Craig glanced across at her. 'You're better than that. If he has got another woman. Maybe you should …' He raised his eyebrows.

She looked at him and shrugged. 'I like him, Craig.'

'Do you love him?'

She shrugged again. 'I'm not sure I love him.'

He stared across at her as he pulled up at some lights. 'If you were my girlfriend, I wouldn't want anyone else.'

She forced a smile and placed a hand on his arm. 'Thanks.'

'I mean it.'

'What are you doing today?' she said.

Craig lowered his brow. 'Is that an offer?'

She laughed. 'Just curious.'

'I'm meeting Sean.'

Lindsey's smile fell from her face. 'Sean Grant?'

'What's up?'

'Nothing. I've heard things.' She stared out of the window.

Craig tapped her arm. 'He's all right. Bit of a lad. I've known him since school. He's all mouth, really.'

Lindsey turned back to face him. 'Is he still working for …' She sneered. '*Conrad Hudson?*'

'Yeah. Why?'

'He's another one I wouldn't trust.'

'Yeah? Sean's never mentioned anything to me.'

'You're a nice lad, Craig, but people get judged by the company they keep. The stories I've heard about Hudson … from Alex.'

'What stories?'

She turned to look out of the window again. 'Forget it. Alex would be furious if he knew I was saying anything.'

'I'll put Sean off. We could go for a coffee.'

'Not today,' she said. 'Another time, maybe.'

Craig nodded. The remainder of the journey conducted in deafening silence. He reached the top of a road near to Lindsey's house and pulled over.

'Stop here,' she said.

Craig brought the car to a halt. 'Sorry if I've upset you.'

Lindsey opened the door and turned to face him. 'Watch your back, Craig.'

'Will I see you again?' He winked.

Lindsey stepped out and pushed her head back through the door. 'Give me a call.' She opened her bag and jotted her number on a till receipt. 'Tomorrow.' Bending down, she handed him the paper and kissed his cheek.

Craig beamed. 'Ok.' He watched as Lindsey walked off along the road and around a corner.

Alex Cooper slumped into the armchair. 'Get me a drink, babe.'

Amanda sidled closer. 'I thought you'd want to go to bed?'

'Not yet. I need to ask you something. A favour.'

She fixed a drink and handed it to him. 'What sort of favour?'

'Conrad Hudson.'

She leant against the wall. 'What about him?'

'He's screwing me over. I've managed to get all sorts of contacts, but I'm not seeing a fair cut of the money. I want my rightful share.'

'But how can you do that?'

Cooper patted the arm of his chair, and Amanda sat. 'He runs these parties.'

She shuffled on her seat. 'What sort of parties?'

'He has people up at his house. Likes to invite bigwigs. MPs, judges, coppers. Plies them with drink and drugs, and then uses this as leverage.'

'How do I come in?'

Alex patted her leg. 'He has girls there too. Create the right atmosphere and these people lower their guard.'

'You want me to …?'

'Babe,' Cooper said. 'You know I love you. If I can get my fair share, you and I can enjoy ourselves a bit more.'

'What would you want me to do?'

He cupped her chin with his hand. 'Get some photos or footage and then, well … You get the drift?'

'You want me to sleep with these men? Is that what you're asking, Alex?'

He stood and placed an arm around her shoulder. 'I thought we had something good, babe.'

'But …'

'We could go to The States,' he said. 'You've always said you wanted to go there.'

She beamed. 'New York?'

'New York, Las Vegas. Wherever you want, babe.'

'I love you, Alex. But—'

He pulled a long, black case from his inside pocket. 'I got you a gift. Look.'

Amanda plucked it from him. Inside the case was a necklace. 'It's lovely.'

'Let me put it on for you,' he said. Stepping back, he held out his hands. 'There. Isn't it gorgeous? My little angel.'

Amanda slowly ran the necklace through her fingers. 'I love it, Alex.'

He leant in and kissed her neck. 'I don't want you to do anything you feel uncomfortable with. If you don't want to help me ...'

'It's not that,' she said. 'I don't want anyone but you. I don't want to sleep with anyone but you.'

'This could be worth thousands. You and I could go somewhere ... Somewhere across the world. With the money, you and me, we'd have it all. We could live in the US.'

'Really?'

He pulled her close. 'Yeah. Do you want to go to bed?'

Her head dropped, and Alex lifted up her chin. 'Come on then. I've missed you.'

They climbed the stairs and entered the bedroom. Alex paused. 'I'm going to sort one of those new flats for you. The ones in the centre of town. Our own little love nest.'

Amanda beamed and stepped across to him. 'Oh, would you?'

'Yeah.' He unbuttoned his shirt and tossed it onto a chair. 'Nothing's too much for my little angel.'

She kissed his chest. 'I do love you, Alex.'

He unfastened his trousers and stepped out of them. 'Prove it,' he said. 'Do this thing for me, and I'll give you whatever you want.'

She nodded. 'Good girl,' he said.

'But won't they suspect something?'

He pulled off his boxers and cupped her chin again. 'I've got someone on the inside. He can get you in. He organises the girls for the parties.'

'Ok. You will look after me, won't you?'

'Of course, babe. I won't let anything happen to you.' He slipped into bed, eyeing Amanda as she undressed.

Amanda slept as Alex padded downstairs. He crept into the dining room and closed the door behind him. Taking out his mobile he called.

'Alex,' Colin said. 'What do you want?'

'Payback time, Colin.'

'What do you want?'

Alex sat. 'When's the next party?'

'Next Saturday,' he said. 'Why?'

'The right honourable James Whittaker-Brown.'

'What about him?'

Alex put his hand over the mouthpiece and listened. There was no noise from the sleeping Amanda. 'He'll be there?'

'Yeah,' Colin said.

'Apparently, he likes his girls a little younger.'

'I've got someone sorted,' Colin said. 'She's twenty-four but looks much younger. It should satisfy the pervert.'

'I want you to get someone in for me.'

'I'm not sure I can do that, Alex.'

'Do you want Conrad getting hold of those missing invoices.' The phone went quiet. 'Well?'

Colin blew out. 'No.'

'Right. Get Amanda inside.'

'Jesus, Alex. She's seventeen for Christ sake. She's just a kid.'

'It's no good getting all moral now.'

'The girls I provide know what they're doing. They've all done this sort of thing before. They get well paid, and I look after them.'

'Amanda's cool with it. You can look after her. Channel your avuncular personality.'

'What are you planning?'

'You don't need to know. They'll be some money in it for you.'

Colin sighed. 'I'll see what I can do.'

'Good. I'll be in touch.' Alex hung up. The door opened, and Amanda ambled in. She yawned. 'What time is it?'

'Come here, gorgeous,' he said.

CHAPTER SIXTEEN

Graveney pulled the phone from his pocket. 'I'll put you on loudspeaker, Bev. I've got Mac here with me.'

'Hello, Mac,' she said.

'Hi, Bev. I take it this is the result of the post mortem on Tommy Robinson. AKA Robbo?'

'It is. The same MO as the first murder.'

'Same people then?' Graveney said.

'Looks that way. I'll send the full report over.'

'Thanks,' Graveney said. 'We'll speak later.'

Mac rested his elbows on his desk and eyed Graveney. 'You and Bev seem back to your old selves.'

'Bev and I are in the past. I'll make sure it stays there.'

'Good,' Mac said. 'The murders ... These two don't mess around. What's your take?'

'I think it's some kind of sex crime. Otherwise, why mutilate him like they did?'

Mac rubbed his chin. 'Yeah. We still don't know who the girl is?'

'Not yet. We're digging into the soldier's background to see if anyone matching her description turns up.'

'Keep me up to date.'

Graveney stood. 'I will.'

'We're on for the dinner party then?' Mac said.

'Yeah. Louisa said she'll babysit.'

'Great. Fancy a pint tonight?'

'Not tonight. I've a couple of errands to run. Tomorrow's better?'

'Ok,' Mac said, as Graveney stood and walked towards the door.

'Peter.' Graveney turned. 'Everything ok? You seem a little preoccupied.' Mac nodded towards the phone. 'Are you sure ...?'

'Like I said, Mac. It's history. An error of judgement on our part. I've got a bit of a headache, that's all. I'll be all right tomorrow.'

Mac leant forward. 'The Grewgrass Lane murders? Any news?'

Graveney felt pain shoot across his temple but fought to disguise it. 'We've hit a bit of a brick wall. Lindsey Armstrong is definitely involved somehow.'

Mac's phone rang. 'We'll chat later. I've been expecting this call.' He picked up the phone. 'One second, Sir.' Graveney opened the door and left. Mac furrowed his brow. 'Sorry about that, Sir,' Mac said. 'You were saying …'

Graveney stumbled along the corridor, past preoccupied people and into his office. He closed and locked the door, his legs almost failing him as he leant on his desk for support. He worked his way around it and slumped into his seat. The room spun. He closed his eyes, trying desperately to wrestle back control of his senses. He lay his head on his desk and sucked in air, the unsteadiness gradually receding. Graveney opened his eyes. Marne sat opposite.

She pushed a hand through her hair. 'Hello, Peter.'

Graveney's mouth dropped open. She seemed so real. Only a light haze around the outline of her form betrayed her.

'Steph,' he said, the corners of his mouth lifting into a smile.

'Have you missed me?'

'You're not real. I do know that.'

'Of course you do. But I'm in here.' She tapped the side of her head. 'You and I are one.'

'Why … Why did you do it? I ...' His eyes filled with tears and he swallowed hard.

Marne smiled and threw back her head. 'Don't think too hard, Peter. Sometimes things happen for a reason.'

Graveney stood and staggered around his desk. His head swam. The pain returned, but much more intense.

'The case, Peter,' Marne said. 'What's going on?'

He dropped to his knees and looked up. Marne knelt close to him and placed a hand on his cheek. 'Why did Lindsey do time for a murder she didn't commit?'

'I don't know.' He closed his eyes and grimaced. The pain now excruciating.

Marne's eyes widened. 'Unless she did something else. Something as bad, or worse.'

He pushed himself up and groped for his chair. 'Who did she kill?' she persisted. 'Who did she murder?'

Graveney fell onto his chair. The pain in his head reached a crescendo and then subsided. His eyes, clamped shut from the onslaught, blinked open. Marne was gone. He blew out hard, burying his face into his hands.

Graveney, hand shaking, raised the coffee cup to his lips and swigged. Someone knocked on his office door and tried the handle. Graveney composed himself, got to his feet, and answered.

Hussain stood outside. 'Rav,' Graveney said. 'Come in.'

Hussain narrowed his eyes, entered and sat.

'I was on a pressing call,' Graveney said. 'What's up?'

'Karl Smith?'

Graveney slumped back in his chair. 'What about him?'

'We've found a possible alias for him. Karl Jenkins.' He pushed a photograph across the table to Graveney.

Graveney examined it. 'It certainly looks like him. An address?'

Hussain smiled. 'Life's never that easy, Guv. He was living with his girlfriend.' Hussain opened his notebook and flicked through the pages. 'Alison Preston.'

Graveney leant forward. 'Was?'

'He disappeared two months ago. She reported him missing, but he's a big boy. You know the drill.'

'Where was he living?'

'Stockton,' Hussain said.

'Ok.'

'You all right, Guv? You look a little ...'

Graveney stood and put on his jacket. 'Yeah, fine. Bit of a headache, that's all. Let's go and talk to his girlfriend.'

Hussain pulled the car up outside a house. He checked the address in his notepad and pointed towards the building. 'It's the one with the blue door.'

The police officers got out and knocked on the door. A woman opened it and glanced between the pair. The smile she wore slowly dissolving.

Graveney held out his credentials. 'Alison Preston?'

A deep frown etched its way across her brow. 'Yeah.'

'Detective Inspector Graveney and this is my colleague Detective Sergeant Hussain. Can we come in?'

'Is this about Karl?'

'Yes,' Graveney said. She moved aside allowing the officers to enter, closing the door behind them. She led them into a sitting room and motioned for them to sit.

'Can I get you officers a drink?' she said.

'I'm fine,' Graveney said. Hussain shook his head.

She perched on a seat opposite. 'You said it was about Karl?'

'It is.'

She forced a smile. 'Have you found him?'

Graveney glanced at Hussain before fixing his attention back on Alison. 'We're looking to interview Karl in relation to an ongoing investigation.'

'I don't understand,' she said.

'Has Karl ever mentioned anyone called Sean Grant?'

She pondered for a moment. 'No.'

'Karl was friends with Sean way back. Sean was found dead a few weeks ago. We're interviewing people who knew him when he disappeared.'

'I've only known Karl for three years,' she said. 'He didn't talk much about his past. He told me he had family in Middlesbrough but didn't really get on with them.'

Graveney looked at Hussain, who opened his notebook and leant forward. 'You reported Karl missing two months ago?' Hussain said. She nodded. 'He's not been in touch since?'

'No. It was Oliver's birthday last week. He loves Oliver—'

Graveney narrowed his eyes. 'Oliver?'

'His son,' she said. 'Why wouldn't he get in touch. I … could …' She put a shaky hand to her face.

Graveney plucked a tissue from the box to the side of him and handed it to her.

Alison dabbed at her eyes. 'I never knew what Karl did. Sometimes he'd have lots of money and sometimes … But he always provided for us. He was …' She dabbed her eyes again. '*…is,* a good dad.'

Graveney and Hussain glanced at each other. Graveney leant forward. 'Do you think someone's harmed him?'

Alison stood and walked across to a dresser. She rifled through a drawer and pulled something out. Returning to her seat, she held out a plastic bag. 'I found this when I searched through his things.' She clutched something tightly in her other hand.

Graveney took the bag from her and studied it before handing it to Hussain. 'Cocaine?' Hussain said.

'Maybe.' He fixed his attention back on Alison. 'You don't know anyone he mixed with?'

She shook her head and handed Graveney a small book. He flicked through it, a series of names listed on the first sheet, the remainder blank, apart from the final page. He scrutinised it for a moment and handed it to Hussain.

'Did Karl ever mention anyone called Lindsey Armstrong?' She frowned, and Graveney continued. 'Or Jimmy Jefferson?'

She pondered for a moment and shook her head again. 'No. Do you think …?' she said.

'I don't know what to think,' Graveney said.

A baby's cry could be heard upstairs. Alison stood. ' I'm sorry, that's my son.'

'I think we've finished here,' Graveney said. He looked to Hussain who nodded. The two officers stood. 'If you remember anything else or if Karl gets in touch, can you give me a ring?' Graveney pulled a card from his top pocket and handed it to her. She led them out, and Graveney paused at the threshold. A dusty memory stirred in his mind. He placed a hand back into his pocket and ran his fingers along its length. He was sure he felt something else inside it. Something familiar. Something resembling a key. The same feeling as before. He pushed the uneasiness aside.

Graveney followed Hussain outside and into the car. He slumped into the passenger seat.

'Drugs?' Hussain said.

'Looks that way. There are a few of those names I recognise.'

'What do we do?'

Graveney huffed. 'We'll hand it over to the drug lads. This investigation is complicated enough. See if they can come up with anything.' He blew out. 'If he's had a fallout with one of his mates, we need to know.'

Hussain accepted the package containing the powder and dropped it into an evidence bag.

'Did you look in the back of the book,' Graveney said. Hussain shook his head. Graveney stared at him.

Hussain fished the book from his pocket, and flicked through the pages, stopping at the final page. In bold capitals was written, *Lindsey,* and a date. Hussain looked up. 'Lindsey?'

Graveney tapped the page. 'I'd put money on that being Lindsey Armstrong's release date.'

'I'll check it as soon as we get back,' Hussain said.

'We need to speak with Lindsey Armstrong again.'

Hussain fired up the engine. 'Shall I arrange an interview?'

'Yeah. Can you drop me in town?'

'Whereabouts?'

'Near the Cleveland Centre. I'm meeting a mate of mine for a drink. He's up here for a few days.'

Graveney pushed the car door closed and set off into the centre. He hurried along its length and exited at the far end on Newport Road. Making his way around the corner, he dashed along Albert Road and into The Hospitality Inn.

He took out his phone and called. 'It's me. I'm downstairs. What room are you in?'

'216,' a voice said. Graveney hung up, peered around and started up the stairs. He knocked, and the door opened. 'Glass of wine, Peter?' Bev said.

Graveney tossed his coat onto a chair and grabbed hold of Bev, pushing her up against the wall. 'Later,' he said, his hand pulling roughly at her skirt. He spun her around, pushed her onto the bed, and stared at her.

Marne stared back, a huge grin filling her face. 'I knew you couldn't resist me,' she said.

Graveney pulled at his clothing and edged closer. He paused above her, his hand now resting on her throat. 'I've missed you,' she said.

'Peter,' Bev said, taking hold of his arm.

He opened his eyes as his senses slowly delivered him back to wakefulness. 'Bev.'

She placed a hand on his cheek. 'You were shouting in your sleep.'

He pushed himself upright and rubbed his eyes. 'What time is it?'

'Don't worry. You haven't slept long. You went out like a light.'

He flopped back onto the bed. 'You ok?' Turning to face Bev, he placed a hand on the side of her face.

Bev bent lower and kissed him. 'Never better.' She smiled. 'I'm going to get a shower.'

Graveney furrowed his brow, his eyes drawn to the other side of the room. On the chair, a naked Stephanie Marne. She lifted a finger to her lips. 'Shh,' she said.

Bev followed his gaze. 'What are you looking at?'

Graveney turned back to face Bev. 'Nothing. Do you mind if I join you in there?'

Bev kissed him on the lips. 'Not at all.' She took hold of his hand and led him towards the bathroom. Graveney meekly followed, but couldn't resist a final glance back at the now empty chair.

Graveney and Bev exited the hotel and into the carpark. They headed towards Bev's car, as Graveney nervously glanced about.

'Where do you want me to drop you?' Bev said.

'At the Marton Arms.'

'Going for a drink?'

'Yeah. I'm meeting an old mate.' The pair climbed inside.

Ben glanced across at Graveney. She placed a hand on his. 'You ok?'

He forced a smile. 'Yeah.'

'Sure? You seemed a little distant today.'

Graveney rubbed his chin. 'Remember the chat we had?'

Bev narrowed her eyes. 'Which one?'

Graveney turned away and stared out of the window. The rain dropping outside, diffused the different coloured lights from shops as they passed.

'Hey,' she said. 'What's up?'

'I've been hallucinating .... Quite a bit.'

'I see.' She glanced his way again. 'You should get it checked out. To be safe. You did have a knock on the head.'

Graveney faced her again. 'I don't want it to affect my job. Mac already thinks I'm working too hard.'

'And are you?'

'No. These two cases. The Grewgrass Lane bodies, and the murders of Hudson's men. I can't help but think they're connected. They have to be.'

'It could be a coincidence?'

'I'm not buying that.'

Bev pondered for a moment. 'I've a friend who works in psychology. I could ask her to talk to you.'

'Am I going mad, Bev?'

She gave a throaty laugh. 'What? Madder than normal?' Graveney smiled. She placed a hand on his again. 'It's outside of my field of expertise, Peter. It could be anything. We won't know until—'

Graveney dropped his head. 'You won't tell anyone, will you?'

Bev pulled the car over. She put a hand on his cheek and turned his face to hers. 'Of course not. You know I wouldn't.'

Graveney looked away. 'I know, it's just ... Do you remember Stephen Stewart? He had a—'

She pulled him close. 'Hey. We'll get this sorted. Like I said, it could be anything. I'll call her tomorrow. Don't worry.' She kissed him and hugged him tightly. 'We'll get to the bottom of it.'

CHAPTER SEVENTEEN

Conrad Hudson placed the newspaper down and reached for his mobile as it vibrated. 'Yeah.'

'I've got Harry on the phone, Sir.'

'Put him through.'

'Can we meet, Conrad?' Harry said.

'Have you got something?'

'Yeah.'

'We'll meet for lunch. I'll fetch the boys. 12.30 at Stephano's.' He hung up and pressed a button on his phone.

'Yes, Mr Hudson?' a female voice said.

'Can you book me a table for four at Stephano's, Karen? The usual table.'

Hudson entered the restaurant and was met by a uniformed man. 'Good Afternoon, Sir,' he said. Hudson followed the man as he led him to a table in the far corner.

'The usual, Angelo,' he said.

A man talking with someone at a table on the other side of the room ended his conversation and headed over to Hudson. 'Conrad,' he said, holding out his hand, he smiled pleasantly. 'How are you?'

'Very well. What about you, Howard? How's business?'

'Business is booming.'

'Still not interested in a sleeping partner?'

Howard pursed his lips. 'No. I'm doing fine as it is.'

'You could open a second restaurant. I've got a possible location in mind. With your reputation ...'

The waiter returned and placed the drink in front of Hudson, nodded at the two men and left.

'Like I said, Conrad, I'm fine as I am.'

'Well if you change your mind?' Hudson said.

'I won't.' He smiled. 'Enjoy your meal.'

'We're having a little party at the end of the month. Why don't you come along?'

Howard stopped. 'What sort of party?'

Hudson raised his eyebrows. 'The best kind. The sort which caters to everybody's tastes.'

Howard stepped closer. 'You don't know my tastes.'

'I know everyone's. It pays to. Tell Patsy you're on a business trip and I'll sort the ideal person for you. Free of charge.'

'I still won't sell you a share of this.' He waved his hands around the room. 'It's my life's work.'

'Of course not. But I could use your expertise.'

Howard eyed Hudson. 'In what?'

'I'm thinking of opening somewhere myself. I could do with your input.'

'I'll think about it.'

'You do that. You'll love it.'

Howard hesitated for a moment then walked away as Harry, Taffy and Charlie approached.

'Take a seat, boys.' Hudson said. 'Something to eat first, then Harry can tell us what he's found out.'

Hudson waved across to the waiter who made his way over to the table.

'Was everything ok?' the waiter said.

'Excellent, Angelo.' He handed him a £50 note. 'Can you give us a bit of privacy? Make sure we're not disturbed.'

'Of course, Mr Hudson.' He collected the empty bowls and left them to it.

Hudson settled back in his seat and viewed the men in turn. 'Now you've been fed and watered, we can get down to business. Harry?'

Harry dipped into the inside pocket of his jacket and pulled out a photo. He pushed it across the table towards Hudson. 'Amanda Hewitson's sister. Her name's Jen.'

Hudson picked up the photograph and studied it before passing it to Charlie.

Harry pulled out a notebook. 'She's done time. She has a list of petty offences, and finally ended up in prison.'

'What about her family and friends?' Hudson said.

'Not a lot.' Harry said. 'She pretty much burnt her bridges, and disappeared off the radar about a year ago.'

'What prison was she in?' Hudson said.

Harry glanced at Hudson. 'Durham.'

Hudson smiled. 'Taffy. Have you still got that mate who works there?'

'Yeah.'

'See if you can find out who she was in with. Maybe they're still in contact with her.'

'I'll do it now, Boss.'

Graveney pulled into the car park of the clinic. He found a parking space and stopped, switched off the engine and rested his head against the steering wheel.

'Lindsey's the key to this,' Marne said.

'I know.' He exhaled. 'I know.'

'What's up, Peter?'

'You're not real, Steph. You're dead. I watched you put a bullet through your head.'

Marne giggled. 'I know. Stung a little.'

'I'm seeing someone. Someone who'll help me.'

'I'm helping you.'

Graveney opened his eyes and glanced to his left. Marne gazed at him. She lifted a hand and placed it on his cheek. Graveney almost recoiled. He could feel it, and yet, it didn't feel real.

'Bev can't replace what we had. What we had was special. Bev isn't dangerous enough.' Marne roared. 'Too prudish.'

Graveney pulled his face away and looked towards the building. 'I'm hoping Dr Hope can help me.'

Marne laughed. 'Appropriate name.'

Graveney turned back to face her. 'I miss you so much,' he said. 'But this can't go on.'

'Have it your way, but drugs or therapy won't remove me forever. I'll always be inside you. Only I understand the darker side of Peter Graveney.'

Graveney opened the door and marched towards reception. He paused and glanced back at the empty car before heading inside.

'Take a seat,' Dr Hope said. 'Can I get you a drink, Peter?' Graveney shook his head. Dr Hope flicked on the kettle and prepared herself one.

'You and Bev are friends?' Graveney said.

'Yeah. We were at medical school together. How's she doing?'

'Very well. Did you hear she moved back to Teesside?'

Dr Hope eased into a seat opposite him with a cup in hand. 'Yes, I did. We chatted briefly last week.'

Graveney glanced around the room. 'Bit of a surprise.'

'Why?'

Graveney stared at Dr Hope. 'It just was.'

'So,' she began. 'I know little about you, Peter. Bev told me you're looking for some advice.'

Graveney rubbed his chin. 'I had a bang on the head a few weeks back. Since then, I've ...' He rubbed his chin again. 'Since then, I've suffered from hallucinations.'

'I see. And you think the two are linked?'

'I suppose. You're the expert.'

Dr Hope jotted something in her notebook and looked up. 'What form do the hallucinations take?'

Graveney put his hands up to his face and rubbed his eyes. He slowly lowered them. 'A woman. An ex-colleague.'

'Ok. This ex-colleague. Are you still—?'

'She's dead. I was there when ...'

'I see. When you see her, does it appear real?'

Graveney lowered his eyes. 'She touched me, and I felt it. Her hand on my skin. It wasn't quite real, but I could feel something.'

'You obviously had an emotional attachment to this woman. The trauma of her dying—'

'She killed herself. Shot herself through the head as I watched.'

'Do you blame yourself for this?'

'It's not like that. It's complicated.'

'Complicated how?'

Graveney straightened in the chair and folded his arms. 'That's not important.'

Dr Hope nodded and made more notes. 'Ok. Let's talk about the hallucinations themselves.'

'We had a relationship.'

Dr Hope stared at him. 'I see.'

'You don't. We were colleagues. It was unprofessional. I shouldn't have allowed it. But she didn't kill herself because of me. Ok?'

'Ok.'

Graveney stared upwards. 'I know they're not real. I do know that.' He stared at Dr Hope. 'I'm worried there may be ...' He half-laughed. 'Brain damage.'

'Why do you find it amusing?'

'It was already damaged.' She tilted her head. He false-smiled her. He couldn't hide his dislike of talking about himself. To a friend or partner, he could just about bear it. But to a professional? Someone capable of stripping away the emotional veneers he'd managed to cover himself with.

'Maybe I should be the judge of that?' she said.

Graveney sneered. 'You're not as confident as you appear.' Five minutes in her company and she was already under his skin. He recognised that. But couldn't understand why. She was getting to him, and he was allowing it to happen. He felt weak. He felt fragile. This wasn't how it was supposed to go.

'Go on … please.' Her voice calm and gentle.

Attack is the best form of defence he said to himself. Let's see how clever she really is. 'Behind your calm exterior, you massively doubt yourself,' he said.

Dr Hope made notes. 'Why would you say that?'

'Because it's true. I have an ability. Your face betrays you. I can see every nuance you display.'

'Maybe we should concentrate on you, Peter.'

'You're attracted to me. It's so bloody obvious.' Graveney felt his self-control begin to crack.

Dr Hope made notes. 'Go on.'

'You make notes when you don't know what to say. It's your defence mechanism.'

She studied him. 'I'm a professional, Peter. I …'

Graveney lifted his eyes briefly. 'Have you heard of thin-slicing?' The pair momentarily locked eyes before Dr Hope tore hers away.

'A little. I've read articles on it.'

'I'm quite good at it. It's a help and a hinderance. A gift and a …' He closed his eyes.

'Curse?' she said.

Graveney stared at her. 'I don't mean to do it. I can't help it. Before my accident, I could manage it. Keep it under ...' He felt his control crumble. Brick by brick it tumbled.

'And now?'

'And now I can't.' He stared wide-eyed at her. 'I have multiple streams of information swamping me. I'm struggling to handle them. They're relentless.'

'And you're reading me now?'

'Yes.' He studied her. 'I see every facet of your personality. You appear confident but are wracked with self-doubt. You instinctively write notes when you need time to decide what to say. You're attracted to me. I can tell. Don't get me wrong. I'm not saying you'll act out your attraction. Most people don't.'

'It would be unprofessional of me.'

'You're uneasy now. You fear you've lost control of this session. My words are just that, but they continue to chip away at the wall of pseudo-confidence you've erected.'

'Peter, I think …'

'Your pupils, the flush of the skin around your neck, the way you grip the pen. Everything. In glorious, fucking, technicolour.'

Dr Hope held up her hands. 'Peter. I don't doubt what you say, but this is not why we're here.'

Graveney brought his hands up to his face again. Suddenly he felt overwhelmed with embarrassment. The thoughts which usually swirled around his mind, tethered by his self-control, now free and unrestrained. He wrestled back control. Slamming the door to the torrent of words spilling forth just in time. 'I'm sorry … I …' He placed a hand on his temple as a bolt of pain arrowed its way across it.

'Are you ok?' she said, as she leant in towards him.

'Headache ...' Was all he could muster.

She placed a hand on her chin. 'Are you comfortable with me? I could always get a male colleague to handle your treatment.'

Graveney shook his head. 'I was way out of order, Doctor. It was wrong of me to … I can only apologise for my terrible behaviour.'

She smiled professionally. 'Don't worry. I've had far worse.' Graveney studied her features. She was being honest.

'Thanks.' The maelstrom in his head abated.

'I think the best thing is for me to organise a scan. Let's see what's going on in that head of yours.' She stood. 'I'll make a call and see if we can arrange one sooner rather than later.'

Graveney stood. 'Thanks again.' He placed a hand on her arm and glanced down. 'I'm sorry for what I said. It was …'

She smiled and gently tapped his arm. 'I won't be long.'

Graveney watched her leave and turned to face Marne sat in the chair opposite. He slumped into his own.

'Naughty, naughty, Peter,' she said. 'You're up to your old tricks again.' Graveney ignored her, closed his eyes, and leant back in his chair.

Heather opened the door to her friend Maddie. She beckoned her inside and into the living room. 'Have a seat.'

'Is everything all right?' Maddie said. 'You sounded a bit upset on the phone.'

'I think Peter's having an affair.'

Maddie brought a hand up to her mouth. 'What makes you—'

'I just know.'

'Who with?'

'I don't know.'

'Are you sure you're—?'

'Maddie, I know. I've known Peter long enough.' She reached for a tissue and dabbed at her eyes. 'I thought he'd change, with us getting married.' She laughed unconvincingly. 'Leopards ...' She threw her head upwards and sighed heavily.

'What are you going to do?'

Heather shook her head. 'I can't accept what he's doing. I need to know for sure.'

Maddie leant forward and clasped her friend's hand. 'Are you going to confront him?'

'If I do, he'll only deny it. I need a favour.'

'Anything,' Maddie said.

CHAPTER EIGHTEEN

1999 - Lindsey headed away from her house and around the corner to meet Craig waiting in his car.

'Hi,' he said. 'Glad you could make it.'

'I'm sick of sitting around in the house waiting for no one to call.'

'Where to?'

'Surprise me.'

Craig pulled away. 'Alex doesn't know about this, does he?'

'Why would I tell him?'

'It's just …' He forced a smile. 'I need the job.'

Lindsey glanced across at him. 'We can't keep this a secret forever. Not if you're serious.'

'Of course I'm serious.'

'There are other jobs,' Lindsey said.

'Not for me. No qualifications to talk of. I'm lucky to have got this one. Someone I know put a word in for me.'

'Oh yeah. Who, Sean?'

'Yeah, Sean.'

Lindsey crossed her arms. 'He works for Conrad Hudson.'

'Yeah, I know.'

'Alex doesn't like Conrad Hudson. He called him bad news. Your friend, Sean … Well, let's say I've heard things about him too.'

'I told you. I've known Sean since school. He's not as bad as he's painted.'

'What do you do for Alex?' she said.

'Pick him up and drop him off. That sort of thing.'

'Women's' houses?'

Craig shuffled in his seat. 'Listen, Lindsey. I won't lie to you. I like you a lot. Alex ...' He furrowed his brow. 'Alex likes the girls.'

'Yeah, well. I've had enough of Alex. He asked me to do something for him.'

'What?'

'Conrad Hudson runs these parties. Powerful people attend them. I think there are drugs and ...' She stared out of the window. '... girls.'

'Right. Sean hasn't mentioned them. And where does Alex come in?'

'He wanted me to go to one and get some information from a man.'

'What sort—?'

'I don't know. He never went into specifics, but you get the picture.'

'What did you say?'

'I told him to take a running jump,' she said.

'Good for you.'

'Alex doesn't like you saying no. He's been a bit distant with me lately. Probably moved onto his next shag.'

Craig glanced across at her. 'Are you bothered?'

She shrugged. 'Not really. It was fun while it lasted.'

'Good. I know a nice little pub. We could have lunch?'

'I'd like that,' she said. 'Very much.'

The pair ate their lunch and as they talked, Lindsey became more attracted to Craig. She watched him at the bar as he got served and made his way back over to her.

He held out a glass. 'I got you another half. I'm on Coke. I'd better not risk my licence.'

'Thanks.' Her phone sounded and she read the text. She quickly typed a reply and threw it into her bag.

'Who was that?'

'Who do you think?'

'Alex?'

Lindsey scoffed. 'The cheeky bastard wants to meet me at a hotel.'

Craig lowered his eyes. 'What are you going to do?'

'He can sod off. I'm not interested in him anymore. I'd rather stay with you.'

Craig beamed. 'Great.'

'Where do you live?' Lindsey said.

'Hemlington. In a flat.'

'Why don't we have these and then go back there?'

'Are you sure?'

She leant across the table and kissed him on the cheek. 'I'm sure.'

Lindsey stretched across the bed and kissed Craig. 'I enjoyed today,' she said.

'So did I. Maybe we could have another day out? Go to the pictures or something?'

'Yeah, I'd like that.' Lindsey sat up and viewed her watch. 'I'll need to get going.'

'Come on then.' Craig jumped out of bed and pulled on his jeans. 'I'll drop you off.'

They were heading out the door when Craig's phone sounded. He studied the name. 'Alex,' he said. Lindsey viewed him as he answered.

'I need a lift, Craig,' Alex said.

'Yeah, no problem. I need to fill up and put some air in one of the tyres. I think there's a slow puncture. I'll be as quick as I can though.'

'Yeah, no rush. Give Terry at Stepney's a ring. He'll have a look at the tyre for you.'

'I will.' Craig hung up and looked at Lindsey. 'Alex,' he said, holding up the phone.

'I heard. Be careful, Craig. That's all I'm saying.'

He pulled her close. 'I will.'

Craig drew to a halt outside Alex's house, took out his phone, texted and waited. A long ten minutes passed by until Alex came bounding outside. He jumped in beside Craig and drew in a large breath.

'All right, Alex?' Craig said.

'Not really. Jean's giving me earache about going out again. Women. Who needs them?'

Craig started the engine. 'Where to?'

'Amanda's. I've binned Lindsey. She's ignoring my calls.'

Craig glanced across. 'Oh yeah?'

'The ungrateful bitch. I asked her to do one small favour. You'd think all the money I'd spent, all the gifts I'd lavished on her …'

'So, it's over for good?'

'I was willing to give her a second chance. So, I texted her today. She said she didn't want to see me anymore. Told me she'd met someone else. Good luck to him. Let's see how she likes it when she's eating Macdonald's happy meals, instead of the food I buy for her.' His phone rang. 'Alex Cooper.'

'Alex. It's Colin.'

'I was wondering when I'd hear from you.'

'Conrad's having a party at the end of the month. I've managed to get Amanda in.'

'Great. Our friend?'

'He's going to be there. There's a problem, though.'

Cooper sighed. 'What?'

'He likes them under twenty.'

'That's ok,' Cooper said.

'He prefers blondes. Amanda's brunette.'

'That's not a problem either. I'll buy her some hair dye.'

'I'll phone nearer the time with details.'

'There's one more thing,' Cooper said. 'I need you to get some recording equipment in there.'

Colin gasped. 'Christ, Alex. Are you mad?'

'No. I want it set up so we have some leverage against him. It's pointless setting him up with Amanda if we haven't got it on tape. He could prove useful to me. There could be a lot of money involved.'

'If Conrad was—'

'Make sure he doesn't then. Listen,' Cooper said. 'I'll make it worth your while.'

Colin mumbled. 'Ok.'

'Good man. I'll be in touch.'

Cooper eyeballed Craig. 'You never heard any of that.'

'Heard any of what?'

Cooper smiled and searched through his phone. 'Babe. I'm on my way over.'

Cooper let himself into the house. 'Babe,' he said. 'It's me.'

Amanda came racing into the hall and threw her arms around him. 'I thought you were never coming,' she said.

'Business.' Cooper lifted her chin from his chest and gently stroked her hair. 'Have you ever considered changing your hair colour?'

Amanda stepped back from him and pulled a face. 'Don't you like the colour of my hair?'

'Of course, babe,' he said.

Amanda stroked her hair. 'I'll change it if you don't like it.'

'I wouldn't want you to do anything you didn't want.' He placed his hand on Amanda's cheek and kissed her.

'I'd do anything for you, Alex. You know that.'

He took hold of a piece of her hair. 'Blonde?'

'Blonde?' she said. 'I've never imagined myself as a blonde.'

'You could go somewhere posh. My treat of course.'

She kissed him. 'Whatever you want.'

'And the eyebrows. We'd need them tinted.'

Amanda giggled. 'Are you trying to turn me into some sort of bimbo?'

'You'll look sophisticated,' he said. 'Some top-notch shoes and clothes as well.'

'Can we go to London?'

'If you want to,' he said. 'I've got a factfinding trip next week. I'm sure I could wangle you a train ticket. We'd have to be discreet, though.'

'We will,' she said.

Cooper pulled Amanda close to him. 'How about we open the bottle of champagne I brought last time, and take a bath in that huge tub upstairs.'

Amanda giggled again. 'I'll go and get the bottle. You'll have to open it, though.' She pulled herself free of him and disappeared into the kitchen.

Cooper took out his mobile and texted Colin Pybus. 'We need to meet up.'

He popped the phone back into his jacket pocket and slid his coat off, tossing it over the bannister.

Amanda appeared at the door naked, holding a bottle and two glasses. 'Shall we?' she said.

Alex Cooper pulled into the layby and came to a stop next to a red car. He got out and headed around to the passenger door and jumped inside next to Colin Pybus.

'Strange place to meet, Colin,' Cooper said.

'I don't want any of Hudson's lads clocking me, do I?'

'Fair point.'

'About the weekend,' Pybus said.

'Everything ok?'

'I still think it's incredibly risky. If Hudson—'

'Don't worry about that. He won't find out. Just get Amanda in there, and fix her up with you know who.'

'I'll do my best, but I can't guarantee—'

Cooper grinned. 'You'll manage. Have you sorted out the recording equipment?'

'I've got a Dictaphone. I'll give it to Amanda on the night.'

'Good lad.'

Cooper gripped hold of the door handle, and Pybus took hold of his arm. 'You've warned her to be careful?' Pybus said.

'Of course. She'll be fine. There'll be a good drink in this for you, Colin. I'll see to that.'

Pybus swallowed. 'As long as we don't get caught.'

Cooper smiled and patted Pybus on the cheek. 'Don't worry. I'll see you on Saturday.'

CHAPTER NINETEEN

Graveney stood at the end of the bar nursing a Jack Daniels and Coke. He held up his glass, the barmen finished serving a customer and moved over to him.

'Another?' he asked Graveney.

Graveney drained his glass. 'Get one yourself,' he said, pushing a note across the bar.

'Thanks.' The barman winked at Graveney, allowing the double measure to slightly overflow into the glass as he filled it.

Graveney glanced over his shoulder as a group of people entered and made their way into one of the corners. He briefly studied them and turned back to face the bar.

The barman indicated behind him. 'Doctors. From the clinic up the road.'

Graveney spun around on his stool again and studied them once more. His eyes met with Dr Hope's. She nodded across at him and waved as the man next to her continued to talk. Dr Hope placed a hand on the arm of her companion and stood. She mouthed something to the group and ambled across.

Graveney smiled as she reached him. 'Are you following me?' he said.

'That wouldn't be ethical.'

Graveney gestured towards the bar. 'Drink, Doctor?'

'I'm fine, thanks. I thought you'd be heading off home?'

'Didn't fancy the long drive. I'm a bit tired as well.'

Dr Hope glanced across the room. 'They'll be talking about us. I just know it.'

'Us? Why?'

'Gossip. People love to gossip,' she said.

Graveney leant in closer. 'Have a drink. Give them something to gossip about.'

Dr Hope threw back her head and laughed. 'They don't need any encouragement.'

Graveney drained his glass and looked across at the barmen who moved over to him. He plucked a note from his pocket and laid it on the counter. 'Same again, and whatever the lady's having.'

The barman glanced at Dr Hope. She placed a hand on Graveney's arm. 'You're persistent, I'll give you that.'

Graveney smiled at her through the mirror behind the bar. 'A small glass of Merlot,' she said.

The barmen placed down their drinks and held out Graveney's change. Graveney waved it away and spun around on his stool to face Dr Hope.

'You're a lot more confident out of the clinic,' he said.

Dr Hope looked into his eyes. 'I'm relaxed. A couple of glasses with dinner helped as well.'

'Who are they?' He looked towards the group in the corner.

'Colleagues from the clinic.'

'No partner then?'

Dr Hope smiled. 'I'm single.'

'Really?' Graveney said.

'But you're not.' She nodded at the ring on his finger.

'Banged to rights,' Graveney said. He held up his hand. 'Does it matter? Being married, I mean?'

Dr Hope tilted her head to one side. 'It would to your wife.'

Graveney edged nearer, moving his mouth closer to her ear. 'I won't tell. I'm good at keeping secrets.'

'Does this ever work, Peter? This little boy lost strategy?'

Graveney leant away. 'Sometimes.'

She patted his arm again. 'Not tonight, though. I should get back.'

Graveney smiled to himself. 'Yeah. I'd better get to bed.'

Dr Hope headed back across to her group. She watched as Graveney eased himself from the stool, waved at the barman and unsteadily made off.

'Who was that?' a woman next to Dr Hope asked.

Dr Hope glanced towards the exit Graveney left by and tucked a strand of hair behind her ear. 'A friend of a friend,' she said, looking back towards the door.

Graveney stopped in the lobby and felt for his room key, dropping it to the floor as he finally pulled it from his pocket. He stooped and snatched it from the ground and staggered up the stairs, assisted by the bannister on his ascent. Maddie edged from behind a column and watched as he disappeared around the corner.

Graveney slumped onto the bed and groaned.

'That didn't go as planned,' Marne said.

Graveney avoided looking at the seat in the corner of the room. He stood, staggered across to the table and poured himself a large glass of Jack Daniels.

'How embarrassing,' Marne said. 'Trying to seduce your therapist.'

He placed his hands on the table top and leant forward, supporting his slightly tottering form. He looked towards the door as someone knocked, stood tall, rubbed his face and ambled over to it, pulling it open.

His eyes widened. 'Maddie?'

'Peter,' she said. 'Can I come in?'

Graveney stepped aside. 'Of course. Long way to come for a—'

'I'm doing this for Heather.'

Graveney picked up the bottle and another glass. 'Drink?'

Maddie waved him away. 'Heather thinks you're having an affair.'

Graveney sipped from his glass. 'And?'

'I suggested following you to allay her fears. Get her to believe you're not being unfaithful. But now I'm here ...'

Graveney grinned. 'But now you're here ...?'

'Who was the woman in the bar?'

Graveney narrowed his eyes. 'Police business.'

'You expect me to believe that? Heather's my friend, Peter. Heather's—'

Graveney edged closer to her. 'Friends don't do what you're doing. Friends don't sleep with their friend's husband.'

Maddie lowered her eyes to the floor. 'I hate what we're doing. I hate what ...'

Graveney took another sip. 'No one put a gun to your head.'

'Why do it, Peter? She adores you.'

Graveney slumped onto the edge of the bed. He glanced across into the corner at a smiling Marne. 'It's who I am. Who I've always been. I'm too old and too set in my ways to change.'

Maddie sneered. 'A convenient get-out.'

Graveney put down his glass with a bang and stood. 'Then go. The door's there. No one asked you here.'

Maddie's eyes locked on his. 'You bastard.'

Graveney moved nearer, and pulled her close, allowing their lips to meet. 'I know,' he said. 'I know.'

Maddie slipped from the bed, dressed, headed towards the door and paused to view the slumbering Graveney. She left quietly. Outside she leant up against the wall, and shakily dabbed at her eyes with a tissue. Maddie blew her nose, and hurried off, her guilt a heavy load.

Graveney arrived home later in the day. He pulled up outside the house and collecting his overnight bag, made his way inside. Heather brooded at the table with a cup of tea in her hand.

'Hi,' he said. 'You ok?'

Heather placed her cup on the table and fixed Graveney with a stare. 'You're having an affair.'

Graveney stopped and gazed at her. 'Don't be—'

'Please don't lie to me, Peter. I've suspected for a while. Maddie confirmed it.'

Graveney widened his eyes. 'Maddie?'

'I had her follow you yesterday. To a swanky hotel.'

Graveney felt a lightning bolt of pain shoot across his temple. He reached out for the wall for support.

Heather stood. 'Are you ok?'

Graveney forced a smile. 'Fine, fine.'

She turned away from him and peered into the garden. 'I think it's best if you leave.'

Graveney recovered his equilibrium. 'Look, Heather. I don't know what Maddie told you, but ...'

'Peter,' she said, as she spun around. 'She saw you with a woman. Why lie?'

Graveney searched for a plausible answer. 'Maddie was mistaken. It was police business.'

'How convenient,' she said. 'I just know, Peter. The fact you stand there and lie ...' Heather brought her hands up to her face and rubbed it. '... makes me so angry.'

'But the kids ... what will you tell them?'

Louisa appeared at the kitchen door holding Max. She joined Heather.

Heather glanced at Louisa, who squeezed her arm with her free hand. 'Your flat's empty at the moment,' Heather said. 'You can stay there.'

Graveney lowered his head. 'If you're sure it's what you want?'

Heather pulled a tissue from her pocket and blew her nose. She took Max from Louisa and headed into the kitchen, closing the door behind her. Graveney moved forward.

Louisa stepped between him and the door. 'Leave her, Dad.'

'Louisa.' Graveney held out his hands. 'Please ...'

She shuffled back a few steps. 'I love you, Dad. But at this moment, I hate you. You should go.'

Graveney's shoulder slumped as he accepted defeat. 'Luke?'

'I'll tell him,' she said.

'I'll get my things and ...' He pointed upstairs. Louisa folded her arms and glared.

Graveney trudged down the stairs carrying a suit holder and a large suitcase. He paused at the door to look at Louisa holding Max. He walked forward and placed a kiss on his son's head, mouthed a sorry to Louisa, and then he was gone.

Graveney watched from outside the shop as Maddie exited with a man. He jumped out of his car and raced across to her.

'Have you a minute?' Graveney said. His anger patently obvious.

The man with Maddie stepped closer. 'Is everything all right?' he said to Maddie.

Maddie patted his arm. 'It's fine, James. I won't be long.' He eyeballed Graveney and moved away from them, stopping at a corner.

'Why?' Graveney said.

Maddie glanced up and down the road. 'I don't want a scene, Peter. If you start shouting …'

Graveney nodded and held up the palms of his hands. 'Ok. I promise.'

Maddie motioned towards the car, and they both jumped in. Graveney turned and stared at her.

Maddie met his stare. 'You don't deserve her. You really don't.'

Graveney sneered. 'And you …?'

'I'll have to live with what I did.'

'What if I told her about us? Told her while you were supposed to be spying on me, you were shagging me?'

Maddie gave him a defiant look. 'Do it. She almost certainly won't believe you. And if she does, she'll hate you even more.'

Graveney moved his face closer. 'You bitch. This is my life you're—'

'Don't lecture me, Peter. You have no morals where women are concerned. You had a good life, a wonderful woman.' She half-laughed. 'But you couldn't keep your cock in your pants, could you? This is your fault. No one else's. If you're looking for scapegoats, look in the mirror.'

'And I suppose none of it was your fault?'

Maddie put a hand up to her eyes as tears cascaded the length of her face. 'I'll never forgive myself for allowing this to happen. But you … You made it so difficult to say no … you manipulate, Peter. You …'

Graveney lowered his head. 'I don't mean to hurt people …' Maddie rolled her eyes at him, his voice clearly lacking conviction.

'Get some counselling,' she said. Maddie bolstered her resolve. 'Stop treating the women in your life like doormats.' Graveney lifted his head to look directly at her. Maddie slightly tilted her head. For a moment, Graveney spotted the remorse in her eyes. Sensed the affection she still had for him. 'Stop turning your relationships into train-wrecks.' She glanced upwards. 'Think about what you're doing to others.'

Maddie grasped the handle, her hands shaking and Graveney took hold of her arm. 'I'm sorry,' he said. 'Sorry for hurting you.'

Maddie faced him. Graveney recoiled slightly, surprised to see more tears in her eyes. She false-laughed. 'I'll survive. Heather's the one you should worry about.' Maddie yanked open the door and left.

Graveney brought his hand up to his head and rested it on the steering wheel. The pain, a searing one, thankfully brief. He lifted his head and rubbed at his eyes, catching sight of the smirking Marne through the rearview mirror.

Graveney dropped his luggage into the hall and raced through into the kitchen with a carrier in hand. He pulled the bottle of Jack Daniels from the bag, opened the bottle and swigged greedily. The liquid a warm sensation as he swallowed. He caught his breath, plucked a glass from the cupboard, and filled it to the top.

'Is that all you're going to do.' Marne said. 'Get drunk?'

Graveney stared at the wall. 'Yeah. Why not?'

'What about the case?'

He looked up to the ceiling and blew out hard. 'The case?'

'Lindsey's the key to it. You must see that?'

He allowed his head to rest against the cupboard door. 'Why are you haunting me, Steph? Why can't you leave me alone?'

Marne appeared at his side, moving her mouth next to his ear. 'Forget about Heather and Maddie. Bev too. You don't need any of them. You've got me.'

Graveney brought a hand up to his face and rubbed. 'You're not real, Steph.' He gazed at her, lifted a hand to her face, but stopped short. 'You're in here?' He tapped his head with his finger.

'It's all you need, Peter. I'm part of you now.'

Daybreak bludgeoned its way into Graveney's flat, spilling blinding, searing-heat across his prone form. He groaned and slowly hoisted himself into a sitting position. The bottle rolled from his lap and onto the floor, banging and bouncing noisily before coming to a clanking stop against the hearth. He swung his feet around and planted them unsteadily onto the floor. The union of feet and the unforgiving hard surface sending shockwaves through his body which slammed into his skull. Graveney groaned, his hands instinctively coming up to cover his face from the painful brightness screaming in from the window. He stood fully, assisted by items of furniture, and gingerly trod towards the bathroom. His body pinballing from wall to wall as he finally reached the sink. Graveney filled the basin, and plunged his head into the ice-cold liquid, gasping as the glacial slap shivered him to his core. He grabbed for a towel and patted his face and head. Looking into the mirror,

Graveney exhaled loudly, as the ghosts of a thousand dolorous eyes glared back. Pushing a hand through his matted hair, he headed for the kitchen. The doorbell chimed, and Graveney groaned again as nausea churned his guts. He trod towards the door and pulled it open. Mac stood outside, a scowl filling his face. Graveney turned and headed away as his friend followed him inside.

'Peter,' Mac said. 'Heavy night?'

Graveney slumped onto the arm of the settee. 'Yeah. Night in with my friend Jack.' He pointed to the empty bottle still resting against the hearth.

'Heather told Becky what happened.'

'Obviously,' Graveney said. 'You wouldn't be here otherwise.'

'You ok?'

'Fantastic. Never felt better.'

Mac's eyes glanced across at the empty bottle again. 'Maybe you should take a few days off.'

'I've had hangovers before, Mac.'

Mac straightened. 'Let me put it another way, Peter. Take the rest of the week off.'

'Is that an order?'

Mac smiled tightly. 'Get yourself straight. Pull yourself round.'

Graveney held up a hand. 'One minute.' He raced for the bathroom, slamming the door behind him. Mac waited. The sound of Graveney wretching the only noise in the eerie silence.

Graveney came back out. 'You were saying.'

'The two cases you're working on? The Cooper murder and Conrad Hudson's men?'

'What about them?'

Mac rubbed at his chin. 'I'm going to assign another senior officer to assist you. Maybe he can work on one, while you—'

'They're linked, Mac.'

'We don't know that, do we?'

'I do.'

'A hunch?' Mac said.

Graveney sneered. 'Hudson is living with Cooper's wife. How can you say they're not linked?'

'I'm not. I'm saying we don't have evidence to prove they are.'

Graveney winced as a blistering pain shot across his temple. Marne watched him from behind Mac, grinning.

'What does he know, Peter?' she said. 'We know, don't we?'

'What's up, Peter?' Mac said. 'There's something you're not telling me.'

'Like what? Heather's kicked me out. She thinks I'm having an affair.'

'And are you?'

'Is this as my friend or my superior?'

Mac forced a smile. 'A friend.'

'Sometimes in life, miscarriages of justice happen. I was away on … I was away. Heather put two and two together and came up with five.'

'Away where?'

Graveney swallowed. 'Private business. Nothing to do with the force.'

'So you're not having an affair. Explain to Heather.'

'Mac,' Graveney said. 'Heather's right. It's just …' He scoffed. 'I'm getting hanged for the wrong crime. Some might call it poetic justice.'

Mac shook his head. 'Take the rest of the week off.'

'Friend or superior.'

Mac stared at Graveney. 'I'll see you on Monday.' He moved towards the door and stopped. 'I'll brief DI Robertson for you. I'll tell the team you're unwell. Monday, Peter. I don't want to see you until then. Are we clear on this?'

'Perfectly, Sir,' Graveney said, as Mac exited.

'Why would Lindsey admit to a murder she didn't commit?' Marne said. 'It doesn't make sense. Why, Peter? Why?'

Graveney rubbed his face and slumped into the armchair. 'Why indeed?'

CHAPTER TWENTY

Graveney pulled his car into Middlesbrough Police station and parked. He checked his appearance in the mirror, satisfied he got out and headed inside. He made his way past colleagues, exchanging pleasantries, attempting to give off an air of confidence he hardly felt.

He stopped outside Mac's office, took in a large lungful of air, and knocked. Mac's muffled voice from within beckoned him inside.

Mac was on the phone, he placed a hand over the mouthpiece. 'Have a seat, Peter.'

Graveney waited as Mac finished his conversation and hung up. 'How are you?' Mac said.

Graveney suppressed the urge to snap at him. 'I'm good.'

Mac leant in closer. 'I've been giving the murders a good deal of thought. I was going to get you to continue with the investigation of the bodies found at Grewgrass Lane, and give the murders of Conrad Hudson's men to DI Robertson.'

'But ...?' Graveney said.

'I was thinking about what you said. Maybe the two are linked. So what I'm proposing is you, and DI Robertson work together. Any problem with that?'

'None, Guv.'

'Peter ...' Mac said. '... we aren't going to fall out over—?'

'Mac ...' Graveney said. 'You were right. My head was all over the place last week. Sometimes you don't see it when you're on the inside looking out.'

'And now?'

' And now, I'm fine.'

Mac nodded. 'Good. Maybe a drink later? And a chat? It would be good to catch up away from work.'

'I'm laying off the booze for a while,' Graveney said. 'Maybe next week.'

'It's a date,' Mac said.

'Has anyone been to see Lindsey Armstrong and Jimmy Jefferson?'

Mac leant back in his chair. 'We put it off until your return. You'll need to fill DI Robertson in. He knows the bare bones of the case, but any insights would be helpful.'

'He's buttering you up,' Marne said, as she appeared to Graveney's right. 'See, he can't do without you.' Graveney closed his eyes briefly.

'Everything all right?' Mac said.

'Yeah,' Graveney smiled. 'I was giving it some thought. I'll pop and see Robertson now.'

'Good. Keep me informed.'

Graveney stood and turned.

'It's good to have you back, Peter,' Mac said.

Graveney paused at the door. 'Thanks ... Mac. I appreciate it.' He left, raced along the corridor and into the toilet. Leaning over the sink, he splashed his face with cold water as the nausea he felt slowly dissipated. He looked up and stared at his reflection in the mirror. Marne stood behind him. He watched as she wandered closer and put her head close to his ear. 'They're lost without you, Peter,' she said. 'The other coppers are useless.'

Graveney headed along the corridor and stopped outside a door marked 'DI Robertson.' He knocked and poked his head inside. Robertson glanced up from what he was doing. 'Hi, Peter. Come in.'

Graveney entered, placed two coffees on the desk, and sat. 'How are you, Neil?'

'Good,' Robertson said. 'Have you spoken to the Guv?'

'Yeah. Wants us to put our heads together. See if we can crack this case.'

Robertson picked up one of the coffees. 'Cheers,' he said. 'I've got a good overview of the two cases, but I'll need you to fill me in with the minor details.'

'I think the cases are linked,' Graveney said.

Robertson laced his fingers and placed them on his round belly. 'Yeah?'

'Lindsey Armstrong is the key.'

Robertson opened a file. 'I was reading about her. She killed her boyfriend, and—'

'I don't think she did,' Graveney said.

'Why?'

'Gut instinct.' Graveney rubbed his face. 'She knew Alex Cooper and Sean Grant.' Robertson nodded, and Graveney continued. 'There's more she's not telling us, I'm sure. Conrad Hudson is having a thing with Jean Cooper.'

'What about Hudson?' Robertson said. 'Do you think he killed his own boys?'

'No. Someone is targeting and killing his men. Someone from his past.'

'I read the post mortem reports,' Robertson said. He picked up a file and waved it. 'The mutilation ... Struck me as significant.'

'Sex Crime?' Graveney said.

'Yeah. Looks as if someone is trying to send out a message.'

Graveney tapped the desk. 'That's what I thought. Hudson's men did something bad to someone. Probably rape?'

'I'd say so.'

'I'd like to go and see Lindsey Armstrong again though.'

Robertson rubbed his chin. 'You don't think she's the woman with the big guy, do you?'

'No. But as I said, she's definitely involved somehow.'

Robertson stood. 'Well, what are we waiting for?'

Graveney joined him at the door. Robertson paused. 'Are you ok with us working together, Peter?'

'Yeah, fine.'

'Only ... I know you like your own team. I know you have your own methods.'

Graveney smiled and patted him on the arm. 'It's fine. Two heads are better than one.'

CHAPTER TWENTY-ONE

Lindsey closed the door to her mother and father's house. She rattled the handle to confirm it was locked.

'Hi, Linds,' Jen said.

Lindsey spun around. She smiled and hurrying forward, hugged her. 'What are you doing here?'

'I was in the area,' Jen said. 'You finally got out then?'

'Yeah. How did you find me?'

'I asked people. Not too many jailbirds kicking around.'

Lindsey laughed. 'Yeah.'

Jen nodded towards the "SOLD" sign outside the house. 'Moving on?'

'It was Mam and Dad's. I'm moving to a nicer area. A new life.'

'On your own?'

Lindsey beamed. 'No. He's called Jimmy.'

'Does he know…?'

'Everything,' Lindsey said. 'Shall we go for a coffee?'

Jen smiled. 'Yeah.'

'Ok. I know a nice little coffee shop not too far from here. Maybe a slice of cake as well?'

'Yeah. I'd love one.'

Lindsey placed the cup and plate in front of Jen and sat opposite. 'So, what've you been up to?'

'This and that. Not a lot out there for an ex-offender.'

'Yeah. I've been lucky. Jimmy got me a job in a shop a friend of his owns.'

'How's Maggie?'

'She gets out next year. She's coming to live with us.'

Jen sipped at her coffee. 'I've got a friend too. Joey.'

Lindsey moved in closer. 'Male?'

'Yeah.'

Lindsey raised her eyebrows. 'Only I thought you—?'

'Inside you do what you have to. Billie helped me adjust to prison life, and … well, you know.'

Lindsey placed a hand on her arm. 'Yeah, I know. I didn't mean to pry.'

'You're not. I knew him from way back. He was in the army for a lot of years.'

'Squaddie?' Lindsey said.

'Yeah. He's had a few problems with PTSD. He lived rough for a while, and I happened to spot him one day. He's much better now.'

'Good. You look happy. Healthier.'

Jen unzipped the bulky parka she was wearing and patted her bump. 'That'll be this.'

Lindsey beamed. 'Oh, my, God. Brilliant'

Jen moved closer and glanced left and right. 'I need a favour, Linds.'

Lindsey leant forward. 'Yeah. I'll do what I can.'

Jen raised her eyebrows. 'Amanda?'

Lindsey rubbed her face and sucked in a breath. 'That was some time ago, Jen.'

'I've come by some information.'

'What sort of—?'

'I don't want to involve you,' Jen said. ' It could get tricky.'

'I've told you all I know. It was a long time ago.'

'Colin Pybus?'

Lindsey stroked her chin. 'I knew Colin. He was mates with Alex. He worked for Conrad Hudson.'

'I know. Colin told me stuff.'

Lindsey gazed outside, deep in thought. 'I'll be honest, Jen. Conrad Hudson is not the sort of man to mess with. He's a—'

'I know all about Hudson. Colin told me what they did to Amanda.'

Lindsey put her hand over her eyes and rubbed at them. 'I suspected something happened to her. It was only when you told me inside. What did Colin say?'

Jen sniffed, as her eyes filled with tears. 'They raped and murdered her. One of four men dumped her body somewhere. I need to know where. The least she deserves is a decent burial.'

Lindsey dropped her head. 'I understand, but—'

'I know it won't bring her back. But I need to know where she is.' Jen picked up a napkin and blew her nose. 'She was my sister, Linds.'

Lindsey leant forward and hugged her. 'Ok. I understand. Is Colin helping you?'

'Colin's dying. I don't think he'd have told me otherwise. He had a thing for Amanda and blames himself for not saving her.'

'These men who ...?'

'You don't want to know.'

'What's the favour?'

Jen stared into the eyes. 'I need somewhere to stay. Somewhere no one knows me.'

Lindsey considered for a moment. 'How long?'

'Couple of weeks. That's all.'

Lindsey put her hand into her pocket and pulled out a key. 'My mam and dad's place. I've got the keys until next month. You can stay there.'

'I'm grateful for this.'

Lindsey touched her arm. 'Be careful. These men ...?'

'Don't worry. They've got their's coming.'

Lindsey closed her eyes and blew out. 'Just be careful, Jen. Be careful.'

Jimmy was painting when Lindsey returned home. 'I'm up here,' he shouted.

Lindsey paused at the foot of the stairs. 'I was going to cook some lunch before I got cracking.'

'I've had a bacon sandwich,' he said.

'Ok. I'll make myself something, and then I'll join you.'

The doorbell sounded, and Lindsey spun around. The clear shape of two men stood outside through the glass. She edged closer and tentatively opened the door. Graveney stood there with Robertson.

Lindsey crossed her arms. 'Don't you coppers ever give up?'

Graveney smiled. 'Can we come in, Lindsey?'

She stepped aside and theatrically welcomed them inside. Jimmy appeared at the top of the stairs with a paintbrush in his hand. Spotting the officers, he ambled down.

'We need to ask a few more questions,' Graveney said.

Jimmy nodded and followed Lindsey and the officers into the lounge. Lindsey slumped onto a settee, and sternly folded her arms.

Jimmy looked across at Graveney and Robertson. 'Can I get either of you two a drink?'

Graveney shook his head. 'I'm fine,' Robertson said.

Jimmy eased himself next to Lindsey.

'You said you had questions?' Lindsey took hold of Jimmy's hand and squeezed.

'Karl Jenkins?' Graveney said, fixing Lindsey with a stare.

'Who?' Lindsey said. Jimmy swallowed hard.

'Karl Jenkins is Karl Smith,' Graveney said.

'Good for him.' She met Graveney's stare.

'He was living in Stockton,' Graveney said.

Lindsey huffed. 'I thought we'd done this? I've told you all I know. Karl and Craig were mates.'

'Karl has disappeared off the map,' Robertson said. 'He went missing a while ago.'

Lindsey refolded her arms. 'And?'

Graveney smiled. 'We're interviewing anyone who knew him. Anyone who may ...'

'For Christ's sake. I've told you everything. I haven't seen Karl for years.'

Robertson opened the file he held. 'You were the victim of a hit and run some time ago. Nobody was ever arrested for it.'

'Probably a drunk,' Lindsey said.

Graveney viewed Jimmy. 'You were there when it happened?'

Jimmy looked away. 'I didn't see who it was. I was inside the pub and heard a commotion. Me and a group of others came outside as a car raced away.'

'One of the witnesses said it appeared deliberate,' Graveney said.

Lindsey scoffed. 'I was daydreaming. I stepped out in front of a car, and he hit me—'

'He?' Graveney said, taking the file from Robertson. 'In the report—'

'Oh, for God's sake,' Lindsey said. 'It was a slip of the tongue. I don't know who was driving the car.'

Jimmy gripped hold of Lindsey's hand. 'No one saw the driver, Inspector,' he said. 'I was the first out, and I couldn't tell you if it was a man or a woman.'

Robertson opened his notebook. 'A witness claims the car screeched before it hit you. It doesn't sound like an accident.'

Lindsey false-smiled. 'A boy racer, perhaps?'

Graveney edged closer and fixed Lindsey with an icy glare. 'I think Karl Jenkins was the driver. I think Karl Jenkins tried to kill you.'

Lindsey looked away, her hand moving down to her leg as a pain shot through it.

Graveney glanced at Robertson. 'I think we should have a word with you two at the station.' Robertson nodded, and Graveney continued. 'Make things a little more formal.'

Lindsey turned back to face Graveney. 'Do what you want.'

Graveney stared at Jimmy. 'What about you, Jimmy?'

Jimmy swallowed hard again.

Lindsey scowled across at Graveney and Robertson as Graveney switched on the tape recorder. 'Interview with Lindsey Armstrong.' He glanced at his watch, recording the time and date. 'Can you state your name for the benefit of the tape, please?'

'Lindsey Armstrong,' she said.

'Officers present,' continued Graveney, 'Inspectors Peter Graveney and Neil Robertson. Miss Armstrong has waived the right to legal representation at this stage.' He glanced at her.

'Yes,' she said.

Graveney leant forward. 'We've brought you here, Lindsey, to help with our enquiries regarding—'

Lindsey puffed out her cheeks. 'Karl Smith was driving the car.'

Graveney looked at Robertson and then back to Lindsey. 'Karl Smith tried to kill you?'

'Yes.'

'Why would he do that, Lindsey?' Robertson said.

'He killed Craig and he knew sooner or later, I'd find out.'

Robertson furrowed his brow. 'But you spent—'

'I know.' She laughed sarcastically. 'I spent fifteen years in prison for a crime I didn't commit.'

'Why?' Graveney said.

Lindsey took a deep breath and began.

Robertson and Graveney stood outside the interview room.

'What's your gut instinct?' Robertson said.

Graveney rubbed his chin and glanced back along the corridor. 'I think she's telling the truth. I think Karl Smith killed her boyfriend, and she may well have believed she killed Sean Grant. It's plausible.'

'What do we do?'

'She was incapacitated when Karl disappeared. So she probably didn't kill him. If he's dead.'

Robertson nodded towards the interview room door. 'Jimmy Jefferson?'

'Let's see what he has to say,' Graveney said.

Jimmy looked up as the officers entered. They sat opposite and carried out the tape recorder formalities before focussing their attention on him.

'Sorry for the delay, Jimmy,' Graveney said. 'Lindsey had quite a bit to say.'

'When can I see her?'

'Soon,' Graveney said. 'She's told us some interesting things, but we'd like to hear your side.'

Jimmy slouched. 'Ok.'

Robertson glanced at his pad. 'Who knocked down Lindsey?'

Jimmy rubbed his face. 'Karl Smith.'

Graveney nodded. 'And Lindsey's boyfriend, Craig?'

'She didn't kill him. Karl did.'

Graveney leant back in his seat. 'Go on,' he said.

Jimmy joined Lindsey in the reception at the police station. They hugged, and Graveney watched as the pair of them exited.

Robertson joined him and followed Graveney's stare outside. 'Jefferson?' Robertson said.

Graveney pushed his hand through his hair and turned to face Robertson. 'I'm not sure if he's hiding something.'

'Karl Smith? Do you think he had something to do with his disappearance?'

Graveney shrugged. 'We'll check his alibi on the day Karl Smith went missing.'

Graveney dialled a number and waited. A female voice answered on the other line. 'Tetricide Chemicals,' she said.

'Good morning. My name's Inspector Graveney from Cleveland Police. I'm checking up on one of your employees.'

'Oh, yes?'

'James Jefferson.'

'Jimmy. He's not in any trouble, is he?'

'No. Nothing like that. It's routine, really. He gave me this number. Can you check a date for me? Jimmy said he was at work all day.'

She repeated the date back to Graveney as he read it out. 'I'll check,' she said. 'I'll just put you on hold for a few moments.'

Graveney waited as the on-hold music played in his earpiece. He opened his drawer and pulled out his diary. A piece of paper fell from the pages and onto the floor.

'Hi there,' she said.

'Yes,' Graveney said. He bent and scooped up the paper, popping it onto his desk.

'Jimmy worked a twelve-hour shift. Eight 'til eight.'

'That's fine,' Graveney said. 'Thanks for your help.'

'No problem.'

Graveney hung up and plucked the paper from his desk. He stared at the name of Helen Trainor written on it. He picked up his phone and dialled.

'Yes, Guv,' Hussain said.

'Meet me downstairs in ten minutes, Rav. We need to go across to Guisborough.'

'Whereabouts in Guisborough?' Hussain said.

'The Kings Head, on the High Street.'

'What's this lead, Guv?'

Graveney rubbed his eyes and yawned. 'Probably nothing. It's someone who knew Robin Slaney.'

'The gardener who worked for Hudson?'

'Yeah.'

Hussain furrowed his brow. 'You think Hudson had something to do with Cooper's murder?'

'Maybe. It's just another line of inquiry.'

Hussain put the car into gear and pulled away from Middlesbrough police station.

Hussain found a parking spot on the High Street and pulled up. The officers climbed from the car and headed inside the public house. Graveney looked about, the pub half-full of diners and drinkers. He made his way to the bar, smiling at a young barmaid who moved across to him.

'What can I get you guys?' she said.

'I'm looking for Helen Trainor,' Graveney said.

'She's on her break. She shouldn't be too long.'

Graveney pulled out his identification. 'Police. It is quite urgent.'

'Ok. I'll go and get her.'

Graveney smiled again as the barmaid disappeared.

'Nice pub,' Hussain said. 'I've never been in here.'

'I've had a couple of good meals,' Graveney said. 'With the family.'

The barmaid returned. 'Helen's coming.'

'Thanks,' Graveney said.

An older woman came through into the bar. She stopped in front of Graveney and Hussain. 'Can I help you, gentlemen?'

Graveney stepped nearer. 'Nothing to worry about, Miss Trainor. Just routine stuff.'

'You can come through into the back.' She lifted the hatch and Graveney and Hussain followed her through into the rear of the pub.

She pointed to a table and chairs. 'Have a seat. Can I get you two a drink?'

The officers sat. 'Not for me,' Graveney said. Hussain shook his head as she joined them at the table.

'We're making enquiries about someone you know,' Graveney said. 'Robin Slaney.'

The woman's eyes widened. 'Robin? That was a long time ago.'

'Do you know where he lives?' Graveney said.

'No. I haven't seen Robin since …' She glanced upwards. '1999 … I think.'

'How well did you know him?' Graveney said.

She pursed her lips. 'Robin worked at a huge house out in the country, as a gardener. He lived near to the pub I worked in.'

'Which pub?' Hussain said.

'The Fighting Cocks, in Hartburn'

Graveney nodded. 'Go on.'

'He and I became close.' She lowered her eyes. 'Really close, if you know what I mean?'

'You and he had an affair?' Graveney said.

'I'm not proud of what I did. I didn't know he was married, at first. It was later he told me, and by then … well, I'd fallen for him.'

Graveney looked at her. 'We're not here to pass judgement on your life, Helen. It's information we're after.'

She smiled. 'We had a thing for about six months. We used to meet two or three times a week. Robin was married to a Portuguese woman—'

'Anabela?' Graveney said.

'Yeah. He told me his marriage was on the rocks.' She sneered. 'Don't they all? I was younger, more gullible. I believed him.'

'What was he like, back then?' Graveney said.

'Funny and handsome. I'd recently come out of a bad relationship, and Robin cheered me up.'

'Did he know anyone else in the pub?' Graveney said.

'There was a couple of older men he'd drink with. They were keen gardeners. Robin gave them plants and stuff.'

'Do you know their names?' Hussain said.

'It'd be a waste of time. They're both dead.'

'How did your relationship with Robin end?' Graveney said.

'His wife found out about us. Not who I was, but that Robin was seeing someone. She went ballistic, understandably. She hadn't settled in England and gave Robin an ultimatum. Either they returned to Portugal, or she'd go on her own. Robin told me he had no intention of going there. He told his wife to go, and he'd follow. In hindsight, he was a bit of a coward. He should've told her straight.'

'And?' Graveney said.

'Turns out he was lying to me. I thought he was going to leave her, but he went back with her.'

'How do you know?' Graveney said.

'I tried ringing him when he didn't come to my house. I was livid. I drove to where he worked and knocked on the door.'

'Stranton Manor?' Graveney said.

'Yeah, that's it. I met his boss … Mr—'

'Hudson?' Graveney said.

'That's it. Hudson. He said he'd left for Portugal.'

'Can you remember the date?' Hussain said.

'It was so long ago.' She closed her eyes and thought. 'I really don't.'

'Has he ever been in contact since?' Graveney said.

'No. I tried ringing his number, but it went to answerphone. I left messages. Loads of them, but he never got in touch. I put it down to one of life's lessons.'

Graveney glanced at Hussain. 'I think that's everything,' Graveney said. 'You've been helpful.'

'Can I ask what this is about?'

'It's an ongoing enquiry,' Graveney said. 'Thanks again.' He took out a card and handed it to her. 'If you remember anything else …'

She showed them back through into the bar, and the officers made their way outside.

'What do you think, Guv?' Hussain said.

'The missing persons are stacking up, Rav. He never went back to Portugal. There's no record of him still living here either. In 1999, he disappeared off the face of the earth.'

CHAPTER TWENTY-TWO

1999 – Sean and Karl parked their car up the street from Mary Jefferson's house. Karl grabbed hold of Sean's arm. 'Are you certain that no one's in?'

Sean sighed. 'I told you, Mary lives there alone. She threw her old man out weeks ago. She goes to a fitness class tonight.'

'And the lad?'

'He lives with his dad.'

'How do we get in?' Karl said.

Sean smiled. 'She has a spare key hidden out the back. I used to let myself in when I was seeing her.'

'She may have moved it.'

'If she has, we get in through the downstairs toilet window. The locks are a bit iffy. You'd think a copper would have his house better secured.'

'Ok,' Karl said. 'We'll go there first and get as much valuable stuff as possible.'

Sean clenched his fists. 'I can't believe Craig didn't show. He's changed since he met Lindsey.'

'Yeah well,' Karl said. 'He isn't here, so it's you and me.'

Sean pulled a small packet of white powder from his pocket and spread it out across the dashboard. He took £10 from his wallet and rolled it into a tube. Sniffing half of the cocaine he handed the note to Karl. 'Dutch courage,' Sean said.

Karl did likewise. Dabbing his finger into the last bits of powder, he rubbed it on his gums. 'Let's go.'

The pair pulled on leather gloves and crept from the vehicle. Making their way up to the house, they slipped noiselessly down the side of the property. Karl followed his friend as he made his way to the rear and stopped near to the kitchen door. Sean glanced around, sure they weren't being watched, he stooped and lifted the rock. Below it lay a key. He plucked it from the ground and held it up for Karl to see.

'The stupid bitch must have forgotten about it,' Sean said.

Karl took hold of the key. 'She'll know it was you.'

Sean smirked. 'We had an affair for six months. That'll take some explaining to her old fella.'

'Even so. When we've finished, we'll put it back.'

'I'll force a window,' Sean said. 'Make it look more realistic.'

'What about the alarm?'

'It didn't work. She's been meaning to get it repaired for ages. But I know the code. 1,2,3,4.'

Karl handed Sean the key and led him towards the house. Sean turned and opened the kitchen door as Karl followed him inside and through into the hallway. The pair pulled a small torch each from their pockets and switched them on.

'Look in the cupboard under the stairs,' Sean said. 'See if there's a holdall or something.'

Karl dropped to his knees and rifled through the cupboard.

Sean put a hand on his friend's shoulder. 'I'll start upstairs. There are some nice bits of jewellery. You do the lounge.'

Pulling a bag from under the stairs, he held it aloft. 'This should do,' he said.

Sean headed upstairs while Karl concentrated on the living room.

Sean pushed the last bits into a bag and grabbed hold of it. He gave the room one last look and raced towards the door. He stopped, as the sound of a car reversing onto the drive caught his attention. Running towards the window, he carefully pulled the curtain aside a little and glanced down. Mary Jefferson's car was parked below. He hurried from the bedroom and to the top of the stairs.

'Mary's coming,' he said.

Karl appeared at the foot. 'You're kidding?'

'No.'

Karl waved Sean away, slipped into the downstairs toilet and waited. Trying to control his heavy breathing, he listened as a key was inserted and the front door swung open. He shrank further into the cloakroom when the hall light was lit.

Mary tossed her handbag onto the table, pulled off her coat and draped it over the bannister. She pulled open the toilet door and gasped as Karl grabbed her and put his hand across her mouth, dragging her back into the hall. Mary struggled, her muffled cries escaping the vicelike grip of Karl's hand.

'Shut the fuck up,' Karl said.

Sean appeared halfway down the stairs. 'What's happening?'

'I told you to stay out of sight.'

Mary's eyes widened when they met with Sean's. Karl pulled the struggling Mary into the dining room and Sean followed him.

'Get something to tie her up with,' Karl said.

Sean glanced at Mary and disappeared into the kitchen, returning moments later.

Sean nervously paced the length of the kitchen as Karl came in from the dining room.

'What are we going to do?'

Karl walked past him and stared outside. 'She's seen us.'

'I said we should've worn masks.'

Karl spun around. 'Well we didn't, did we? You said the place would be empty.'

Sean rubbed at his face and paced the floor again. 'Christ, this is a mess.'

Karl grabbed hold of him. 'Have you any more stuff?'

'Yeah. A bit.'

'I need a hit.'

Sean reached into his pocket and pulled out the packet, his hands trembled as he dropped it. Karl stooped and picked it up. Laying out the powder, the pair snorted as before. Karl threw his head backwards, exhaled loudly and stared directly at Sean. 'She would have identified us,' Karl said.

Sean furrowed his brow. 'What do you mean, would …?'

Karl strode forward and gripped hold of Sean. 'It had to be done.'

Sean extricated himself from his friend, backed away and hurried into the dining room. Mary's limp body slumped on a chair. Her eyes fixed in a lifeless stare. He gasped.

Karl appeared next to him. 'It had to be done.'

Sean's mouth gaped. 'What have you …?'

Karl grabbed hold of him again. 'You're as much to blame. You said she'd be out. There'd be no one home. That's what you said.'

'But …'

'But nothing. It's done.'

Sean dropped onto a chair opposite Mary. He stared at her. 'What are we going to do?'

'We'll dump her somewhere.'

He clamped his eyes shut. 'This is a nightmare.'

'Do you want to go to prison for a long time?' Karl said, and pushed Sean's arm. 'Do you?'

'Of course not.'

'Right,' Karl said. 'Get your shit together then. We dump her. We were never here. The road's quiet. We can take her car.'

Sean looked up at his friend. 'Ok.'

Karl pulled him to his feet. 'If anyone saw her return, they'll assume she's going back out. As long as we don't get seen.'

'Where are we going to …?' He glanced back at Mary.

'Out in the sticks. We'll cover her over. Bury her.'

'What about DNA? Won't they be able to …? I've got previous.'

'Leave it to me,' Karl said.

2018 - Graveney waited in the consultation room, staring vacantly outside at the tree-lined perimeter of the clinic. He felt tired, and his head ached with a familiar fuzziness through lack of sleep. Leaves from the trees tumbled downwards as a gust of wind shook them free. He turned as the door opened, and a male doctor entered carrying a file.

The doctor smiled and sat. 'How are you feeling, Peter?'

'Ok.'

'Good.' He opened the file in front of him. 'I've examined the scans, and there's nothing at all to worry about. No abnormalities. I've checked your medical notes, and I know you suffered a bang on the head some time ago.' Graveney nodded. The doctor looked up and smiled again. 'There's no lasting damage. No bleeds.'

'I'm still getting headaches,' Graveney said.

'Without any physical cause, we need to explore other avenues.'

Graveney half-smiled. 'Stress?'

'Have you got a particularly stressful job, Peter?'

'I'm a police officer.'

'Ah, I see. Well, we can't rule out the possibility of it having a baring. What about your home life?'

'I've separated from my wife, but I was getting the headaches before then.'

The doctor rubbed his chin. 'I deal with the physical causes, rather than psychological. I think the best thing to do is refer you back to Dr Hope.'

Graveney looked past him. 'Yeah, ok.'

The doctor stood and offered a hand which Graveney shook. 'I'll make the necessary arrangements,' he said.

'Thanks,' Graveney said. He stood and left, making his way downstairs and back to his car. Slumping into the seat, he placed his head against the steering wheel. His phone sounded. Graveney sighed heavily and answered it without even looking at the name.

'Peter, it's Bev.'

'Hi, Bev.'

'How did it go?'

'Apparently, I'm going mad.'

Bev laughed. 'Going? Gone you mean.'

'Yeah. I've got to go back and see your therapist friend. See if she can pull me back from the brink.'

'She's good, Peter. I'm sure she'll help.'

'I'm on my way back to my flat,' he said.

'Flat? I—'

'Heather threw me out.'

'She doesn't—?'

'No. She doesn't know about us. She suspected I was having an affair. Put two and two together and came up with five. But she wasn't far wrong, was she?'

'I'm sorry, Peter … I didn't mean for this to—'

'Shit happens, Bev.'

'Do you want to talk?'

Graveney rubbed at his forehead. 'I won't be back until late.'

'I don't mind. If you still want me to … I can make an excuse and get away.'

Graveney glanced in the rear mirror. Marne smiled and shook her head.

'Yeah,' Graveney said. 'Why not. I'll ring when I'm home.'

'Ok,' she said.

Graveney crept from the bed and the sleeping Bev. He closed the door to the bedroom and made his way into the kitchen, closing the door behind him. He took out his mobile and dialled a number. It rang for several moments before switching to answerphone. 'Hi,' a female voice said. 'You've reached the number of Liz. Sorry, I can't take your call at the moment. Leave a message, and I'll get back to you.'

Graveney hung up, placed the mobile on the worktop and trudged back to bed.

CHAPTER TWENTY-THREE

1999 – Sean followed Karl, in Mary's car, as he sped along country lanes. The vehicle slowed and pulled off onto a track. Karl continued and pulled up under the canopy of trees. Sean drew up behind him. The pair got out of their respective cars and met at the rear of Mary's. Karl opened the boot, and the two men stared at the body inside. Silently they grasped hold of it.

Sean stared at the body in the ditch as Karl returned with a petrol can. 'You can go,' Karl said.

'Where?'

'On the Northallerton road there's a council depot,' Karl said.

'I know where you mean.'

'About 500 metres past there you'll find a layby. It used to be part of the road before they straightened it up. Meet me there.'

'How long will—?'

Karl patted his arm. 'Not long.'

Sean turned and strode off. Karl waited for the roar of the car in the distance before dowsing the body with petrol. Pouring a trail of the fuel from the body, he stopped about twenty metres away and pulled a piece of paper from his pocket. With his lighter he lit it and stooping, ignited the petrol. He watched as the fire rapidly made its way back towards the body. There was a whoosh as the body, engulfed in a fireball, illuminated the surrounding area. He glanced about, but nothing stirred. The flames gradually died down, before eventually going out. Making his way over to the body, he brought his hand up to cover his nose and mouth as the smell of charred clothes and flesh filled the air. Moving quickly, he concealed the body with leaves, branches and other bits of woodland detritus.

He stepped back, surveyed his handiwork, and satisfied the body was fully covered hurried back to Mary's car.

Karl raced across the open ground and jumped in the car next to Sean. 'Go,' Karl said. 'Her car's going to go bang in a minute.'

Sean found first gear and roared away, the car screeching as he accelerated. They continued, putting distance between themselves and the burning vehicle. The sound of an explosion in the distance caused Karl to spin around in his seat.

'Craig's to blame for this,' Sean said.

Karl looked across at him. 'Why?'

'If he hadn't bottled it, all this shit wouldn't have happened. One of us could have kept watch outside.'

'Well it did,' Karl said. 'There's nothing we can do now.'

'I'm going around there.'

Karl frowned. 'Where?'

'Craig's.'

'We need to sort out an alibi first. Craig can wait.'

Sean screeched to a stop. He spun to face Karl. 'You've been calling the shots all night. Stop ordering me about.'

'Listen,' Karl said. 'All I'm—'

Sean grabbed Karl by the throat and pushed him against the door. 'You say one more word …'

Karl's eyes widened. 'Ok.'

Sean let go of him and turned away. He banged his head on the steering wheel. 'I need some gear. Something to wash away this nightmare.'

Karl stayed silent. Sean looked up and stared through the windscreen, pushed the car into gear, and roared off again.

Jimmy crept forward towards the flat and peered through the window at Lindsey and Craig, the pair oblivious to the onlooker. Craig rose from his seat and held out his hands as he moved closer. She pushed him away and, removing something from around her neck, tossed it at him. Craig glanced to the floor and reached for Lindsey as she pushed past him. Brushing him aside, she raced off.

At the sound of the door opening, Jimmy slipped behind a wheelie bin and watched as Lindsey stormed outside, jumped into her car, and sped off. He waited and slumped against the wall. Zipping his coat up higher, he glanced up the road as a familiar car came into view. Jimmy, his interest piqued, slunk back behind the wall out of sight.

Karl Smith and Sean Grant jumped from the car and bounded inside. Jimmy edged his way around to the window again and peered through the gap in the curtains. He watched as the three men talked. The conversation became more heated as Craig pushed Sean in the chest. Sean grabbed at him as Craig swung his arm, catching Sean square on the chin. He fell as Craig towered over him pointing a finger at his stricken friend. Karl stepped between them, but Craig brushed him aside. Sean jumped to his feet and careered into Craig, the pair tumbling over the arm of the settee and onto the floor. They grappled, Craig, gaining the upper hand, punched Sean again. Unable to stop the assault, he threw up a defensive arm as Craig pulled back his fist. Craig stopped, gasped, and dropped to his knees. He looked at Sean who glared back at him before Craig slumped forward onto his face, a knife stuck squarely between his shoulder blades. Sean jumped to his feet and glowered at Craig. Karl grabbed a towel from the kitchen and wiped the handle of the knife, took hold of his friend's arm, and shook him forcefully. Sean glanced from the body to Karl, who shook his arm again. Karl spoke, and Sean stared at him. The pair raced outside, and into their car.

Karl found the gear and drove off. As he sped away, he spotted someone in his peripheral vision creep around the corner of the building out of sight.

He nudged Sean. 'It was the Jefferson kid.'

'Christ,' Sean said. 'What do we do?'

He stared at his friend. 'We make sure he doesn't talk.'

Lindsey parked around the corner from Craig's flat. Her anger slowly dissipating. If Craig was determined to go with Sean, so be it. But she wanted no part of it. If he wanted a life of crime, it was up to him. She thought he had changed. Assumed he would side with her and not Sean. Sean was poison. He was heading for deep trouble and would pull Craig down with him. If he was adamant he was going, then there was nothing she could do. She would go back and give him a final ultimatum. It was her or Sean. Lindsey pushed the car into gear and set off, travelling the short distance she screeched to a halt outside his flat. She bounded up the path, narrowly missing a woman pushing a child's buggy as she stomped towards the building. The woman muttered something under her breath as Lindsey sped by. The door was slightly open as she reached the property. 'Craig!' she shouted as she pushed it open. She entered and crept forward. A feeling of something, not quite right, engulfed her. 'Craig?'

Lindsey gasped and brought her hands up to her mouth as she spotted the prone form of her boyfriend on the carpet. She hurried across to him, dropped to the floor, hardly noticing the blood she now knelt in. She lifted Craig's head and viewed his lifeless eyes. Lindsey pulled him close. Tears tumbled down her face, her mind whirred, and dizziness washed over her. She pushed herself to her feet and fumbled for her mobile. Staring at it, the phone and her hands covered in blood. Stumbling back, the sight of the crimson liquid causing her to recoil. She had to leave, get away from the horror confronting her. Pushing the mobile back into her pocket and swallowing hard against the bile rising in her throat, she staggered towards the exit, only preventing herself from falling by leaning on the doorframe. Forcing herself to view the terrible scene one final time, she fled, jumped into her car and roared off.

Lindsey pulled the car off the road and parked beneath a dense canopy of trees. She leant forward and placed her head on the steering wheel. Tears running unabated, dropped onto the floor. The image of Craig, the blood which covered him, taunted her. Lindsey studied her hands and the semi-dried patches covering them. She pulled the phone from her pocket and shakily dialled.

'Emergency. Which service, please?' a female voice asked.

Lindsey tried to talk. Her throat constricting, hanging on grimly to her words.

'Which service, please?' the voice repeated.

She tried to speak again. Her heartbeat hammered in her chest. She brought a bloodstained hand to her face and closed her eyes, dropping the phone into the footwell. She reached down, picked it back up and ended the call. Throwing the mobile onto the passenger seat, Lindsey jumped from the car and raced around to the boot. Finding some wet-wipes inside, she set about cleaning her hands. Pausing, she gazed at her t-shirt and viewed the large patches of deep-red marring it.

'What are you doing?' she mumbled. 'You have to tell someone.'

Her mind raced. Why had she left Craig's flat? She had to tell someone. Who had killed him? Would the police blame her? The woman with the pushchair. She brought her hands to her face and rubbed it. 'Think, Lindsey.' She couldn't go home. What would her mam and dad say? The police would trace her phone, but she hadn't done anything. 'Oh, Craig,' she said. 'Who did it to you?' A moment of clarity swept over her and she dived back into the car, lowering the window she tossed her phone outside. Opening the glovebox, she snatched up Craig's mobile and pushing it into her pocket, set off again.

2018 - Dr Hope sat opposite Graveney. She examined the notes in front of her for a few moments and lifted her head. 'Your scan came back fine.'

'Doesn't explain why I'm getting headaches and ...' Graveney lowered his head and closed his eyes.

'Hallucinations?' she said.

'Yeah.'

'We need to explore other avenues, Peter. You've been referred back to me to get to the bottom of this.'

Graveney scoffed. 'Stress. That's what the doctor said.'

Hope looked at Graveney. 'It's quite possible.'

Graveney stared past her and outside. He hated talking about himself. Hated opening up. The Peter Graveney he knew was not a particularly pleasant character, in his mind anyway. An emotional rollercoaster heading for destruction. The words of Maddie hectored and taunted him.

'What are you thinking, Peter?'

Graveney turned back to face her. 'I'm not a fan of this. Having your innermost thoughts laid bare. I've normally had a bit ... a lot to drink when I spill my guts.'

'Do you like a drink?'

'Too much. And not enough.' He forced a smile.

'We don't need to do this. You have to feel comfortable.' She studied him. 'But it could help you a lot.'

'Could it?'

Dr Hope tilted her head. 'I think it will.'

Graveney studied her for a moment and then looked past Dr Hope at Marne who wagged her finger at him. 'Yeah.' Graveney focussed his attention back to Dr Hope. 'Let's do it. In for a penny ...' Marne shook her head.

'You mentioned a colleague of yours who ...'

'Stephanie Marne,' Graveney said.

Graveney narrowed his eyes as Dr Hope jotted something down. She glanced up. 'Is my taking notes ok? I could tape the session if you like?'

Graveney shook his head. 'It's fine. It's just ... I'm normally the one taking notes.'

'What do you do for—?'

'I'm a police officer. Detective Inspector.'

Dr Hope scribbled some more. 'And Stephanie Marne?'

'My sergeant.'

'You said she killed herself while you were there?'

Graveney gazed past Dr Hope at Marne, who, using two fingers pretended to shoot herself. He brought his trembling hands up to his face.

'Are you ok, Peter?'

Graveney pulled his hands down his face and stared at Dr Hope. He took a deep breath. 'She shot herself in front of me. Put the muzzle in her mouth, and blew her brains out.' Graveney resisted the urge to smile as Dr Hope winced.

'And you blame yourself?' Returning to her former demeanour, she wrote something down.

Graveney stood and turned away from the searchlight of her questioning. 'It wasn't like that. We were having an affair … She didn't kill herself because of me. There were other factors … It was complicated.'

'Did you love her?' Dr Hope said.

Graveney scoffed and turned around to face her again. 'We had this …' He searched for the words. 'I was addicted to her. Everything about her, but mostly … the sex. It was the sex.' He studied her again as Dr Hope scribbled some more. 'Look,' Graveney said. 'I know I said I was fine with you taking notes, but I'm not. I don't want what's in here ...' He tapped his head with a finger. '… ending up on paper.'

Dr Hope placed the pen and notepad down. 'I can do without them.'

Graveney sagged back in his chair. 'Steph had family members who were murdered. My colleagues and I knew nothing about this.' He swallowed the large lump of emotion lodged in his throat. 'She took it upon herself to track them down and kill them.'

'Are you angry at her for this?'

'No. I was angry she manipulated me.' He half-laughed and threw back his head. 'I see through lies and deceit. It's so easy. Steph was different. She climbed inside my head and lives there today.'

'Did you love her?' Dr Hope repeated.

'I still do.' Graveney sneered. 'She mangled me and bent me out of shape. The sex I had with her was …' He rubbed his forehead. '… phenomenal.' He stared deep into Dr Hope's eyes. 'Nothing has ever come close. Nothing ever will.'

'How do you view women, Peter?'

Graveney rubbed at the two-day growth of beard. 'I love women. I love being with them. I want to protect them. I worry about them. The predators who wait in the outside world for them. They've no idea how vulnerable they are.'

'It's only natural,' Dr Hope said. 'You're a policeman. You must see some awful things.'

'Why do women trust men, Doctor?' He raised his eyebrows. 'Men are children. They say women are the weaker sex. They aren't. Men are. It's only our physical strength that gives us an advantage. Emotionally, we're cripples.'

'Not all men are like that, surely?'

'My dad was a bastard.' Graveney allowed the words to loiter. He studied Dr Hope, who seemed unfazed. 'He beat Mam black and blue. She put up with it for my brother and me.'

'Did he beat you and—?'

'Of course. We were to blame for his shitty life. We were the cause of his misfortune. He told us often enough. Every bit of bad luck he had was down to us.'

'Did you hate him?'

Graveney grimaced. 'With a passion. I longed to grow up and kill him. I'd imagine what I'd do when I was strong enough.' Graveney lowered his eyes to the floor.

'How do you feel about him now?'

Graveney looked up and shrugged. 'He's long dead. What does it matter?'

'Sometimes, we carry this emotional baggage through life. It can deeply affect us.'

Tears formed in Graveney's eyes. 'Maybe his childhood was as crap as mine. Maybe his dad beat him. Maybe he was sexually or physically abused. Maybe, maybe ...' The last two words increased in volume. He smiled at Dr Hope. 'What's your first name?'

'Tanya,' she said.

'Life throws some awful things our way, Tanya. Things we have no control over. Things we find difficult to deal with. But it's up to us how we choose to handle them. Are they going to make you stronger, or crush you? My dad poured his life, his existence, into a glass and pissed it all away. It was his choice.'

'Was it the drink which killed him?'

'No. I did,' Graveney said. Marne threw up her hands beyond Dr Hope's shoulder. Dr Hope slightly tilted her head, lowered her eyes, and stared at Graveney.

'I tripped him, and he fell down the stairs. He died later in hospital from his head injuries.'

'How old—?'

'Twelve.' Graveney stared defiantly. 'Old enough to be responsible.'

'You were only a child. I don't think the police would—'

Graveney huffed. 'I know all about police procedure. It's just ...'

'Just?'

'Maybe he might have changed, had I ... Given enough time, I mean. I may have found out why he did what he did to us. Why he drank himself stupid. He must have been so unhappy.' Graveney dropped his eyes to the floor again, and stubbornly held onto the tears.

'Your mum?'

Graveney coughed and rubbed his face. 'She died when I was in my late teens.'

'It must have been hard for ...' Dr Hope glanced at her watch. 'We should schedule another session. I think we have more to discuss.'

Graveney looked away from her. 'I don't think I want to, Tanya. I've kept that particular secret to myself for years.' He lifted his head, and the two of them locked eyes. 'It took you less than an hour to break down the wall and ...' His eyes glistened again. 'I can't let anyone get close. Not again.'

She forced a smile. 'It's better sometimes … to tell someone, Peter. These things eat away at us.'

He shook his head and stood. 'Sorry.' He turned away from her in time as the first tears tumbled from his eyes and down his cheeks.

CHAPTER TWENTY-FOUR

1999 - Sean and Karl viewed Jimmy Jefferson's house, from their car, a couple of hundred yards away. Sean lay the cocaine on the dashboard and snorted some of it through a rolled-up note.

He nudged Karl with his shoulder and pointed towards the remaining white powder.

Karl waved his hand. 'I need a clear head, Sean.'

Sean grunted. 'What about the Jefferson kid?'

'We need to warn him off.'

'We got some valuable things from the house. We may need to keep our heads down. What happens if he's gone to the police?'

Karl grabbed Sean's arm. 'We don't even know what he saw.'

Sean's phone sounded. He stared at the name and glanced at Karl. 'It's Conrad Hudson. What should I do?'

'You've got to answer it. Don't let on about me, though.'

'Mr Hudson,' he said.

'Sean. I need a favour.' Karl put his ear to the mobile. 'Do this right, son, and I'll look after you.'

'Yeah, of course.'

'Are you alone?'

He glanced at Karl. 'Yeah.'

'Good. I want you to pick up a car and get rid of something for me.'

Sean swapped ears. 'What something?'

'In the boot is something I want burying. Something that mustn't turn up in the future. Do you understand?'

Sean sniffed and rubbed his nose. 'Absolutely.' He glanced across at Karl again.

'Once you've got rid of the package, torch the car.'

'Ok,' Sean said.

'In the front of the car, in the footwell, you'll find a bag with money in it. The money's yours.'

'Thanks, Mr Hudson. I appreciate this. There's …'

'There's what?'

Sean looked at Karl again. 'We had a bit of bother tonight—'

'We?' Hudson said.

'I meant me. Craig …'

'Alex's driver?'

'Yeah. We got into a bit of an argument over his girlfriend at his flat.'

'And …?'

Sean rubbed his face. 'He pulled a knife on me. We got into a fight. I think he may be dead.' Karl pushed him in the side and scowled.

'For fuck's sake, Sean,' Hudson said. 'I thought you were reliable.'

'I am, Mr Hudson. It was—'

'I need reliable people, Sean. People I can trust.' Hudson sighed. 'I'll give this some thought.'

'Please, Mr Hudson. I'll do anything to make this right.'

'I'll ring you back in two minutes.' Hudson rang off.

Karl glowered at him. 'Why did you tell him about Craig?'

'He has friends. Contacts. He may be able to help. I thought …'

Karl looked skywards and exhaled.

Sean's phone sounded. 'Yeah, Mr Hudson?'

'Right, Sean,' he said. 'Your luck's in. I'm going to help you out. I'll send some of the boys over there. I can't promise anything until I know if he's been found yet. If he has, you're on your own. You understand?'

'Yes, perfectly.'

'Are you sure no one else saw you?'

Sean closed his eyes. 'Well … It's a little …'

'What?' Hudson snapped.

'There was this kid. He may have seen me.'

Hudson sucked in air. 'You're priceless, Sean. You really are. Who is he?'

'He's a copper's son.'

Hudson false-laughed. 'This just gets better. His name?'

'Jimmy Jefferson.'

'Eddie Jefferson's boy?'

'Yes, Mr Hudson.'

Hudson groaned. 'Ok. Where does he live?'

'He lives with his dad in Coulby Newham.'

'Address, Sean,' Hudson said. 'I'll need an address.'

'I can find out and text it to you.'

Hudson sneered. 'Do that. One more thing …'

'Yes, Mr Hudson?'

'We'll need a patsy for Craig Embleton's murder. This girl you two fought over. How close are you?'

Sean glanced at Karl and winked. 'Not close at all.'

'Good. I'll keep in touch.'

Hudson raced from his study. He spotted Robbo in the hallway and waved him across.

'Yes, Boss?' Robbo said.

'I want you and one of the boys to go across to Craig Embleton's flat.'

'Cooper's driver?'

'Yeah. That dickhead Sean has gone and killed him. Be discreet. Make sure he is dead. If there's a weapon, bring it back with you.'

'What happens if he's been discovered?'

Hudson rubbed his chin. 'Forget it and come back here. Sean's on his own.'

'Why not let him take the fall?'

'He's a relation of a mate of mine, and he could be useful. I'm going to get him to dump Cooper's body. We've all got alibis. When the moment's right, we'll drop him in it. Sean will think I'm doing him a favour, and he'll be more amenable.'

Robbo blew out hard. 'It's a bit risky. Is he reliable? We don't want a mess, Boss.'

Hudson smiled. 'It'll be ok. Besides, I don't want Jean suspecting I had anything to do with Alex's disappearance.' Hudson winked. 'She doesn't know about Sean Grant.'

'Ok, Boss. You know best.'

Jimmy paced upstairs in his bedroom. He couldn't decide what to do. His dad was at work, on a nightshift, so he couldn't talk to him. Not yet. He could phone 999 and report it. How could he explain what he was doing there, though? It wasn't clear to him what he had seen. Had Karl really stabbed Craig? He was unsure now. Maybe he hadn't. He couldn't be certain. He put his head in his hands and rocked back and forth. The doorbell sounded, shaking him from his thoughts. He stood, glanced at his watch and trudged down the stairs. It must be Billy, his mate, from over the road. He'd texted earlier to say he was coming around. Jimmy reached the door and pulled it open.

Two men stood outside. 'Jimmy Jefferson?' the taller of the pair said.

Jimmy's heart rate increased. 'Yeah,' he said softly.

They stepped inside, pushing Jimmy along the hall. The smaller of the men closed the door, and Jimmy backed away, his progress halted by the wall behind him.

The taller man stepped closer and pulled a gun from his pocket. 'Whatever you think you saw at Craig Embleton's flat today, you didn't.

You were never there. You know nothing. Have you got that?' The man pushed his face closer.

Jimmy recoiled. 'Yeah.'

'Just because your dad is a copper won't help you either. If anything, anything at all gets out …' He glanced across at his friend. '… we'll be back. I'll put a bullet through that head of yours.' He placed the tip of the gun onto Jimmy's forehead. 'But not before my friend here, has cut your dad to pieces in front of you. Understand?'

Jimmy swallowed hard. 'Yeah,' he whimpered, tears now rolling down his face.

The man gently patted his cheek. 'Good lad.' The pair turned and stopped at the threshold. 'We'll be watching you,' he said, slipping the weapon back inside his coat.

Jimmy shook. With legs like jelly, he slumped to the floor, brought his hands to his face, and sobbed.

Hudson answered his phone. 'Yeah, Robbo.'

'We've been to the flat and he hasn't been discovered yet. He's definitely dead.'

'No one saw you?'

'I'm pretty sure no one did. I recovered the knife. Do you want me to dump it?'

'No. I'm texting you an address. I want you to hide it at the property.'

'Inside the house?' Robbo said.

'It doesn't have to be inside. Outside. In the garden. A shed, anything like that. Hopefully, the police will find it when they search.'

'And if they don't?'

'We'll give them a helping hand.'

Karl slipped outside as Sean snorted cocaine in the bathroom. Craig's number lit up on his mobile. He rubbed his chin and thought hard about answering.

'Yeah, Craig?' he said.

'Karl, it's Lindsey.'

'Lindsey. Everything all right?'

'Craig's dead,' she said, through tears.

'What?'

'I went to his flat, and he's been stabbed. I don't know what to do. I haven't anyone else to turn to.'

'Jesus,' he said. 'Have you phoned the police?'

'I panicked, Karl. I left. I …'

'Did anyone see you?'

Lindsey sniffed and wiped her nose. 'Maybe. A woman. What do I do? Who did it?'

Karl stared back at the house. 'Sean was going around to see him. He's been a bit edgy since he came back.'

'You think ...?'

'Sean was pretty mad at Craig. He wanted him to go on a job with him.'

The phone went silent. 'Are you still there, Lindsey?'

'Yeah.'

'Maybe you should call the police?'

Lindsey hung up. Karl looked at the handset and smirked.

Lindsey parked up the road from Sean's flat. She gripped the wheel tightly, her knuckles white. Sean and Karl bounded outside and jumped into a car. Their engine roared into life and they screeched away, closely followed by Lindsey. She followed the pair as they raced towards Guisborough, finally pulling the vehicle into the car park at the foot of Roseberry Topping. Lindsey watched from nearby as Sean, carrying a holdall, set off up the hill with Karl not far behind him. She waited. The thoughts inside her head a whirlpool. Visions of Craig, lying bloodied and dead, bludgeoned their way into her mind. Lindsey rested her head on the steering wheel and sobbed, allowing the feeling of loss to engulf her. Minutes passed before she steadied herself. The grief replaced with anger and loathing for Sean. She peered towards where he and Karl had gone, threw open the car door, slammed it shut again and set off after them.

Sean stopped halfway up the hill and turned to face Karl. 'I'll get the stuff.'

'Hurry up,' Karl said.

Sean hurried towards a rock and dropped to his knees. 'I'll be two minutes.'

Karl spun around on hearing a noise behind them and moved aside as Lindsey, armed with a large branch, advanced. Swinging it wildly above herself, she brought it down with a thud across Sean's head. He let out a groan and tumbled forward onto his face. Lindsey stood, allowing the would-be weapon to fall from her grasp.

Karl raced across to her. 'Lindsey! What the hell—?'

'He killed Craig. I ...'

Karl squatted next to Sean and placed two fingers onto his friend's neck. He waited, stood and turned to face Lindsey. 'You've killed him,' he said.

Lindsey gasped and brought a hand up to her mouth. 'I didn't mean to ...'

Karl raced across and took hold of her shoulders. 'Look at me,' he said.

Lindsey dragged her stare away from Sean. 'Go,' he said. 'I'll sort this out.'

She lowered her head and paused before setting off back down the slope. Karl smirked and looked at Sean, who groaned.

Sean pulled himself up and tentatively placed a hand on the back of his head. 'What the hell—?'

'Lindsey.' Karl sniggered. 'Lindsey hit you with a branch.'

Sean struggled to his feet. 'Lindsey?'

'She thinks you killed Craig. She's on her way to the police.'

'Why didn't you stop her?' Sean said.

'She was mental, Sean. Proper wound up.'

'What do we do?'

'The car Hudson wanted you to get rid of,' Karl said.

'What about it?'

'Didn't he say there was money in it?'

Sean winced as he touched his head again. 'Yeah.'

'We dump the car as he asked you to and grab the money.'

'Are you mad?' Sean said. 'If Lindsey's on her way to the police ...'

'Hudson said he was going to sort that out for you. All we need to do is make ourselves disappear for a while.'

Sean pondered. 'It's a bit risky.'

'We need money. I've a mate who lives in Spain. He may be able to get us a job over there until the heat is off.'

Sean moved towards the hole. 'What about the stuff we nicked from Jefferson's place?'

'Get that as well. The more money we have, the better.'

Lindsey pulled her car up outside her parents' house. She lay her head on the steering wheel and let out a long-held breath. What should she do?

She hadn't meant to kill Sean. And Craig, she brought a hand to her mouth and gasped. Her head cleared. She had to change, get rid of her clothing, and deny she was at Craig's tonight. She would claim the woman with the pushchair, if she came forward, was mistaken about the time. Lindsey jumped out of the car and crept towards the house. All was quiet. She remembered it was the night her mam and dad went to the club, and the house would be empty. Lindsey let herself in and climbed the stairs to her room. She showered and changed, putting the bloodstained clothing into a bin bag. Grabbing her coat and car keys, she headed along the hall, but as she reached it, someone knocked. Lindsey gulped in a lungful of air and opened the door. Two men stood outside. The pair brandished their badges.

'Lindsey Armstrong?' the elder of the two said.

She blinked. 'Yeah.'

'Detective Inspector Harris,' he said. 'This is my colleague ...' He nodded towards his younger companion. '... Detective Sergeant Waters. Can we come in, Lindsey?'

Lindsey moved aside, and the two officers entered. They waited for Lindsey to close the door and followed her into the lounge.

'Is everything all right?' she said.

Harris glanced at Waters. 'You better have a seat, Lindsey.' She lowered herself onto an armchair and stared at the two officers, trying desperately to remain in control of her nerves.

'Your boyfriend,' Harris said.

'Craig?'

'Yes. I'm afraid I've some bad news.'

Lindsey lowered her head and fixed her eyes on the floor, afraid to make eye contact with the two officers, as Harris explained Craig's body had been found at his flat.

'Do you understand what we're telling you, Lindsey?' Harris said.

'He can't be dead. I saw him earlier.' The tears in Lindsey's eyes, genuine.

'What time was that, Miss?' Waters said.

'Four ... five. Between four and five.'

'How did he seem?' Harris said.

'We had a bit of a tiff. I stormed out. He was supposed to be taking me to the pictures, but he told me he was going out with a mate.'

'Right,' Waters said, making notes in his pad. 'This mate?'

'Sean,' she said. 'Sean Grant.'

'Do you know where this Sean Grant lives?' Harris said.

Waters jotted the address down as Lindsey relayed it to him.

'You think Sean ...?'

'We're not sure yet,' Harris said. 'At the moment we're trying to assess Craig's last movements.'

Lindsey stretched across and plucked a tissue from a box on the table nearby. 'Are you sure it's him?'

'We need a formal identification,' Waters said. 'But we're pretty sure it is.' Waters glanced across at Harris and continued. 'He was in trouble with the police a couple of years back. Nothing major.'

'I know about his past. Craig told me. He told me everything.'

Harris coughed. 'We're having difficulty locating his parents. A neighbour told us you were his girlfriend.'

Lindsey sniffed. 'His proper dad hasn't been around for years. His mother is in Spain with Craig's stepdad.'

'Do you know when they get back?' Harris said.

'No. They go for weeks sometimes.'

'Would you be prepared ...?' Harris said.

Lindsey brought her hands up to her face and sobbed.

Harris moved next to her. 'If it's too much?'
Lindsey looked down. 'No. I'll do it.'

Karl and Sean pulled onto the industrial estate. Sean stared across at a car parked on the opposite side of the road. 'That must be it,' Sean said. 'Why don't we get the money and do a runner?'
Karl huffed. 'I don't think Hudson is the sort of person we want to mess with.'
Sean rubbed at his nose. 'I could do with some sniff.'
Karl glowered at him. 'We need to keep a clear head. Let's get rid of this car and then we can take off. Are you with me on this?'
Sean sagged. 'Are we both going to take the car?'
'How the hell will we get back if we do?'
'Yeah,' Sean said. 'Never thought of that.'
'I'll follow you. That way, we can dump it and then shoot off.'
Sean placed a hand on the back of his head, and gingerly dabbed it. 'That bitch, Lindsey, really smacked me.'
'Well,' Karl grinned. 'Hudson is going to deal with her.'
Sean smiled. 'Yeah.'
'I know a place to dump the car,' Karl said.
'Where?'
'Do you know Grewgrass Lane in New Marske?' Sean shook his head, and Karl glanced upwards. 'Follow me.'
Sean jumped out of the car and raced over to the other vehicle. He bent down and fumbled beneath the driver's front wheel, finally emerging triumphantly with a set of keys. Sean gave the thumbs up and got inside. Karl put his car in gear and sped off, closely followed by his friend.

Lindsey exited the police station and, making her way around the corner, took out her phone.
Karl answered. 'Lindsey. What's happening?'
'I've just left Middlesbrough Police station. I've identified Craig's body.'
'Oh, Jesus. I'm sorry, Linds.'
'I'm fine. What happened to Sean?'
'I dumped his body in a hole on Roseberry Topping. Don't worry, no one will find it.'
'Karl, I'm grateful for this.'
'What did the police say?'
Lindsey swallowed. 'They asked me loads of questions. They know I was at Craig's flat, but I think they believe me that I left.'
'You didn't tell them you returned?'
'No. I wish I'd phoned them when I found him. What if they find out?'

'You can't change your story now. And what with Sean ...'

'Yeah.'

'What about me, Linds?'

'I won't mention you. This is between us.'

'Listen, Linds. I have to go. Keep me informed.'

'Will do,' she said.

Karl pulled his car into a small layby at the top of Grewgrass Lane. Sean slid to a halt behind him. Karl searched beneath his seat and snatched up a large knife from under it. He slipped the knife into the inside pocket of his coat and climbed from the car. Sean put down the window as Karl approached.

'Move over,' Karl said. 'I'll drive from here.' Sean moved into the passenger seat.

'Do we look and see what's in the boot?'

Karl lowered his brow. 'I don't think we want to see what's in there, do we?'

Sean grimaced. 'Maybe you're right.'

Karl put the car in gear and glanced across at Sean. 'Did you find the bag?'

Sean grinned and motioned behind him. 'It's in the back. I'm not sure how much there is, but it must be thousands.'

Karl laughed sped off. After about a mile, he pulled off onto a small track and continued a bumpy ride along it. He came to a halt in front of a large body of water. A battered old sign, the paint peeling with age, with DEEP WATER written across it.

'This is it,' Karl said.

'What do we do?'

'If we remove those two bits of wood ...' He pointed to a fence in front. '... and let the handbrake off, I reckon the car will roll into it.'

'I think you're right.'

He moved to open the door, and Karl took hold of his arm. Sean turned to face his friend again, as the knife was plunged into his chest. He let out a low groan, his eyes fixed on Karl as he tried to speak, but only an incoherent sound escaped his lips as he slumped forward against the dashboard.

Karl watched as the car slowly rolled towards the water and dropped down with a splash. It glided a little on the surface before the vehicle slowly filled with liquid. He watched as first the wheels, then the door, and finally the roof slid gently below the surface of the inky black water. He pulled Sean's phone from his pocket and tossed it into the water. Smiling to himself, he picked up the bag, slung it over his shoulder, and headed back to his car.

Lindsey sat with her mother and father at the dinner table.

Her mother gazed across at her. 'Do the police know who did it?' she asked.

Lindsey fidgeted and looked away. 'No. They just said they're making enquiries.'

Her dad patted her arm. 'I'm so sorry, Linds. I don't know what to say.'

'It's terrible,' her mother said. She took out a tissue and blew her nose. 'The poor lad. What his family must be going through.'

Lindsey dropped her head down. 'I'm going to bed.'

Her mother glanced at her father. 'Are you sure you'll be all right?' she said.

Lindsey stood. 'I need some time on my own.' She trudged her way upstairs. She reached the top and pushed open the door to her bedroom, closed it gently behind her and fell onto her bed as tears flowed incessantly.

It was the sound of her name that roused her from her slumber.

'Lindsey,' shouted her dad up the stairs.

She stood sleepily and made her way to the window. Pulling the curtain aside, she looked down at a familiar looking car parked outside the house. Lindsey wiped away tears, got dressed and headed downstairs. The two officers from earlier stood at the bottom of the stairs, along with her mother and father.

Harris stepped forward. 'Lindsey Armstrong ...' he said. 'I'm arresting you on suspicion of murder. You do not ...'

Lindsey's mind drifted, her brain hardly registering what he was saying. She heard her mother and father protesting as she was led outside and into the car. At first resisting the temptation to look back, Lindsey finally glanced over as the vehicle pulled away. The image of her mother, her father's arm draped protectively around her shoulders, the last sight before the car turned the corner.

CHAPTER TWENTY-FIVE

1999 - Hudson picked up his mobile and grunted.

'It's Robbo. The call to the police. Do you want me to ring?'

'Did you make the knife easy to find at her house?' Hudson said.

'It's behind the back of a shed. Any thick copper should find it.'

'Hold back on tipping-off the police.' Hudson said. 'They might find it on their own.'

'I've got Tina ready if we need to make a call. I gave her a few hundred.'

'Great,' Hudson said. 'Are you sure she won't say anything?'

Robbo scoffed. 'The stuff I've got on her, she wouldn't dare.'

Hudson sucked in a deep breath. 'We may have another problem. Sean Grant isn't answering his phone.'

'What about the car with Cooper in it?' Robbo said.

'He's supposed to be dumping it tonight.'

'Do you want me to check on it, Boss?'

'Yeah, do that. Ring me straight away.'

Lindsey, with her solicitor, looked at the two officers across the table from her. 'I didn't kill Craig.'

Harris glanced at his notepad. 'You said you and Craig quarrelled?'

Lindsey bit her nail. 'Yeah. But I didn't kill him. It was just a tiff. The sort people have all the time.'

'What was the quarrel about?' Harris said.

'Craig was supposed to be taking me out, but he told me he was going out with mates.'

'Who?' Waters said.

'I don't know. He has … had a large circle of friends.'

'What time did you leave after this argument?' Harris said.

'I've told you.'

'Tell us again,' Waters said

Lindsey rubbed the tiredness from her eyes. 'About four-thirty.'

'Which coincides with the time of death,' Harris said. 'There or thereabouts.'

'Craig was alive when I left.'

Harris drummed his fingers on the desk. 'We have a witness who says she saw a woman head into the same block of flats where Craig lived. She has positively identified you from a photograph.'

'I told you I was there. But Craig was alive when I left.'

'What were you wearing when you visited your boyfriend's?' Harris said.

'I can't remember.'

Waters pulled out a plastic-covered photograph and slid it across the table towards Lindsey. 'Was it these?'

Lindsey glanced at them. 'It could've been.'

'We found them at your parents,' Waters said. 'They'd been washed and dried.'

Lindsey stared down. Harris paused as someone tapped on the door.

'Interview suspended,' he said. Turning off the tape, he stood and headed outside.

A female, plainclothes officer, stood there. 'The blood in her car matches her boyfriend's.'

'Good.'

'And …' she said. '… we found something in the garden of her mother and father's.'

'What?'

'A knife. It has blood on it. Forensics are running a check on it now.'

'Good work,' he said. Turning, he re-entered the interview room. Harris returned to his seat and steepled his hands together as Waters started the recorder back up.

'We found traces of blood in your car, Lindsey,' Harris said. 'It matches Craig's.'

Tears queued in Lindsey's eyes. 'I didn't kill him. He was dead when I found him.'

'Why didn't you—?' Waters said.

'I panicked … I just panicked.'

'I think,' the solicitor said. 'I need a moment with my client.'

Waters looked across at Harris, who nodded.

'One more thing, Lindsey,' Harris said. 'We found a knife at your mam and dad's house.' Lindsey's eyes widened, then narrowed. Her brow knitted deeply. 'It has blood on it.'

Hudson snatched up his mobile and answered it. 'Yeah, Robbo?'

'The car's gone, Boss.'

Hudson growled. 'I've tried ringing Sean again, but he's not picking up.'

'Maybe he's done what you asked. Give it until tomorrow.'

Hudson scoffed. 'There's something not right here. I knew I shouldn't have trusted that dickhead.'

'Like I say. See what tomorrow brings.'

'Do you know where he lives?' Hudson said.

'Yeah.'

'Pop around and see if he's there. Be discreet.'

'Ok. Did you see the news?'

'What news?' Hudson said.

'They've arrested Lindsey Armstrong. They must have found the knife.'

Hudson grunted. 'She's the least of our worries.'

CHAPTER TWENTY-SIX

Conrad Hudson stormed through the double doors and into the workshop of the enormous factory. A man lay trussed on top of a bench, two others standing, guard-like, either side of him. One tall and slender, the other small and portly.

Hudson reached the men. 'This better be good, Slim?'

'We found him messing around the containers, Boss,' Slim said. 'He had this.' Holding up a camera, he allowed Hudson to take it.

Hudson scrutinised the bound and gagged man. 'Who is he?'

The slender man looked at his companion and then back at Hudson. 'He won't say. He has no ID on him.'

'We've tried knocking it out of him,' Chubby said. 'But he still won't talk.'

Hudson tossed aside the camera and loomed over their victim. He held out a hand. 'Get me one of the circular saws, Slim.'

The tethered man's eyes widened. Slim handed Hudson the saw and plugged it in. Hudson grinned at the man and started up the tool. The blade hovered close to the man's left leg, above the ankle. Hudson pressed down, allowing the blade to slice into the leg. The man screamed. The sound only partially muffled by his gag. Tears rolled from his eyes and over the sides of his face.

Hudson pulled off the gag. 'This is how it works, my friend. I'll stand here all night and cut pieces off you until you tell me what I want to know. If you're smart, you'll do that now before you become totally disabled.'

The man gasped, beads of sweat dotting his face. 'He'll kill me,' he whispered.

'Jesus,' Hudson looked upwards. '*He's* not stood here holding a saw, is he?' Hudson switched the tool on again.

The man gulped. 'He said he was working for Scott Macintyre.'

Hudson frowned. 'Who did?'

'The man who asked me to take the pictures. I don't know his name.'

'Macintyre?' Hudson said. 'That wanker.'

'The man paid me £1000 and threatened me.'

'If you're fucking lying ...' Hudson moved the blade close to the man's other leg.

'Please. That's all I know. He had a gun. Warned me he'd kill me if I told anyone about it.'

'Where did you meet him?' Hudson said.

'In The Crown.'

Hudson turned off the machine and rubbed his chin. 'Macintyre's getting bold. He's trying to muscle in,' he said to Slim, and walked towards the exit.

'What do you want us to do with him?' Chubby said.

Hudson paused at the door and spun around. He strolled back over to the man, stopped, and stared at him again. 'Looks as if he needs A&E to me.' Hudson put his face close to the man. 'You look the type who can keep your mouth shut. If I were you, I'd get as far away from Teesside as possible. Scott Macintyre may want a word with you.'

The man groaned. 'I'm a dead man.'

Chubby glanced at Slim and pulled a face. 'Anywhere in particular?' Slim said to Hudson.

'Christ,' Hudson through up his hands. 'Have I got to think of everything. Bandage his leg, and drive him to a hospital. Leave him there. And don't get seen.'

Hudson pondered for a moment. 'Have a word with Taffy. He'll tell you the best place. And get this mess cleared up.'

Taffy walked into the office, and Hudson turned around. 'Where the hell have you been?' Hudson said.

'Chasing down leads on the man and woman. Why?'

Hudson poured himself a large whisky. 'I'll tell you why. I've been pissing about extracting information from some bloke.'

'Which bloke?'

Hudson slumped into the chair. 'Those two new guys you took on caught him taking photos at the yard.'

Taffy rubbed his chin. 'Right. Who is he?'

'Some tosser. He was paid by a bloke working for Scott Macintyre.'

'Which bloke?'

Hudson shrugged. 'No idea.'

Taffy raised his eyebrows. 'Scott Macintyre? He's getting brave. It doesn't sound the sort of thing he'd do.'

'Well, that's what he said.'

Taffy narrowed his eyes. 'Maybe.'

'We've got a shipment coming in tonight. I don't want any mishaps. Macintyre's small-time, but we've enough on our plate without that wanker causing us problems.'

'Maybe we need to send him a message.'

Hudson drained his glass, got up, and refilled it. 'Maybe we do. We can afford to have a few bags of the coke make its way over to his place, and then maybe the police should pay him a visit.'

'I'll get onto it, Boss.'

'I'm not happy with the two new guys,' Hudson said. 'Are you sure they're trustworthy?'

'Yeah. I've checked them out myself.'

Hudson sat back down and took a sip of his drink. 'Anything new on the man and woman?'

'Nothing. It looks as if they've gone to ground.'

'Someone must know them,' Hudson said. He stood and downed his drink. 'Someone must have seen the big guy. He'll stick out like a sore thumb.'

'We're still checking. They'll turn up. And when they do ...'

'Yeah,' Hudson said. 'When they do, I want to be there.'

CHAPTER TWENTY-SEVEN

Graveney leant against the bar, nursing a Jack and Coke. In truth, he didn't feel much like drinking. He had decided to stay over at the same hotel as the last time he visited Dr Hope. What was the point of driving home to an empty flat? He lied to Mac and told him he had a dental appointment in the morning and would be a little late. Mac hadn't suspected. Or if he had, he covered it up well which Graveney doubted. His friend, like so many others in his life, was an open book. Graveney sipped at his drink, the taste lacking the usual pleasant flavour. It was strange, he mused, how alcohol can take on the mood of an individual. He felt neither happy nor sad. Just bored really. This would be his last drink. He glanced at his watch, downed the remainder, and slipped from the stool.

'Early night?' the barmen said.

'Yeah. I'm up at six in the morning.'

The barman waved as Graveney trudged from the bar and into the foyer. He turned towards the stairs and slowly started his ascent.

'Peter.'

Graveney looked at Dr Hope.

'I thought you'd gone home,' she said.

'I couldn't face going back to an empty flat.' Graveney inwardly berated himself for his clear attempt at sympathy.

'Are the family away?'

'Long story.'

'I see,' she said. She glanced towards the restaurant. 'I'm meeting a few of my colleagues.'

Graveney rubbed his eyes. 'I was just off to bed. I thought an early night might …'

Dr Hope stepped close to him. 'If you need to talk,' she said quietly.

'Like I said at the clinic ...'

Dr Hope waved at a woman who entered the hotel and made her way into the restaurant. 'Maybe a less formal chat. I get the feeling it's the whole clinic thing you dislike?'

He gazed into her eyes and watched the fleeting traces of attraction spread across her face. She coughed and glanced towards the restaurant. 'I should get going.'

'I'd like that,' Graveney said. 'A chat, I mean.'

She smiled and slightly tilted her head to one side. 'You'll feel a lot better for it.'

'We'll see. You'd better get going,' he said. 'Your friends will be talking.'

'I'll be in touch.' With that, she turned and hurried towards the dining room.

Graveney watched her leave and then continued his ascent of the stairs.

Graveney splashed cold water on his face and leant against the sink for support. He gulped greedily for air. His head ached, even though he hadn't had much to drink the previous night. He looked up and stared into the mirror, hardly recognising the face looking back at him. Marne folded her arms and glowered at him.

'You ok, Peter?' Graveney glanced towards the bathroom door. A naked Dr Hope stood at the threshold, staring at him. 'You were miles away.'

He turned to face her fully. 'Bit of a headache, that's all.'

She ambled closer and lifted a hand to rest on his cheek. 'What's going on in that head of yours?'

Graveney laughed sardonically. 'You don't want to know.'

'I've got half an hour before I need to go. If you want to talk.'

'I can think of better things to do than talk.'

'Oh, yeah. Like what?'

Graveney pulled her to him. 'We'll think of something.'

Graveney started the engine of his car as his mobile sounded. He glanced at the screen, the name DI Robertson calling.

'Hi, Neil,' Graveney said.

'Peter. What time are you in?'

Graveney glanced at the dashboard clock. 'I should be there by twelve, why?'

'I had a drink with an old mate of mine. We used to work together until he headed onwards and upwards. He's running a task force dealing with major drug crime.'

'Go on,' Graveney said.

'A name cropped up. Conrad Hudson.'

'Right. Have they got anything on him?'

'No. It's hearsay at the moment,' Robertson said. 'But I thought maybe the murders of his men could have something to do with that.'

Graveney rubbed his chin, deep in thought.

'What are your thoughts, Peter?'

'It's the sexual mutilations the bodies had. Why do that to them if it's only about drugs?'

'Who knows,' Robertson said. 'Maybe someone is trying to muscle in on his turf?'

'Can we meet this mate of yours?'

'I'm way ahead of you. He's going to pop in this afternoon.'

'I'll see you then.' Graveney hung up, put the car into gear and sped off.

Jen shook Joey awake and held out a cup of tea to him. He pushed himself up and swung his legs onto the floor next to the bed. She bent and kissed his head.

'You ok?' she said.

He nodded and took a sip of tea.

'I've been out while you slept. I followed our next target.' She pulled a photo from her back pocket and handed it to him. Joey placed his cup down and taking it from her, studied it. He walked across and pulled her close.

'You shouldn't go out on your own ...' He placed his hand on her bump. 'These men are dangerous.'

'I'm fine.' She leant and kissed him. 'Besides, they'd spot you easily. It looks as if they're going around in pairs.'

'What if they spotted you?'

'What, a pregnant girl?' She laughed. 'That wouldn't worry them. I went in the daylight because I thought they'd be less suspicious.'

He viewed the photo again. 'When?'

'Tonight.'

Joey continued to stare at the photo. 'Yeah, tonight sounds good.'

Robertson entered Graveney's office accompanied by a man.

'This is DI Matt Daniels,' Robertson said.

Graveney offered his hand. 'Have a seat.'

Robertson and Daniels sat. Graveney picked up his empty mug. 'Either of you two want a drink? I was about to get one myself.'

'I'll get them,' Robertson said. 'Matt's in a bit of a rush.' He glanced at Daniels. 'Tea, white, no sugar?'

Daniels nodded. Robertson looked at Graveney. 'I'll be back in a minute.'

'So,' Graveney said. 'Neil was telling me you've some information about Conrad Hudson?'

'Yeah. I'm part of a task force trying to discover who's supplying the drugs which are flooding Teesside. His name keeps cropping up.'

'You don't have anything concrete then?'

Daniels leant back in his chair. 'Not so far. There are large consignments of cocaine getting into the country somehow. There's a much wider investigation looking to discover how they're getting them in.'

Graveney's eyes widened. 'I'd an inkling Hudson was involved in drugs, but I wasn't aware it was on such a large scale.'

Robertson returned and placed the drinks on the table before taking his seat next to Daniels.

Daniels picked up his mug and swigged. 'His kitchen-making factory is a front. We've been watching it and there have been some dodgy characters coming and going.'

Graveney rubbed his chin. 'I take it Neil told you about the murders of his two guys?'

Daniels smirked. 'I don't think anyone will mourn their passing. They all had previous.'

Graveney bent forward, picked up his coffee, and took a large mouthful. 'We thought with the level of mutilation that took place, it might be a sex crime.'

'It could be,' Daniels said. 'Or maybe somebody, who's trying to take over his patch, is sending out a stern message.'

'Yeah.' Graveney leant back and took another large gulp of coffee. 'I still think it's someone from his past. There are too many coincidences for my liking.'

'I'll ask about,' Robertson said. 'See what the word on the street is.'

Graveney looked at Daniels. 'If someone is trying to muscle in, who would that be?'

Daniels shrugged. 'Not sure. I don't know of anyone on Teesside brave enough to take him on.'

'Has Neil told you about Lindsey Armstrong?' Graveney said.

Daniels glanced at Robertson. 'No. Who's Lindsey Armstrong?'

Graveney went on to explain how they discovered Lindsey Armstrong had links to Alex Cooper and also Sean Grant.

Daniels pondered. 'You don't think she's the one who murdered Hudson's men, do you? The woman with the big bloke?'

'No. But she's definitely involved somehow.' Graveney tapped the side of his head. 'Something in here. Something nagging at me.'

Robertson raised his eyebrows at Daniels. 'Peter does this thing,' Robertson said. 'Thin-slicing.'

Daniels frowned. 'Thin-slicing?'

Graveney smiled. 'It's a technique I learnt. You can tell if people are hiding things or not being totally honest. It's not a lie detector, and it's certainly not infallible, but ...'

'But ...?' Daniels said.

'Despite the fact Lindsey Armstrong and her present boyfriend, Jimmy Jefferson, told us a lot, I still think they're hiding something.'

'It could be the murders of Hudson's men, then?' Daniels persisted.

Graveney blew out. 'No. But they may know who killed them. And why.'

Robertson stretched back in his chair and looked at Daniels. 'They both have alibis.'

'For both abductions?' Daniels said.

'For both,' Graveney said, as an idea chugged into his head. 'I think we should check out Lindsey Armstrong's past. Find out who she mixed with inside. Maybe ...?'

Daniels glanced at his watch and stood. 'Looks as if you two have your work cut out here.'

'Can we keep in touch?' Graveney said. 'In case we come across any information which may help each other.'

'Absolutely. Neil has my number.' Daniels leant across and shook hands with Graveney.

'Thanks,' Graveney said.

CHAPTER TWENTY-EIGHT

Graveney looked up from his paperwork as Hussain popped his head around the door. 'I thought I'd had a bit of peace from you for a few hours.' He smiled at his junior. 'You look pleased.'

'I've got some names,' Hussain said. 'People Lindsey Armstrong knew inside.'

'You'd better get DI Robertson. He'll want to hear this.'

Hussain turned and left. Graveney tapped his chin with his finger. He was sure Lindsey Armstrong was involved. It was too much of a coincidence, or was he wrong? He rubbed his face as doubts crept into his mind. 'Coincidences do happen, Peter,' he mumbled.

Robertson entered, closely followed by Hussain. The pair sat opposite Graveney, still deep in thought.

'You ok, Peter?' Robertson said.

'Yeah. Just mulling over these cases.' He looked at Hussain. 'Ok, Rav. Give me what you've got.'

Hussain opened his notebook. 'Armstrong shared a cell with three people during her time inside.'

Graveney sighed. 'It doesn't necessarily have to be someone she shared a cell with.'

'I know, Guv, but we needed to start somewhere.'

Graveney folded his arms. 'Go on.'

'The first year she was in with a woman called Sophie Allay. She was a petty criminal. Theft, shoplifting, possession of a class A. She was released years ago. Died from a drug overdose in 2010.'

Graveney sighed again. 'So not her then.'

'The second—'

'Rav ...' Graveney said. '... I want helpful information. Telling us people it can't possibly be, isn't.'

Robertson chuckled. 'Let him enjoy himself, Peter.' Hussain smiled at Robertson.

Graveney waved a hand and leant back in his chair. 'Go on.'

'The second has done quite well for herself. Runs a charity for ex-offenders down south,'

'And the third?' Graveney said.

'Margaret Southey. She's still inside for the murder of her husband.'

Graveney threw up his hands. 'And?'

'A lot of the staff have moved on, but one remembers Lindsey Armstrong well. She also remembers her taking a young girl under her wing. The prison officer could only remember her first name. Jen.'

'And this, Jen?' Graveney said.

'We checked the name against inmates and came up with two. One's back inside doing six years for GBH and the other was released eighteen months ago.' Hussain pushed a photo across the table towards Graveney. 'Jennifer Hewitson, Guv.'

Graveney leant forward and studied it. 'Where is she now?'

Rav grinned. 'There's more.'

Graveney fixed Hussain with a stare. 'Rav, my patience is wearing thin.'

'She's from York.'

Graveney smiled. 'At last. Where—?'

'She was last sighted in York two months ago. No one knows where she is now.'

'So, we're no further forward?'

'York fits with the squaddie,' Robertson said.

Graveney closed his eyes and brought his hands together under his chin, deep in thought. 'We need to revisit Lindsey Armstrong. See if she's been in contact with her. I'm sure if this, Jennifer Hewitson is ...' Graveney viewed the photo again. '... in Middlesbrough, she'd have got in touch with her old prison friend.'

Robertson raised his brow. 'Now's as good a time as any, Peter.'

'Yeah,' Graveney said. 'While we're out, Rav ...' Hussain looked at him. '... look into her family. See if anyone was sexually assaulted or murdered.'

'Sounds promising,' Robertson said, getting to his feet.

Graveney stood and pulled on his coat. 'It certainly does, Neil, it certainly does.'

Lindsey was in the kitchen when she heard the doorbell sound. She wiped her hands with a cloth and headed into the hall. She paused, the form of the two men outside clearly visible, before pulling open the door.

Graveney smiled at her. 'Good afternoon, Miss Armstrong. Can we talk?'

Lindsey stepped aside, waived the officers past her and led them into the lounge. 'Take a seat,' she said, and slumped into an armchair.

'Is your boyfriend not in?' Graveney said.

'He's at work.'

'You've met my colleague Detective Inspector Robertson.' He nodded towards his companion as he pulled out his notebook.

'I thought we'd finished our business.' She folded her arms sternly. 'I've told you everything I know.'

'Jennifer Hewitson?' Graveney said.

Lindsey stared at the officer. 'What about her?'

'You know her?' Robertson said.

Lindsey switched her attention to Robertson. 'Yes. But that's the reason you're here, isn't it?'

Graveney studied her. 'How do you know her?'

'We were inside together. She was this young, frightened kid and I took her under my wing. Being inside's not nice. It's full of criminals.'

Graveney smiled to himself. She was rambling on. He allowed her to talk, her unease palpable.

'She reminded me of myself when I first went in ... I … Why?'

'When did you last see her?' Graveney said.

Lindsey paused, about to speak, when a timer sounded in the kitchen. 'Excuse me a moment.' She stood and headed for the kitchen and closed the door, trying to gather her thoughts. She leant against the worktop breathing deeply and composed herself. Opening the oven, she pulled out the dish and plonked it on the work surface. She composed herself, took another deep breath, and headed back to the lounge.

'Sorry about that.' She positioned herself opposite the officers once more. 'You were saying?'

'We were asking you about Jennifer Hewitson. The last time you saw her?'

'2007, 2008. When she was released.'

'You haven't seen her since?' Robertson said.

'No. Why?'

Graveney fixed her with a stare. 'Are you sure?'

'What is this?' Lindsey's voice rose in pitch. 'Are you going to pop around here every time someone who I used to know crops up in your enquiries? I'm trying to get on with my life. I'm trying to keep the past where it belongs.'

'Ok, Lindsey,' Graveney said. 'It's just routine.'

'Piss off, Graveney. I haven't got time for this. If we're finished, I'd like you to leave.' Lindsey stood.

Robertson looked at Graveney. 'We're done,' Graveney said. 'Thanks for your help.'

'Yeah, yeah,' Lindsey said.

The two officers stood and made their way outside. Lindsey exhaled and rubbed at her face. She raced into the kitchen and snatched up her mobile.

Graveney slipped into the passenger seat next to Robertson. 'What do you think?' Robertson said.

'She's lying. I'm sure of it.'

'About Hewitson?'

'Yeah, she's seen her recently.'

Robertson peered back towards the house. 'How can you be certain?'

'It would take me ages to explain. But take it from me, she's seen her recently.'

'We're not even sure Hewitson's the woman we're looking for,' Robertson said, and turned back to face Graveney.

'Then why lie?' Graveney tapped his chin with a finger. 'Maybe Lindsey Armstrong is involved in the murders. Maybe we're looking for more than the other two.'

'What do we do?' Robertson said.

'What can we do at the moment but keep a close watch on Armstrong and wait for her to slip up.'

Lindsey phoned the number again. It rang several times, then went to answerphone. She groaned and tossed the mobile onto the counter. She quickly snatched it back up and viewed the name as it rang. It said, *pizza*.

'Hi, Linds,' Jen said. 'What's up?'

'I've had the coppers around asking about you?'

'Me?'

'Yeah.'

'What did they say?' Jen said.

'They asked me if I knew you. I told them we were inside together. Then they asked when I'd last seen you.'

'What did you say?'

'I lied. I told them I hadn't seen you since prison.'

'Cheers, Linds. Appreciate that.'

'What's going on, Jen?'

'You don't want to know. It involves Conrad Hudson.'

'Jesus, Jen. I told you he's dangerous. He—'

'He murdered Amanda. Well, one of his guys did.'

'If you have evidence, tell the police.'

Jen scoffed. 'What will they do? They're all corrupt. They're in his pocket.'

'Even so—'

'They raped her, Linds. Raped and murdered her.'

Lindsey put a hand to her mouth. 'I know. I'm sorry. But getting yourself killed won't bring her back.'

'She's buried somewhere. One of them knows where, and I'm going to find out.'

'What about Hudson? He'll be after you.'

'He's got his coming, too. I'm not afraid of the scumbag.'

'The house … Has anyone seen you there?'

'No. We've been careful. We come and go at night, and we've been very quiet.'

'Good,' Lindsey said.

'We're going to be on the move soon. I've found another place out of town. I'm grateful for your help.'

'Jen. Just be careful. Conrad Hudson is a dangerous man. Alex Cooper told me about him years ago. Alex believed he could handle him and look where he ended up.'

'I'll be fine,' Jen said.

'What about the baby?'

'When I've found Amanda. When the men responsible for her murder have paid for it, then Joey and I will move on.'

'I'll only get in contact if I need to.'

'I'll let you know when we've moved out and where I've left the keys.'

'Good luck,' Lindsey said.

CHAPTER TWENTY-NINE

Hudson gulped at his large whisky and placed the empty glass on his desk. Taffy came in and stopped in front of him.

'Have you done it?' Hudson said.

Taffy slouched down onto a chair. 'I've just had a message that the stuff's been planted at his club.'

'Get someone to call the police.'

Taffy rubbed his chin. 'Are we sure it was Macintyre? It's not like him. He knows he couldn't take you on.'

'He's obviously getting bold.' Hudson sneered. 'He's heard about Billy and Robbo. He thinks he has a chance of taking over my business.'

'But it's ...'

'Taffy.' Hudson huffed. 'The man we caught said it was one of Macintyre's men who told him to take the pictures.'

'It doesn't ring true. What if it wasn't Macintyre? He has a handy crew. Do we want a war when we're weakened?'

'Macintyre is an insignificance. I've only left him alone because he didn't cause us any grief.'

Taffy cocked his head. 'Why would one of Macintyre's men get someone to take photos?'

'Christ, Taffy. I don't know. Just make the call. He won't know it's me who's set him up.'

'He'll probably guess.'

'So. He can't prove it. I'll deny it. Macintyre's upset quite a few people over the years.'

Taffy stood. 'Ok.'

'Where's Harry?' Hudson said.

'He's trying to locate the big guy and the woman. Well, that's what he told me.'

Hudson ignored the comment. 'I've been thinking. Someone on Teesside has to be helping them.'

'Have another word with Colin Pybus, Boss.'

Hudson scoffed. 'I thought of that. He died on Friday. His funeral's next week. He wouldn't tell us anything, anyway.'

Taffy laughed. 'Are you going?'

'Not a bad idea. See who turns up. We'll take someone along with a camera and get some snaps.'

Taffy's mobile sounded, and he quickly answered. 'Hi, Bob.'

'I've got some news,' Bob said. 'Amanda Hewitson's sister was banged up in Durham Prison.'

'And?'

'She was close to a few women while inside. One's still in there. The other two have been released. One's interesting.'

'Why?' Taffy said.

'She lives in Middlesbrough. Lindsey Armstrong.'

'Address?'

Bob relayed the address as he wrote it down. 'There's a good drink in it for you.'

'One more thing,' Bob said. 'The police were asking questions about her.'

'Who? Hewitson?'

'No … Lindsey Armstrong.'

'Cheers,' Taffy said. He hung up and looked at Hudson. 'We could have a lead. Hewitson was inside with someone called Lindsey Armstrong.'

Hudson furrowed his brow. 'Where do I know the name from?'

'Craig Embleton.'

Hudson's mouth dropped open. 'Cooper's driver?' Taffy nodded. Hudson continued. 'She's the girl we fitted up for his murder.'

'Could she know?' Taffy said.

Hudson stood and walked over to the drinks cabinet. He poured two large whiskies and handed one to Taffy. 'Colin couldn't have told her,' Hudson said. 'He didn't know.'

'Who did?'

'You, me and Billy.'

'Shall we pick her up?'

Hudson picked up his glass and took a swig of his drink. 'No. I think we need to be canny here. If the police know about Armstrong, they may be watching her.'

'One of the new lads?'

'Yeah,' Hudson said. 'Send them around to keep an eye on her address. Do it in shifts. Day and night. And warn them not to be seen.'

'Ok, Boss.'

Slim and Chubby waited outside Lindsey's parents' house. Darkness was drawing in and Chubby yawned.

'This is a waste of time,' he said. 'There's no one here. The house has been sold.'

'Taffy told us to wait here,' Slim said. 'So we do what we're told.'

'What about something to eat?'

'There's half a sandwich and some crisps in the back.'

Chubby scoffed. 'I want something warm.'

'Get down!' Slim said. The pair bobbed down in the front of the vehicle as someone came out from behind the houses.

'It's only a pregnant lass,' Chubby said.

'Wait ... There's a man with her, loitering in the alley.'

Chubby followed his companion's eyes as he strained to see in the fading light. 'He looks tall.'

The woman glanced up and down the street before heading around the corner. A vehicle started, and a blue Transit trundled along the road. It stopped at the top of the alley and the big guy jumped in. Slim watched as the van moved off and out of sight.

'Phone Taffy,' Slim said. 'I'll follow them.'

Taffy downed his pint and patted Charlie on the arm. 'I'll drop you off,' Taffy said.

Charlie emptied his drink and slipped from the stool. 'Yeah. Nothing left for us to do tonight.'

Taffy's mobile rang. 'Yeah, Chubby?'

'We're following a van. There's a woman and a big guy in it.'

'From Lindsey Armstrong's house?' Taffy said.

'Yeah. The one in North Ormesby.'

'Keep after them. I'll phone the boss.'

Taffy turned to Charlie. 'Follow me.' The pair headed outside and waited.

Taffy phoned Hudson. 'Yeah,' Hudson said.

'The lads are following the girl and the big bloke. They were at the house in North Ormesby.'

'Where are they now?'

'Not sure. I'll give them a ring and phone you back.'

Joey looked over his shoulder. He glanced across at Jen. 'We're being followed,' he said.

Jen peeped into the mirror. 'Which one?'

'The red Mercedes,' Joey said.

'What do we do?'

'We could lose them, or sort them out.'

Jen sucked in a lungful of air. 'What do you think?'

'When we stop at these lights, jump in the back and I'll drive.'

They pulled up at the red light, and Jen clambered from her seat and climbed into the back.

'Grab the guns,' he said.

She rummaged through a holdall and pulled out two pistols. She checked they were loaded and placed one on the seat next to Joey. Joey accelerated and pulled off at the next exit. The car behind struggled to keep up. The heavy traffic allowing the Transit to gain distance on them. Pulling onto an industrial estate, he brought the vehicle to a halt. He motioned for Jen to get out, which she did, and the pair jogged across the road and down the side of a building.

'You wait here, ' he said. 'Keep out of sight. They'll be here shortly.'

Joey hid nearby to the van behind a wall and waited as the red Mercedes came into view. It slowed to a crawl and stopped. The two men jumped out with pistols in hand and made their way forward. On reaching the rear of the vehicle, Slim made his way around one side as Chubby slid around the other.

Slim glanced at his mate. 'They must have gone inside there.' He nodded towards a vast compound housing dozens of caravans and trailers.

'Maybe they're moving house,' Chubby said.

'Yeah. Phone Taffy and tell them where we are, I'll stand guard in case they turn up.'

Chubby plodded back towards the car. Slim darted across to the high fence of the compound. He peered through the railings and inside. Nothing moved. As he turned back around, the fist caught him square on his jaw. He crumpled to the ground, unconscious. Joey seized his feet and pulled him into the undergrowth.

Chubby sat in the front seat, his right leg dangling outside of the car, and phoned.

''Yeah, Chubby,' Taffy said.

'They've stopped on an industrial estate in Thornaby. Slim thinks they've gone inside a compound housing caravans.'

'Could be where they're staying?'

'That's what we thought. They appeared as if they were leaving the house in North Ormesby.'

'Where's Slim?' Taffy said.

'He's having a look around.'

'You two sit tight. I'll phone Conrad. He'll want to be there, I'm sure.'

'Ok.'

'What's the address?'

Chubby gave Taffy the address and rang off. He lumbered out of the vehicle and stopped. The cold, hard metal of the gun pressed against his neck. 'Do as I say and you may see the morning,' Joey said. Chubby stood motionless. Joey pushed his victim towards the van and inside the back. He waved at Jen, who raced across and jumped into the front.

'Park around the back of the compound.' Joey said to her. 'We can see the road from there.' She started the engine and roared off.

Taffy phoned Hudson. 'Yeah, Taffy?'

'Slim and Chubby followed them to an industrial estate not far from here. I thought you might want to be there.'

'I do. You come and pick me up, and send Charlie across to where they are.'

'I'm on my way.' Taffy looked at Charlie. 'Get over to this address.' Handing him a piece of paper, he patted him on the arm. 'I'm off over to Conrad's.'

Charlie snatched the paper from his hand and hurried off.

Taffy pushed his mobile into his jacket pocket and followed his friend out of the door.

Jen and Joey waited out of sight until a blue BMW pulled onto the estate. It drew to a halt behind the Mercedes, and Charlie got out. He glanced about, the road eerily silent. His phone sounded.

'Chubby. Where are you?'

'We're around the back of the compound,' he said. 'They're inside a caravan.'

'I'm on my way.' Jumping back into his vehicle he slowly drove around the compound, pulling up opposite the van. He eased himself out and drew his gun. 'Chubby. Slim,' he whispered, creeping closer to the Transit.

He reached the side door and peered inside. A bound and gagged Chubby and Slim lay on the ground. He spun around, the gun knocked from his hand flew across the floor. He lunged at Joey, the big man easily swatted him aside and knocked him facedown towards the tarmac. As he pulled himself upward, the giant boot of his attacker met him squarely on the jaw. Charlie groaned and slumped to the ground, blood and several teeth splattering the surface in front of him.

Charlie's phone sounded inside his pocket. Joey flipped him over with one mighty push from his boot. The now unconscious victim stared up at him with eyes half-open as Jen joined Joey. She rifled through Charlie's pocket, pulling his mobile free. She viewed the name, "Conrad Hudson" and slid it into her pocket. Joey lifted Charlie up, carried him to the back of the van and dropped him inside.

'He's not answering,' Hudson said to Taffy.

'He's probably left it in his car or something.'

Hudson rubbed his chin. 'Put your foot down. I don't like this.'

'We're not far away. Try again, Boss.'

Hudson dialled once more as the car screeched onto the industrial estate and skidded to a halt behind the BMW and Mercedes. The pair jumped out and with handguns raised, they crept towards the vehicles. Hudson looked at his phone as a muffled voice shouted through it. He placed the handset to his ear.

'Is that you, Hudson?' Jen said.

'I know who you are, you bitch,' he spat.

'I've got your friend here, Hudson. We're going to carve him open like a pig. This is for Amanda. Tell your pal, he's next.'

'Fuck you,' Hudson said.

'Then we're coming for you, my friend. Colin told us everything. I've got something special planned—'

Hudson hung up and raced toward the BMW. He wrenched open the door and dragged Slim from inside, ripping off the tape which covered his mouth.

'What happened, you piece of shit?' he screamed. 'How could you let them get away?' He placed the muzzle of the pistol next to Slim's head. 'I should blow your fucking brains out.'

Taffy grasped hold of his arm. 'Boss,' he said. 'It's not their fault.'

Hudson glared at Taffy, the scowl etched across his face only partially diminishing. 'Keep these two idiots away from me.' He let go of Slim and stomped back towards the car.

CHAPTER THIRTY

Graveney made his way along the corridor and into DI Robertson's office. 'Morning, Neil,' he said.

'I've had a call from DI Daniels.'

Graveney sat. 'Oh, yeah?'

'He arrested Scott Macintyre yesterday. For possession of a Class A drug.' Graveney grinned, and Robertson continued. 'He thought it was a little suspect as it was via a tip-off.'

'How does this concern us, though?'

Robertson placed his hands behind his head and leant back in his chair. 'He was released on bail, but one of the uniformed lads heard him mumble a name to one of his heavies.'

Graveney smiled. 'Conrad Hudson?'

Robertson winked. 'That's what it sounded like.'

'Could be those two are having a turf war. Maybe Hudson was just flexing his muscles.'

'Hudson's murdered men. Possibly Macintyre had something to do with it?'

'I'm not convinced,' Graveney said.

There was a knock at the door and Cooke entered. 'Have you a moment?' She glanced between the two officers.

'Fire away,' Graveney said.

'Jen Hewitson had a sister called Amanda. Amanda disappeared in 1999. She's never been heard from since.'

'Right,' Robertson said. 'That's interesting.' He looked at Graveney and raised his eyebrows. 'She could be the key to the murders.'

'Who reported her missing?' Graveney said.

'A friend of hers.' Cooke flicked over the page of her notebook. 'Seranne Dryburn. She lived with Amanda for a couple of years.' Cooke tore a piece of paper from her book and placed it on the desk. 'That's her address.'

'Great work,' Robertson said.

Hussain appeared at the door. 'We've got another murder. Charlie Warrender.'

Graveney glanced at Robertson. 'Another of Hudson's men.'

Graveney pulled the car to a halt outside an old, dilapidated house. He and Robertson got out and joined Hussain.

'What do we have?' Graveney said to him.

'Same MO as the other two. Dr Wilson's in there now.'

Robertson surveyed the terrain. 'Who owns the land?'

'It was owned by a neighbouring farm, Guv,' Hussain said. 'But it was sold to a developer some time ago. They're building over there.' He pointed past Robertson's shoulder.

The DI followed his gaze. 'Don't suppose anyone saw anything?'

'It's a bit remote out here,' Hussain said. 'Wynyard's over there, but I don't think the locals would think it unusual if vehicles were coming and going.'

Graveney nodded. 'Keep asking about, Rav. You never know.' Graveney gestured to Robertson. 'Shall we?' he said, moving towards the crumbling structure. The pair trudged across to the building and stopped outside.

Bev Wilson made her way over to them. 'I wouldn't come any nearer, boys. The building's in a bit of a state.' She smiled at Robertson. 'How are you, Neil?'

'Good, Bev,' he said.

She turned her attention to Graveney. 'Same as the other two. I'll have to do a post mortem to be certain, but it looks identical.'

'When will that be ready?' Graveney said.

'Tomorrow. I'll phone.'

'Ok,' he said, avoiding eye contact and then marched away.

'Thanks, Bev,' Robertson said, and followed his colleague. He caught Graveney up. 'Everything all right, Peter?'

'Bit of a headache,' he said.

Robertson glanced back at the building. 'Dr Wilson's attractive.'

'Is she?' Graveney said. He fumbled in his pocket for his mobile.

'I thought with your reputation, you'd ...'

Graveney peered across at the building. 'It's hard to find someone attractive who's been cutting up cadavers all day.'

Robertson chuckled. 'I never considered that.'

Graveney checked his phone. He had two missed calls and a text message. He read the message. 'I've got a call to make. I'll be with you in a minute.' He stepped away from Robertson.

'I'll crack on, shall I?' Robertson shouted after him.

Graveney headed out of earshot and dialled.

'Hi, Peter,' Liz said. 'How are you?'

'I'm well. How's sunny Majorca?'

'A bit overcast today. Sorry I missed your call. I've been having a bit of trouble with my mobile.'

'I was phoning to see how you are,' he said. 'You know. The bar?'

'The bar's doing great. Things are winding down a bit now. It'll give us a chance to spruce the place up a bit.'

'Good.'

'What's up, Peter?'

'Heather and I ... She threw me out.'

Liz sighed. 'Sorry to hear that.'

'Don't you want to know why?'

'I think I can guess,' she said.

'Shit happens. But it was my own fault.'

'I don't judge, Peter. Listen, why don't you come across for a few days. Relax and enjoy the sun and sangria.'

'I'd love to,' he said. 'But I'm in the middle of a complicated case.'

'You have to think about yourself sometimes. There are other policemen, I'm sure.'

Graveney pushed a hand through his hair. 'I had some time off the other week. I wish I'd thought about it then.'

'I'm always here. You know that.'

'I do. Can I ring tomorrow? We'll chat more.'

'I'd like that,' Liz said.

'Send your sister my love.'

'I will.'

'Speak tomorrow,' Graveney said.

He hung up and ambled back across to Robertson. 'Sorry, Neil. Personal.'

'No worries. I've rung the Guv. He said he wanted to be kept in the loop.'

'Good. I think we're done here. We need to pay Amanda Hewitson's friend a visit.' Graveney pushed his hand into his pocket and pulled out the crumpled paper. 'Seranne Dryburn.'

'Ready when you are,' Robertson said, striding off towards the car.

Graveney caught sight of Wilson as she exited the building. She peered across at him and gave a half-hearted wave. Graveney gave a cursory lift of the hand and followed Robertson.

The officers arrived outside a house in Thornaby. Graveney checked the address on the piece of paper he held, before the officers got out and made their way up the path to the property. He knocked. A dog inside barked furiously, and as the door opened the animal pushed its nose through the gap. A man inside held on firmly to its collar. 'Yeah?' he said, peering around the corner of the half-opened door.

'Police, Sir,' Robertson said. 'Can you put the dog into another room, please.'

The door closed and a muffled noise was heard inside as the man, Graveney presumed, tried to get the intransigent canine to do what he wanted.

'Bloody hate dogs,' Robertson said.

Graveney laughed. 'Why?'

'You wouldn't believe how many times I've been bitten.'

The door re-opened. 'Sorry about that.' The man frowned. 'Police you said?'

Graveney and Robertson held out their badges. 'Inspectors Graveney and Robertson,' Graveney said. 'We're looking for Seranne Dryburn.'

'Seranne?' the man said. He turned. 'Seranne,' he shouted. 'It's for you.'

The door to a room behind him opened and a woman in her late thirties came out. 'Yeah?'

'Nothing to worry about,' Graveney said. 'Routine stuff. Do you think we could have a minute?'

'Of course,' she said, and beckoned them inside. The two officers followed her into the lounge. 'Have a seat.' Graveney and Robertson sat. The man wandered in and perched on the arm of a chair next to the woman.

'This is my husband. Is it—?'

'As I was saying,' Graveney said, 'it's routine stuff. Your husband can stay.'

Graveney pulled out his notepad. 'Do you remember someone called Amanda Hewitson?'

'Amanda? Yeah. We shared a house for a while.' She furrowed her brow. '1998 to about 1999, I think.'

'You reported her missing in 1999?' Robertson said.

'Yeah. It's a long time ago now.'

'Take your time,' Graveney said.

'She told me she was going to a party but didn't come home. I got a bit worried after a day or two, so I called the police.'

'What happened?' Graveney said.

'They took details and told me they'd be in touch.'

'And did you speak to the police again?' Robertson said.

'I left a message a few days later. I told them it was ok.'

'Why would you tell them that?' Graveney said.

'She'd moved in with her fancy man.'

Graveney glanced across at Robertson. 'Fancy man?'

'Yeah. Amanda had this rich older man on the go.' She mused for a moment. 'Alex. That was his name.'

'Alex?' Robertson said. 'Are you sure?'

'Yeah. She wouldn't tell me, but I overheard her on the phone one day. It was definitely Alex.'

'I don't suppose you recall his surname?' Graveney said.

'No. I never met him either.'

'Anything else you remember about him?' Robertson said.

'Not really. As I said, I never met him. He'd send a flash car to pick Amanda up. I chatted to the driver a couple of times.' She glanced at her husband. 'He was handsome and a bit of a lad, if you know what I mean?'

Graveney smiled. 'And this driver—?'

'Craig,' she said.

'Craig. He never told you anything?' Graveney said.

'No. He was too busy flirting.'

'I don't suppose you know his surname or where he lived?'

'Wouldn't matter anyway. He was murdered by his girlfriend years ago.'

Graveney looked up from his notes. 'Murdered?'

'Yeah. She stabbed him to death. The police thought it was a crime of passion. Having met Craig, I could—'

'Was his girlfriend called Lindsey? Lindsey Armstrong?' Graveney said.

She rubbed her cheek. 'Yes. I think it was. She got life.'

'Would you recognise Craig again from a photo?' Robertson said.

'I think so.'

Graveney looked back over his notes. 'When you said Amanda had gone off with this Alex, how did you know?'

'Some guy came around. Said Amanda had sent him for her things. He gave me a few hundred quid towards the rent from her. The strange thing was, he didn't take much of her stuff.'

'What happened to the rest?' Graveney said.

'I kept some of it and gave the remainder to a charity shop.'

'And you never spoke to Amanda again?' Graveney said.

'No. We weren't what you'd call close. Just housemates, really. After Alex arrived on the scene, she got even more distant. I assumed she'd got lucky with a rich sugar daddy.'

Graveney glanced at Robertson, who nodded. 'I think that's all, Seranne,' Graveney said. 'Thanks for your help.'

The two officers stood and headed towards the door. 'We'll send someone with a photo for you to look at,' Graveney said.

'Thanks again,' Robertson said.

Once outside, they made their way across to the car. 'Well,' Robertson said. 'That was interesting. It's got to be Alex Cooper.'

'I think so.' He stared at Robertson. 'It's funny how Lindsey Armstrong's name keeps cropping up, isn't it?'

Robertson rubbed his chin. 'It certainly is. I think we need another word with the young lady.'

'It's still circumstantial though,' Graveney said.

'Yeah. But sooner or later, something will fall into place.'

CHAPTER THIRTY-ONE

Graveney stood and viewed the whiteboard in the incident room. Photos of the three murdered men, who worked for Hudson, evenly spaced around the perimeter. Pictures of Sean Grant and Alex Cooper next to these. Dotted at various intervals were names. Craig Embleton, Karl Smith. In the middle, taking centre stage, a mugshot of Lindsey Armstrong, her boyfriend's name written next to it with a question mark. Lines from everyone else connecting Lindsey to them. Next to this whiteboard, another. In the middle of it, Joseph Purdey, Jennifer Hewitson and Lindsey Armstrong. Graveney rubbed his chin as Hussain approached.

'Yes, Rav,' Graveney said, without looking away from the board.

'Seranne Dryburn has seen the photo. She confirmed it was Craig Embleton.'

Graveney grunted. 'We're going to chat with Lindsey Armstrong this morning.'

'What are your thoughts, Guv?'

He turned to face Hussain. 'I think Hudson's men murdered Amanda Hewitson. I think her sister, and Joseph Purdey, possibly with the help of Lindsey Armstrong, murdered three of them.'

'Armstrong's alibis check out,' Hussain said.

'Yeah, well. She may not have been there when they were abducted, or murdered, but she's involved. I'm sure.'

'Jimmy Jefferson?' Hussain said.

'Possibly.'

'Do you want us to check on his whereabouts when Hudson's men were abducted, Guv?'

'Yeah,' Graveney said, and Hussain left, passing Robertson on his way out.

Robertson stopped next to Graveney. 'Lindsey Armstrong?' he said.

'Yeah. I'll give Bev Wilson a ring first. She should've finished the post mortem.' Robertson followed Graveney as he headed back to his office. The pair sat. Graveney called Bev and put the phone on loudspeaker as she answered.

'Hi, Peter.'

'Morning, Bev. I've got DI Robertson here with me so none of your bad language.'

Bev chuckled. 'I'll be on my best behaviour. Morning, Neil.'

'Morning, Bev,' he said.

A rustling of paper could be heard before she began. 'Same MO as the other two murders. There were signs he'd suffered a beating before death.'

'The others had as well?' Robertson said.

'Yes, but not as severe. The other two men's injuries were subtle. This time it appeared frantic. I'm tempted to say rushed.'

Graveney glanced at Robertson. 'An attempt to extract information, perhaps?'

'Maybe they were in a hurry. They possibly had more time with the other two, or maybe it was just anger.'

Robertson tutted. 'What information are they after?'

'Where Amanda Hewitson is,' Graveney said.

'Who's Amanda Hewitson?' Bev said.

Graveney explained what he and Robertson suspected and that they believed the murders were related to her disappearance.

'Well, they went a bit overboard on the beating. Charlie Warrender suffered a massive heart attack during it. Luckily for him, the evisceration and mutilation took place after death.'

'I bet he was over the moon with that,' Graveney said.

Robertson grimaced. 'Could be they didn't get the information they wanted.'

'Maybe,' Graveney said. 'Anything else we need to know?'

'No. I think that's about everything.'

Robertson stood. 'Thanks, Bev.' He looked at Graveney. 'I've got a call to make, Peter. I'll see you downstairs.'

'Five minutes,' Graveney said.

Robertson left. Graveney waited for him to exit and close the door behind him before focussing his attention back on Bev. 'How are you?' he said.

'Can we talk?' she said.

'Yeah. Neil's gone.'

'When am I going to see you again, Peter? It's been ages.'

'I know, but, with the case and that. I've been run off my feet.'

'You're not ...?'

'Of course not, Bev. What about tonight?'

'I should be able to manage that. Your flat?'

'Yeah,' Graveney said. 'About eight?'

'Eight's good. I've missed seeing you, Peter. It's hard when I only see you at work.'

'I know, I know.'

'I … I … love you, Peter.' She coughed.

'Listen, Bev. I need to go. We'll talk tonight. I promise.'

'Ok. Eight.'

'Eight.' Graveney hung up and put his hands over his face. He remained like this for a few moments before removing them. Marne sat across from him, shaking her head.

Lindsey threw open the door. Graveney and Robertson stood outside and she beckoned them in.

'The length of time you two spend around here,' she said, 'I should charge you rent.'

'We need another chat, Lindsey,' Graveney said.

'Really?' She false-smiled. 'And here's me thinking you came around for my sparkling wit.'

'Can we come in?' Robertson said.

'Of course. You know the way into the lounge. Grab a seat, boys. I'm making a cuppa. I'll be with you shortly.'

The two officers made their way into the lounge while Lindsey headed for the kitchen. She closed the door behind her, raced through into the utility room and into the toilet. Dropping to her knees, she vomited.

Lindsey entered the living room carrying a tray with a teapot, cups, sugar, milk and biscuits on it. She smiled at the officers. 'There's no reason we can't be civilised, is there?' She poured out three cups, added milk to hers and picked up her drink. Graveney and Robertson followed suit before taking a sip of the tea and placing their cups down.

'Now,' Lindsey said. 'What is it you wanted to talk about?'

'Amanda Hewitson?' Robertson said.

Lindsey fidgeted. 'Jen had a sister.'

'Had?' Graveney said.

'Has … Has a sister.'

Graveney studied her. Lindsey at first met his stare, and then looked away.

'We spoke to a friend of Amanda's,' Robertson said. 'Seranne Dryburn.'

Lindsey folded her arms and crossed her legs. 'I've never heard of her.'

'Amanda lived with her for a while,' Graveney said. 'Until she disappeared in 1999.'

'Can't help you. I had other things on my mind back then.' She false-smiled the officers again.

Graveney threw open his notebook. 'Let me tell you what we know, Lindsey.' He fixed her with a glare. Lindsey stared back at Graveney as he studied her. 'Amanda had a rich boyfriend by the name of, Alex. Could it be the same Alex you knew?'

Lindsey shrugged. 'How would I know?'

Graveney smiled. 'Alex had a driver who he would send to pick Amanda up. His name was Craig.'

Lindsey dropped her eyes to the floor. 'Why do you keep bringing Craig into it? I told you I didn't kill him.'

'I know you didn't.' Graveney continued. 'I believe you. But you see how it looks from our point of view.' He glanced across at Robertson. 'Every step of the way, every time we find a new lead in this investigation, your name crops up.'

'Alex and I had an affair. It ended after we argued. It wouldn't have mattered. I'd already fallen for Craig.'

'Why didn't you tell us this earlier?'

Lindsey bit her lip. 'I met Craig through Alex.'

'Did you ever meet Amanda?' Robertson said.

'Once. I saw her talking to Alex. I got a little jealous over it.'

'Did you know Alex was seeing Amanda?' Graveney said.

'I guessed. We were in a hotel, and someone called Amanda rang him. I put two and two together.'

'Is it what you fell out over?' Graveney said.

'... Yeah.'

Graveney noticed the pause. He leant closer to her. 'You're lying, Lyndsey.'

Lindsey rubbed at her face. 'He wanted me to do something for him.'

'What?' Graveney said.

'He had a business partner. Alex used to supply contacts. People who could help with their business. He thought his partner was holding out on him and wanted to know if he was.'

'Who was this partner?' Robertson said.

Lindsey gulped. 'Conrad Hudson.'

Graveney sighed loudly. 'Why didn't you tell us this earlier?' He glanced at Robertson and threw up his hands.

'I don't know.' Tears appeared in her eyes. 'I remember reading Alex had disappeared, with the money he stole from the council, while I was on remand. It was ages later I met up with Jen inside. She told me her sister had disappeared.'

'You knew it was Amanda?' Graveney said.'

'Not at first. But as she told me more, I guessed. I assumed Amanda had left with Alex.'

'Until?' Graveney said.

'Until you fished him out of the pond.'

'What do you think happened?' Robertson said.

'I'm not sure. I thought maybe Hudson killed Alex, but when Amanda's body didn't show up ...'

'Have you met Jen recently?' Graveney said.

'Once. I gave her the keys to my mam and dad's house. She needed a place to stay. I didn't think anything of it.'

'Didn't you ask what she was doing in Middlesbrough?' Graveney said.

'She told me she was trying to trace her sister. Middlesbrough was the last place she'd been seen, it seemed natural to start here.'

'Where is she now?' Robertson said.

'I've no idea.'

'You do realise—?' Robertson said.

'I honestly don't know.'

'Have you a number?' Graveney said.

'No. I met her near my mam and dad's house.'

Graveney clenched his jaw. 'Keys.' He held out his hand. 'And your mobile.'

Lindsey pushed the phone across the table towards him, stood and disappeared into the hall. She returned moments later with a set of keys and handed them to Graveney.

Graveney stared into her eyes. 'I hope you've told us everything. If you're keeping—?'

'That's everything. All I know.' She stared back as teardrops dripped from her eyes. 'I lost fifteen years of my life and spent all my twenties inside. I saw my mam and dad prematurely age and die. All I want is to be left alone. All I want is the past to stay where it belongs. That's all. Please.'

Graveney furrowed his brow. 'Ok, Lindsey. We'll leave it there for now.' He held up the keys and phone. 'You'll get these back in due course. And if you hear from Jen ...?'

She smiled unevenly. 'I'll phone.'

Graveney motioned at Robertson, who stood. 'We'll let ourselves out,' Graveney said.

Lindsey watched through the window as they drove off.

'What do you think?' Robertson said. 'Has she told us everything?'

'I'm not sure. We'll see.'

Slim and Chubby loitered in the car a hundred metres from Lindsey's mam and dad's house.

'This is a waste of time,' Chubby said. 'They won't come back here.'

Slim looked upwards. 'Hudson wants us two here, just in case. He's the one who pays us.'

Chubby stared at Slim. 'Don't you get the impression Hudson's losing it a bit.'

Slim turned to his friend. 'I'd keep those thoughts to yourself, if I was you.'

Both men glanced to the right as three vehicles drove into the road. Realising who was inside the cars they slipped down below the dashboard.

'It's the coppers,' Chubby said.

'Yeah,' Slim said. 'I'll phone Taffy. It's a waste of time us being here if they are.' He pushed his hand into his pocket and pulled out his mobile, quickly locating and calling a number.

'Yeah, Slim?' Taffy said.

'The police arrived mob-handed at the house. What do you want us to do?'

'Stay put and out of sight. See what happens and let me know.'

'Ok.' He rang off and turned to Chubby. 'He wants us to stay put and see what happens.'

Graveney and Robertson jumped from the car. They were quickly joined by several armed officers.

'We're waiting for bomb disposal to arrive,' Graveney said, addressing the officers. 'I want you two.' Looking at Rav and Jack. 'Around the back. Keep an eye out and let us know if you see any movement from inside.'

'Sarah,' Graveney said. 'You and a couple of others knock on doors. Ask if anyone saw anything.'

'How long will the bomb disposal be?' Robertson said.

Graveney glanced at his watch. 'Should be here in fifteen minutes. We'll sit tight until then. We don't want another Pearl Street.'

Robertson chuckled. 'Yeah. Coffee? There's a shop around the corner.'

'Love one. And maybe a Jack Daniels.'

Robertson grinned. 'Me too. I'll send one of the guys.'

A man in military uniform approached Graveney and Robertson. He stopped and handed Graveney a set of keys. 'We've done a complete sweep of the house. It's clean.' Graveney and Robertson thanked him and wandered over to the others.

Graveney glanced around at the officers. 'It looks as if our suspects have scarpered. I want the house searching from top to bottom. Let's see if we can come up with any clues as to where they've gone.'

They headed towards the house and Graveney pulled Lindsey's mobile from his pocket. 'Sarah,' he shouted to Cooke. She stopped, moved back towards him. 'Yes, Guv?'

He held out the phone. 'I want you to check out the numbers on this. It's Lindsey Armstrong's.'

'Lindsey Armstrong's?' Cooke took the mobile from him.

'Yeah. We've reason to believe she's been in contact with Jennifer Hewitson. One of these numbers could be hers.'

'Will do, Guv.'

Robertson sipped at his coffee. 'Tenner says we'll find nothing from the house.'

Graveney slipped his hands into his pockets. 'I wouldn't take the bet, Neil. These two have been pretty clever so far.'

Conrad Hudson placed his elbows on the desk and viewed Harry and Taffy seated in front of him. 'Where's Slim and Chubby?' Hudson said.

'They're on their way now,' Taffy said. 'It didn't sound promising.'

Hudson tapped the desk. 'This Lindsey Armstrong, she's the key.'

'You think she knows where they are?' Harry said.

'She was in Durham with the woman ...' Hudson said. '... and obviously allowed her to stay at the house.'

'Maybe she doesn't know what Hewitson's up to,' Harry said.

'She mightn't,' Taffy said. 'But she may be able to contact them.'

Hudson picked up his glass and drained it. 'I think we should pay Miss Armstrong a visit. Nothing heavy. Just a little bit of pressure. Let's see if she'll talk.'

'I'll wait until the lads get back,' Taffy said. 'And then I'll go.'

'Do you want some company?' Harry said.

Taffy glanced at him. 'No. I'll take one of the boys.'

Jen glanced about. Happy she wasn't being watched she jumped into the vehicle. Joey, who was sleeping, woke. Jen handed him a coffee and a paper bag. 'I got you a bacon and sausage bun.'

He placed the drink on the dashboard and opened the bag. 'Brown sauce?'

Jen pushed a hand into her pocket and pulled out a sachet of HP. 'Of course.'

He planted a kiss on her cheek. 'The last man?' he said, and took a bite of his sandwich.

'He knows where she is. We need to get that from him.'

'And Hudson?'

'Then we can sort him out.' She turned away and looked out the side window.

'You ok?'

Jen turned back around to face him. Her eyes glistened with unshed tears. 'Yeah.' She reached across and kissed him on the cheek. 'I will be when we get those two.' Her phone sounded in her pocket and she pulled it free. She stared at the name. 'It's Lindsey.'

'Aren't you going to answer it?'

'She hasn't sent a text,' she said.

Joey furrowed his brow. 'A text?'

'I told Lindsey to text me before she phoned. That way I'll know it's her.' Joey frowned. 'In case someone else has the phone,' she continued. 'We don't want to walk into a trap.'

'Maybe she forgot?'

'Maybe.' The phone stopped ringing. Jen rubbed her temple and waited. There was no message.

'What are you going to do?'

'I don't know. I could phone her house, I suppose. But the police may have it bugged.'

'Should we go around?' Joey said.

'We'll sit tight for the moment. Maybe she forgot to message. We'll give it until tomorrow.'

Slim and Chubby entered and made their way over to the other three men.

'What's happening, lads?' Taffy said.

Slim stepped forward. 'The police searched the house. They had the bomb disposal there as well, from what we gathered.' He glanced across at Chubby, who nodded back at him. 'They haven't found anything. Graveney and another DI were there.'

Hudson leant back in his chair. 'Are you sure?'

'They didn't bring anything out, Mr Hudson,' Slim said.

'And they didn't look pleased,' Chubby said.

'It looks as if those two have flown the coop,' Taffy said.

'Yeah,' Hudson rubbed his chin. He stood and filled a glass full of whisky. 'Get the Armstrong woman.'

'Are you sure you—?' Harry said.

'Of course I'm sure. She knows something.'

'The police may be watching her,' Harry said.

Hudson took a gulp of his drink. 'Well, don't let them catch you then.'

'Where are we going to take her?' Taffy said.

Hudson returned to his desk and scribbled down an address. 'I've bought a piece of land between Darlington and Northallerton. I'm hoping to build some houses on it. There's an old, derelict farmhouse there. Take her there and let me know when you have her.'

'We'll go across to her house now,' Taffy said. 'Do a recce. See if the police are kicking around.'

'What do you want me to do?' Harry said.

'Do you need another pair of hands?' Hudson said to Taffy.

Taffy glanced across at Harry and narrowed his eyes. 'No, I'll be fine. I'll take Slim and Chubby.'

Graveney and Robertson came out of the house. Graveney threw his hands up and stared back towards the building. 'Well, what a bloody waste of time that was.'

Robertson grunted. 'They've obviously moved on. But where?'

Cooke marched up to the officers and stopped. 'Have you a minute, Guv?' she said.

'Yeah,' Graveney said. 'Fire away.'

'I've checked through the numbers on Lindsey Armstrong's phone. They all check out bar one. The contact says, pizza.'

'And?'

'There was no answer. Just an automated answerphone. It's a pay as you go mobile, so we can't trace it.'

'It could be Jennifer Hewitson?' Robertson said.

'Yeah.' Graveney rubbed his chin. 'Maybe. Armstrong will deny it, though.'

'Shall we pull her in?' Robertson said.

Graveney rubbed at his eyes. 'We could have another chat. We'll finish up here.' He glanced at his watch. 'We'll go over first thing in the morning. Catch her on the hop.'

Robertson consulted his watch. 'Yeah. It's been a long day, Peter. I'm done in.'

Hussain exited the house carrying a plastic bag. He held it up for the officers to see. 'We found this,' he said. 'It's gum. Still soft too, so it's recent.'

'Get it over to forensics,' Graveney said. 'See if it matches with either Jennifer Hewitson or Joseph Purdey.'

'Is there anything else you want me to do?' Cooke said.

'Round up the other guys,' Robertson said. 'Knock on doors and see if anyone saw a van or anything. A make and colour would be good.'

Graveney closed the door to his flat behind him and tossed his house and car keys onto the table. He yawned, stretched and rubbed at the knot on the back of his neck. He was tired. All he wanted was a shower and his bed. A sharp pain shot across his temple, causing him to wince. The dagger-like prick quickly receding into a dull ache. Graveney plodded his way into the kitchen and eased off his jacket. The need for a drink outweighing anything else.

He slumped into the armchair, clutching the quarter-full bottle in his hand. Closing his eyes, he leant back his head as tiredness pulled at his eyelids. The bell to his flat sounded. Graveney opened his eyes and groaned, casting a glance towards the clock on the wall. Hauling himself from the seat, he trudged into the hall and pulled open the door. A smiling Liz stood outside.

'Hi, stranger,' she said.

Graveney stepped forward and hugged her. 'What are you doing here?' He moved aside and beckoned her in.

'I was worried about you.' She carried on through into the kitchen as Graveney followed. 'I've a bit of business I need to be over here for. I thought I'd kill two birds with one stone.'

'I was having a nightcap,' Graveney said. 'Will you join me?'

'A small one, Peter. I'm driving.'

Graveney collected two glasses and a new bottle from the cupboard. He handed Liz the empty glass and tilted the bottle over the top, slowly pouring a small amount inside. 'It's great to see you.'

Liz perched on a stool. 'Come on then.' She took a sip of her drink and raised her brow. 'Tell me all about it.'

'What's to tell? I'm living in a flat again.'

'You and Heather. There's no chance …?'

Graveney slumped onto a stool opposite. 'I don't know. I texted her last week and she ignored it.'

'She may not have seen it.'

Graveney smiled. 'Nice try, Liz.'

'The other woman?'

'She's unimportant.' Graveney looked up and shook his head. 'It's complicated.'

'What about Louisa?'

'She's still mad at me, but we've arranged to meet up for a coffee tomorrow. Louisa and Heather are close.'

Liz placed a hand on his arm. 'But you and her—?'

'She'll come around, I'm sure.' He took a sip of his drink. 'Listen.' He hopped from his stool. 'Why don't you stay the night. I'll sleep on the sofa. You can have—'

'I've met someone … back in Spain.'

A frown appeared on Graveney's face. 'I see.' He quickly painted on a smile. 'Great. Has he a name, this paramour?'

'Bernie.'

'English?'

'Irish.' She said. 'He works at my bar. He's …' She paused. '… He lost his wife and packed his job in, booked a flight and jumped on a plane.'

Graveney patted her arm. 'Good for you.'

'He's special. So gentle.' Liz's eyes filled with tears. 'I …'

'Love him?'

'Yes, I think I do.'

'Well if anyone deserves happiness, you do.'

'So, you see why I can't—?'

'I do. You don't have to explain. You don't need to rush off, do you?'

Liz smiled tightly. 'I suppose I could get a taxi back to the hotel and pick my car up in the morning.'

'I could drop it off for you. Leave me the keys.' Liz fished inside her handbag and pulled them out.

'Leave them on the table. I'll get a quick shower, and then you can tell me all about your bar ... And *Bernie.*'

Louisa pulled her car into a parking spot behind the back of Graveney's flat. She snatched her phone from the dashboard and gulped in a deep breath. Still annoyed at her dad but it had tempered into something more comfortable to cope with, rather than the way she felt when Heather told her of his infidelity. She loved him. For a long time, he had been her world, but she felt so disappointed with him, not least for the massive upheaval he had caused. She had arranged to meet him the next day for a coffee but decided to visit first, not wanting an argument with him in public. Heather appeared to have taken it in her stride, had been stoic even. But Louisa suspected she was donning her brave face and in reality, was devastated. Louisa stepped from the car and checked her mobile, pausing as a familiar woman headed towards the flats carrying a bag. She almost shouted, but stopped herself as the woman pressed the bell on Graveney's door. Louisa opened her car and slid inside unnoticed by Bev, who waited for the door to be answered.

Liz heard the bell sound and as Graveney was still showering, answered it. Bev stood outside glancing nervously left and right.

Liz smiled. Bev stared at her as the silence crawled by.

'Can I help you?' Liz said.

'I ... I was looking for Peter.' Bev glanced beyond Liz, along the hall.

'He's in the shower. I'll give him a shout?'

Bev glanced left and right, looking desperately for a means of escape. '... No ... that's fine ... I'll ...'

Graveney came out of the bathroom wearing a pair of jogging bottoms and a t-shirt. He glanced along the hallway and spotting Bev beyond Liz, stopped open-mouthed.

'Bev?' he said, but as he moved along the corridor she strode off.

He raced outside and caught up with her. 'Bev. Where are you going?' He grabbed her arm and turned her around.

She glanced back at the flat. Liz had closed the door now. 'Sorry to bother you. I didn't know—'

Graveney looked back towards the building. 'Liz is just a friend. She's popped over from Spain—'

'I should never have come.'

'It's not how it looks.'

'And how does it look, Peter?'

Graveney deciphered the emotions which flooded her features. Anger, resentment and disappointment. 'I forgot you were coming.'

'Obviously I'm not as important as your friend.' She closed her eyes and brought a hand to her mouth.

'Don't be stupid,' he said. 'She called around unannounced.'

Bev thrust the carrier towards Graveney. 'There's a bottle of wine here. Enjoy!' She spun on her heels and raced back towards her car. Graveney chased after her but faltered, as if knowing the futility of the situation. He looked on helplessly as the car roared into life and screeched past him, tears cascading down Bev's face the final view he had of her. He threw up his hands and stomped back inside, slamming the door behind him.

'I take it me being here was bad timing?' Liz said

Graveney shook his head. 'No. It's not your fault.'

'Do you want to talk?'

Graveney banged the bottle down and looked at her. 'No, I want a bloody drink.'

Louisa popped up from her hiding place below the dashboard. She stared towards the flat and brought her fist down onto the steering wheel. 'Bastard,' she said to herself. 'How could he?'

She put the car in gear and sped off, her feelings for her father somewhere between hatred and volcanic.

Liz stared at the unconscious form of Graveney. He had hit the bottle with total abandon and passed out around eleven. He told her everything about Bev and Aimee, about Maddie and his therapist. Liz listened as he spewed forth his inner thoughts. But the thing that shocked her most was the graphic detail he laid bare regarding him and Stephanie Marne. She had never suspected. Part of her felt betrayed, although there wasn't an exclusivity when she had been with Peter, but she had no idea the depth of his deception. Now a loathing for him washed over her. The Peter Graveney she thought she knew didn't exist. Yet still there remained an affection for him. Liz shook her head, at odds with her feelings. Her phone beeped, indicating her taxi had arrived. Liz pulled her gaze away from him, and left.

CHAPTER THIRTY-TWO

Graveney was dragged from his slumber by the doorbell ringing. He hauled himself to his feet and trudged into the hall. A delivery man stood outside.

'Hi there,' he said, pleasantly. 'I've got a package for your neighbour next door, and—'

'Yeah.' Graveney yawned. 'You can leave it here.'

The deliveryman handed the parcel to him, smiled and disappeared. Graveney grunted and tossed the package onto the hall table. He headed into the kitchen and downed a large glass of juice and two paracetamols.

After showering and changing he forced a small amount of breakfast inside him. Reaching the door, he groaned as he remembered Liz's car parked outside. Quickly retrieving the keys, he jumped into her car and headed off.

He reached the hotel and raced inside. The receptionist smiled as he approached.

'Morning, Sir,' she said.

'Can I leave these keys here? They're for a friend of mine. She's in room 212.'

'Yes of course.' The receptionist took the keys from him and deposited them in a pigeonhole behind her. 'No problem, Sir. Anything else I—?'

'No, thanks,' Graveney said. Once back outside he took out his mobile and phoned Louisa. It went straight to answerphone. He searched his contacts and texted Bev. 'Can we talk?' he typed.

His mobile sounded. 'Hi, Neil.'

'Do you want a lift in?' Robertson said.

'Can you pick me up from The Golden Lion hotel?'

'Yeah, sure. Now?'

'Anytime you're ready.'

He phoned Liz. 'Hi,' she said.

'Sorry about last night. I hope I wasn't a pain?'

'No. I'm on my way back later today, so probably won't have time to pop around again.'

'That's ok,' Graveney said. 'I've got a bit on myself. Maybe when you're next over?'

'Yeah. I hope you sort yourself out.'

Graveney grunted. 'Yeah. I'm my own worst enemy.'

'Good luck, Peter.'

'Are we still good, Liz?'

'Of course. You've left the car?'

'Yeah. The keys are in reception.'

'Thanks for that. Look after yourself, Peter.'

'I will.' They hung up, and Graveney viewed the phone. There was a certain finality to their conversation. A feeling the relationship they had was somehow tarnished. He exhaled and walked to the entrance to the hotel. He slumped onto the wall outside and checked his phone. There weren't any messages. He rubbed at his eyes as the headache he'd had since he woke moved up a notch. When he opened them, Marne stood next to him.

She sneered. 'Look at the state of you, Peter. Getting pissed on a school night.'

Graveney ignored the gibe and stared across the road. Marne lowered her mouth to his ear. 'What did you say to Liz last night? And Bev? How are you going to sort that out? What a mess your life is, Peter. What a complete shit storm. Forget about them. Concentrate on the case. Lindsey's phone. Use it against her.'

Graveney stood as Robertson's car pulled up near to him. 'The women in your life hate you,' Marne said, as he slid inside next to Robertson.

Robertson pulled the car to a halt outside Lindsey's house. Graveney snatched up her mobile and house keys before climbing out. Robertson followed him up the drive, stopping at the front door.

Taffy slid to a halt fifty metres from Lindsey's house and switched off the engine. He glanced across at Slim. 'Graveney and Robertson are here.'

'Coppers?' Chubby said, as he leant forward from the back seat.

'Yeah.'

'What do we do?' Slim said.

'We wait while I phone Conrad.'

Hudson chatted with Harry in his office when someone tapped on the door. A woman entered and rushed across to his desk. 'I'm sorry to—' She turned as two men came after her. 'These men just—'

'It's ok. I'll deal with them.'

The woman glared at the men and made her way out.

'Scott,' Hudson said. 'And to what do I owe this visit?'

'You know damn well, Hudson. You got someone to plant coke on my premises and then phoned the police.'

'Have a seat, boys,' Hudson said. 'Harry ...' He glanced to his right. 'Get Mr Macintyre and his friend a drink, will you?'

'I haven't come here to socialise,' Macintyre said. 'I came here for answers.'

'Very well,' Hudson said. 'Cards on the table. I did have the coke planted. It was to teach you a lesson.'

Macintyre's jaw dropped open. 'A lesson. For what?'

'You know what.'

'I don't know—'

'You had someone take photos at my factory.'

Macintyre glanced at his friend. 'What's he on about?' he said.

The man shrugged. 'Don't know, Scott.'

Hudson sneered. 'Of course you know. One of your guys paid someone to take pictures. We caught him.'

'I haven't a clue—'

Hudson stood. 'Don't give me that, Macintyre.'

'Why would I do that?' Macintyre said.

'Because you're trying to muscle in. You think you can move in on my patch. You're getting too big for your boots.'

Macintyre slowly shook his head. 'You're losing it, Hudson.' He nudged his friend. 'Come on.' He stopped and faced Hudson again. 'You haven't heard the last of this. Maybe you're not as strong as you think, Conrad. You've lost a few of your boys. The way I heard it, someone's picking you off one at a time.'

Hudson snarled. 'You'll never be man enough. I'll fucking crush you.'

Macintyre sneered, and slowly ran a finger from his neck to his groin. 'Way I heard it, Conrad, your boys were butchered like pigs. I look forward to the same happening to you.'

Hudson made a lunge for Macintyre, but Harry grabbed hold of him. 'He's not worth it, Conrad.'

Macintyre nudged his friend again and hurried off.

Hudson slumped back into his chair. 'Get me a drink, Harry.'

Harry filled a tumbler and handed it to him. Hudson shakily held the glass and drank greedily from it.

'What do you want to do?' Harry said.

'I want that bastard dead.'

'What about Taffy?'

'Taffy?'

'Yeah. Won't he try and talk you out of it?'

Hudson drained his glass and banged it down. He stared up at Harry. 'Taffy doesn't need to know.'

Harry smiled to himself. 'You're the boss.'

Jimmy showed Graveney and Robertson through into the lounge. Lindsey remained motionless as they entered.

'Have a seat,' Jimmy said.

'This is only a short visit,' Graveney said. He reached into his pocket, took out the keys and phone, and placed them onto the coffee table in front of Lindsey. 'Your friend's gone from the house.'

Lindsey glared at him. 'And?'

'Nothing,' Graveney said. 'One of the numbers you have stored on your phone?'

Lindsey gazed back at the floor. 'Which number?'

'Pizza.'

'It's a number for the local pizza shop I use.'

'Which one?' Robertson said.

'Around the corner from Mam and Dads' house.'

'Ok,' Graveney said. 'If Jennifer Hewitson gets in touch?'

Lindsey looked up again and stared at him. 'You'll be the first I ring, Inspector.'

'We'll see ourselves out,' Graveney said.

Jimmy perched on the edge of the armchair and put his arm around Lindsey. 'You ok?' he said.

Lindsey glanced up at him. 'Yeah. Fine.'

Graveney and Robertson climbed into the car.

'What do you think?' Robertson said.

'She's lying. The pizza shop near her parents' house was shut ages ago.'

Robertson rubbed his chin. 'Right. And you think it's Jennifer Hewitson's number …?'

'Yeah.'

Robertson frowned. 'Then why give her the phone back?'

'DS Cooke tried ringing the pizza shop number. But no one picked up. Maybe she knows it wasn't Armstrong ringing.'

'How?'

'Not sure. But I bet she's going to get in touch with her now.'

'Then?' Robertson said.

'We take the phone off her again, and see what pattern she used. Did she ring twice, for instance, or send a text?'

'How long are you going to give her?'

Graveney glanced at the clock on the dashboard. 'The time it takes to grab a cup of coffee.'

Robertson chuckled. 'I know a cracking little coffee shop.'

Harry slipped his way along the corridor. He paused at the door, glanced both ways and entered the toilet cubicle. He took out his phone and searched his contacts. Finding the name, he dialled.

'Hi,' Jen said.

'I haven't got long,' he said. 'Hudson knows about Lindsey. He knows you were inside together, and also you were staying at her parents' house.'

'Shit. What's he going to do?'

'He's got some lads there now. He plans to abduct her.'

'Jesus, Harry. Lindsey wasn't supposed to—'

'I know, but she is. Can you ring and warn her?'

Jen blew out hard. 'I think the police or someone else has her phone.'

'Can you and Joey get around there?'

'Yeah. We'll go now.'

'They're in a black Mercedes. Keep me informed.'

Jen raced from the cottage and over to the van. Joey spun around on hearing her footsteps.

'We need to go, Joey. Lindsey's in danger.'

'What will I need?' he said.

'There could be a few of them.'

'I'll be two minutes.'

Slim glanced across at Taffy. 'How long do we wait?'

Taffy continued to stare across the road at Lindsey's house. 'We'll wait until she leaves the house, or it gets dark. We don't want every Tom, Dick and Harry seeing us.'

Jimmy emerged from the house and set off up the street.

'That must be her fella,' Chubby said, nodding towards Jimmy.

'It'll be easier if he's not around,' Slim said.

Taffy rubbed his chin. 'Yeah.'

Jen grabbed for her phone in her pocket as it vibrated. She read the message. 'It's from Lindsey.'

Joey glanced across from the driving seat. 'Are you sure?'

'Yeah. She should phone any second.' The mobile rang.

'Hi,' Jen said.

'The police have been here,' Lindsey said. 'They've been over to my mam and dads'. I couldn't phone to warn you because they had my mobile.'

'It doesn't matter, Linds. We've moved out and found somewhere else.'

'Good. I was—'

'Listen, Linds. You're in danger.'

'Danger?'

'Yeah. Conrad Hudson is sending some men to pick you up. He knows we were in Durham together.'

'What does he want with me, though?'

Jen sucked in a lungful of air. 'I don't know, but Hudson's a bad bastard. If he thinks you know where I am ...'

Lindsey raced across to the window and glanced up and down the street. 'I can't see anyone.' She edged back across the room and perched on the edge of an armchair.

'Me and Joey are on our way across to you now. Stay inside, and don't answer the door to anyone.'

'Ok,' Lindsey said.

'What about your fella?'

'He's popped to the shop to get some milk.'

'Does he know about us?'

Lindsey shuffled her feet. 'Most of it. I've told him the police are just following up leads. He knows I ran into you, but he knows nothing about the house.'

'It might be best if you kept it that way. See you in five minutes.'

Lindsey hung up and put the phone on the coffee table. The doorbell sounded. She gulped and crept towards the door and glanced through the glass panel. Two figures stood outside. Searching for a makeshift weapon, she picked up a heavy-based lamp from the hall table as the doorbell chimed again.

'Lindsey,' Graveney said through the letterbox. 'It's the police.'

Lindsey let go of the lungful of air she'd been holding onto, returned the lamp and headed for the door. Graveney and Robertson stood outside as she opened it.

'We need another chat,' Graveney said.

'... Yes ... of course.'

'You ok, Lindsey?' Graveney said.

'I'm fine.' She moved out of the way to allow the officers inside. Graveney and Robertson ambled into the lounge.

'What is it you want?'

Graveney plucked the mobile from the coffee table. 'This.'

She dropped into an armchair. Graveney opened the phone and found the last person Lindsey had contacted. He turned the phone screen around to face her. 'You sent a message five minutes ago to *pizza*.' He smiled. 'Oh, and look here. You phoned the shop, too.

Lindsey folded her arms and stared at Graveney. 'I fancied a margarita.'

'Where's Jimmy?' Graveney said.

'He's gone for milk.'

'I think you'd better write him a note,' Graveney said. 'We're going on a trip to the station.'

Graveney and Robertson led Lindsey from her house and into the car, while Taffy, Slim and Chubby watched from up the road.

'That's screwed it up,' Taffy said.

Slim leant forward. 'What do we do?'

'I'll phone Conrad.' He pulled out his phone and dialled.

'Yeah, Taffy.'

'Graveney and Robertson have taken Lindsey Armstrong into custody.'

'When?'

'Just now, Boss.'

'She must know something. We need her to use as a trap to catch the other two. But while she's in police custody ...'

Taffy glanced to his left as Jimmy walked along the road towards his house. 'Leave it with me, Boss. I may have another solution.'

'Ok. Keep me informed.'

Chubby leant forward. 'What are you planning, Taffy?'

'Lindsey Armstrong's boyfriend.' He pointed across the road as Jimmy disappeared inside. 'If we can get him it might make her play ball.'

'But she's at the police station,' Slim said.

'She'll probably get bailed. I'll see if I can find out why she's there. If and when she gets released, we get her to come to us.'

'It's a bit risky taking him in broad daylight,' Chubby said.

'We'll wait until it's dark.'

'So, we sit tight then?' Slim said.

'Yeah.' He leant back in his seat. 'We sit tight.'

CHAPTER THIRTY-THREE

Joey brought the van to a stop a hundred metres away from Taffy's car, and out of sight of their vehicle.

Jen peered up the road. 'That's their car.'

'It doesn't look as if they've got her yet,' Joey said.

'We'll wait.'

Graveney and Robertson sat opposite Lindsey and her solicitor. Graveney went through the routine with the tape recorder.

He folded his hands together and looked across at Lindsey. 'Can I remind you, Lindsey, you are still under caution. Do you understand?'

'Yes.'

Graveney placed Lindsey's phone in the middle of the table. 'Do you recognise this?' he said. 'For the record, DI Graveney has placed a mobile phone on the table.'

'It's my mobile.'

'One of the numbers on your phone has a contact name of *pizza*. Is that right?'

'Yes.'

'Whose number is it?' Graveney said.

'Jen Hewitson's.'

Robertson leant closer. 'Yet, earlier today you claimed the number was for a pizza shop.'

'I did.'

'Why did you lie to us, Lindsey?' Robertson said.

'I don't know. I just did.'

'You are aware Jennifer Hewitson is wanted in connection with a number of murders?' Robertson said.

'I wasn't then, but I am now.'

Robertson glanced across at Graveney, who scoffed.

'I think we all know you knew,' Graveney said.

The solicitor leant forward. 'I've spoken with my client, Inspector. She's aware she acted foolishly previously. However, she is prepared to help in any way she can.' He looked towards Lindsey, who nodded.

'Ok,' Graveney said. 'We'd like you to contact Jennifer Hewitson.'

Lindsey inhaled. 'How do you normally contact her?' Robertson said.

She let out her breath. 'I send her a text message, and then phone.'

'Why do you send her text messages?' Robertson said.

'So, she knows it's me. When she sees the message from me, she expects me to phone soon after.'

'We want you to send her a text,' Graveney said. 'Then phone her and arrange a meeting.'

Lindsey glanced at her solicitor. 'Ok.'

Graveney picked up the phone and handed it to Lindsey. 'Send exactly the same text as before,' he said.

Lindsey typed the words *ten-inch margarita* and pressed send.

'How long do you wait?' Robertson said.

'About a minute.' Lindsey waited and watched the second hand on the clock on the wall complete one minute, then dialled. She listened as it rang for a few moments and then went to answerphone.

'She's not answering,' Lindsey said.

Graveney glanced across at Robertson and frowned. 'Why isn't she answering?'

Lindsey shrugged. 'I don't know. Maybe she knows I've been arrested.'

'Try again,' Graveney said.

Lindsey dialled a second time. She waited then hung up. 'Answerphone.'

Graveney fixed her with a stare. 'Are you sure you've done it right?'

'Of course I'm sure. I—'

'Inspector,' the solicitor said. 'My client has been extremely helpful.'

'Ring again,' Graveney said. 'Leave her a message asking her to get in touch, urgently.'

Lindsey paused and dialled again. '... Hi, Jen, it's Lindsey. Can you ring me back? It's urgent.' She hung up and held the phone out to Graveney.

Graveney shook his head. 'We wait.'

Jen and Joey, outside Lindsey's, watched Hudson's men parked up the road. Her phone sounded, and she studied it. 'She's left a message.' Jen listened to the recording. 'She says she needs to speak. Said it's urgent.'

'Are you sure about the text?'

'She typed ten-inch margarita. Which was the text last time. The text this time should have been twelve-inch margarita. It's what we agreed.'

'A mistake?' Joey said.

'Lindsey wouldn't make a mistake.'

Joey glanced along the road. 'It can't be Hudson's men who have her, they wouldn't still be here. Are you sure it's their car?'

'I'm sure.' Jen's eyes widened. 'The police. Maybe it's the police who have her.'

'You think the coppers are in there?' Fixing his gaze on the property, he looked at Jen. She narrowed her eyes.

Jimmy came bounding out of the door. He jumped into his car and roared off.

'That's Lindsey's boyfriend,' Jen said.

'Shall I follow?'

'Wait,' Jen said, motioning towards the Mercedes which set off after Jimmy. 'Follow Hudson's men.'

Robertson glanced at his watch. He looked at Graveney. 'I don't think she's going to ring.'

'No,' Graveney said, his eyes fixed on Lindsey.

Robertson motioned towards the door and stood. Graveney followed him, as the two of them headed outside.

'We can't hold her indefinitely,' Robertson said.

'No. She's still holding out on us, I'm sure.'

'On the face of it ...' He blew out his cheeks. '... It looks as if she's helped us. The chief will see it like that.'

'We let her go?' Graveney said.

Robertson shrugged. 'I think we have to.'

Graveney sagged and trudged back into the interview room, followed by Robertson.

'We're releasing you on police bail, Lindsey. If Jennifer Hewitson gets in touch with you—'

Lindsey waved a dismissive hand. 'I know.'

'Can we remind you,' Robertson said. He glanced towards Lindsey's solicitor. 'That preventing us from—'

'I know. I understand what you're saying. If she gets in contact, I'll let you know.'

'I think Lindsey's been helpful so far, gentleman,' the solicitor said. 'I'll discuss the legal implications with my client.'

Graveney gathered his notes together. 'Ok.' He plucked the phone from the desk. 'We'll keep this for the time being.' He held the mobile aloft and marched off.

'I'll get one of the officers to show you out,' Robertson said, following after Graveney

Robertson caught Graveney up and took hold of his arm. 'What do you think?'

Graveney stopped. 'Hewitson knew it wasn't Armstrong phoning her, somehow.'

'How can you be sure?'

Graveney half-smiled. 'Her face betrayed her.'

Lindsey entered the reception of the police station. She bounded outside, flagged down a passing taxi and jumped in. Jimmy, who'd been in the bathroom, came out. He wandered across to a seat and slumped down. The desk sergeant came out of the office behind his desk and looked across at Jimmy.

'You still here?' he said.

'I'm waiting for my girlfriend?'

'She left a couple of minutes ago.'

'Are you sure?' Jimmy said.

'Of course I'm sure.'

Jimmy jumped to his feet and raced outside. He hurried across the road and climbed into his car. He fumbled for his mobile and dialled Lindsey.

Graveney opened the drawer to his desk and glanced at the name on the screen, 'Jimmy.' He slammed the drawer shut.

Taffy reached the Mercedes and spotting Chubby asleep in the driver's seat, banged on the window. Chubby jumped to attention as Taffy slid in beside him. 'Where's Slim?' Taffy said.

'He's popped over the road for some food.'

'I hope you haven't missed the boyfriend,' Taffy said.

'He's still inside the police station. I'm sure of it. His cars over there,' he said, nodding towards Jimmy's vehicle.

Taffy scowled at him. 'Phone Slim and tell him to get his arse here.'

The rear door opened and Slim jumped in. Taffy spun around in his seat and stared at him. 'Who told you to disappear?'

'No one, Taffy. I thought—'

'I don't care what you thought. You two better buck up your ideas. Conrad's not keen on either of you. I've gone out on a limb here. If you two let me down …' He glared at each in turn.

Jimmy phoned the house again. No one answered. He hung up in frustration. His mobile sounded.

'Hello,' he said.

'Hi, Jimmy,' Lindsey said.

'Where's your phone?'

'I had to get another one. The police kept mine.'

'I was at the station,' Jimmy said. 'I must have missed you when you came out.'

'Sorry,' she said. 'The police wanted to ask me some more questions.'

'What about?'

'Jen Hewitson,' Lindsey said.

'The woman you were inside with?'

'Yeah. They want her in connection with some murders.'

'What murders?'

Lindsey glanced outside of the front window, glancing up and down the street. 'This is not the best time to talk, Jimmy.'

He groaned. 'What murders?'

'Conrad Hudson's men.'

'Jesus, Lindsey.'

Jimmy started up his car. 'So, this questioning is just routine?'

Lindsey closed her eyes. 'Not exactly. I let her stay at Mam and Dad's house. She said she needed a place for a while.'

'What is she doing in Middlesbrough? What's her connection to Conrad Hudson?'

'I'm at Mam and Dad's.'

'Why?'

'I'll tell you everything when you get here.'

'I'm on my way.'

'Get some wine,' she said. 'I need a drink.'

The men in the Mercedes watched as Jimmy's car drove off. Taffy slapped the side of Chubby's head with the heal of his hand. 'I thought you said he was still inside?'

Chubby lowered his head. 'Sorry, Taffy.'

Taffy glared at him. 'Follow his car, you idiot.' The Mercedes started and set off after it.

Jen and Joey pulled up outside Lindsey's mam and dad's house.

'What do we do?' Joey said.

'You wait here. Watch for Hudson's men.' Jen picked up her pistol and pushed it inside her coat pocket.

'I'm pretty sure we weren't followed.'

'I know,' Jen said. 'Strange that. Maybe they were spooked by the police.'

'Be careful.'

Jen leant across and kissed him on the lips. 'Don't worry, I'll be fine. Keep your eyes open.' Joey nodded. She picked up a piece of paper and scribbled on it, folded it up, kissed Joey again, and jumped out of the vehicle.

Lindsey paced the length of the living room, waiting for Jimmy. She paused as she heard something pushed through the letterbox. Glancing into the hall, she spotted the paper on the floor and crept over to it. Lindsey looked through the glass in the door, trying to decipher if anyone was outside. No one was there. Bending down, she snatched up the paper, read it and smiled to herself. Quickly locating the back-door key, she opened the door and hurried outside. On reaching the gate, she threw back the bolt, opening it a small amount. A smiling Jen stood there.

Jen glanced up and down the alleyway. 'Well?' Turning back to face Lindsey. 'Are you going to let me in?'

Lindsey beckoned her friend inside and locked the gate behind her. She turned and threw her arms around her friend.

'Mother Maggie?' Lindsey said, holding up the paper.

'I wanted you to be sure it was me. Inside, Maggie was like a mother to both of us.'

'She was.' Lindsey smiled. 'Are we ok here?'

Jen rubbed her face. 'Not sure. Joey's outside keeping watch. He'll phone if anyone turns up.'

'How did you—?'

'We followed you from the police station. Hudson's men were there as well. We weren't followed here though. Not quite sure why not.'

Lindsey headed indoors with Jen in hot pursuit. 'Could they have missed me?' Lindsey said.

Jen briefly placed a finger on her lips. 'Maybe. Either way, we need to get you away from here.'

'Jimmy's on his way over. I'll have to wait for him.'

'Phone him en route. We can't risk staying here. They may be getting more men. We need to go now.' Jen stepped forward and placed a hand on Lindsey's arm.

Lindsey's head dropped. 'Where will I go?'

'You can stay with us. They need you to get to Joey and me.'

Lindsey frowned. 'Ok.'

'Lock up, and we'll go out the back. Joey's waiting at the far end of the alley.' Jen put her hand inside her pocket and pulled out a key with a small keyring attached. 'The key to the house. I forgot to give you it back.'

Lindsey examined the familiar key, but with an unfamiliar keyring. Jen held the keyring up. 'I put this on. Look after it.'

'What is it?'

'Just look after it.'

Lindsey plucked it from her and followed Jen through into the kitchen. They stepped outside, and Jen raced towards the gate as Lindsey locked the back door and hurried to join her friend.

'What now?' Lindsey said.

Jen took out her mobile and dialled. 'I'll phone Joey.' The pair waited.

'Hi,' Joey said.

'Is the coast clear?'

'Yeah. There's no sign of them.'

'We're coming along the alley. Open the side door so we can get in.'

'Will do.'

Jen glanced at Lindsey and took in a deep breath. 'Ready?' Jen said. Lindsey nodded, and the pair made their way into the alley. They raced along its length and stopped at the large gate barring their exit. Lindsey fumbled for the key and clumsily tried to insert it into the lock. Jen took hold of her hand and then the key, quickly pushing it home. The gate opened with a large creak and the two of them stepped outside. Joey's van stood parked beyond the gate with the side door open. Jen raced to the end of the alley and looked both ways. A woman walking a dog ambled along the road, but apart from that, nothing stirred. Jen gently nudged Lindsey who jumped inside the back of the van, closely followed by Jen.

Jen perched up behind Joey's seat and placed her hand on his shoulder. 'Back to the cottage,' she said.

Joey started up the engine and slowly turned into the road and along the street. He reached the junction, glanced both ways and pulled out accelerating along the road, through lights and finally joined the dual carriageway.

Jen patted him on the shoulder. 'No one's following.'

'Should I phone Jimmy?' Lindsey said.

'Yeah,' Jen said. 'Lindsey this is Joey. Joey, Lindsey.'

The pair smiled at each other. Lindsey reached into her pocket for her phone and called Jimmy.

'Hi,' Jimmy said.

'Where are you?'

'I've just pulled up at your mam and dad's house.'

'I'm not there. Go home and I'll call shortly.'

'Why?' Where are you?'

'I can't explain now. I'll phone soon. Don't worry, I'm safe.'

'Ok. Love you.'

'Love you too,' Lindsey said. She hung up and looked at Jen. 'Where are we going?'

'We've rented a cottage outside of Yarm. We're going there.'

Jimmy pushed his mobile back into his pocket and started the engine. The back door to the vehicle opened, and Taffy climbed inside.

A startled Jimmy swivelled to face him. 'What the—?' He stared at the gun Taffy held.

'If you want to see tomorrow,' Taffy said, 'do as I say.'

Joey pulled the van up at the cottage, the three alighted from the vehicle and headed inside.

'I'll rustle up some drinks,' Jen said. 'Have a seat.'

Lindsey eased into a chair and pulled out her mobile. 'I'll give Jimmy a ring.'

'You do that.' Jen patted Joey on the back. 'Hide the van out of sight. In case anyone clocked us.'

Jen busied herself in the kitchen, making tea for the three of them. She turned around as Lindsey entered and held out a steaming mug.

'They've got Jimmy,' Lindsey said.

Jen put the mug aside. 'Who?'

'He said he'd kill him if I phone the police or told anyone else.'

Jen stepped forward and placed her hands on either side of Lindsey's arms. 'Did he say who he was?'

Lindsey shook her head and slumped into a chair. 'No. He wants me to meet him.'

Jen moved next to Lindsey. 'It must be Hudson's men. They're trying to get to Joey and me.'

Lindsey stared at her friend. 'What do we do?'

'Did they mention us?'

Lindsey shook her head again. 'No.'

Both women turned as Joey entered. 'I've hidden it out back,' he said. He scrutinised the two women. 'What's up?'

Jen jumped to her feet. 'We have a problem. Hudson's men snatched Lindsey's boyfriend.'

Joey stepped closer to Lindsey. 'We'll get him back.'

'Where did they say you had to meet?' Jen said.

Lindsey rubbed her eyes. 'He told me he would text.'

'Good,' Jen said. 'They might not know you're with us. And if not ...' She sat back down. '... we'll have the element of surprise.'

'What should I get?' Joey said.

'Everything. It's time to sort these bastards out, once and for all.'

CHAPTER THIRTY-FOUR

1999 – Amanda, and a group of other young women, followed Colin inside the house. He led them through a series of doors, stopped and turned to face them.

'Most of you know the score. For those that don't, Trisha …' He placed his hand on the arm of a middle-aged woman who appeared at his side. '… will help with make-up and clothes.'

'I've brought my own things,' a blonde woman next to Amanda said.

'You wear what we give you,' Colin said. 'Mr Hudson is particular on this.' Colin wandered across to a table in the corner and picked up a masquerade mask. 'You wear these at all times. Do you understand?'

The women looked at each other and nodded. 'Good,' Colin said. 'One last thing …' He paused for effect. 'You'll be getting well paid for tonight. Mr Hudson values discretion. Nothing of what you see or hear leaves this house. Is this understood?'

Again, the woman nodded. 'If any of you don't adhere to this …' He stepped closer and viewed the women one by one. '… you will regret it.' He smiled. 'Have a good time. But most importantly, make sure our guests have a good time. If any of the guests get a little too loud or aggressive, let me or one of Mr Hudson's men know.'

The women chatted amongst themselves, and Colin made his way over to Amanda. 'A word.'

Amanda followed him outside and into another room. He stopped and faced her. 'How are you?' he said.

Amanda glanced around the opulent room. 'I'm good, Colin.'

'Are you sure about this?'

'About what?'

Colin rubbed his chin. 'What Alex wants you to do.'

'He said it'd be ok.'

Colin stepped closer and placed a hand on her arm. 'You're better than this, Amanda. What Alex wants you to do is dangerous. If Conrad finds out—'

'But Alex loves me. He's promised to take me to America.'

Colin sneered. 'He doesn't love you. If he did, he wouldn't be asking you to do this. You must see that?'

Amanda smiled. 'You don't understand what we have. Alex loves me. I'll be fine, Colin.'

Colin took hold of her hand in his. 'Please be careful. For me.'

She smiled again. 'I will.'

He stepped back from her and put a hand inside his pocket. He pulled out a Dictaphone and held it out to her. 'I've got this. You press this button to begin recording.' She nodded. He continued. 'There's about half an hour of recording time. You must put it somewhere out of sight. Make sure he doesn't spot it.'

'What do I do with it after?' she said.

'Get it back to me. I'll make sure Alex gets it.'

'What about the man. How will I know who he is?'

'I'll identify him for you. His name's James Whittaker-Brown. Get yourself ready. I'll see you later.'

Conrad Hudson wandered around the palatial room, talking and shaking hands with guests. The young women mingled with older men. Some flirted and whispered into the ears of their partners. Occasional laughter filled the room. Uniformed waiters circulated, carrying drinks and canapes on trays. Hudson's men, dressed in black tie, stood at various entrances and exits around the room.

Hudson paused his conversation with a man. 'Excuse me,' he said, and wandered across the room, intercepting another man at the door. 'James,' Hudson said. 'So glad you could make it.'

'It looks a lively affair,' Whittaker-Brown said.

Hudson waved across a waiter, lifted a glass of champagne from the tray and handed it to his companion. 'All my parties are lively affairs.'

'That favour you wanted …?'

Hudson smiled. 'Yeah.'

'I may have a solution.'

Hudson ushered him into a corner. 'Tell me more.'

'The man we need on our side is Teddy Jennings.'

Hudson narrowed his eyes. 'Will he play ball?'

Whittaker-Brown chuckled. 'I've come by some information. Information which will encourage him to help us.'

'You have it?' Hudson said.

'It's yours for a price. You'll need to deal with him yourself. He sees me as a sort of confidante.' Whittaker-Brown took a swig of his drink.

'He's an idiot, though. I can nudge him in the right direction. Get him to do what you … what we want.'

'The consignments?' Hudson said.

'Teddy will wave them through. He has discretion on such matters.'

'Good. Your payment?'

'The usual, old-boy. My account in Switzerland.'

'I'll let you know when the money's there. In the meantime, enjoy the evening.'

'I will. The women …' He surveyed the room. '… Are they all fair game?'

Hudson laughed. 'Of course. Fill your boots. They've been vetted. They'll be discreet.'

Amanda glanced across as Colin came into the room. He looked back at her and paused next to Whittaker-Brown before walking on. Amanda made her way over to him.

'Hello,' she said.

Whittaker-Brown turned around. 'Hello yourself,' he said, looking Amanda up and down. 'What do they call you, then?'

'Amanda.'

'Would you like a drink, Amanda?'

She nodded. 'Yes, please.'

Whittaker-Brown stopped a passing waiter. 'Now,' he said, handing her the drink. 'What's a pretty little thing like you doing at a party like this?'

Billy Turner strode into the room and over to Hudson. 'Can I have a word, Conrad?'

Hudson glanced away and back to the man he was talking with. 'Sorry about this, I won't be a minute.' Hudson glared at Turner and motioned for him to follow him. 'This better be good, Billy. That's David Wainwright.'

'Sorry, Boss. It's just … Alex Cooper's here.'

'Cooper? What the hell does he want?'

'He said he wants a word with you,'

'Where is he?'

'I showed him into your study.'

'Right,' Hudson said. 'I suppose I need to have a word. Do me a favour, keep Whittaker-Brown happy. He's important to me.'

Turner followed Hudson's stare. 'Who's the little blonde with him?'

'No idea. Some new girl,' Hudson said.

'She seems familiar.'

'Yeah, well. As long as she puts a smile on his face, I don't care who she is. I'll be back shortly.'

Turner watched as Hudson left, then stared back across the room at Whittaker-Brown and the young woman with him. He furrowed his brow. Where had he seen her before? He pondered.

Hudson entered the room. Cooper relaxed in a leather, high backed chair with a large brandy in his hand, grinned.

Hudson eyed Cooper. 'To what do I owe this pleasure, Alex?'

Cooper held up his glass. 'I fixed myself a drink. You don't mind, do you?'

'No, not at all. I might join you.' Hudson poured himself a drink and positioned himself in a chair opposite Cooper. 'I thought we agreed, Alex. I thought we agreed, you and I would keep a low profile.'

Cooper waved a dismissive hand at Hudson. 'Don't worry, Conrad. No one knows I'm here. Only that big ape of yours.'

'What is it you want?'

Cooper smiled. 'A larger slice.'

'We discussed this. You do all right.'

'Was that Whittaker-Brown's vintage Jag I saw outside?'

Hudson took a long, large sip of his drink. 'There would be no point in me lying.'

'You have forgotten, Conrad? I was the one who put him your way. I did the legwork, and now you're going to reap the benefits.'

'Losing at the casino again, Alex?'

'I only want a fair share. You'd be nothing without my contacts. You'd still be scratching around, running that fleapit of a nightclub you used to own.'

Hudson ground his teeth. 'Anything else you need to get off your chest, Alex?'

'I know every little detail of your operation. When. Where. How.' He grinned at Hudson. 'That safe hidden behind the painting over there.' He stepped closer to the wall behind Hudson. 'I'm sure you have some spare cash. For emergencies.'

'If you spill the beans on me, Alex, you'll implicate yourself.'

'Who said anything about spilling the beans. I'm trying to negotiate a better deal for myself, that's all. It's business.'

Hudson stood and wandered across to the painting, pulling it from the wall revealing a safe behind it. He entered a code and opened the door. Inside, papers and bundles of notes half-filled the cavity. Hudson snatched two large wads and tossed them onto the table close by. 'There's a hundred-grand there. It's all you're getting. There won't be anymore.'

Cooper leapt to his feet and raced across, grabbing hold of the money. 'Cheers, Conrad.' He waved the notes in the air. 'You know it's the sensible thing to do.'

Hudson gritted his teeth and clenched his fists. 'You and I can still be good together,' Cooper said. 'I've other contacts.'

'As I said, Alex, that's your lot. I think you've had more than you deserve. *There won't be anymore*.'

Cooper grinned. 'We'll see. There's always more.' He turned.

Hudson snatched hold of a bronze statue from the table and brought it crashing onto Cooper's head. Cooper grunted and dropped to his knees before slumping forward onto his face. Hudson stepped closer and sneering brought his foot down hard on Cooper's head.

'You piece of shit,' he said, kicking and stamping until Cooper stopped moving. Hudson stepped back and viewed the carnage. Cooper lay motionless, his head surrounded by blood. Hudson blew out hard. Stepping over the body, he shakily picked up his half-full glass of brandy and threw the contents into his mouth. He paused to gather his thoughts, raced across to the door and locked it.

Taffy watched from the terrace as the last of the cars, dropping guests off, drew away from the house. His phoned sounded.

'Yes, Boss?' he said.

'I need you to come to my study. We've got a problem.'

Taffy closed the huge front door and hurried along the corridors. He stopped outside Hudson's study and knocked. The door was unlocked and opened a small amount before Hudson opened it fully and beckoned him inside.

'What's up?'

Hudson pointed across the room. Taffy edged closer and stopped a couple of metres from the body. 'Christ,' he said. 'What the—?'

'He was trying to put the squeeze on me. I just lost it.'

'Did anyone else see?'

'I don't think so.'

Taffy exhaled loudly. 'Is he dead?' Hudson shrugged. Taffy wandered across, knelt down, and then stood. 'We'll need to get the body out and dump it.'

Hudson gulped at his drink. 'He said no one knows he's here.'

Taffy stared at Hudson. 'He must have got here somehow.'

Hudson brought a hand up to his mouth. 'What if the lad he uses to drive brought him here?'

Taffy bent near to the body again and searched through his pockets. He held a set of car keys aloft. 'Looks as if he drove here.'

'His car,' Hudson said. 'Find his car.'

'I'll get the other boys to help.' Taffy removed his mobile and rang. 'You'd better get yourself cleaned up, Boss,' he said.

Hudson looked at his shoes, dried blood covering the top of them. 'I need to change and get rid of these clothes.'

'Billy,' Taffy said into his phone. 'Fetch Robbo and come to Conrad's study. We've got a situation.'

Cooper's body, wrapped in black plastic bags, lay on the floor of the study. Hudson, having changed and showered, sipped a large brandy. There was a tap on the door and Taffy opened it. Robbo and Billy slipped inside.

Billy tossed Taffy the set of car keys. 'We found Cooper's car. It was parked out of sight near the old cottage.'

'Good,' Taffy said. 'No one can see it from the road.'

Hudson looked up. 'Cooper said he'd been discreet.'

'We need to dump the body and car, Boss.' Taffy said.

Hudson stood. 'I've given it some thought.' He wandered across to the table and re-filled his glass. 'We need to distance ourselves from this.'

'It doesn't look as if anyone saw him here,' Billy said.

Hudson slumped back into his chair. 'He hinted at something.'

Taffy glanced at the others and then at Hudson. 'What?'

'I don't know. But he has something,' Hudson said.

'Are you sure you're—?' Taffy said.

'I'm certain. He was cocksure. Arrogant even. I gave him money tonight but when I told him there would be no more, his words were, "We'll see." He had something that gave him an air of confidence I haven't seen before.'

'What did you give him money for?' Taffy said.

Hudson sneered. 'He figured I owed him for putting Whittaker-Brown my way.'

'Could Whittaker-Brown be the leverage?' Robbo said.

Billy clicked his fingers. 'That's her.'

'Who?' Hudson said.

'I saw Whittaker-Brown with one of the girls tonight. Her face seemed familiar. I wracked my brains for ages. A pretty, young thing. It's just come to me. I saw her at the casino a few months ago ...'

'And?'

'She was with Cooper.'

Hudson stood. 'Are you sure?'

'Yeah. She's changed the colour of her hair to blonde. But it was definitely her.'

'And she's here tonight?' Taffy said.

Billy widened his eyes. 'Yeah.'

'Go and check if Whittaker-Brown's car is still outside,' Hudson said to Robbo.

Robbo slipped out through the door.

'What do we do?' Taffy said.

Hudson perched on the arm of the chair and took a sip of his drink. 'We need to clear up this mess. Put Cooper's body in the boot of his car first.'

Taffy rubbed his chin. 'We'll need to dump it.'

'I've got a better idea,' Hudson said. 'I'll get Sean Grant to do our dirty work.'

Taffy grimaced. 'Are you sure? Can we trust him?'

Hudson laughed. 'Of course not, he's an idiot. He's going to be our fall guy, though.'

'Bit risky, Boss.'

'Drive the car somewhere,' Hudson said. 'There's a hundred-grand I gave Cooper. I'll tell Sean Grant he can keep it. I never told you this, but Cooper has been embezzling money from the council. I've a friend who works there. He was keeping tabs on Cooper for me.'

'How come the missing money hasn't been noticed?' Taffy said.

'It was convenient for me to cover it up.'

'I'd have let the tosser get found out,' Billy said.

'I couldn't. He'd have sung like a canary. Even if I'd been able to talk myself out of it, mud sticks. It would have been too much grief.'

'And now?' Taffy said.

'Now it's convenient for that little secret to see the light of day. I'll make a call in the morning.'

There was a tap on the door and Robbo re-entered. 'Whittaker-Brown's car is still out front,' he said. 'I've checked around the grounds, and everything's quiet.'

'Good,' Hudson said. 'We wait until he's gone. Get the girl. I want to know if Cooper had her spying for him. She doesn't leave this house until we're sure she's not a plant.'

Taffy looked across at Robbo and Billy, and then back towards Hudson. 'We'll get Cooper's body in his car,' he said. 'That's the most important thing.

'I'll give Sean Grant a ring. Let's get this in motion.'

'What about Colin?' Taffy said.

Hudson's eyes widened. 'Ask him how the girl got in here?'

'We'll need to clean up this mess.' Taffy said, looking down at the large bloodstain on the carpet.

'Take the carpet up. I was thinking of redecorating this room.' He curled his lips. 'Stash the carpet in one of the outbuildings until Monday. We'll put it in the incinerator at the factory. Leave no stone unturned, boys. I want any trace of Cooper being here tonight, erased.'

Some of the guests left. Others, who had paired off with the women, headed for the bedrooms. Whittaker-Brown sat on the edge of the bed and pulled off his shoes. He leant across and filled two glasses from a bottle and handed one to Amanda.

'Are you ok?' he said. 'You seem a little nervous.'

'No … I'm fine.'

'Have a drink of wine and come and sit next to me.' He patted the bed.

'I need to go to the loo,' she said. 'I'll be two minutes.'

'Of course.' Standing, he undid his trousers and pulled them off. Folding them neatly, he draped them over the back of a chair. 'I'll be waiting for you.'

Amanda entered the en-suite and closed the door behind her, locking it. She walked across to the mirror, viewed her reflection and swallowed hard. Opening her handbag, she pulled out the Dictaphone and studied it. Satisfied she could work the device she undressed.

Amanda opened the bathroom door. Whittaker-Brown, propped up in bed, grinned at her. She stood, in black stockings and suspenders, smiling at him. 'Will I do?'

He licked his lips. 'Oh, yes.'

She placed her handbag, with the Dictaphone running, next to the bed and climbed in.

Taffy reached Cooper's car and stared down at the deflated front tyre. He cursed, opened the boot and rifled through it.

Ten minutes later, he slid to a halt outside the French windows.

'Where the hell have you been?' Billy said.

'The car had a flat. I had to change the wheel.' Taffy threw open the boot and glanced about as Billy and Robbo carried the package containing Cooper's body towards the vehicle. They heaved it inside, and Taffy pushed the boot shut.

'Take the car to where we agreed,' Taffy said. 'One of you drive, the other follow behind. Don't forget to put the money in the footwell. Then get back here as soon as possible.'

'I'll drive it,' Billy said. He pulled on his gloves and plucked the keys from Taffy. 'We'll be as quick as we can.'

Taffy trudged back inside and closed the doors behind him. He wandered over to the drinks table and poured himself a brandy.

Hudson came through the door. 'Everything all right?'

Taffy sucked in air. 'The car had a flat. I changed the wheel and the lads are dropping it off now.'

'Good,' Hudson said. 'I think I'll have one of those.' He nodded towards the glass in Taffy's hand.

'What about Sean Grant?' Taffy said.

'I'll ring him now.' Hudson searched his contacts and dialled. 'Sean. I need a favour. Do this right, and I'll look after you.'

'Yeah, of course,' Sean said.

'Are you alone?'

'Yeah.'

'Good,' Hudson said. 'I want you to pick up a car and get rid of something for me.'

'What something?'

'In the boot is something I want burying. Something that mustn't turn up in the future. Do you understand?'

'Absolutely.'

'Once you've got rid of the package, torch the car.'

'Ok,' Sean said.

'In the front of the car, in the footwell, you'll find a bag with money in it. The money's yours.'

'Thanks, Mr Hudson. I appreciate this. There's ...'

'There's what?' Hudson glanced at Taffy.

'We had a bit of bother tonight—'

'We?' Hudson said.

'I meant me. Craig ...'

'Alex's driver?'

'Yeah. We got into a bit of an argument over his girlfriend at his flat.'

'And ...?' Hudson said.

'He pulled a knife on me. We got into a fight. I think he may be dead.'

'For fuck's sake, Sean,' Hudson said. 'I thought you were reliable.' Taffy frowned at Hudson.

'I am, Mr Hudson. It was—'

'I need reliable people, Sean. People I can trust.' Hudson sighed. 'I'll give this some thought.'

'Please, Mr Hudson. I'll do anything to make this right.'

'I'll ring you back in two minutes.' Hudson rang off.

'What's up?' Taffy said.

Hudson looked upward. 'Sean's killed Craig.'

'Craig?'

'Cooper's driver,' Hudson said. 'They got into a fight over a girl.'

Taffy looked upwards and shook his head. 'Well, that's just great. We can't use him then.'

Hudson stared deeply into his glass. 'He knows now.'

'Knows what?' Taffy said. 'You didn't tell him anything.'

'When the police catch up with him, he may hear about Cooper going missing. He could put two and two together.'

'I can't see—'

'We may be able to contain it somehow.'

'Conrad,' Taffy said. 'It'll make it even more complicated.'

'We've got the girl to think about,' Hudson said. 'We've enough loose ends here. I'll ring Sean back. See if we can retrieve the situation.'

'But, Boss—'

'Taffy,' Hudson said. He glared at the other man. 'Who's in charge here?'

Taffy held up his hands. 'Ok.'

Hudson took out his phone, rang Sean and put it on speakerphone.

'Yeah, Mr Hudson?'

'Right, Sean. Your luck's in. I'm going to help you out. I'll send some of the boys over there. I can't promise anything until I know if he's been found yet. If he has, you're on your own. You understand?'

'Yes. Perfectly.'

'Are you sure no one else saw you?'

'Well ... It's a little ...'

'What?' Hudson said.

'There was this kid. He may have seen me.'

Hudson sucked in air. 'You're priceless, Sean. You really are. Who is he?'

'He's a copper's son.'

Hudson false-laughed. 'This just gets better. His name?'

'Jimmy Jefferson.'

'Eddie Jefferson's boy?'

'Yes, Mr Hudson.'

Hudson smiled to himself. 'Ok. Where does he live?'

'He lives with his dad in Coulby Newham.'

'Address Sean?' Hudson said. 'I'll need an address.'

'I can find out and text it to you.'

Hudson sneered. 'Do that. One more thing ...'

'Yes, Mr Hudson?'

'We'll need a patsy for Craig Embleton's murder. This girl you two fought over ... How close are you?'

'Not at all.'

'Good. I'll keep in touch.'

'What now?' Taffy said.

'Get onto a couple of the other boys. When I get the address from Sean, I want you to send them around to the Jefferson kid's house and put the frighteners on him. Make sure he keeps his trap shut.'

'Ok. The girl?'

Hudson glanced upwards. 'Loiter near the room. If she comes out, don't let her leave the house.'

Amanda woke. She glanced across at the sleeping form next to her and slid out of bed. Quickly dressing, she gathered her other stuff together and headed for the door. Whittaker-Brown shifted slightly in the bed as she reached for the handle. Pausing, and satisfied he wasn't waking, she opened the door and glanced outside. It was deathly quiet, and no one was about. Amanda stepped into the corridor and padded her way along the landing. Finding herself at the top of a flight of stairs, she made her way down. On reaching the bottom she paused again, trying to remember the layout of the house.

She took out her phone and texted Alex. 'I'm trying to get out. I'm at the bottom of the large stairs.' She dropped onto a chair and waited.

Her phone pinged with a message. *Turn left and walk down the long corridor,* it said. *At the bottom, turn right and head for the room at the end.*

Amanda sprung to her feet and hurried along the passage, following the instructions she had been given. She reached the door, glanced back along the empty hallway, pushed it open and stepped into the darkness.

'Alex?' she whispered.

A man stepped from behind the door and grabbed hold of her. Amanda fought as a piece of cloth was held across her face until she ceased struggling, her kicking and thrashing slowly coming to a stop as she slipped into unconsciousness. The figure scooped up her limp body and carried her through the open French doors.

Hudson, having endured only a few hours of fitful sleep, hauled himself from his bed and got dressed. He sat on the edge of a chair and rubbed his eyes. Dawn broke, and sunlight pushed itself through open curtains into his bedroom. His mobile sounded. Hudson snatched up the handset and answered. 'Yeah, Taffy?'

'Can you come to your study, Boss?'

'I'm on my way.'

Hudson checked his appearance in the mirror and headed downstairs. As he reached the bottom, Robin Slaney, the gardener, entered from a side door.

'Mr Hudson,' he said.

Hudson stopped. 'Yes, Robin?'

'I'll be leaving this week.'

'That's fine. I'll see your money and P45 are forwarded to you. Leave your address with the housekeeper and I'll send them on.' Hudson motioned to move again.

'Will you be able to give me a reference?'

'Yes, yes,' Hudson said. 'All that will be sorted out. There'll be a little extra for you. For all your hard work.' Hudson glanced towards his study door. 'I'm a little busy. I'll see you before you leave, though.'

'Thanks very much,' Slaney said. 'It's been a pleasure working for you … Did Mr Cooper sort his car out?'

Hudson paused again with his fingers on the door handle, then slowly turned. 'Mr Cooper?'

'I spotted his car parked near the copse last night.' Hudson furrowed his brow. 'I noticed it had a flat tyre,' Slaney continued. 'I wasn't sure Mr Cooper was—'

Hudson waved a hand dismissively. 'Oh, that. Yeah. We sorted him out this morning.'

Slaney smiled and hurried off.

'Where are you off to now?'

'Over to the greenhouses. I've a little to do before I go.'

'Good man,' Hudson said. 'When are you going to Portugal?'

'In a couple of days.'

'I'll get one of the lads to drop you at the airport.'

'Are you sure, Mr Hudson? I could jump in a taxi.'

'I wouldn't hear of it.'

'Thanks,' Slaney said. Hudson watched as Slaney disappeared through the doors and outside. He slowly rubbed his chin, took hold of the door handle again and entered. Taffy stood inside cradling a cup of tea in his hand.

'The girl?' Hudson said.

'We're holding her in one of the outbuildings. Robbo and Billy are entertaining her.' He pushed his hand inside his jacket pocket, pulling out the Dictaphone. 'She had this with her.' Hudson examined the device. 'She was taping herself and Whittaker-Brown,' Taffy continued. 'Cooper was behind it.'

Hudson picked up the machine. 'We'll keep this. In case we need it in the future.'

'I take it you want the girl to disappear?' Taffy said.

'For good.'

'What if someone knew she was coming here?'

Hudson slumped into a seat. 'We'll take the risk. I'm hoping people will assume Cooper left with her after stealing the cash.'

Taffy stood. 'We'll deal with the girl.'

'We may have another problem.'

Taffy paused and gazed upwards. 'What?'

'Robin Slaney saw Cooper's car here last night. He's leaving to join his wife in Portugal soon.'

'He'll be out of our hair then?'

Hudson shook his head. 'I don't want any loose ends. Slaney's a loose end.'

'When?'

'I've told him I'll sort out a lift to the airport for him. I don't want him making the flight.'

'This is getting messy, Conrad.'

'We've a lot to lose. Me, you and the boys. We can't leave anything to chance.'

Taffy's shoulders drooped. 'I suppose.'

'I want you to deal with this. It's between you and me. Robbo sometimes drinks with Slaney. I don't want sentiments getting in the way. You understand?'

'Yeah. I understand.' Taffy said.

Hudson picked up his mobile and phoned. 'Conrad?' a voice bathed in tiredness said.

'I need you to do something, Jeff. The little cleaning up operation I asked you to do for me.'

'Alex Cooper's money?'

'Yeah. I need it to come back into view.'

'But you—?'

'I know what I said. That was then, this is now. Just make sure it gets seen.'

'Ok.'

'There's a drink in this for you,' Hudson said. 'I don't forget my friends.'

Taffy glanced around before entering. Billy turned with a drink in his hand. 'You're missing all the fun,' Billy said. He moved towards a door. 'Robbo and Charlie are still in there.'

'The fun's over. Conrad wants this dealing with.'

Billy banged on the door. 'Come on, you two. Get your pants on.'

Taffy and Billy waited as noise was heard from within, and a dishevelled Robbo pulled open the door. 'What's up?'

Taffy glanced past Robbo at Amanda. She lay naked, whimpering on an old mattress in one corner. Charlie was fastening his trousers. Taffy pulled Robbo outside and beckoned Charlie to join him before closing and securing the door to the room.

'The cards?' Taffy said. Billy nodded to an old table in the corner.

Taffy strode across and picked up the cards. He shuffled them and placed them face down on the table. Robbo, Charlie and Billy took one. They each looked at their respective card before putting it back down. Taffy picked up the remaining card and glanced at the Ace of Spades. He deposited his on top of the other three.

'We'll meet here in thirty minutes.' The men filed outside. Taffy secured the door with a padlock. He held up the key for everyone to see and hung it onto a nail to the side of the door.

'Thirty-minutes,' he repeated, as all four of them headed back towards the house.

Colin Pybus watched the four figures disappear inside, waited a few moments and darted across to the outbuilding. He checked around, his heart thumping madly, and reaching for the key he stopped as a noise alerted him that someone was coming.

Taffy came into view. He halted and stared at Colin. 'What are you doing?' Taffy said.

'I was looking for you guys.'

'Why?'

'Oh … I was wondering if you'd like a bit of breakfast.'

Taffy strode across to him and glared into Colin's eyes. 'Creeping around places can get you into trouble, Colin.'

'I know … I'm sorry … It's just …' Colin glanced towards the building.

'I'm going to cut you some slack here … because I was mates with your old man.'

'I know—'

Taffy draped an arm around Colin's shoulder. 'But your dad's not around anymore. Only you and your mam. How is your mam by the way?'

'Eh … fine.'

'Who'd look after her if anything happened to you? It's an awful world out there. A woman's vulnerable on her own. You understand what I'm saying?'

Colin swallowed hard. 'Yeah.'

'The girl? Whose idea was it?'

'I … please, Taffy … I don't know anything.'

'You're lucky I've enough on my plate.' He slowly patted Colin's cheek. 'Forget about her and anything else. You understand?'

Colin's shoulders dropped. 'Yeah.'

'Run along, Colin. Like a good boy.'

Colin extricated himself from Taffy's grip and hurried towards the house. He paused at the threshold for a final look. Taffy stood looking at him with the door to the outbuilding now open. He glared at Colin. Colin lowered his head and raced inside.

Taffy drove the van along the bumpy track for half a mile before turning off the road. It trundled along slowly until finally coming to a halt. Jumping from the vehicle, he made his way around the back. He glanced around in all directions and pulled open the door. The trussed-up body lay inside. Grabbing one end of it, he tugged it towards the doors and outside onto the floor. Slowly, meticulously, he dragged it towards an already prepared hole. Pausing to gather his breath, he blinked as dawn broke in front of him. With one mighty heave, he pushed the body over the lip of the trench and watched as it rolled down the side and into the bottom. He made his way back to the van, returning to the hole moments later with a spade and began covering the body with earth. He stopped and leant on the implement. The body no longer visible in the partly filled trench. Taffy picked up the spade, made his way back to the van, and threw it inside.

Taffy drove back along the track towards the main road. He stopped at the end, jumped out, and walked a small distance towards a white rock, marking the entrance to the track. Lifting the rock, he deposited an envelope beneath. Taffy glanced around and listened, but only the chirping of nearby birds broke the silence. He got back in his van, threw the vehicle in gear, and roared off.

The tractor pushed the remaining earth into the hole. The driver manoeuvred his vehicle back and forward over the top to flatten it down before he turned the machine around, and bounced its way along the same route as the van. Stopping at the entrance to the track, the driver jumped out, retrieved the package from under the stone, and carried on the quotidian life of a farmer.

CHAPTER THIRTY-FIVE

The car, with Lindsey inside, drew to a halt in the layby. Jen and Joey travelling behind her, pulled off the road and out of sight some distance away. Joey handed Jen a pair of binoculars.

'I can't see anyone,' she said.

Joey took them. He scanned the horizon, paused, and pointed into the distance as Jen looked again. Set back from the road stood an old farmhouse, a black Mercedes parked outside.

Jen pulled out her phone and waited for Lindsey to answer.

'Hi,' Lindsey said.

'Are you sure you want to do this?' Jen said.

'I don't have a choice. They've got Jimmy.'

Jen glanced across at Joey. 'We'll be right behind you. Don't take any risks. Tell them what they want to know.'

'Jen,' Lindsey said. 'You're heavily pregnant. You can't risk—'

'I can still fire a gun. Don't you worry about me.'

'I'm going to set off now. I'm leaving my phone inside the car so you won't be able to contact me.'

'Ok,' Jen said. 'Take care.'

Lindsey hung up, pulled open the glovebox and threw in the phone. She took a deep breath, opened the door, and stepped outside. A chill breeze caused her to gasp. She pulled the top of her jacket tight around her neck and set off.

Jen pulled the gun from her pocket and checked it was loaded. Joey placed a hand on her arm. 'You're staying here.'

She frowned at him. 'What are you on about?'

He placed a hand on her swollen stomach. 'We can't risk you or the baby.'

'But—'

Joey placed a finger to her lips. 'Shh,' he said. 'You'll need to stay here in case we need to make a quick getaway.'

Jen's shoulders slumped. 'I love you, Joey.'

They kissed. Joey jumped from the vehicle and hurried around to the back. He fumbled around while Jen watched Lindsey, through binoculars, make her way across to the house. Joey returned wearing a large black jacket. He thrust a handgun into his pocket and snatched Jen's from the dashboard. 'I'll see you two soon,' he said, kissed her again, and then was gone.

Lindsey headed along the lane towards the house. As she neared, a man exited. He held a gun in his hand which dangled next to him. He walked forward to meet her and gripped hold of her arm. Lindsey, half-walked, half-dragged, was pushed into the building. Taffy, perched on the edge of an old table, looked up as she entered. She glanced towards Jimmy, fastened to a chair, on the far side of the room.

Taffy stood. 'Nice of you to join us, Lindsey.'

'I didn't have a lot of choice.'

'Don't worry,' Taffy said. 'We haven't harmed him. We need a little help from you.'

Lindsey joined Jimmy, who stood and hugged her.

'All very touching,' Taffy said. 'But …'

Lindsey glared towards him. 'What do you want. We haven't any money.'

Taffy laughed and then glared at her. 'If you're going to treat me like a fool.' He edged closer. 'This will end badly.'

Lindsey glared. 'What then?'

'The Hewitson girl and her boyfriend. Where are they?'

'I don't know. They were staying at my parents' house for a while but when the police arrived, they legged it.'

A third man entered. 'It's all quiet outside,' he said.

'Good,' Taffy said. 'Let's hope it stays that way.' Taffy held out his hand. 'Your mobile.'

'I haven't got it. The police have it.'

Taffy loomed closer. 'Why would the police take it?'

'They know I knew Jen from Durham. They think I've been in touch.'

'And have you?'

'I've her number stored on the mobile. They got me to ring her, but she didn't answer. That's why they still have it.'

'Right,' Taffy said. 'Then you'd better think of a way of getting in touch with her and her fella. Because you and your boyfriend.' He pointed at Jimmy. 'Are going nowhere until they turn up.' Taffy pushed a chair towards Lindsey with his foot. 'Have a seat.'

Chubby entered holding a mobile. 'There's a call from someone called Archie, at Chestnut Farm,' he said.

Taffy snatched the phone from him and hurried outside. 'Yeah,' he said.

'It's Archie, Taffy. I've dug the holes for you.'

'Why did you do that? I said wait for my call. We're not ready for them yet.'

'I thought—'

'I don't care what you thought.'

'It's just my son's away at market today—'

'Listen you old, drunken bum. You dig the fucking hole when I say and not before. Fill them back in. In future, don't go making decisions on your own. Otherwise, the next hole you dig will be for you. Are we clear on this?'

'Yes,' the voice said.

Taffy hung up and dialled another number.

'Yeah,' Hudson said.

'Lindsey Armstrong claims she doesn't know where they are,' Taffy said.

'She must know how to get in touch with them?'

'She has a number, but Graveney has the mobile.'

Hudson grunted. 'She's fucking lying. Persuade her it's for the best. Do what you need to. Find out where those two are and then get rid of her and her boyfriend.'

'What happens if she doesn't know?'

'We've wasted a day, haven't we?' Hudson hung up.

Taffy walked across to Slim, who stood at the end of the lane. Slim spun around on hearing footsteps.

'Slim,' Taffy said. He glanced around the countryside. 'Tell the others to keep a good lookout. I don't want anyone turning up unannounced. Have a drive up to the main road. See if there are any cars or vans about.'

'Ok,' he said.

The man stood close to the gate. He took a long draw of his cigarette, dropped the butt at his feet and stamped it into the earth. His phone sounded.

'Yeah,' he said.

'Any movement?' Slim said.

The man scanned the countryside. 'It's all quiet here.'

'Keep your wits about you. The big guy and his girlfriend might turn up any minute.'

'Will do.' He pushed the phone back into his pocket and pulled out his packet of cigarettes as the butt of a pistol cracked against his skull.

He crumpled to his knees before falling forward onto his front with a thud. Joey grabbed his legs and pulled him behind a wall. He secured his hands and pushed a piece of tape across his mouth. Joey stood upright and pushed the man's revolver inside his own waistband. He surveyed around him and crept onwards towards the house.

Slim's phone sounded. 'Yeah,' he said.

'There's a blue van parked about half a mile away,' a man said.

'Anyone about?'

'No, it's empty.'

'It could be a dog walker,' Slim said.

'There's a pair of binoculars on the front seat.'

Slim grunted. 'Keep out of sight and wait. Give me a ring if anyone turns up.'

Slim hung up and dialled Taffy. 'Yeah, Slim?'

'One of the lads found a van parked not far away. It has a pair of binoculars on the front seat.'

'Really?'

'It could be a bird watcher,' Slim said.

'If it was,' Taffy said. 'He'd have taken them with him.'

'I've told him to keep a watch out for anyone returning.'

'Good. Keep me informed.'

A second man lay taped and unconscious. Joey knelt on the ground and stared towards the house, now no more than a hundred metres from him. He narrowed his eyes, checked in all directions, and keeping low, made his way silently along a drystone wall which shielded him from anyone inside the house.

The man at the van scanned the length of the road, he leant back against a fence, masked from the passing traffic by a large shrub. The crack of a twig caused him to turn but when he did, he found himself staring into the muzzle of a handgun.

Jen glared at him. 'I knew the van would attract one of you.'

The man eyed her up and down. The heavily pregnant woman in front of him somewhat incongruous. He smirked. 'There are others on their way.'

Jen sneered. 'Don't let how I look fool you. My boyfriend taught me well. I could easily put a bullet in that head of yours.'

The smile fell from his face. 'Take your gun out,' she said. 'And toss it over here. If you try anything ... Well, you know how it goes.'

The man slowly removed his pistol while continuing to stare at Jen and threw it towards her. The gun landed a few feet to the left, and she stooped to pick it up.

'Now,' she said. 'Why don't you call up the cavalry.' The man sneered. Jen raised her weapon higher. 'This gun will make a mess of your head. I'm sure whatever Hudson pays you isn't enough for that.'

The man held up the palms of his hands and slowly removed his mobile. 'What do you want me to say?' he said.

'Tell them you've spotted someone near to the van.'

The man dialled. 'I'm near to the van. I've spotted a woman.'

'... It could be them ... I'll wait here.' He hung up and looked at Jen.

'Well done,' she said. Jen pulled a set of handcuffs from her pocket and threw them over to him. 'Put those on.'

The man complied. She waited for the click of the shackles and then motioned to her left. He walked forward, through a gap in the wall, and into a small copse of trees.

'This will do,' she said. He halted and turned to face her. 'Lie on the floor face down.'

The man did as he was told. Jen bent down and pushed the gun into the nape of his neck. 'Stay still, and you won't get hurt.' Pulling out another set of cuffs, she clicked them around his ankles. She removed a roll of tape from her jacket pocket, tore off a strip and pushed it across his mouth. Standing, she glanced at the prostrate form and then headed back towards the van. She reached the gap in the wall, dropped onto her knees, and waited.

Joey peered over the top of the wall towards the house. A couple of men exited and jumped into a car. He watched as the vehicle sped off along the driveway towards the road. One man stood, sentry-like, outside the house. Joey surveyed the land. Creeping along and around to the back of the property, he leapt the wall and ducked behind an old piece of rusty farming equipment. He felt for his gun and closed his fingers around the handle. Moving closer and keeping low, he glanced from side to side. Reaching the rear window, he peeped through a gap in the curtains at Lindsey and Jimmy secured in the middle of the room on chairs. Across from them, an armed man stood watch. Joey reached into his pocket and pulled out the photo. He studied it and then stared at the man. It wasn't him. Neither was it the man at the front of the house. Pushing the snap back into his pocket, he crept towards the door. He waited, gave the area one last look then turned the handle. It was locked. Skirting the building, he paused at the corner of the wall leading to the front and glanced past it. The man at the front stared into the distance, and Joey waited.

Jen watched from her concealed viewpoint as the car pulled up. Taffy and another man got out. Her eyes narrowed when she recognised him from the photo, her lips slowly curled into a grimace.

'Check his car,' Taffy said.

The second man raced across to the vehicle. 'It's empty.'

Taffy peered about. 'Something's not right. Get on the phone to Tommy. Get him down here.'

The man pulled his mobile from his pocket and phoned, allowing it to ring. He looked towards Taffy. 'He's not answering.'

Taffy scrutinised the van. 'Look in the van.'

The man did as he was asked. Trying the rear door first, and then the side doors. 'It's locked.'

Taffy gazed away from the wooded area and up and down the layby. 'This could be a ruse to lure us away from the house.'

'What do we do?'

Taffy pulled his gun from his jacket pocket. 'We'll go back to the house. Make sure everything is ok.'

The pair walked over to their car and got in. The man glanced across at Taffy. 'Where do you think Tommy is?' he said.

Taffy rubbed his chin. He could've gone after someone, I supp—'

He stopped mid-sentence as he felt the cold metal of the gun on the back of his neck. 'Either of you two moves an inch, and I'll take his head off,' Jen said. She tossed a large black tie-wrap towards the man. 'Fasten his hands and feet together.' The man complied.

'Where's your mate?' Taffy said.

'He'll be sorting your friends out, hopefully.'

Jen switched her attention back to the other man. 'Gun,' she said.

'In my pocket.'

'Take it out slowly. Don't do anything clever or I'll make a mess of that head of yours.'

He slowly pushed a hand inside his jacket and retrieved the gun.

'Throw it out of the window,' she said.

'Now his.' She nodded towards Taffy. The man repeated the process.

Jen leant forward. 'Get out slowly.'

The man climbed from the car and waited as the heavily pregnant Jen, clambered out. He smirked at her.

She stood impassively. 'Just because I'm pregnant, doesn't mean I can't kill you.'

She motioned with the gun, and the man walked around to the back of the car. 'Open it.'

The man lifted the boot and gaped at her.

'Get in,' she said.

'You're kidding?'

'I don't care if you're dead or alive,' she said. 'But you're going in there.'

The man peered into the boot and back at Jen. He grunted loudly, climbed inside, and Jen slammed the boot shut.

Joey felt his mobile vibrate inside his trouser pocket. He pulled out the phone and read the message from Jen. *How's it going?*

He quickly typed a reply. *There's two of them left. One inside, and one outside.*

I've got three of them here. She messaged. *One in the woods, one in the boot and the other's fastened up in one of the cars.*

Be careful x, he texted.

You too, x.

Joey pushed his mobile back into his pocket and paused as the man stood in front of the building, headed inside. He silently crept along the wall of the cottage, ducking lower when he reached the window. Once he neared the door, he stood upright again. He listened as voices from inside drifted out. Pushing his back up against the wall, he paused as footsteps crunched on the gravel path. Joey waited, grabbed him from behind and thrust an arm across his throat.

'Don't move a muscle,' Joey whispered. 'I've got a gun in your back.' The man ceased his struggling. 'I want you to call your friend and tell him to come outside. Don't make it sound as if you're panicking. Tell him you want to show him something. Have you got it?' The man nodded.

'Do anything stupid and you're dead.' Joey said. 'Understand?' The man nodded again, and Joey removed his arm. He held out his hand. 'Give me your gun.'

He handed it to Joey. 'Go ahead,' Joey said.

'Slim,' the man shouted. 'What do you think of this?'

'What?' Slim said.

Joey waited as Slim came out carrying a gun. 'What?' Slim said. The other man motioned behind him, and he turned to find Joey with a gun pointing at him.

'Drop it,' Joey said. Slim allowed the weapon to fall to the ground. 'Are there any more in there?' Slim shook his head. 'Good. Inside.'

The two men entered, closely followed by Joey. Lindsey and Jimmy sat next to each other, taped to the chairs.

'Unfasten them,' Joey said.

The men released the pair. Joey placed a hand on Jimmy and motioned towards the windowsill. 'Tape them to the seats.' Jimmy snatched the tape from the window and began fastening the now seated duo onto their chairs.

Jen glanced up and down the road. Only light traffic passed by, and with the layby being set back, it was out of sight of vehicles. She headed back towards the car with Taffy in it but stopped. A sharp pain in her stomach caused her to suck in air. Her mobile sounded.

'Hi,' she said, trying to keep the pain in check.

'I've got them free,' Joey said. 'Can you drive the van up?'

'Yeah. I've got the last man. The one who knows where Amanda is. He won't talk.'

'Can you get him into the van?'

'I ...' Jen panted as another pain shot through her.

'Jen,' Joey said. 'Are you ok?'

'I think I'm going into labour.'

'But it's too early.'

Jen grimaced. 'Tell that to the baby.'

'Stay where you are. I'll use one of the cars here. I'll be as quick as I can.'

Jen stumbled towards the vehicle with Taffy inside and threw open the door. She placed the muzzle of the gun onto the side of his head. 'Where's my sister buried, you fucking murdering bastard.'

Taffy cocked his head at her and smiled. 'If I tell you that, I'm a dead man.'

'Tell me where and I'll make it quick. You know what happened to your friends.' Jen grimaced again.

He grinned. 'Looks as if your little bastard wants a piece of the action.'

'Tell me,' she screamed, gripping hold of the door for support. The pain arriving in regular spasms. She looked down as warm liquid trickled from between her legs.

Taffy chuckled. 'Hudson will slice that kid of yours in front of you.'

Jen swung the weapon at his head but only succeeded in connecting with the headrest as he ducked. Taking his opportunity, he pushed forward forcefully with his shoulder. She fell backwards, hitting her head hard on the floor, the gun in her hand slipping from her grasp. He bent down, grabbed hold of the strap around his ankle and pulled, but the restraints held firm. His urgency mounting as Jen stirred, he pulled again, and again until finally, the strap gave way. Taffy jumped from the car and searched for the gun, spotting it a couple of metres from Jen, who stretched desperately for the weapon. Taffy stepped forward and grasped hold of her hair with his still fastened hands, dragging her away from the gun as she despairingly grasped at thin air. She fought him, clawing at his hands with her nails. He threw her hard against the car, Jen slamming into it with a thud. She grimly hung onto the car for support as her knees buckled, and she struggled for breath.

Taffy laughed and smacked his tethered hands against the side of her head. 'Let's give the bastard of yours a little help, shall we?'

Jen slumped to the floor, blood running along the side of her face where it had connected with the vehicle.

He loomed over her again and raised his foot up. 'Let's kick the fucker out.'

Jen rolled to the side as his foot came crashing down, narrowly missing her. He grabbed at her hair again, pulling her to her feet and banged her face into the top of the car. Blood exploded from her nose, coating her teeth in a sickening red grin. Taffy paused, still holding onto her hair as a car screeched into the layby. He let go, dropping her like a ragdoll, and dived for the gun. Jen forced herself upright and careered into him as the pair of them fell into a crumpled heap. He grabbed the weapon and pointed it at Jen who instinctively threw out an arm as he tried to level it.

Joey leapt from the vehicle and dropped onto one knee firing rapidly, the bullets whistling past Taffy's shoulder as he dived behind the back of the car. Jen crawled towards her boyfriend and the vehicle as Joey advanced, pulling a second weapon from his pocket as he continued to pin Taffy down. He reached Jen and pulled her into his arms while still firing. Lindsey and Jimmy emerged from the car and fired past Joey towards Taffy. Joey placed Jen down, continuing to provide covering fire as Lindsey and Jimmy helped the struggling Jen into the van.

Joey tossed Jimmy the keys. 'Get the van started.'

Jimmy caught them and jumped into the driver's seat. The engine sprung into life. He waited nervously as Joey emptied his gun at the car. The roar of another vehicle caught his attention, and a black car skidded into the opposite end of the layby. Joey pulled his final gun from his pocket and trained it on the vehicle. The front doors burst open, and two men jumped out. Joey turned and ran towards the van with Jimmy inside, but dropped onto one knee when a bullet hit him in his thigh. He struggled upright, the van about forty metres from him. A second bullet ripped into his side. He slumped to the floor and looked back as Jimmy exited the van.

Joey waved him back. 'Go! Get Jen out of here. Just go.'

Jimmy raced back to the vehicle and jumped back inside. Jen struggled to her knees and stared helplessly out the window as Lindsey held tightly onto her.

'Joey,' Jen screamed. The pair locked eyes as Joey, now laying on his side, continued to fire at the car. Jimmy quickly performed a U-turn and raced from the layby. Another car, with Hudson inside, approached them as he screeched onto the road. The two vehicles narrowly missed each other as the car slid from the tarmac and skidded to a halt in a ditch by the side of the road. Jimmy floored the accelerator and disappeared into the distance.

Hudson prised himself from the now deflated airbag and groaned loudly. He stared across at the driver, who shook his head as if clearing it.

Hudson rubbed at the nape of his neck. 'Are you ok?'

'Yeah, I think so.'

Taffy pulled himself forward and felt his thigh, his jeans covered in red as blood slowly seeped through them.

One of the men, tall and thickset, edged around the vehicle. 'You ok, Taffy?'

'I've been shot. I think it's only a flesh wound, though.'

'The van with the others has gone. But we've pinned down the big guy.'

Taffy's eye's widened. 'Don't kill him. Mr Hudson will want that pleasure. Get him into the car. The police will be crawling all over here any minute.'

The man strode away. His mate stood with his gun pointed towards the motionless Joey. He reached his friend, glanced at him and then fixed his eyes back on Joey.

'He's not dead, is he?'

The man pointing the gun shook his head. 'I heard him groan. He's out of ammo.'

'Let's go and get him. Taffy wants him in the car.'

The two men crept closer, continuing to train their weapons on Joey. The tall man stopped and nudged the motionless figure with the toe of his boot. Joey groaned as the man stooped and plucked the spent weapon from his grasp.

'You don't look so clever now, soldier-boy,' he said. And with his boot he pushed Joey onto his back. 'Mr Hudson's going to slice you to pieces, you murdering bastard.'

Joey grinned and stared towards his own left hand. The two men's eyes followed his stare. The tall guy's brow furrowed into deep ridges as the realisation of what was in the wounded man's hand dawned on him. Joey pulled open his jacket with his right hand, revealing more grenades hanging from his belt. 'This is for Jen and Amanda.' The one in his hand slipped from his grasp and rolled nearer to the men, as the tall one glanced across at his partner in disbelief.

Taffy managed to haul himself upright next to the car, but as he stood straight, the concussive force of the explosion hit him full on, sending him backwards. He landed with a thud on the ground, unconscious, as debris and human detritus rained down.

Hudson instinctively ducked behind the car, trying to decipher what had happened. He looked across to the layby. Thick, black smoke plumed upwards from the canopy of trees and the noise of sirens drifted into earshot. Glancing to his right, he narrowed his eyes as the flashing lights in the distance snaked their way towards him. The driver staggered around to Hudson's side and pulled at the door, the buckled metal finally giving way on the third yank.

'Are you ok, Mr Hudson?'

'Yeah.' He panted. 'Go and check across the road. See if anyone's still alive.'

The man hurried away from him, as Hudson slumped onto the ground.

Jimmy pulled the van up out of sight as vehicles, with sirens wailing, sped past. He swivelled and faced his girlfriend and the prone Jen.

He stared at Lindsey. 'How is she?'

'Not good. She needs a hospital. She's in labour.'

Jen opened her eyes and grabbed hold of her arm. 'No hospitals. They'll be looking for me.'

'The explosion?' Jimmy said. 'What ...?'

Jen closed her eyes and groaned as a spasm of pain shot threw her side and tears mercilessly pushed out through her tightly closed eyelids. 'Joey. He had hand grenades. He said it'd be a last resort.'

'Why didn't he use them on Hudson's men?' Lindsey said.

'The one called Taffy. He knows where Amanda's buried. We had to take him alive.' She let out a loud sob.

Lindsey placed a hand on her arm as she groaned again. 'We have to think of your baby, Jen. I can't ...'

Jen grimaced and motioned across to her jacket. 'My phone.'

Lindsey quickly retrieved the mobile and gave it to her. Jen fumbled for a number and handed it back to Lindsey. 'My friend Alison. She's a nurse. She'll know what to do.' Jen groaned once more, loudly.

'What about what's gone on?' Jimmy said.

'Alison's sound,' Jen said. 'We go back a long way. She won't say anything.'

Lindsey pressed the call button and waited. 'Hi, Jen,' a female voice said.

'It's not Jen, it's her friend Lindsey. Jen needs your help. We're in a spot of bother. She's in the early stages of labour. I don't know what to do.'

'Where are you?'

'Between Northallerton and Darlington,' Lindsey said.

'Good. Head towards Darlington, and as you pass through Croft, there's a turnoff onto a lane. Look out for a large white stone at the entrance to a private road with *Whinstone House* painted on it. It's quite secluded so you shouldn't be spotted.'

Lindsey glanced towards Jimmy. 'We'll be as quick as we can.'

Jimmy put the van back into gear and swung it around, checking both ways as he reached the main road. The wailing of sirens, aided and abetted by the Doppler effect, could be heard in the distance. He pulled onto the road and sped off.

CHAPTER THIRTY-SIX

Graveney checked his mobile for messages. There were none. Bev was clearly still annoyed with him and ignoring his calls. He would visit her and try to sort it out. Louisa was acting strangely too. She hadn't turned up at the coffee shop, and when he phoned her, she was offhand, angry even. But when he asked her what was wrong, she hadn't been forthcoming. She had agreed to meet him later today, reluctantly it appeared. He picked up his empty coffee cup and stood as his phone sounded. He groaned, slumped back onto his chair and snatched it up. 'Graveney.'

'There's been an incident not far from Northallerton,' Hussain said.

Graveney sighed. 'That's outside of our jurisdiction. We've got enough—'

'Involving Hudson, Sir.'

'Ok. You've got my attention, Rav.'

'A mate of mine knows we're investigating the murder of Hudson's men. Apparently, there's been an explosion and gunshots.'

Graveney jumped to his feet and pulled on his coat. 'Find the location and the senior officer dealing with it, will you?'

'Yes, Sir.'

Graveney bounded out of the office nearly bumping into DI Robertson. 'Have you heard?' Graveney said.

'I was on my way to see you,' Robertson said. 'Could be the soldier and the woman.'

'Does the Guv know?'

'I've just finished chatting with him. He wants to be kept abreast of developments.'

'I've asked Rav to find out the name of the investigating officer. Let's go and see what's happening.'

Graveney pulled the car up at the police cordon. He put down his window and held out his credentials. 'DI Graveney, and this is my colleague DI Robertson. We're here to see DI McCullagh. He's expecting us.'

The uniformed policeman opened the barrier and let them through. Graveney stopped the car by the side of the road. The two officers got out and strode towards three men standing together, chatting.

Graveney stopped near to the men. 'DI McCullagh?'

The older of the three stepped forward and held out a hand. 'DI Graveney?'

'Yes. This is my colleague DI Robertson.'

The three men shook hands. 'Follow me,' McCullagh said.

Graveney looked towards the vehicle wedged in the ditch. 'What happened here?'

'Hudson's car,' McCullagh said. 'He told me his boys were up at the house in the distance.' He scoffed. 'Apparently, they were ambushed.'

'What happened in the layby?' Robertson said.

'The bomb disposal are over there. There was an explosion.'

'Any witnesses?' Graveney said.

'One.' McCullagh took out his notepad. 'Gerry Llewellyn.'

Graveney grinned and glanced at Robertson.

'You two know him?' McCullagh said.

'Oh, yeah,' Robertson said. 'Gerry 'Taffy' Llewellyn. His reputation precedes him.'

'He's Hudson's right-hand man,' Graveney said. 'A string of previous. None of it for traffic offences.'

McCullagh smiled. 'He's on his way to the hospital.'

Graveney raised his brow. 'Serious?'

'Gunshot wound. Not life-threatening, though.'

'Pity.'

'Where's Hudson?' Robertson said.

'He's up at the house.'

'Mind if we have a chat with him?' Graveney said.

McCullagh held up his hands. 'Not at all. Is this to do with the investigation you're working on?'

'Yeah,' Graveney said. 'We're hunting two people, a man and a woman, for the murder of three of his men.'

McCullagh rubbed his chin. 'The man could be dead. Llewellyn told us a man blew himself up, taking two of Hudson's men with him.' McCullagh held out his hand. 'Follow me.'

Jimmy poured the boiling water into the teapot and stirred it. The door opened behind him, and he spun around. Lindsey came in.

'Anything?' he said.

'Alison said not long.' Lindsey gazed at the floor.

Jimmy moved across and lifted her head. 'What's up?'

'Jen's in a bad way.' Lindsey rubbed her face. 'Alison's worried. For her, and the baby. She should be in hospital.'

'The police and Hudson's men will be looking for her.'

'I know. But what if—?'

'Hey,' Jimmy said. He placed his hands either side of her face. 'Let's not think about that.'

He filled two mugs with tea, handed them to Lindsey, and kissed the top of her head. 'You'd better get back.'

'I love you,' she said, and then she was gone. Jimmy leant against the worktop and gave a huge sigh. He stared outside into the garden as darkness slowly claimed the day.

Conrad Hudson stood talking with one of his men as Graveney, Robertson and McCullagh entered. He spun around as footsteps sounded behind him.

Hudson sneered. 'What are you doing here, Graveney? No crime to fight in Middlesbrough?'

Graveney moved nearer. 'An interested party.'

'Why aren't you out there catching the lunatic who did this?'

'Lunatic?' Graveney said. 'The way I heard it, Taffy, your boys saw one of them blow himself up.'

'Taking two of my men with him.'

'Why is someone doing this, Hudson?' Graveney said. 'Why does someone want your men dead? What did they do?'

Hudson stepped closer. 'I've done nothing wrong, copper. I'm the injured party here. And I ...' He pushed his face nearer to Graveney. 'I don't have to say anything. You want to ask me questions—?'

'This is just informal, Mr Hudson,' Robertson said.

'I haven't got time for this,' Hudson pushed past Graveney and headed for the door.

'Amanda Hewitson?' Graveney shouted.

Hudson hesitated. 'If you've anything to ask me ...?' He stared at each officer in turn, allowing his eyes to rest on Graveney. 'You can do it with my legal representative present.' He turned and raced outside, closely followed by his heavy.

Robertson looked to Graveney. 'What are you thinking?'

'We need to find the woman,' Graveney said.

McCullagh took out his pad again. 'We got a description of the van and a partial licence plate from one of Hudson's men.' He tore out the paper and handed it to Graveney.

'Thanks,' Graveney said.

'Any weapons found?' Robertson said.

McCullagh smiled. 'No. I reckon it was five to ten minutes after the explosion that the first police car got here. It looks as if they did a clean-up operation.'

'Will it be ok to give you a call when you have the results of the forensics ...?' Graveney paused.

'Bryn,' McCullagh said. 'Yeah, no problem ...'

'Peter,' Graveney offered his hand, and McCullagh shook it.

'Neil,' Robertson said. He shook McCullagh's hand. 'Thanks again, Bryn.'

'Let me know what you find out,' McCullagh said.

'I will,' Graveney said. He looked towards Robertson, who followed him as the pair headed off.

'What did you think?' Robertson said.

'There was someone else here.'

'Someone else?'

'There were two chairs in the corner. Out of place in such a dilapidated room. Almost as if they'd been brought specifically.'

'Something to sit on, perhaps? For his men?'

Graveney stopped and stared at Robertson. 'One had gaffer tape on its arms. And on the window ledge ...'

'A roll of gaffer tape?'

'Yeah.' Graveney walked on and stopped at the car. 'Who would he have taken and brought here?'

'Lindsey Armstrong.'

'Exactly. He was obviously trying to flush out Purdey and Hewitson.'

Robertson tapped his chin with his index finger. 'And bit off more than he could chew?'

'Let's give Armstrong another visit,' Graveney said.

'Surely she wouldn't be stupid enough to take Jen Hewitson to her home?'

'Probably not. But sooner or later she'll meet up. She has to.'

'What about Taffy Llewellyn?' Robertson said.

'Maybe we should pay him a visit first. He was the last to see Purdey alive.'

Jimmy glanced towards the hall as the sound of a baby crying sounded. He stood and paced along the corridor, stopping at the closed door and tapped.

Lindsey opened it and popped her head through.

'Do you need anything?' Jimmy said.

'We could do with another cuppa.' Lindsey stepped outside and closed the door behind her.

'The baby?' Jimmy said.

'Alison is checking her over. She thinks she's fine.'

'It's a girl then?' Jimmy looked down. 'And Jen?'

Lindsey lowered her head and blew out. 'Alison's worried about her. She thinks she needs to go to hospital.'

'We could—'

'She won't go. She's worried Hudson will find her. She won't leave her baby either.'

'What are you going to do?'

Lindsey held out her hands. 'We don't know. But if she gets any weaker, we'll have no choice.'

'Ok. I'll make the tea.'

Lindsey took hold of his arm. 'We need some milk, nappies and clothes.'

'Where do I get those from?'

'Go into Darlington. You can't risk going home to Middlesbrough. Not yet anyway.'

'I'll go now.'

Harry stood as Hudson stormed into the room. 'Conrad?'

'I need a couple of the boys to go to James Cook hospital.'

'Why?'

Hudson grunted. 'Taffy and the boys got jumped by Hewitson and her boyfriend.'

'Where?'

Hudson filled a glass with whisky and took a large gulp. 'I've got some land out near Northallerton. An old farmhouse. We had some bait.'

'What kind of bait?'

Hudson slumped into a chair. 'We took Lindsey Armstrong and her boyfriend out there. We thought it would flush the others out.'

'Well, clearly it did.' Harry maintained his outer calm, but inwardly he was worried.

'What happened? Did anyone die?'

Hudson sneered. 'Yeah, that bastard soldier. But he took two of the boys with him.'

'And Hewitson?'

'She got away with Armstrong and her fella. Nearly killed me.' Hudson stood. 'Taffy's injured. Not life-threatening, but I need him protected. She might come after him again.'

Harry gulped. 'What about the police?'

Hudson threw out a dismissive hand. 'Graveney and Robertson came sniffing around.' He looked upwards. 'It's not even their area.'

Harry stood. 'I'll get onto the boys now.'

'Phone my lawyer too. I pay him enough. I don't want Graveney bothering me.'

'Ok. Anything else?' Harry said.

'Taffy told me the girl's heavily pregnant. He roughed her up a bit. She'll need hospital treatment. Pull some strings. I want her found.'

'She could be anywhere.'

'Harry … It's what I pay you for. Taffy will be out of action for a few weeks. I need you to take up the slack.'

'Of course, Conrad. Leave it to me.'

'One more thing,' Hudson said. 'Loose ends.'

'Loose ends?'

Hudson emptied his glass. 'Armstrong and her boyfriend.'

Harry stared across at him. 'Now?'

'Now. When you find the pair, lose them. You understand?'

'Absolutely.'

Hudson refilled his glass. 'While we're on the subject of loose ends, have you sorted Macintyre yet?'

'I was just waiting for your final say so.'

'Taffy's out of the way. It would be a good time.'

Harry nodded. 'I'll make a call. Get someone from out of town to sort him.

'Yeah. Good idea.'

Harry raced from the office, took out his mobile and dialled. Lindsey answered. 'Hello.'

'Who's this?' Harry said.

'A friend of Jen's.'

'Can I speak to her?'

'Jen's a little poorly, and—'

'Is that Lindsey?'

Lindsey paused. 'How do you—?'

'Listen, Lindsey. It's vitally important I speak with Jen. She'll want to talk, I'm sure.'

Lindsey sighed. 'I'll check if she's awake.'

Harry waited as he heard footsteps, muffled talking and then the sound of a door closing. 'Hi,' Jen said.

'Jesus, Jen. What happened?'

'Joey's dead.'

'I heard. I'm sorry to hear that. Hudson's looking for you. He wants me to search hospitals. He said you're injured.'

Jen shifted her position in bed with the baby in her arms, and the phone cradled to her neck. 'I've had my baby. A little girl.'

'Is she ok?'

'She's fine. But she doesn't have a dad.'

Harry rubbed his face. 'I'm sorry, Jen. I'm so sorry.'

'Llewellyn's still alive. I still don't know where Amanda's buried.'

'Don't worry about that now. You need to get yourself better. For you and the baby.'

'Promise me, Harry. Promise me, if I don't make it, you'll put a bullet through his head for me.'

'Maybe I can get some help to you, a doctor?'

'I've got help here.'

'Lindsey and her boyfriend?'

'Yeah,' Jen said, her voice now bathed in tiredness.

'Hudson wants them out of the way.'

'Why?'

'He sees them as loose ends. I can delay it for so long, but I don't want him getting suspicious.'

'What was your mother's name, Harry?'

'Elizabeth. Beth. Why?'

'I'm going to call her after your mum.'

'Keep me informed, Jen. Please.'

'I will.'

Harry quickly dialled a second number. 'What the hell happened?'

'I tried ringing you but it went to answerphone,' the male voice said. 'The big guy killed himself and a couple of men with him.'

'I heard,' Harry said. 'I've spoken with Jen. She's in a bad way. Now her fella's gone we won't have them to assist with removing Hudson.'

'What are you thinking?'

'We'll have to come up with another strategy,' Harry said. 'One more thing?'

'Yeah.'

'Hudson's given me the green-light on Macintyre.'

'Should I make the call?'

'Yeah,' Harry said. 'This weekend. Use your mate.'

Lindsey came back into the bedroom. 'Everything all right?' she said to Jen.

'Yeah. Can you take Beth, please?'

'Beth?' A memory flickered deep within Lindsey's mind and then extinguished.

'I'm calling her Beth.'

Lindsey accepted the baby from her and hugged the infant tight. 'You need to go to hospital, Jen. Alison hasn't got the expertise. We're all worried.'

Jen eased onto her side away from Lindsey's stare. 'Hudson will find us if I do.'

'He mightn't. He may—'

'He's already looking for me in hospitals.'

'How do you know?' Lindsey said.

'I just know. I just … know.' Her eyes dropped as sleep gathered her up.

Lindsey's shoulders slumped, she paused and closed the door behind her. Alison stood outside, worry etched deeply across her features.

'What did she say?' Alison said.

'She won't go. She's adamant.'

Alison motioned towards the bedroom. 'She's getting weaker by the hour and could have internal injuries. Jen took quite a beating. I'm surprised the baby survived.'

'What are you saying?' Lindsey said.

'She's going to die. We'll take her to a hospital away from Teesside. Where the men, who are after her, won't find her.'

'She won't go,' Lindsey said.

'She won't be able to put up a fight much longer. When the time comes, we'll take her.'

Lindsey cradled the baby and kissed her on the top of her head. 'What about her baby?'

Alison pulled out a piece of paper and held it out to Lindsey. 'She gave me this.'

'What is it?' Lindsey took the paper and read.

'She wants the baby to go to her cousin in Lincoln. She told me they'd been trying for a baby for years. Apparently, her and Jen are extremely close.'

Lindsey peered towards the bedroom door. 'But she'll survive. Won't she?'

Alison shrugged. 'I don't know.'

'You and Jen. How did you become friends?'

'We got into a bit of bother when we were kids. Jen covered for me. I've never forgotten that.'

'Is that why you helped?' Lindsey said.

'Yeah. I could've ended up in prison. Jen gave me a chance to change. I did. When she asked me to help, I was only too willing. I don't care what she's done. She told me about Amanda.'

The door opened, and Jimmy entered carrying shopping bags. 'I think I got everything.' He stared at Lindsey. Unshed tears sparkled in her eyes. 'You ok?' he said.

'Yeah. Have you met Beth?'

Jimmy smiled. 'Beth. I love that name.'

CHAPTER THIRTY-SEVEN

Taffy sat in the chair next to his hospital bed as the man stuffed the last of his belongings into a holdall.

'Is that everything?' the man said.

Taffy grunted. 'Yeah.'

'Shall I fetch a wheelchair?'

Taffy glared at him. 'What the hell do I want a wheelchair for? I'm not a fucking invalid.'

'I thought ... with your leg ...?'

Taffy hauled himself out of the chair and picked up the walking stick leant against the bed. 'It's bad enough I'm using one of these.'

The two men turned towards the door as someone knocked and it opened. Graveney and Robertson entered.

Taffy groaned, slumped back into his chair, and tossed his stick onto the bed. 'What do you want, Graveney?'

'A couple of questions.'

'About what?'

Graveney pointed at Taffy's injured leg. 'Isn't it obvious?'

'I told the other copper everything. It wasn't even on your patch. Why are you pestering me?'

Robertson stepped closer. 'We know that, but we are investigating the murder of three men who worked for your employer.'

Taffy huffed and looked towards the man. 'Meet me downstairs,' he said to him. 'Take the bag.'

He picked up the bag, eyed both officers in turn, and then left.

'Fire away,' Taffy said.

'Joseph Purdey?' Graveney said.

'He's dead, Graveney. Blew himself to bits. Killed a couple of good lads as well.'

'Jennifer Hewitson?' Robertson said.

'What about her?'

'Where is she?' Graveney said.

'How the hell should I know? Isn't that your job? How hard can it be to find a heavily pregnant, gun-toting headcase?'

Graveney glanced at his partner. 'Pregnant?'

'Yeah, pregnant. You know, expecting, up the duff.' Taffy smirked. 'The kid will have to get along without a dad, though.'

'So,' Graveney said. 'What happened?'

Taffy drummed his fingers. 'The two of them ambushed us.'

'What were you doing at the cottage?' Robertson said.

Taffy smirked. 'Cleaning up for Mr Hudson.'

'Bit of a comedown for you, isn't it?' Graveney said.

'I do what I'm told.'

'Why all the men?' Robertson said.

Taffy false-smiled. 'Many hands ...'

'So, you and your mates were spring cleaning?' Graveney said. 'And Purdey and Hewitson turn up? They start shooting and then Purdey kills himself?'

'That's about the size of it.'

'And of course, you didn't shoot back,' Robertson said.

'Those two bastards killed three good men. We have a right to protect ourselves.' Taffy stood again. 'Now if you've finished?'

'Lindsey Armstrong?' Graveney said.

Taffy picked up his walking stick and glared at Graveney. 'Never heard of her. Who is she?'

Graveney observed him. 'Ok, Taffy. Thanks for the chat.'

The two officers turned and exited the room. Taffy scoffed. 'Pair of tossers.'

Once outside the building, Robertson paused. 'What do you think?'

Graveney looked back towards the hospital and rubbed his chin. 'He's heard of Armstrong. We need to find her. If only for her own safety.'

'We'd better get over to her house,' Robertson said.

Graveney walked on. 'Yeah. But I'll be amazed if she's there.'

Jimmy carried the unconscious Jen towards the vehicle and carefully placed her on the mattress in the back of the van. Lindsey and Alison joined him outside.

'Are you two ok doing this?' Alison said to them both.

'Yeah,' Jimmy said. 'I'll take her inside, and then leg it.'

'They'll be able to identify you,' Lindsey said.

Jimmy shrugged. 'What else can we do?'

'I'll wait here,' Alison said.

Lindsey stepped into the back and clasped hold of Jen's hand. 'Hurry, Jimmy ... She's fading fast.'

Jimmy jumped into the van and started it up. Alison watched as they made their way out of the drive and onto the road. She shivered as a chill breeze cut through her thin clothing and then headed inside.

Jimmy pulled the van up outside the hospital. Climbing out of his seat he jumped into the back. 'Are you sure?'

Lindsey turned to look at him, tears running the length of her face. 'She's not breathing and I can't feel a pulse.'

Jimmy tilted Jen's head back. Putting his ear close to her mouth, he listened. He blew two breaths into her and began to pump her chest. Lindsey watched on helplessly as he continued. Beads of sweat appeared on his head as the minutes ticked by.

'Phone for an ambulance,' he said.

Lindsey fished out her phone and dialled, giving the person on the other end details as Jimmy continued CPR.

'They're on their way,' she said.

He was panting heavily now. 'Can you do this?'

'I think so.'

He showed her what to do, and Lindsey continued as Jimmy jumped up. He grabbed hold of a cloth, wiping clean the steering wheel and other surfaces. Climbing outside, he rubbed all the door handles, inside and out.

He spun around as flashing lights heralded the arrival of the ambulance. 'Come on, Linds,' he said. 'We have to go.'

Lindsey bent forward, kissed Jen on the top of her head and followed Jimmy outside. The pair darted to their right and into some bushes, creeping silently into the night. They paused for a final look as the paramedics jumped from their vehicle and headed into the back of the van.

Graveney raced through the doors of the coffee shop and, spotting Louisa at a table in the corner, he made his way over to her. Graveney slid onto the seat opposite and Louisa glanced up at him.

'Hi,' he said.

'Hi.'

'Another coffee?'

She stared down at the table. 'I'm fine. This is my third.'

Graveney frowned. 'Sorry about that. Work stuff.'

Louisa tutted. 'Well, here I am. You said you wanted to talk. So, let's talk.'

Graveney placed his hand on hers, but Louisa pulled away. 'What's up, Louisa? You can't still be mad at me for Heather?'

Louisa pinched her lips. 'Heather's fine. She's getting along nicely without you. Marriages break down all the time.'

'Well, why so distant?'

'Bev Wilson?' she said.

'What about her? You know about Aimee.'

'You're still having an affair with her.'

Graveney was stuck for words. 'What makes you think—?'

'Please don't lie to me, Dad. I was at your flat the other night. I came around to chat. I saw her.'

Graveney brought his hands up to his face. 'Listen—'

'I don't want to hear your excuses. She's married. She has a child. Your child. Not content with making a mess of your own relationship, you go around spoiling someone else's.'

'She's an adult, Louisa. No one put a gun to her head.'

Louisa sneered. 'You're a misogynist.'

Graveney half-laughed. 'What?'

'You are. You claim to love women, but you treat them like shit.'

'Now wait a minute, young lady—'

'No, you wait a minute. I saw Bev at the barbecue. It's obvious she's in love with you. Bloody obvious. You could have kept her at arms-length. But no, Peter Graveney, the great womaniser, can't.'

'It's over now. It was ill-judged.'

'Good. Who's next in line. How many more woman have you bedded? How many more are you shagging, *Dad*?' The last word spat at him through gritted teeth.

Graveney glanced around as people close by stared across. 'This is hardly the place.'

'No. You're right.' She stood. 'I'm going.'

'Louisa,' he said. 'Please ...'

'Don't get in touch with me. Not for a while, anyway.'

'I need to see Luke and Max.'

Louisa threw her handbag across her shoulder. 'Speak with Heather. Get your life in order. Stop ruining other peoples' lives. Just stop it.'

Graveney said nothing as Louisa tearfully stared at him. She grabbed her bag, glared and fled. Graveney wanted to follow but fought the urge. He remained for a couple of minutes, then left. Once outside, he switched his phone back on. It beeped indicating he had messages. He listened to them one by one, opened his contacts and dialled Robertson.

'Hi, Peter. Just to keep you up to date on Lindsey Armstrong and Jimmy Jefferson. We're keeping tabs on their house. Nothing yet, though.'

'What about her parents' house?'

'There too. No one's seen them. They've gone to ground. We're checking on friends and family. Nothing yet.'

'Ok.'

'You all right, Peter?'

'Long week, mate. I'm going home for a shower.'

'See you on Monday.'

'Yeah, Monday.'

Graveney headed home, but not before stopping at a shop to get a meal for one and a bottle of Jack Daniels. He trudged inside, placed his shopping down and went for a shower. After dressing, he slumped in front of the television with a glass in hand and drank. A third of the way through the bottle, he pulled out his mobile and searched through his contacts.

'Peter,' Dr Hope said. 'To what do I owe this pleasure?'

'How are you?'

'... Fine ... Just swamped with work.'

'Listen, Tanya. I've got a free weekend. How about you and I get together?'

'I'm going to say no.'

'Oh, right ...'

'Peter, we had a good time. But if I'm honest, maybe we should leave it at that.'

'Right. It's just ... I thought we had something ...'

She sighed. 'I know about Bev.'

Silence crept by as Graveney took a long drink from his glass. 'She told you?'

'We met up the other day.' Dr Hope sighed again. 'If I'm honest it didn't come as a shock. Knowing you as I do.'

'Would it help if I said it was over?'

'Let's put some distance between us, shall we? Put it down to experience.'

'Ok. I get the picture. Maybe I'll ring in a few weeks?'

'... Peter ... I'd rather you didn't.'

'Fine. I should go.'

'Yeah, I think you should. Whatever you're looking for, good luck finding it.'

Graveney hung up and tossed the mobile across the room and onto the settee. He closed his eyes and leant his head back. His eyes snapped back open, and Marne stared across at him.

'How embarrassing, Peter. Your love life just gets better. Why don't you go out and see if you can pick up a slapper?'

He sneered. 'Maybe I will.'

'Look at you. You're a mess. Heather, Louisa, Bev, Tanya. They all hate you. Why torment yourself with women who don't deserve you. Don't understand you like I do?'

Graveney put a hand to his mouth to stifle a sob as tears rolled relentlessly down his face.

'Because you're dead, Steph. Because you're dead.'

CHAPTER THIRTY-EIGHT

Two days later – Graveney knocked on the front door of Lindsey and Jimmy's house. A woman from next door came outside and walked towards her car. 'They're still not back,' she said. Graveney looked at her as the woman jumped into her car.

Robertson strode up the path with his mobile pressed to his ear. He hung up. 'That was the station,' he said to Graveney. 'Jen Hewitson's dead. She never regained consciousness.'

Graveney exhaled. 'We need to find these two.' He tapped at the door. 'Hudson won't want them talking to us.'

'I've tried where they work,' Robertson said. 'They both phoned in sick.'

'They can't hide forever.'

'Maybe Hudson has already found them.'

Graveney looked back at the house again. 'I hope for their sake, he hasn't.'

Lindsey put the cups onto the worktop. 'Another cuppa?' she said to Alison.

Alison looked up from feeding the baby. 'Yes please.'

'Jimmy and I were talking,' Lindsey said. 'We're thinking of going home.'

'You can stay here as long as you like. You know that.'

Lindsey sat opposite her. 'I know. We have to face the music eventually.'

'What are you going to tell the police?'

'I don't know. We'll concoct a story.'

Jimmy came into the kitchen. He shook his head at Lindsey.

'Jen?' Lindsey said.

Jimmy lowered his head. 'It was on the news.'

Lindsey brought a hand to her mouth, a feeble attempt to stifle the sob and Jimmy moved across to hug her. Alison lowered her head as teardrops dripped from her eyes.

Harry entered the office. Hudson glared up at him. 'Yeah, what is it?'

'The Hewitson woman's dead,' Harry said. 'It was on the news.'

Hudson stood and beamed. 'Brilliant. Although I wish I could have finished her off.' He moved across to the other side of the room and pulled out a half-full bottle of whisky. 'This calls for a celebration.'

'What about Armstrong and Jefferson?' Harry said.

'A loose end, Harry. We need it tied up.'

'Maybe they won't go to the police.'

'We can't take the risk.' He handed Harry a glass.

'You could deny any involvement. Blame it on the boys. Tell the cops they were over-zealous. That they acted on their own.'

'You haven't got the stomach for killing, have you Harry?'

'It's just, the police will be watching for her. It's dangerous.'

Hudson sat back in his seat. 'No. I think I prefer my idea. The dead can't talk.'

Harry turned away and smirked.

Harry made his way outside and into his car. He took out his phone and dialled.

'Hello?' Lindsey said.

'Lindsey. I've heard the news.'

'Who are you? What is it you want with us?'

'A friend of Jen's. We need to talk.'

'About what?' Lindsey said.

'You and Jimmy.'

'Why should I trust you?'

Harry paused. 'I work for Conrad Hudson. I was assisting Jen and Joey.'

'They're both dead. Whatever you were—'

'Hudson wants you two dead. He thinks you're going to tell the police it was him who held you and your boyfriend prisoner.'

'Why were you helping Jen?'

'Personal,' he said. 'Me, Jen and ...' He paused. '... and another, have a vested interest in Conrad Hudson.'

'Who's this other?' Lindsey said.

'That's unimportant. Maybe you could assist us in some way.'

'I'm not a killer. Even though he killed Jen and Joey, that was the chance they took. Jen knew the risks.'

'It was one of Hudson's men that planted the knife.'

'What knife?'

'The knife that framed you. The knife found at your parents' house.'

'Why do that?'

Harry sighed audibly. 'It's a long story. If you meet me, I'll tell you it all.'

'How do I know—?'

'Eventually, Lindsey, we have to trust someone.'

Lindsey thought for a moment. 'Where and when?'

Jimmy peered across at Lindsey who was fiddling with her phone. 'I'm not sure about this, Linds.'

'Neither am I, but what choice do we have?'

'Tell the police what we know. That's what we can do.'

'Shouldn't I listen to what this guy has to say first?'

Jimmy put his face in his hands. He blew out hard. 'This could be a trap.'

'Don't you think I know that?' She clasped hold of Jimmy's hands. 'I love you, Jimmy, but Hudson won't leave this. He'll hound us. This could be a way out.'

Jimmy opened the glovebox and pulled out a gun. 'Take this.'

She examined the weapon in his hand. 'I can't—'

'For me,' he said.

She paused and then accepted it from him. 'If I'm not back in twenty minutes, call the police.'

'I still think I should—'

Lindsey put a finger to his lips. 'He said alone.'

Jimmy dropped his head down. 'If anything happens to you, I'll never forgive myself.'

Lindsey leant forward and kissed him on the head. 'It won't.' She opened the door and got out. Pausing, she gave a half-hearted wave at Jimmy and then she was gone.

She headed along the bridle path towards a figure stood next to a fence. He moved to join her as she approached.

Harry held out a hand. 'Hi, I'm Harry.'

'Lindsey,' she said. Accepting his hand, she shook it firmly.

'We'd be more comfortable in my car,' he said, turning towards a vehicle forty metres away.

'I'm fine here.' Lindsey slipped her hand inside her jacket pocket and felt for the weapon. 'A long story, you said.'

'Robin Slaney.'

Lindsey furrowed her brow. 'Never heard of him.'

'Robin Slaney was my half-brother. He worked as a gardener on Hudson's estate.'

'Go on,' Lindsey said.

'He disappeared the day after Alex Cooper went missing.'

'And you think there's a connection?'

'I think Hudson had him murdered.'

'Why?'

Harry shook his head. 'He may have seen something. Something ...' Harry paused as if searching for the appropriate words. '... something he paid for with his life.'

'How does this involve Jen?'

'Jen's sister, Amanda, was murdered by one of Hudson's men. Gerry 'Taffy' Llewellyn.'

'I know about Hudson's involvement in her disappearance. Jen told me.'

'Amanda, Robin and Alex Cooper all went missing around the same time. I managed to get a job working for Hudson. I'm a good accountant. I hid his ill-gotten gains.'

'Jen?'

'I did a bit of investigating, and Amanda's name cropped up. I didn't buy into the story her and Cooper ran off with the money he stole. But it wasn't until his body was fished out, I was sure.'

'Your brother?'

'I think Llewellyn killed him.' Harry sucked in a lungful of air. 'Robin was having an affair with a woman who worked in a pub. His wife found out and she returned home to Portugal. He was supposed to join her. He never did, and no one has heard from him since.'

'You still haven't told me how you know ...' Lindsey closed her eyes and looked skywards. '... how you knew, Jen.'

'Jen had been trying to find her sister. I told her I thought one of Hudson's men murdered her.'

'And her and Joey started killing these men?'

'Yeah. They all raped her sister. Alex persuaded Amanda to tape a sexual encounter with someone. Hudson found out and had her killed. None of the three Jen and Joey killed admitted to murdering her or Robin. None of them knew where she was buried. There's only one left.'

'Llewellyn?' Lindsey said.

'Yeah. Llewellyn.'

Lindsey stared down at the ground. 'Alex asked me to do him a favour. He wanted me to go to Hudson's party and tape some bigwig Hudson had there. He wanted me to have sex with this man so he could extract money from them both.'

'You knew Alex?'

'Yeah. Alex and I had a brief fling.'

'I didn't know.'

'I could've ended up like Amanda.'

'Hudson had the knife planted at your parents' house. He was helping Sean Grant.'

'Why?'

'Sean Grant was supposed to dump Alex's body, and Hudson planned to use him as a patsy.'

'Karl Smith must've murdered Sean,' she said.

Harry nodded slowly. 'I know all about Karl Smith. He was quite talkative, given the right incentive.'

'Where is he now?'

'He won't be troubling you anymore.'

'You killed him?' she said.

'Not yet. But he's served his purpose.'

'I don't want any part.'

'He tried to murder you. He killed Jimmy's mother.'

Lindsey leant back against the fence. 'I didn't know he killed her. He said it was Sean.'

'Well, now you know.'

'What is it you want, Harry?'

'Hudson wants you dead. He won't rest until you are. Together, we can put an end to this.'

'How?'

'By using you and Jimmy as bait,' Harry said.

'I could go to the police.'

'You could, but I wouldn't give you much hope of ever getting to court. Hudson would never allow that. And even if he did go down, he'd never allow you and Jimmy to live.'

'Neither Jimmy nor I are killers. We just want to get on with our lives.'

'What about Amanda?'

Lindsey looked to the floor again. 'Nothing will bring her … or Jen back.'

'Shouldn't she have a decent burial? It's all Jen wanted.'

Lindsey glanced up. 'I need to think about this and talk it over with Jimmy.'

'Of course. Speak with Jimmy. We could end this, Lindsey. Justice for you, Jimmy, Jen, Amanda, Robin and Alex. Surely they deserve that?'

Lindsey stood up straight. 'I'll ring.'

Harry held out his hand. 'Thanks for trusting me.'

She shook it. 'Trust is earned. I haven't made my mind up yet.'

'Let me know soon. The clock's ticking. I can't put Hudson off forever.'

Lindsey turned and hurried off. She reached the car and slid in beside Jimmy. 'He wants us to help bring down Conrad Hudson,' she said.

'Help? How can we help?'

'Hudson wants us dead. He thinks we'll tell the police about them abducting you.'

'We should. This is crazy, Linds. We've done nothing.'

Lindsey placed a hand on his arm. 'They know where Amanda's buried.'

'Jen's sister?'

Lindsey nodded. 'One of Hudson's men knows.'

'What's in it for this guy …?'

'Harry,' she said.

'What's in it for him?'

'He thinks Hudson had his brother murdered.'

Jimmy rubbed his face and groaned. 'This could go—'

Lindsey placed a hand on his cheek. 'I know.'

'You're going to do this, aren't you?'

'Karl Smith,' she said.

'What about him?'

'Harry has him. I think he has killed him, or he is going to. Karl told him stuff.'

'Stuff?'

'Karl murdered your mam.'

'But I thought it was Sean.'

Lindsey squeezed his hand. 'It was Karl. He confessed.'

Jimmy's eyes shone with tears as memories stirred. 'What's he going to do with him?'

Lindsey shrugged. 'I didn't ask him to go into details. But he said Karl won't be a problem anymore.'

'Karl deserves to go to prison. Harry … you, me … we don't have the right to …' Jimmy closed his eyes and slowly shook his head. 'It isn't up to—'

'Karl tried to kill me,' Lindsey looked upward. 'If he's not dead, he may try again. Do we want to be forever looking over our shoulder?'

Jimmy looked away. 'I suppose not.'

'Hudson had me framed.'

Jimmy faced Lindsey. 'Hudson? Why?'

'He covered up for Sean. Sean was supposed to dump Alex Cooper's body, and Hudson was going to use Sean as a patsy.'

'And Karl killed Sean?'

'Yeah.'

Jimmy looked away and stared out of the window. 'What a mess. Why is life so complicated?'

'We'll get through this. It's always darkest before dawn.'

Jimmy smiled. 'Mam always used to say that.' He turned around to face her again. 'Anything else I need to know?'

Lindsey lowered her eyes. 'I think I may be pregnant. Actually, I'm pretty sure I am.'

Jimmy cupped her face between his hands. 'That's brilliant. How far—?'

'Six weeks. With everything going on, I was looking for the right time to tell you.'

'We could up sticks, and go. Escape all this madness. Start afresh, somewhere new.'

'What about your dad? And Maggie?'

'They could come too,' he said.

'How would we explain everything? Besides ...'

'Besides?'

Lindsey lowered her eyes. 'I feel guilty about what happened to Amanda. It could've been me. I need to find her. I need to do this last thing for Jen.'

Jimmy shrugged. 'We've no choice?'

'No, I don't think we have.'

Harry pulled over to the side of the road as his phone sounded. 'Hi, Lindsey. I didn't expect you to call so soon.'

'You've got your bait.'

'And Jimmy?'

'Both of us. What do you want us to do?'

'I'll call.'

'Why don't you just put a bullet through Hudson's head?'

Harry scoffed. 'That'd be too easy. Hudson's a murdering bastard. People like him don't deserve a swift ending.'

'And Taffy Llewellyn?' Lindsey said.

'He knows where Amanda is buried. He doesn't trust me. While he's out of the picture, we can deal with Hudson. Once he's sorted, we can find out everything from Llewellyn.'

Harry hung up and searched through his contacts for a number. On finding it, he typed a message. 'Lindsey and Jimmy are in.'

'I want to hear it from his own mouth,' came the reply.

'You will,' Harry typed.

Nine Months Earlier – Harry cradled the glass of beer while watching the door, his interest piqued every time someone entered.

'Harry?' a female voice said.

He turned around to face the woman. 'Jen?'

'Yeah,' she said. 'I came in the other door. I've been watching you a while.'

Harry stood. 'Drink?'

Jen shook her head. 'I haven't come here for a drink. You said you had information concerning my sister.'

He sat back down. 'I think she was murdered by one of four people who work for Conrad Hudson.'

'Why?'

'She was trying to obtain some information. Hudson found out and ordered her death.'

'How do you know this?' Jen said.

'I have a contact. Someone who witnessed …' He paused and closed his eyes. 'Amanda was raped by them.'

'This contact. Why didn't he tell the police?'

'You don't cross Hudson. My contact was terrified.'

'And now?'

'Now he wants you to know. He wants to meet with you.'

Jen fixed Harry with a stare. 'Where is she …?'

'He doesn't know. If we want to find that out, we need to do our own dirty work.'

'These men,' Jen said. 'Have you their names?'

'Yeah.'

'And you're prepared to give them to me?'

'I need information myself.'

Jen leant back in her chair and studied Harry. 'I'll have that drink after all.'

CHAPTER THIRTY-NINE

Graveney and Robertson waited outside Hudson's factory. Robertson finished his coffee, crushed his cup and dropped it into the footwell. 'It all seems very quiet.'

Graveney exhaled. 'We'll give it another half hour, and—' He looked to his right as a black car pulled up at the gates. The two officers watched as Harry got out, opened the gate, and drove inside.

'Harry Prentise,' Graveney said. 'Hudson's accountant.'

Robertson raised his eyebrows. 'Bit late to be cooking the books.'

Graveney chuckled. 'Probably the best time.'

Hudson put down his book and snatched up his phone as it rang. 'Yeah, Harry.'

'I've got Lindsey Armstrong and her boyfriend.'

'Where?' Hudson turned to face Jean Cooper who eyed him as she sipped at her drink.

'The factory.'

Hudson forced a smile at Jean and pointed to his phone. 'Business.' He left the room and closed the door behind him. He carried on through into the kitchen and shut this door too.

'The factory?' Hudson said. 'Why the hell did you take them there?'

'Where else was I going to take them? You said you wanted to question them.'

Hudson rubbed his chin. 'No one saw you, did they?'

'Don't worry, Conrad. I was discreet.'

'Have you got the lads there?'

'Yeah. Slim and Andy.'

'I'll be twenty minutes,' Hudson said.

Jean entered the kitchen. 'Who was that?'

'Harry. I need to nip to the factory.'

Jean glanced at the clock on the wall. 'At this time?'

Hudson grabbed his jacket from the back of a chair and pulled it on. 'I shouldn't be too long.'

'Ok,' she said. Hudson forced a smile and then was gone. Jean strode into the hallway and collected her coat and car keys.

Graveney answered his phone. 'Yeah, Rav?'

'Hudson's left his home. He seemed in a hurry.'

'Follow him. I have a feeling he's on his way to the factory.'

'Will do, Guv.'

Hudson put his mobile on speakerphone. 'Yes, Boss,' Taffy said.

'How are you?'

'A lot better. I'll be back on Monday.'

'I'm on my way over to the factory. We've got Lindsey Armstrong and her boyfriend.'

'It's a bit risky, taking them there.'

Hudson grunted. 'It wasn't my idea. Harry found them and decided to take them to the factory.'

'Harry? Is he calling the shots now?'

'Well, you've been out of action. And he's helped out.'

Taffy sneered. 'I bet he has. What are you going to do with them?'

'I want to make sure they haven't been blabbing. We don't know what the Hewitson woman told them.'

'Do you want me to come over?'

'Nah. Slim and Andy are there with Harry.'

'Slim?'

'Yeah.'

'Are you sure, Boss. Slim was around here half an hour ago. He didn't mention he was going to the factory. In fact, he said he was going to his local.'

Hudson narrowed his eyes. 'I'm sure he said Slim.'

'Maybe I should come over. Just in case.'

'Yeah.' He furrowed his brow. 'Do that, but keep yourself out of sight until we know what's going on.'

Hudson pushed the door to the factory open and stormed into the room. Lindsey and Jimmy sat on chairs in the middle of the expanse of the warehouse. Harry stood to the side of them, holding a gun.

Hudson paused and felt inside his pocket for his own. 'So ... this is Lindsey Armstrong and Jimmy Jefferson?'

Lindsey narrowed her eyes and stared at him. 'And you're the bastard who had me framed.'

Hudson sneered. 'That was such a long time ago. I'd almost forgotten.'

He stepped closer, glanced towards Harry, and then surveyed the room. 'I thought Slim was here?' Hudson said.

'He's gone to get us a drink. I thought we could at least be civilised.'

Hudson fixed his attention back on Lindsey and Jimmy. 'Your friend, Jen?'

'What about her?' Lindsey said.

'You were helping her?'

'Jen asked me for a favour. A place to stay. That was my only involvement.'

Hudson scoffed. 'You expect me to believe that? You and your friends butchered three of my men.'

'What about the people you've killed?' she said. 'What about all the bodies you've piled up over the years? What about Alex Cooper and Amanda Hewitson?'

'Alex got too big for his boots. His little slapper poked her nose where it didn't belong.'

'I'm glad Jen and Joey did what they did. My only regret is they aren't here to see your demise.'

Hudson laughed. 'My demise? You think Harry, there, will save your skin?'

Harry raised his gun and pointed it at Hudson. 'I'm afraid it's you that has it wrong, Conrad.'

Hudson laughed even louder. 'Now we see your true colours. Taffy was right.'

Lindsey and Jimmy glanced between the pair. Harry aimed his gun at Hudson's head, as Hudson's own weapon hung loosely by his side.

'What are you going to do, Harry?' Hudson sneered. 'Shoot me?

'I want the code to your safe,' Harry said.

'That's what this is about? Money?'

'What about your brother?' Lindsey said.

'A little white lie. Robin drank in the same pub as me. He was an inveterate womaniser. He also had a big mouth if you plied him with enough alcohol.'

'Robin Slaney?' Hudson said.

Harry laughed. 'We concocted a plan, Robin and I. Robin was going to smuggle me into the manor, and I was going to have you open your safe at gunpoint. The two of us would split the money and go our own separate ways. Robin was heading back to Portugal, and you wouldn't suspect him anyway. You'd think it was some random guy who robbed you. Maybe even someone paid by Alex Cooper … Unfortunately, Robin conveniently disappeared the night before we intended to carry it out.'

Hudson stared at the gun in his hand. 'And Scott Macintyre?'

'Scott Macintyre was a thug. He beat a friend of mine so badly, he ended up in a wheelchair. I used the opportunity to pay him back. Thank you very much for that.' Harry reached into his pocket with his left hand and pulled out a small Dictaphone. 'I have your confession on here. Enough to see you locked up for a long time.'

Hudson glanced towards Lindsey and Jimmy. 'And these two?'

Harry smiled. 'Sorry guys. I was hoping Jen and Joey would be here instead of you two. I needed this to happen here so Conrad ...' He pointed towards him. '... can't escape justice.' He glared at Hudson. 'Drop that gun of yours.'

Hudson looked at Lindsey and Jimmy. 'It appears ... we've all been had.'

'When the police arrive ...' Harry said. 'They'll find you incapacitated, Conrad. A bullet to the leg, perhaps. And these two ...' He moved nearer to Lindsey and Jimmy. 'Dead. Shot with your gun. Try talking your way out of that. I'll doctor the recording.' He held up the Dictaphone again. 'So only your voice appears on it. The police will have all the evidence they need to convict you for Alex Cooper's and Amanda Hewitson's murders. Not to mention Scott Macintyre. Which should enable them to mop up your organisation.'

'Looks like you've thought of everything?' Hudson said.

'Looks that way.' Harry slipped the recorder into his pocket. 'For good measure, I'll send a copy to Jean. She'll sing like a canary. You can think of me sunning myself somewhere warm.'

Harry turned to face Lindsey and Jimmy. 'You have something. Something Jen gave you?'

'What are you talking about?' Lindsey said.

'Jen gave you something. She told me. For safekeeping?'

Lindsey involuntarily felt her jacket

'That's right,' Harry said. 'Hand it over.'

She pulled the key from her pocket and tossed it across to Harry.

He grinned. 'It has all the information Joey stole from your safe, Conrad. With the rest of the information you're going to furnish me with, I'll have all your contacts in my pocket.'

'Good plan.' Hudson said. 'Just one flaw.'

Harry narrowed his eyes. 'I don't think there—'

The revolver muzzle rested on the back of Harry's neck. 'I think I'll take that,' Taffy said.

Harry swivelled, and Taffy held out his hand.

'I was wondering when you'd show up,' Harry said.

'The gun,' Taffy said. 'Give me the gun, or I'll put a bullet through your head.'

Harry swung his hand, carrying the gun, striking Taffy hard. Taffy stumbled backwards and crashed to the floor. Hudson made a move for his own weapon but Harry, who turned swiftly, fired. Hudson dropped to the ground as the bullet ripped through his thigh. He groaned, blood quickly pooling around his leg. Harry smirked as Taffy fired. The bang, bang, bang of his revolver hammer falling on empty chambers sounded behind him. Taffy stared bemused at the weapon in his hand.

'Blanks, Taffy,' Harry said. 'I'll think you'll find they're blanks.'

Slim stepped out of the shadows. 'You should always check your weapon, Taffy. Especially one given to you by other people.'

'Have you met Robin Slaney's half-brother?' Harry said, glancing between Taffy and the moaning Hudson, who was trying desperately to stem the blood flow from his leg.

Slim ambled forward and kicked Taffy in the head. Taffy's skull cracked against the floor as it was thrown backwards.

'Fill your boots,' Harry said to Slim.

Slim surveyed the room and spotted a forklift in the corner. He raced across to it, jumped inside and started it up. Hudson groaned as he pulled himself into a seated position. Slim drove slowly towards Taffy, stopping short of him before continuing over his legs. Lindsey and Jimmy winced as the sound of cracking bones echoed in the room. Taffy screamed in agony, his legs now useless, as Slim reversed the machine and scooped up the helpless victim. Slim hoisted the forks high, tilting them before allowing the crumpled body of Taffy to fall to the ground with a thud. Taffy lay unconscious, his broken limbs arranged in a grotesque mess. Slim moved forward again and using the tip of the fork, pressed it into Taffy's stomach and pushed his body slowly forward until it reached the far end. Slim lifted his motionless victim off the floor, but this time pushed the machine against the wall. Taffy's body flopped against the bloodied forks. His torso fixed to the breeze blocks like a butterfly pinned in an album. He made no sound as Slim jumped from the machine and surveyed his handiwork.

He turned to view the others. 'I think I'm finished here.'

Harry roared with laughter. 'I think you are.'

Slim joined Harry who pulled a pair of gloves from his pocket and slipped them on, stepped across to Hudson and recovered Hudson's gun. 'One last loose end.' He sneered. 'Isn't that what you always say, Conrad?'

Hudson gritted his teeth. 'Fuck you.'

Harry raised the gun at Lindsey. 'Sorry about this, but you know—' Lindsey glared back at him and noticed a movement in the darkness.

Harry groaned loudly and reached for his side as a searing pain tore through it. The sound of the shot still echoing around the warehouse.

He turned as armed police entered the room. Slim grabbed hold of him and pulled him to the side behind some machinery. Harry fired back, the bullets whistling above the heads of Lindsey and Jimmy who pushed himself sideways, deliberately falling into Lindsey. The pair huddled on the floor as he wrapped his body around her in a defensive shield.

'I'll kill you, you treacherous bastards,' shouted Hudson, as he reached for his gun and pointed it at the retreating Harry and Slim.

He groaned and slumped to the floor as multiple bullets from police weapons exploded into him. Hudson lay motionless, a massive circle of red pooled out from his body and covered the concrete.

Harry and Slim edged towards a door at the far end of the workshop, firing at the police as they did so. Slim grimaced and dropped to one knee as a bullet pierced his side, and another hit him in the thigh. Harry looked down at his stricken friend.

'Help me, please,' Slim said. 'Harry ...'

Harry paused at the door and stared back at Slim, raised his weapon, and shot him through the head. Harry hurried through the heavy metal door and locked it from the other side. He limped towards the rear of the building, paused at a door which led outside and slowly opened it peering into the carpark. His car twenty-metres away, agonisingly close.

'Going somewhere?' Jean said.

Harry spun around. 'Jean? We need to get away.'

Jean raised a gun and pointed it at him. 'There's only one way out of this for you.'

'Don't be stupid, Jean. I've got the tape.' He slowly pushed a hand inside his pocket and pulled out the Dictaphone. 'It's all on here. Conrad killed Alex. He admitted it.'

'I heard everything. I heard what you said.'

Harry opened his palms outward. 'Some of what I said back there ...'

'You lied to me. You did this for money.'

'Jean.' He edged closer. 'I was just—'

She squeezed the trigger and Harry stumbled backwards clutching at his neck, as copious amounts of blood spurted from the wound. He leant against the wall and slowly slipped to the floor. Harry tried to speak but unsaid words stalled in his throat, just a gurgling sound emitted as his head dropped to his chest. Jean staggered backwards and stared at the still-smoking gun in her hand. She gulped in a large lung full of air and brought her free hand up to her mouth to stifle her rising nausea. Pulling her gaze away from the bloody corpse in front of her, she stepped over him and through another door. She glanced about and moved into the furnace room. Throwing open the door to the raging flames, she tossed the gun inside, took off her coat, and threw this in as well. Jean closed the furnace and made her way back out and up a flight of stairs. She entered the office and gently closed the door behind her. Racing over to the large radiator she pulled out a set of handcuffs, dropped to the floor and clicked one end to her wrist and the other to the metal.

Jimmy finally looked up, as armed police swarmed into the room. Graveney made his way across to them.

'You two ok?' he said.

Jimmy and Lindsey sat up and glanced between themselves and Graveney. They nodded at each other. 'I think so,' Lindsey said. Clambering to their feet, they hugged.

Robertson halted and stooped next to Taffy. He moved towards Graveney and the others. 'He's still alive,' Robertson said. 'We need paramedics.'

Lindsey moved across to Taffy as Robertson pressed the button on his radio. 'Get the paramedics in here, Rav. We've got a live one.'

Lindsey knelt and put an ear to Taffy's face. 'Amanda,' she whispered, tears rolling down her face. 'Where's Amanda? Please. Do the right thing.'

Taffy's eyes opened a little. '.... F ...' he said. 'Farm ...' His eyes closed again.

Lindsey put two fingers on his neck and felt for a pulse. 'I think he's dead.'

Two paramedics came racing through the doors, headed for the stricken Taffy and began working on him.

Lindsey re-joined Jimmy. 'Did he say anything?' Jimmy whispered.

'Nothing I could make out.'

He placed an arm around her shoulders and gently squeezed her.

Graveney's radio clicked into life. 'We've found a body at the back of the warehouse,'

Graveney waved across at Hussain who had entered the room. 'Get these two outside,' he said to Hussain.

Lindsey took a final look at Taffy as one of the paramedics shook his head at his companion.

'This way,' Hussain said, and Lindsey and Jimmy followed the officer outside.

CHAPTER FORTY

Graveney entered Mac's office and took a seat next to Robertson, placing his coffee onto the desk. 'Sorry about that, Guv. Phone call.'

'Neil's been filling me in on what happened,' Mac said.

Graveney leant forward. 'The forensic guys recovered a Dictaphone from Harry Prentise's body. I'm getting the transcript typed up. You should have it with you by this afternoon.'

'And the gist?' Mac said.

Graveney raised his eyebrows and sighed. 'Where do I begin? Hudson killed Alex Cooper and Amanda Hewitson. He got Sean Grant to dump the body. As we know, someone killed Sean Grant.'

'We think that someone, was Karl Smith,' Robertson said.

'No sign of him?'

'Disappeared,' Graveney said. 'Probably dead.'

'He went missing before the bodies were found,' Robertson said. 'His disappearance could've been a coincidence.' Graveney smiled. 'Peter doesn't think so, Guv.'

'You know me and coincidences,' Graveney said.

'And Harry Prentise's involvement?'

'Purely for money,' Graveney said. 'He recruited the half-brother of Robin Slaney, Kieran 'Slim' Mount, to help him. The idea was to undermine Hudson, and then frame him for the murders of Lindsey Armstrong and Jimmy Jefferson.'

'With the confession Hudson gave on tape,' Graveney said. 'He was looking at a long stretch. If he hadn't been shot and killed.'

Mac leant back in his chair. 'Who killed Harry Prentise, then?'

Graveney glanced across at Robertson and then back to Mac. 'We're not sure. He was shot and injured by one of the armed officers, but when they found him, he'd been shot through the neck.'

'Jean Hudson? Could she be involved in any way?'

'It doesn't appear so,' Robertson said. 'We found her handcuffed upstairs at the warehouse. She told us Harry Prentise fastened her there at gunpoint.'

Mac rubbed his chin. 'There could be a yet unidentified individual?'

Graveney shrugged. 'Maybe.'

'Peter's not convinced,' Robertson said.

'We'll have to see if anything else comes up,' Graveney said. 'Lindsey Armstrong and Jimmy Jefferson swear there was no one else at the warehouse.'

Mac raised his brow. 'Anything more?'

Graveney swigged his coffee. 'Scott Macintyre was murdered by one of Hudson's men we think. We don't know who, though.'

Mac grunted. 'That's Tyne and Wear constabularies problem. Lindsey Armstrong?'

'She didn't kill her boyfriend,' Graveney said. 'She was framed by Hudson.'

'Why?'

'Sean Grant worked for him,' Graveney said. 'Hudson did it to get Grant off the hook.'

Mac rubbed his chin. 'All in all, a good day's work. The chief will be pleased. Amanda Hewitson's body?'

Robertson tapped his pad. 'Not sure. Hudson had an incinerator at his factory. She and Robin Slaney were probably disposed of there.'

'Right,' Mac clasped his hands together. 'Well done you two.' Mac looked at Robertson. 'Can you give us a minute, Neil?'

Robertson stood. 'Of course, Guv.'

Mac fixed his attention on Graveney. 'You ok, Peter?'

'I'm good.'

'Have you seen the kids?' Mac said.

Graveney frowned. 'Not a lot. I was at the pictures with Luke last week. Louisa is meeting me for coffee at the weekend, she's bringing Max along. She's still mad at me. It could be a long road back.'

'If you need a bit of time off ...'

Graveney shook his head. 'I'm fine, Mac.'

'You and I need to get together for a drink sometime.'

Graveney stood. 'Yeah. Maybe next week.'

'No rush with the report on this. There's a lot to write up. But you were right about the cases being linked.'

'A hunch.' Graveney made his way back to his office and shut the door. He sighed heavily and slumped into his chair, closing his eyes deep in thought. When he opened them again, Marne sat opposite. She leant forward and placed a hand on his face. 'Well done, Peter. Not everyone thinks you're a loser.'

Three months later – Lindsey pulled into the layby next to a car. Jean Cooper got out and jumped in beside her. She smiled at Lindsey and handed her an envelope. 'Is this what you want?' Jean said.

'I don't know. It's a bit of a long shot.'

'Well. Do what you want with it.'

'Thanks.'

Jean put her hand into her inside pocket and pulled out a second envelope. 'I've got something else for you.'

Lindsey narrowed her eyes. 'What is it?'

'Money. I thought—'

Lindsey forced a smile. 'No thanks. No offence, but I'd rather not accept blood money.'

'You'd be foolish not to. It'd set you and your fella up.'

'I don't need it. With the compensation I'll get for my wrongful imprisonment, we'll be fine.'

Jean shrugged. 'I understand. I'm shutting down the operation and selling the businesses. I'm giving the bulk to charity.'

'And then?'

'Somewhere warm. The West Indies, maybe.'

'What happened in the factory?' Lindsey said.

Jean bit her lip. 'I followed Conrad there. I sneaked in the building at the rear. Harry was going to kill you and Jimmy, and I would have shot him myself to save you two, but the police beat me to it.'

'Did you shoot Harry?'

'It's best you don't know.'

Lindsey smiled. 'You're probably right. Good luck.' The pair hugged, and then Jean was gone.

Lindsey opened the envelope and stared at the deeds. 'Chestnut Farm,' she muttered to herself.

Lindsey pulled the car up at the end of the farmyard. She got out and walked towards the house.

'Can I help you?' a man said.

'Mr Statham?' she said.

'And you are?'

'Are you Archibald Statham?'

'That's my dad. I'm Robert. Look, what is—?'

She stepped forward. 'Lindsey Armstrong. Can I speak to your father?'

He frowned. 'I'm afraid my dad's not well.' He glanced towards the house. 'He's dying.'

Lindsey lowered her eyes. 'I've got something for him.' She held up the envelope.

'I can give—'

'It'll be worthwhile.'

He studied her and narrowed his eyes. 'What is it you have?'

'The deeds to this farm.'

He blinked. 'I thought—'

'Two minutes with your dad and they're yours.'

'Wait here. I'll see how he is.'

Lindsey followed Robert up the stairs and into the darkened bedroom. The old man in the bed slowly turned his face towards her.

'This is Lindsey Armstrong, Dad,' Robert said.

The old man stared at his son. 'Can you give us a moment?'

Robert nodded at his dad and then left.

The old man coughed and motioned towards a seat next to him. 'Sit,' he said.

Lindsey perched on the edge of the chair next to the old man. 'I've these ... The deeds to this farm.'

He forced a smile. 'Didn't that bastard Hudson have them?'

'I came by them. It's all been done legally. They're yours.'

'Why would you do that?' he said.

'I need some information. There's something buried on your farm.'

The old man looked away from Lindsey. Tears formed in his eyes and tumbled down his cheeks. 'I'm not a bad man, Lindsey. They made me do it. They said they'd take the farm.'

Lindsey leant closer and placed a hand on his arm. 'I'm not here to judge. Tell me what you know, and the deeds are yours.'

Graveney picked up the phone. 'DI Graveney.'

'I've got Lindsey Armstrong on the line, Sir.'

'Put her through,' he said. 'Lindsey. What can I do for you?'

'It's what I can do for you, Inspector.'

'Go on.'

'I want you to meet me somewhere. Come alone.'

'Where?'

Graveney glanced at Robertson. 'You wait here, Neil.'

'This is a bit irregular,' Robertson said.

'I'll be fine.' Graveney jumped out and walked along the track and into the farmyard. Robert stood outside the front door of the property. 'She's over at the top field,' he said. 'Past the red barn.' Graveney set off. As he passed the barn, he spotted Lindsey standing within a field, the perimeter surrounded by trees. He climbed the locked gate and trudged up the incline to the furthermost point and stopped next to Lindsey, who remained still.

'Lindsey.' Graveney followed her stare into one of the corners.

'Amanda Hewitson,' she said.

'How do you know?'

She faced Graveney. 'I just do. The old man was forced to bury her here by Hudson. His son knows nothing about it. Make sure she gets the burial she deserves.'

As Lindsey turned to leave, Graveney grabbed hold of her arm. 'You can't withhold evidence. Who told you she's buried here?'

'What are you going to do, Inspector? Put me back in prison?'

'You're not making this easy for me.'

'Arrest me if you like. I won't talk. Not ever.'

Graveney lowered his eyes. 'Jen's baby? Where is it?'

'She's safe.'

'A girl?'

Lindsey nodded. She peered back into the corner of the field. 'No offence, but I hope I don't see you again.'

Graveney shrugged. 'Enjoy the rest of your life, Lindsey.'

She forced a smile and set off. Graveney watched her stride away. He turned back around and surveyed the ground. The trees around clinging on stubbornly to some of their gold and red foliage. The remainder, lay on the ground, creating a multicoloured carpet of fallen leaves. Marne appeared to his left. He gazed across at her and smiled.

'Getting soft in your old age, Peter?' she said.

'I guess so.' Graveney pulled out his phone and trudged back to the car.

Robertson studied him as he climbed inside. 'Well?'

Graveney looked over towards the farm. 'Amanda Hewitson is buried in one of the fields.'

'Lindsey Armstrong told you this?'

Graveney huffed. 'She wouldn't tell me how she came by the information, though.'

'You could arrest her?'

Graveney turned to face Robertson. 'What would that achieve, Neil?'

'You'd have to come up with a plausible explanation.'

'I'd need your help on this. I won't do it if—'

Robertson patted Graveney on the arm. 'She's already done fifteen years. I think she deserves a break.'

Graveney stared into the distance. 'I think she does.'

Graveney slumped at the dining table with a bottle of Jack Daniels in front of him. He picked up two glasses, placing one in front of himself and the second on the other side of the table.

Marne smiled at him. 'This is how it should be. Just you and me, Peter.'

Graveney half-filled the tumblers and clinked his glass against the other one. 'To us, Steph,' he said. 'To us.'

NOTES ABOUT THE AUTHOR

John Regan was born in Middlesbrough on March 20th, 1965. He currently lives in Stainton Village near Middlesbrough.

This is the author's fifth book and a follow-up to his first – **The Hanging Tree** – A gritty thriller, set in and around the Teesside and North Yorkshire area. His second – **Persistence of Vision** – a sci-fi/fantasy novel. The third - **The Romanov Relic -** a comedy thriller, and the fourth – **The Space Between Our Tears** – a contemporary romance with a twist.

At present his full-time job is as an underground telephone Engineer at Openreach and he has worked for both BT and Openreach for the past nineteen years.

He is about to embark on his sixth novel and hopes to have it completed sometime next year.

August 2019.

The author would be happy to hear feedback about this book and will be pleased to answer emails from any readers.

Email: johnregan1965@yahoo.co.uk.

OTHER BOOKS BY THIS AUTHOR

THE HANGING TREE – Even the darkest of secrets deserve an audience.
Sandra Stewart and her daughter are brutally murdered in 2006. Her husband disappeared on the night of Sandra's murder and is wanted in connection with their deaths.
Why has he returned eight years later? And why is he systematically slaughtering apparently unconnected people? Could it be that the original investigation was flawed?
Detective Inspector Peter Graveney is catapulted headlong into an almost unfathomable case. Thwarted at every turn by faceless individuals, intent on keeping the truth buried.
Are there people close to the investigation, possibly within the force, determined to prevent him from finding out what really happened?
As he becomes ever more embroiled, he battles with his past as skeletons in his own closet rattle loudly. Tempted into an increasingly dangerous affair with his new Detective Sergeant, Stephanie Marne, Graveney finds that people he can trust are rapidly diminishing.
But who's manipulating who? As he moves ever closer to the truth, he finds the person that he holds most dear threatened.
Graphically covering adult themes, 'The Hanging Tree' is a relentless edge of the seat ride.
Exploring the darkest of secrets, and the depths people will plunge to keep those secrets hidden. Culminating in a horrific and visceral finale, as Graveney relentlessly pursues it to the final conclusion.

'Even the darkest of secrets deserve an audience.'

PERSISTENCE OF VISION – Seeing is most definitely not believing!

Amorphous: Lindsey and Beth, separated by thirty years. Or so it seems. Their lives about to collide, changing them both forever. Will a higher power intervene and re-write their past and future?

Legerdemain (Sleight of hand): Ten winners of a competition held by the handsome and charismatic billionaire, Christian Gainford, are invited to his remote house in the Scottish Highlands. But is he all he seems, and what does he have in store for them? There really is no such thing as a free lunch, as the ten are about to discover.

Broken: Sandi and Steve are thrown together. By accident or design? Steve is forced to fight not only for Sandi but for his own sanity. Can he trust his senses when everything he ever relied on appears suspect?

Insidious: Killers are copying the crimes of the dead psychopath, Devon Wicken. Will Jack be able to save his wife, Charlotte, from them? Or are they always one step ahead of Jack?

A series of short stories cleverly linked together in an original narrative with one common theme—Reality. But what's real and what isn't?

Exciting action mixed with humour and mystery will keep you guessing throughout. It will alter your perceptions forever.

Reality just got a little weirder! Fact or fiction…You decide!
Seeing is most definitely not believing!

THE ROMANOV RELIC – The Erimus Mysteries

Hilarious comedy thriller!

Private Detective, Bill Hockney, is murdered while searching for the fabled *Romanov Eagle*, cast for The Tsar. His three nephews inherit his business and find themselves not only attempting to discover its whereabouts but also who killed their uncle.

A side-splitting story, full of northern humour, nefarious baddies, madcap characters, plot twists, real ale, multiple showers, out of control libido, bone-shaped chews and a dog called Baggage.

Can Sam, Phillip and Albert, assisted by Sam's best friend Tommo, outwit the long list of people intent on owning the statue, while simultaneously trying to keep a grip on their love lives?
Or will they be thwarted by the menagerie of increasingly desperate villains?

Solving crime has never been this funny!

THE SPACE BETWEEN OUR TEARS

If tears are the manifestation of our grief, what lies within the space between them?

After experiencing massive upheavals in her personal life, Emily Kirkby decides to write a novel. But as she continues her writing, the border between her real life and fiction begin to blur.

Sometimes even the smallest of actions can have far-reaching and profound consequences. When a pebble is cast into the pool of life, there is no telling just how far the ripples will travel.

A rich and compelling story about love in all its many guises. A story about loss and bereavement. A story about guilt and redemption, regret and remorse. But mainly, chiefly, it’s about love.

Printed in Great Britain
by Amazon

11496149R00161